ALSO BY ALIYA S. KING

Platinum

DIAMOND *Life*

ALIYA S. KING

A TOUCHSTONE BOOK
PUBLISHED BY SIMON & SCHUSTER
NEW YORK   LONDON   TORONTO   SYDNEY   NEW DELHI

Touchstone
A Division of Simon & Schuster, Inc.
1230 Avenue of the Americas
New York, NY 10020

First Touchstone trade paperback edition February 2012

TOUCHSTONE and colophon are registered trademarks of Simon & Schuster, Inc.

For information about special discounts for bulk purchases, please contact Simon & Schuster Special Sales at 1-866-506-1949 or business@simonandschuster.com.

The Simon & Schuster Speakers Bureau can bring authors to your live event. For more information or to book an event contact the Simon & Schuster Speakers Bureau at 1-866-248-3049 or visit our website at www.simonspeakers.com.

Designed by Akasha Archer

Manufactured in the United States of America

10   9   8   7   6   5   4   3   2   1

Library of Congress Cataloging-in-Publication Data

King, Aliya S.
   Diamond life / Aliya S. King.
      p.   cm.
   "A Touchstone Book."
   1. African American women—Fiction.   2. Sound recording industry—Fiction.
3. New York (N.Y.)—Fiction.   4. Urban fiction   I. Title.
   P53611.15713D53 2012
   813'.6—dc23   2011034704

ISBN 978-1-4516-2554-7
ISBN 978-1-4516-2556-1 (ebook)

For Erik . . .
For loving me, underneath it all

The brick office building had just one lone car in the parking lot. Jake's driver pulled the white Maybach up to the door and made arrangements to pick him up in an hour. Along with Boo, his bodyguard, Jake eased out of the car and walked toward the front doors of the building.

Head down, shielded against the bitter, whipping wind, Jake stuffed his hands deep into his pockets and kept in step behind Boo. At over six feet tall and nearly two hundred pounds, Jake didn't need a bodyguard. For today's destination, Boo's purpose was to hide him, not protect him.

He didn't really need Boo to hide him either. Jake looked nothing like he did a few months before, and it was very unlikely that anyone would recognize him. Under a dingy hat, his hair was a misshapen, uncombed afro. His eyes were blood red (concealed by sunglasses), and he was wearing a full beard.

Boo held the door open, and Jake slipped inside. He took the steps two at a time, stopped at the office door, and took a deep breath. He knocked once and then began to turn the knob.

The doctor had her back to Jake, standing at her desk and making notes on a pad.

"Come inside and have a seat," she said, without turning around.

Jake flopped on the couch, lifted his baseball cap, scratched his head, and then pulled his hat back down over his eyes. He took a Poland Spring bottle out of his jacket pocket and set it on the nearby table.

"How are you?" the doctor asked.

"Is that the best you can do? How are you?"

"I'm just starting the conversation, Jake."

"You know how I am," Jake said, his voice flat. "Same as last week and the week before."

"How is your sleeping? Are you still having the dreams?"

Jake grimaced. Each night, he relived the horror of hearing the news about his wife Kipenzi's plane crash. It was a flight he should have been on. (And one he would gladly climb aboard if he could go back in time and the outcome would be the same.)

As soon as he dropped off to sleep, he was standing in the hallway of their penthouse. Just as it happened in real life, Kipenzi was rushing off to catch a flight to Anguilla for a photo shoot and to check on his boy Z, who was about to get out of rehab. Just like in real life, Jake planned to go. But then, he got a last-minute phone call about signing a singer named Bunny to the label. He went to Harlem to meet with the singer and chartered a plane to follow Kipenzi to Anguilla in the morning. And just as in real life, he never saw her again.

That night, he'd gone to bed, fully packed and ready to fly out to see Kipenzi in the morning. The phone rang in the middle of the night and his boy Z was on the other line. He just kept saying *yo* over and over again. Something in his voice told Jake that whatever he couldn't get out of his mouth was going to change his life forever. He hung up on Z without hearing a single word. He called his mother. She answered the phone by screaming out, "Is it true, Jake?!" and he knew immediately that something had happened to Kipenzi.

After making it out of the drug game unscathed, Jake always believed that it was just a matter of time before he would have to pay the price for the dirt he'd done. The pregnant women he'd sold crack to, the weak junkies he exploited, the communities he'd helped to destroy. Ten years after selling his first vial of crack, there had been no retribution from the gods. And then the music industry came calling—an entirely different world of sin.

Ten years in and he hadn't paid the price for those crimes either. Until a year ago everything had been coming up roses.

"I should have never let my guard down," Jake said, more to himself than the doctor. He swigged from his water bottle and kept his eyes fixed on the view outside the window.

The therapist scribbled and nodded.

"That's where I went wrong. I stopped looking back and had the nerve to start planning my future," said Jake. He finally looked the doctor in the eye.

"I was trying to get my wife *pregnant*. All my life I said I never wanted to be a father. I'd seen too much. Done too much. I couldn't see me being anyone's dad. Kipenzi changed all of that. I wanted to have a baby with her. You know how vulnerable you have to be to try and get someone pregnant . . . on purpose?"

The doctor nodded. Jake realized that his voice was getting high-pitched again. It was the warning that he was about to cry, something he'd been able to control, slightly, for the past few weeks.

"Have you thought about taking a break from work to sort of—"

"A break? Have you listened to anything I've said in the past six weeks?"

The doctor flipped back a few pages in her notebook.

"I know you said you were trying to close a deal for a set of headphones . . ."

"Yeah," said Jake. "And I'm running a record label with twenty different artists who all want something from me. I own apartment buildings, a restaurant, a clothing line . . ."

Jake let his voice trail off and took another swig from his bottle.

"Take a break," he said under his breath.

Jake leaned over and grabbed a magazine from the stack the doctor kept on the table between them. He flipped through it absentmindedly and froze when he got to a full-page cosmetics ad featuring Kipenzi. Jake tossed the magazine to the floor as if it had burned his hand.

"I'm sorry, Jake," the doctor said. "I can try to make sure that—"

"That what?" Jake said. "That you scrub this office of any trace of my wife? Can you delete all of her songs from the playlist in your waiting room? Let's start there."

Jake got up and walked over to a window near the doctor's desk.

"And while you're at it, call the billboard company that owns that sign right there. Some days, I think I'm doing okay. Then I see a fifty-foot billboard of my wife's face staring down at me . . ."

"That has to be difficult."

"You can also contact the editors of every magazine on the newsstands and tell them to please stop publishing memorials of my wife to sell a few issues. Be real helpful to be able to walk down the street and not see her face or the scene from the crash."

The doctor motioned for Jake to sit back down and he did, letting out a rush of breath as he slumped on the couch.

"My wife is everywhere except where I need her to be," said Jake. "And that shit pisses me off. Her fans still have her. They have all of her that they ever had. Does that makes sense?"

The doctor nodded.

"I mean, they can still listen to her music, watch her videos, look at her pictures . . . whatever. I don't have a substitute for my wife. But everywhere I go, she's there."

Jake took another swig from his water bottle and then let his head fall back against the couch cushion. He closed his eyes tight.

"We talked about vulnerability last week," said the doctor. She turned a new page over in her notebook. "It's something I think we need to explore."

"Do you ever cure people?" Jake asked, his eyes still closed.

"Excuse me?"

"Do you ever say, 'My job here is done' and then tell someone not to come back?"

"Psychotherapy is not the kind of thing—"

"That's what I thought," said Jake. "Nice hustle you got

going. People pay you three hundred dollars a week to talk. And they never get better. Gangsta."

"Are you saying you think you're never going to get better?"

"I'm saying that if I do, it won't be because of you."

"What's going to help you, Jake?"

Jake sat up and reached for the water bottle. He swished the liquid around in his mouth, and swallowed hard.

"My wife had just retired before she died," Jake said. "She wanted to enjoy what she'd worked for. Sometimes I think I should do the same."

"Why don't you?"

Jake waved a hand.

"It's just a thought. You asked me what would help. I probably need some time off."

"I'll tell you what you *don't* need," said the doctor, taking off her eyeglasses and sitting up in her chair.

"What's that?"

The doctor gestured to Jake's water bottle.

"Vodka's not gonna do it, Jake."

Jake leveled his eyes at the doctor and drained the bottle.

"When'd you realize it wasn't water?" he asked.

"First time you brought it in," said the doctor. "I figured I'd let you tell me in your own time."

"But I didn't say anything."

"It's been long enough, the smell was driving me crazy. Vodka's not actually odorless, in case that's what you thought."

"I'm done for the day, doc."

"Next week, try bringing real water. It might help us get some work done."

Jake stood up and stretched. He made a show of picking up his empty water bottle, getting into basketball-shooting position, and then tossing the bottle toward the trash basket near the doctor's desk. He missed by a foot.

"Alcohol messes up your coordination," said the doctor, picking up the empty plastic bottle and dropping it into the basket.

"What do you think you can do for me?" Jake asked.

"I can help you start grieving."

"*Start* grieving?"

"You heard me," the doctor said. "As long as you're drunk every minute of the day, you're not grieving. You're just numb. When you deal with your wife's death head-on, we can make some progress. Not until then."

Jake burped. He wanted to be polite and cover his mouth, but he was too drunk to care.

Kipenzi always said he was a boor when he was drunk. For a year he'd thought she meant he was boring.

"Next week," said Jake, pointing at the doctor. "No vodka."

"I hope you're going home now to sleep this off . . ."

Jake stood up straight and adjusted an imaginary tie.

"Of course not," he said. "I'm going to work. I'm a big-time executive, you know. You're looking at the president of a major record label! I have acts to sign, deals to make, budgets to approve. You might not know it, but I'm kind of a big deal."

Jake winked and made his way to the door. He stumbled only once.

Three hours later, at a business dinner at Peter Luger's, Jake was only half-listening to Dominic Carerra, his longtime business manager. He was trying to get the attention of the waitress to get a refill on his drink. Holding an empty glass was not a good feeling.

"The headphones deal is just a matter of paperwork right now," said Dominic. "They'll be in stores next Christmas."

"It's a new year, Dominic," said Jake. "What are you going to do differently?"

Dominic was taken aback and sputtered.

"My job is the same every year. Make you more money than the year before."

They both laughed and the sound finally caught the attention of the tiny woman who had taken their orders.

"Let me get a—" Jake said.

The young woman placed a Jack and Coke on the table. Jake wrinkled his eyebrow and looked up at her.

The young woman shrugged.

"Made it already," she said. "I was pretty sure you'd want another."

Jake sized her up. She had her hair pulled back in a bun. And there was a flower tucked behind her ear. Her body was absolutely perfect, almost too perfect. She had small but perky breasts, a tiny waist, and a full ass. And although her body had his mouth watering, it was the eyes that drew him in. Almond-shaped and jet black, her eyes locked with Jake's, and he felt his heart thump harder in his chest. He guzzled his drink to tamp down the feeling and gather his thoughts.

"What's your name?"

"Lily."

Jake pointed to the petals peeking out of her bun.

"What kind of flower is that?"

"Guess."

"Lily?"

"Smart boy."

Jake could see that Dominic was trying to catch his eye. But he ignored him.

"What time do you get off?"

Lily just smiled and walked away.

Jake licked his lips and then drained his drink.

"Are we done here?" Jake asked.

"We just got started," said Dominic. "You're distracted as usual."

Jake kept looking at Lily. There had been only one thing that kept him from killing himself after his wife died: liquor. And with enough liquor in his system, the women started to pile up, one after the other. He seldom woke up alone and usually tossed them overboard quickly. It had taken thirty seconds to decide that Lily would be next.

"I'm right here with you," Jake said, his eyes lingering on Lily as she tended to another table. She leaned over a bit to hear her customer and Jake stared at her neck.

"You should try to make an appearance at Cipriani's tonight if you're up to it. It will look good for the Seagram's deal."

Jake nodded, still watching Lily and rubbing his thick beard.

"I gotta cut my hair and shave for that?"

Dominic cleared his throat.

"Yeah, I think you should."

"Then I won't be there. Send the paperwork about the headphones to the office and I'll sign it," said Jake.

"You also need to talk to Birdie about this reality show VH-1 has on the table," said Dominic.

"What's the problem?"

"He says he doesn't want to do it. Something about his wife not wanting to be involved."

Jake grunted.

"I'll talk to him," said Jake. "He's definitely doing it."

Dominic and Jake shook hands. While Dominic went out the front door, Jake parked himself at the bar. Jake's bodyguard Boo was waiting with his driver outside, but in this dark, cavernous space, he didn't have to worry about being approached by anyone.

Lily came by his spot at the bar and dropped off another drink.

"You didn't tell me when you get off," Jake said.

"I'm not available."

"Did I ask you that?"

"I just thought you should know."

Now Jake *knew* he was taking her home. She was his favorite type: a challenge. One hour and six drinks later, Jake was still alone. And Lily was no closer to leaving with him.

"I'm only giving you one more chance," Jake said, his words slurred.

"No, thanks," said Lily with a smile. "It was nice meeting you, though."

"Look at this," Jake said, struggling to pull his cell phone out of his coat pocket. "I can call anyone on this phone and have them at my house before I can get there." Just as Lily tried to walk away, Jake stopped her by touching her arm.

"Watch this," said Jake. He stabbed a few numbers on the phone and waited.

"Yo," Jake barked into the phone. "Where you at?" Jake listened.

"Take a cab to the house," Jake said. "Be there in twenty minutes or don't come at all."

Lily smiled with her mouth closed.

"Impressive," she said. "I have to get back to work now."

Jake clambered off the stool, losing his balance, and then collecting himself just in time to prevent himself from falling. He touched the flower behind her ear.

"Just remember," said Jake. " That coulda been *you*. You may not know it. But I'm kind of a big deal."

Jake sent a text to Boo, who met him at the entrance and half-carried him back to the car. Jake collapsed into the back seat and reached for the bottle of gin he kept in a side compartment.

By the time he got home, he was out cold in the back seat. The young woman he'd invited over was still in the taxi, waiting. Boo paid the driver to take the woman back home and got Jake into the house.

Jake woke up the next morning without any recollection of Peter Luger's, his therapy session, or a girl named Lily.

2

I hate this."

"Would you relax? Jesus."

Lily sat up slightly and peeled back a corner of the eye gel mask the technician had placed over her eyes. She looked over at Corrine.

"How am I supposed to relax if I can't see?"

"Don't you close your eyes when you're sleeping?"

"But I'm *not* sleeping. I'm in the nail salon. And this thing is making me feel claustrophobic."

"So take it off. Just leave me alone."

Lily took the mask off and placed it on the table on the side of the recliner. She looked down at the basin of water where her feet had been soaking for fifteen minutes. She didn't care for having her eyes closed. She felt too vulnerable. Like someone could be staring at her, judging her while she had no idea. She was used to being stared at and judged. But she needed to see it straightaway. So no eye packs. And definitely no massages. Lily shuddered. Just the thought of someone kneading her muscles while she was wearing nothing but a towel made her heart race.

Lily sat back in her chair and used the lever on the side to recline it completely. She wiggled her toes and smiled. Heaven was a place where you soaked your feet in piping hot water laced with peppermint soap for twenty minutes every day. Lily breathed in deep and tried to relax. Five straight nights at the restaurant, followed by teaching an early morning art class every day had worn her out. Today, she'd planned on sleeping in before Corrine came over unannounced, as usual, and dragged her out of the house for their monthly trip to the salon.

Lily had been having a dream when Corrine called. The man from the restaurant was in it. The cute guy with the afro and the scruffy beard. He was talking to her, whispering something in her ear that she couldn't understand. She kept pulling back to look at his mouth, hoping she'd be able to read his lips. But he would just shake his head and pull her closer so that he could whisper in her ear again. *Do you speak English?* she asked him. He looked at her and said, *Yes, I do*. Lily breathed a sigh of relief and then began to ask him to repeat what he was trying to say. His cell phone rang and he gestured to Lily to give him one second. He started talking on the phone. But somehow it was still ringing . . . And then Lily woke up to the sound of Corrine's ringtone on her cell. She wanted to immediately go back to sleep and find the guy with the scruffy beard and tell him to whisper in her ear once more.

"Maybe if you put the eye pack back on, you'll fall asleep and you can see your Bearded Boyfriend again," Corrine said.

"Shut up," said Lily.

"Did he look like the Brawny guy?"

"No. He was black."

"The Brawny guy is black."

"No, he's not. Anyway. Can we stop talking about him?"

Corrine took off her eye mask and turned to face her friend.

"What exactly happened with this guy?"

"I told you," said Lily. "He was there for a meeting or something. I waited on his table. And I just—"

"You fell in love with him while you were serving him a rum and Coke.'

"No. I did not fall in love with him. And it was Jack and Coke. Not rum."

"But you've been dreaming about him ever since."

"Weird, right?"

"And you don't know his name."

Lily shook her head.

"No clue."

"Wonder why you're not dreaming about Shawn," Corrine said. She raised an eyebrow and smiled.

Lily looked up at the ceiling and then over at her friend.

"Maybe because I know I never want to see him again?"

"Oh come *on*, Lily! You went out with him *twice*. That's it. You know we believe in a three-date rule, unless he's absolutely unsalvageable."

"I won't say I don't like him," said Lily. "It's just . . . I don't like him *enough*."

"Maybe that comes with time," Corrine said.

-Lily shook her head vigorously.

"I'll know right away," she said. "It won't take long to—"

Lily jumped. She jerked her head to the left, expecting to see the bearded guy in the salon.

"Did you just hear a guy talking?" Lily asked.

Corrine looked as if she wanted to call the men with the nets and the straitjackets.

"Lil, there are no guys in here," Corrine said slowly.

Lily looked around again.

"I just heard a guy say, 'I'm kind of a big deal.'"

Corrine sat back and pointed to the television.

"You're losing it, babe. It's a line from a movie. *Anchorman*."

"But that's not playing," Lily said, looking up at the television. "Excuse me," she said to the woman working on her feet. "Can you rewind this for a minute?" Corrine's eyes widened.

"What are you *doing*? There are other people in here, you know. And they're watching—"

Lily bounced in her seat and pointed at the screen. A tall, clean-cut guy with bright eyes was being interviewed.

"Who is that? Right there!"

"Ah," said Corrine. "Please don't sit here and tell me you don't know who Jake is."

"I don't know who Jake is. Should I?"

"Yeah, Lily, you should."

"He sounds *exactly* like the guy from the restaurant. He even said that to me. 'I'm kind of a big deal.'"

"So maybe it was Jake."

Lily shook her head.

"Nah. He didn't look anything like that. I told you. He looked like a mountain man. Really bushy hair and a thick beard . . ."

Corrine rummaged through her purse for her cell phone. She punched a few keys and then turned the screen to show Lily.

"Is *this* your bearded boyfriend?"

Lily squinted and then grabbed the phone for a closer look. It was him. The guy from the restaurant. In the photo, he was climbing into a big black truck. A guy who looked like a bodyguard had a hand outstretched to block the camera's lens.

"That's him! But that can't be the same guy . . ." Lily looked back up at the television.

"Yeah. Your crush is a rapper named Jake. He's huge."

"Why does he look so . . . unkempt?"

"His wife died last year. He's been a mess ever since. You really need to get a television."

"Wait. Who was his wife? The singer? The one who died in a plane crash?"

Corrine looked at Lily and shook her head.

"Yes. He was married to her. She died. And ever since, he's looked like this." Corrine shrugged and threw her phone back into her bag. She leaned over to inspect the color being applied meticulously to her toes.

"You don't seem like you are into the hard-core rapper type . . ." Corrine said, keeping her eyes on her bright red toes.

"I'm not," said Lily. "At all. I'm not into hard-core anything . . ."

Lily and Corrine shared a long look. Lily looked away first, and they both pretended to busy themselves with their magazines. Lily was grateful for the quiet. She was suddenly warm all over and her hands were trembling just a bit. She kept looking up at the television, as if she still expected to see Jake on the screen.

She couldn't fathom that the sharp guy with the easy smile was the same guy from the restaurant who drank too much and slurred his words. He was the complete polar opposite of everything Lily wanted in a man. From his looks to his style. So why had she been thinking about him nonstop? Dreaming about him even . . .

On the other side of the salon, with magazines in their laps and their feet under nail dryers, Lily and Corrine carefully thumbed through ancient magazines.

"See look, here's a picture of Kipenzi and Jake from last year," said Corrine.

Lily leaned over and peered at the photo. The woman was breathtaking—blinding white teeth, and flawless caramel skin.

"She is stunning," Lily whispered.

"She *was* stunning," said Corrine, tossing the magazine to the side. "They were definitely a cute couple, though."

Lily picked up the magazine Corrine had tossed aside and flipped through it. She came to a photo of Jake on his way to Kipenzi's funeral. His lips were set in a thin straight line and he wore oversized shades. He had a five o'clock shadow, the only sign that anything was amiss.

"He's in a lot of pain. I could tell that in the restaurant."

"Don't start, Lily," Corrine said, standing up and slipping into her shoes while blowing on her still-wet nails. "There is no such thing as hyperempathy."

"I'm telling you! I could feel his emotions! As soon as I took his order, I just felt grief and pain and sadness."

Ever since Lily had read Octavia Butler's *Parable of the Sower*, about a woman who bleeds if she even sees someone bleeding, she'd become convinced that she had a mild form of what was known in the book as hyperempathy. For her entire life, she'd felt what other people were feeling—even people she didn't know at all. And as soon as she'd walked away from Jake's table that night, she wanted to go into the break room and sob hysterically. She felt so much heartache radiating from his body that she just wanted to take him in her arms and rock him back and forth, kissing his forehead until he fell asleep.

"You go ahead," Lily said, waving Corrine off when they were all done and had paid for their services. "I'm going to stop by the restaurant for a second."

Corrine dropped her mouth in mock surprise.

"You're hoping your bearded boyfriend is there, aren't you?"

"No. I'm hoping my check is there."

"Uh-huh. Right."

Lily pulled on her warm socks, her all-weather galoshes, and then stood up straight. She blew on her nails a few times to make sure they were completely dry.

"I'm coming with you," Corrine said. She slipped on the oversized shades she wore in all seasons, tipped the salon technician, and started toward the door.

"Corrine, I don't need you to—"

Corrine stopped and turned.

"Whatever. I'm coming. And that is the end dot com," said Corrine.

"You know I hate it when you do that."

Corrine waved down a taxi and threw open the back door.

"Let's go, girl," she said. She slapped Lily on the butt as she climbed in the taxi. "Let's go find your man."

Lily had no idea why she was stopping by the restaurant. She did want her paycheck. But on a Sunday there was nothing she could do with it anyway. She was working the next day, so it would make more sense then. But she had to go. And she felt like she'd know once she got there why she needed to go. As Corrine chatted nonstop about how she'd already broken all her New Year's resolutions, Lily kept her head down, blocking against the wind, as they trudged down Broadway, jumping over puddles of melting snow and ice. As soon as they got to the service entrance to the restaurant, Lily stopped Corrine.

"Okay, I'll admit it. I'm coming here because I think Jake's here."

Corrine made a face.

"Duh. I know that."

"But it's not just that. I feel like he's looking for me."

"And he's telepathically bringing you here."

"Yes."

"Lily, can I be really honest with you?"

"Of course."

"Jake is . . . he's one of *them*. He's rich. He's famous. He's got girls throwing pussy at him like it's a softball."

"Like it's a what?"

"Never mind. I'm just saying I don't want to see you play yourself. It sounds like he gave you some attention and you're making way too big of a deal about it."

Lily glared at Corinne.

"Come on," Corrine said, pulling the door open and holding it for Lily.

The restaurant was nearly empty. And only Manny, Lily's supervisor, was at the bar. He was leaning over, chatting with Samantha, one of the other bartenders.

"Hmmmm. Let's see if there are any platinum-selling rappers who have been inducted into the Rock and Roll Hall of Fame sitting around a deserted restaurant with a rose in their teeth, waiting for their favorite bartender to return so he can profess his love."

Corrine shielded her eyes with her hand and looked around.

"What do you know? He's not here. Gasp."

Lily felt a stinging in her eyes and tried to smile anyway.

"Let's go," she said to Corrine, walking toward the front door.

"Lil?" Corrine walked quickly to catch up and touched her shoulder. "I'm sorry. That was stupid and mean."

"It's okay. It was stupid of me to come back here." Lily waved at Samantha. Manny turned around to see who Samantha was waving to.

"What are you doing here?" he barked. "You're off today!"

"I know, Manny," Lily said. "See you tomorrow."

"Ha. And I told that guy you wouldn't be here tonight."

Lily and Corrine froze in place. Lily spoke to Manny without turning around.

"What guy?" she said.

"The rapper guy. Sat in here with his bodyguard all day today. I told him you wasn't coming in today. Shows how much I know."

Lily and Corrine still didn't turn around to face Manny.

"How long ago was this?" Lily asked.

"What do you mean, how long ago was this? He just walked out. Where were you thirty seconds ago when he was sitting right there?"

Manny lumbered off the stool and walked past Lily and Corrine. He flung open the front door of the restaurant.

"See look, he's right there. Hey, you! Rapper boy! You were right. She did come in. She's right here—"

Lily's mouth dropped. She grabbed Corrine's wrist and they sprinted through the main room, into the kitchen, and out of the service entrance. They ran full speed down a back alley and didn't stop until they were across Broadway.

Both Lily and Corrine were bent over at the waist with their hands on their knees, trying to catch their breath. Corrine pressed her hand to her chest.

"Seriously, Lily. Why the hell are we running?"

"I don't know!" Lily said. "I panicked."

"But you expected him to be there!"

"Well . . ." Lily stopped and gulped for air. "I did and I didn't. You know?"

Corrine took in more deep breaths and then started walking slowly.

"No, Lily. I don't know. Let's go home."

Corrine and Lily limped toward the train without saying a word. Lily felt a warm sensation pulsing through her body. He was there. He was looking for her. She smiled and turned to Corrine.

"He was looking for me," Lily said, still smiling hard.

Corrine looked at Lily.

"Would you give him more than two dates to prove himself worthy?"

Lily looked away. "No. I wouldn't go out without him at all. But the attention's nice. He's cute."

Corrine threw an arm around Lily's shoulders as they walked down the subway steps.

"You're special," Corrine said. "Rappers don't do special."

"Is that what we're calling it now? Special?"

"Isn't it true?"

Lily chuckled.

"Indeed."

3

Birdie ran up the steps of the brownstone and checked the time on his phone. Two minutes. He opened the door, stopped to stomp the snow off his boots, and then ran into the living room.

"Take your boots off before you come in—"

"Go online," said Birdie. "It should be up now."

Alex scrambled to open her laptop and began tapping on the keyboard. She clicked on an icon with her husband's photo. And there was Birdie, his face close up in the screen, rapping along to his first single.

"Look at you!" said Alex, beaming. "I love this video."

The chorus to the song came on and Birdie grabbed Alex and spun her around the room. They both danced and sang along to the song until it went off and another video came on. Breathless, they both flopped onto the sofa.

"Aren't you excited?" asked Alex. "This is huge!"

Birdie shrugged.

"They *would* premiere it on New Year's Eve, when no one's online. It's not gonna get any traffic."

"Oh, come on, we're online!"

"That's because we never go anywhere on New Year's Eve."

Alex leaned over and kissed Birdie on the cheek.

"You are all the party I need. Want some more chips?"

Birdie nodded and Alex climbed over his legs to get to the kitchen. Birdie's hands shot out and he palmed her ass, giving it a tight squeeze.

No matter how many times Birdie saw his wife's butt—firm, high, tight, round, and perfect—he had to touch it. If she got up from the sofa to take her empty ice cream bowl into the kitchen, he'd reach up and feel it without thinking twice about it. Sometimes he wouldn't bother to take his eyes off CNN. Alex often joked that he didn't even realize he was doing it half the time. His hand would dart out before his brain could register.

But sometimes, when she was angry or upset or stressed out over a story, he knew better than to grope her. On these occasions, he had to settle for just staring at it for as long as he could see it. More often that not, she'd turn her head to catch him staring and they'd both laugh out loud.

"Would you have dated me if I had a flat butt?" Alex asked, a bowl of popcorn in her hand. Birdie looked up at his wife, drinking her in. She was wearing his very favorite outfit, a plain white tank top and an old pair of Birdie's basketball shorts. Birdie preferred that combination over anything Victoria's Secret could whip up. And he knew whenever he came home and saw Alex in uniform, they were going to have a good night.

Alex sat down next to Bird, and he threw an arm around her neck and pulled her in close.

"No," Birdie said, kissing his wife on the cheek. "I would have never taken it there with you if you had a flat butt."

"So my cute little face, my bright and vibrant personality, my friendly nature—"

Bird shook his head vigorously and closed the laptop.

"All of the above plus a flat ass equals no."

Alex sat up and adjusted her position on the couch.

"Why'd you do that? The Trip & Step video was on."

"They're an embarrassment to hip-hop," Birdie said, his face a scowl.

Alex smiled.

"I like them. You, my friend, are just getting old."

Alex opened the laptop and Birdie moved her hands and closed it shut again.

"Are you kidding me?" Birdie asked. "They're horrible. They talk about—"

Alex held up a hand. "I know, I know, Birdie. They talk about the same stuff on every song. They're not lyrical. They make up dances to go with their songs. But so what? The kids like it. Why are you hating?"

Birdie gave Alex a look. She exhaled heavily, got off the sofa, and placed a quarter into the Hateration Jar. Some households had a jar for cursing. Birdie had one for using the word *hater*. Instead of coming back to the sofa, Alex began gathering papers and her laptop.

"You're lucky I'm on deadline," Alex said. "I can't deal with you and your old-man issues."

"What's the schedule this week?" Birdie asked.

Alex let out a heavy sigh.

"I don't want to talk about it."

"If you don't tell me when you're . . . you know . . . doing your thing . . ."

Alex pulled out a sheet of paper.

"This week is showtime. Again. Fertility peaks day after tomorrow."

"So we should be doing it, like, now."

Alex nodded.

"And every day this week."

"I think I can manage that," said Birdie, smiling.

Alex looked down at the floor.

"What's wrong?"

"This is just not the way I pictured getting pregnant. I mean, I have to check the color and consistency of my vaginal discharge on a daily basis."

Birdie swallowed hard to keep from scrunching up his face.

"I did not need to hear that."

Alex shrugged and began walking out of the living room.

"Wait, before you go . . . I wanna run some album covers by you."

Birdie sat up straight on the couch and reached for color photocopies of mock album covers. After getting signed by rapper-producer Jake Giles in a seven-figure record deal, Birdie's ten years as an underground sensation were coming to an abrupt close. He'd refused to stray too far from his roots as a backpack rapper—his album was equal parts aspirational and inspirational. But he was still about to enter a whole new world.

"Okay, so you know who Ennio Morricone is?" Birdie asked his wife, gesturing for her to sit next to him.

"No, never heard of him."

"He's a composer for spaghetti westerns. He did the music for Clint Eastwood's *Fistful of Dollars*."

"Is that where you got the name for your song?"

"Yup. Check this out."

Birdie took out a copy of a movie poster featuring a sepia-toned photo of Clint Eastwood holding a rifle. He felt a chill go through him as he held the paper in his hand.

"*This* is my album cover."

Bird stood up and turned around to face Alex. "Can't you see me redoing this photo for my album cover?"

"I could. It's hot."

"And that's my title too—*A Fistful of Dollars*."

"Can't do that."

"Why not?"

"It's bad enough that you chose that title for the first single. Can't make that the album title. That's so corny. Money references? Really?"

"Well, shit, I do want a fist full of dollars. What's wrong with that?"

Alex shrugged. "Nothing. I just worry about what kind of message you're sending."

The doorbell rang and Alex threw on a robe and went to the door. She came back lugging a heavy cardboard box.

"It's for you," said Alex.

Alex sliced the box open, and Birdie let out a low whistle.

There were ten pairs of Air Jordan sneakers, all brand-new and wrapped in plastic. A note was nestled inside. Birdie plucked it out and began to read:

Wishing you much success. Sincerely, your friends at Nike.

It was the sixth time in a month that Birdie had received an enormous care package from a valuable company. There was Moet & Chandon, Ciroc (and every other conceivable brand of champagne), limited-edition leather coats emblazoned with his initials, boxes and boxes of clothes from lines not yet released. And now, yet another box of pristine white sneakers.

"I can't keep all these!" Birdie said. "Help me box them up."

They began to box up the sneakers and labeled them with the addresses of Birdie's cousins across the country.

"So you really don't like *Fistful of Dollars* as the album title?" Birdie asked, tearing off a piece of tape with his teeth.

Alex shook her head and labeled a box with a black Sharpie.

"No. It's not who you are."

"But I signed a deal for a million dollars," Birdie said. "A meeeelion dollars."

"I know, Bird."

"And as soon as word go out on the blogs, people had a fit," said Birdie. "Calling me a sellout, saying Jake was stupid for offering me so much money."

Bird shrugged his shoulders.

"We're selling this brownstone, we're getting the hell out of Brooklyn, and my daughter's going to private school. This baby I'm putting in your belly tonight? He will grow up in the 'burbs. And I don't give a damn about what people say. I want a fistful of dollars in my hands at all times. And I'm not ashamed of that."

"Speaking of moving out of Brooklyn . . ." Alex said. She stood up and looked down at the floor. Bird threw up his hands.

"Don't start, Alex. I'm not living damn near Bushwick so you can feel connected to the 'hood."

"Okay. Hear me out . . ."

Bird shook his head. Any time Alex started out with the words *hear me out*, he knew he was in trouble.

"Nah. I'm not hearing anything."

"Excuse me! Marriage is a partnership, remember?"

"We are not living here," Birdie said. "Period. We don't have to sell the house. I know your dad bought it for you and blah blah blah. So we'll rent it out. But I'm not living—"

"What do you mean 'blah blah blah'?"

Bird put one hand behind his head and blew a quick breath out of his mouth.

"I didn't mean it like that."

"Did you forget that my dad left me the house . . . in his *will*?"

Birdie blinked. "No, I did not forget. And I know that's a sensitive—"

"And did you forget that my dad died right after we got married and he wasn't even *there*."

"Alex, of course, I didn't for—"

"And now you want me to just sell the house he left me?"

There was a deeper reason for Alex's hostility and Birdie knew it. He decided to just rip apart the scab and deal with it.

"Things were weird . . ." Birdie began, knowing Alex would run with it.

"That's an understatement," Alex spat. "You *cheated* on me. "

"I know," said Bird. "So when you decided to give me another chance I didn't want to waste any time."

The previous year had been a tough one for Birdie and Alex. *Vibe* hired Alex to write a story on women married to rappers and, as always, she got in too deep, forging relationships with the women and sympathizing with their plights. At the same time, she was ghostwriting a memoir for Cleopatra Wright, a video model who had messed around with half of the music industry—including, Alex found out later, her own boyfriend. It all came out, as these things always do, and Alex was two seconds away from calling off the wedding and walking away from Birdie forever. When he convinced her to stay, he didn't want to waste any time.

So running down to city hall on a Friday afternoon last year felt right. With Tweet standing between them, holding their simple silver rings, and his lawyer standing right in front of all three of them. Right before the judge started the ceremony, Alex whispered to Bird, "Should we wait and at least do this with my dad?" Bird had told her it was okay. He'd understand. And they would still have the big ceremony in Atlanta later.

Alex's father didn't understand. He was pissed off. And then, a week later, he died. So he died pissed off. An only child, Alex wasn't in touch with any of her cousins or aunts and uncles. So Birdie knew he'd been wrong to marry her without her father being there—or at least having his blessing. But everything was all mixed up and complicated then. He felt like he needed to marry her right that second. But she was devastated when she realized that they would never be able to make it right with her dad. Now that she was digging her heels in and prepping for another epic argument about moving, Bird had to step lightly but stay on task.

"Did you like the house in Jersey?"

"You know I did. It's beautiful. But it's so cliché. You sign a record deal and we move out to the 'burbs . . ."

Alex shuddered and then wrinkled her nose.

"It's so corny."

Bird thought back to his communication classes. *Use "I" statements. Rephrase questions.*

"I think you could be happy in the house in Jersey. Do you?"

"I guess so."

Bird chose that moment to clinch the deal. He wrapped Alex up in his arms and kissed her neck.

"Alex, home is wherever we lay our heads."

"I'm scared, Bird."

"Of what."

"Scared of you changing," said Alex. "Becoming more like the people I interview . . ."

"Like who?"

"Like Jake and Z . . . all the rappers on your new label."

"Can I be successful? Can I go from rapping to running a record label like Jake?"

"Of course! I want you to!"

"But you want me to still be regular. Which, to me, means poor."

"Not poor. Just not too rich."

"You sound insane."

"Are you going to keep your same friends?"

"Alex, I've been friends with Travis, Daryl, and Corey since I was ten years old."

Alex shook her head slowly. "Famous people always end up with a whole different crew," said Alex. "Always."

"Okay. So you think I'm gonna ditch all my friends. What else?"

"I've seen how money and fame change things. Look at this stuff," Alex said, sweeping her hands across the room. "You can afford to buy all this out of your own pocket, but you get it all for free."

"You know I don't keep this stuff," said Birdie. "I like spending my own money."

Alex sighed.

"I just know that for ten years you had a small but dedicated group of people who loved your music. You made enough to support us—"

"Barely."

"The point is, you did. And I could dip into Joe's Pub on a Sunday night and close my eyes and pretend like you were freestyling just for me."

"Half the time I *was* freestyling just for you."

"Just promise you won't change."

"Of course, I'll change. I hope I will. But only for the better."

"No platinum medallions, no drugs, no Bentleys, no *MTV Cribs* looking through our refrigerator, no reality shows . . ."

"Wait," said Birdie. "They're already talking about a deal for a ten-episode reality show leading up to my album release date."

Alex shook her head hard.

"Uh-uh. No way."

"I'll see what I can do. Anything else, your majesty?"

Alex looked up at Bird. He steeled himself.

"No groupies."

"Mr. Washington, come inside please."

Years before, when Bird would stand in line at Bank of America, waiting to deposit one of Alex's freelance checks, he would always wonder why he never saw people going into the back area of the bank, marked with a sign that it was for private banking customers. Was there some kind of separate entrance? The day he got his advance, he finally found out. There was a side entrance, right from the parking lot. He'd never noticed the nondescript, unmarked door. Inside the tiny waiting area were two leather armchairs and a table in between, stacked with the day's newspapers.

"How can I help you today, Mr. Washington?"

The chick had legs for days but no ass. Bird instantly dismissed her from the list of Women He Would Cheat on His Wife with If for Some Reason He Had to Cheat.

"I just want to see my statements for this month. For all accounts."

The woman with the flat ass began tapping her keys.

"Including your investment accounts?"

"Everything."

She tapped her mouse and pages began chugging out of her printer.

"Also. I have a secondary account in my wife's name, opened it this year. A thousand dollars is transferred from my main account into her account each month."

"There is twelve thousand dollars in that account."

He sighed and nodded his head. Alex had not spent a single cent of Birdie's newfound wealth. Ever since he'd signed the record deal and started getting large amounts of money wired into accounts as opposed to getting tens and twenties from a concert promoter in a back room, things had changed.

Alex did not want to spend Bird's money. And it was perplexing. They'd gone over the budget with a financial planner, and a thousand dollars had been on the low end of what she could spend. That included getting her hair done every Friday, something she'd said for years she wanted to do. She could do a weekly manicure and pedicure for her and Tweet. There was money each month for her cell phone bill, internet access, daily Starbucks run, clothes shopping, and date night (which could be a trip to Miami if she so chose).

But she'd never spent a dime. She was still using the money she earned from writing to pay for all of the above and Bird could not understand why. When he got home from the bank, the cleaning service he'd hired was filing out of the front door of the brownstone.

"Leaving already?"

"Sir, the wife says no need. Last week, same thing."

"Next week will be different."

"No different. Some women with no job want to clean house with no help."

"She does have a job. She's a writer."

The cleaning woman blinked. Her face was blank. Bird was glad that Alex wasn't around to see that. Nothing put her over the edge like someone thinking she didn't work.

Bird found her in her usual spot, at the kitchen table. He'd tricked out her home office with every modern tech trinket. And she never went in there.

"You know, Alex," he said, leaning over to kiss his wife on the cheek. "I have to pay the cleaning service whether they actually clean or not."

Alex didn't look up from her laptop.

"So cancel it. I can clean my own house."

"I know you *can*," he said, a smile playing on his lips. "But the point is you *don't*."

"I'm working. Can this wait?"

Birdie nodded and walked into the hallway to several floor-to-ceiling bookcases. He grabbed a copy of *Platinum* off the shelf and walked back into the kitchen.

"You promised me that when you finished Cleo's book, you would take some time off . . ." Birdie said, thumbing through the pages.

Alex finally stopped typing and looked directly at her husband.

"You told me to chill for a year," said Alex. "And I did."

Alex took the book from Birdie's hand and flipped to the page where Cleo had written a message. Alex read it aloud, for what felt to Birdie liked the one-millionth time.

You should ask Ras about that baby he adopted. There's a good story there. And if I know you the way I think you do, you won't be able to resist finding out the truth. You can thank me later.

Alex shut the book and raised her eyebrows.

"I have to find out what Cleo was talking about," Alex said.

"Why?" Birdie asked, shaking his head. "Why?"

"I'm a reporter," Alex shrugged. "That's what we do."

"You know I'm going to Jamaica to work with Ras at his studio. I'm hoping to get a few of his tracks on the album."

Alex jumped up from the table.

"Let me come with you!"

"For what?" Birdie asked. "We'll be in the studio all day and night."

"It can be a working vacation," Alex said. "You can do your thing. I can hang out with Josephine and the baby . . ."

"And snoop around and find out who the baby's parents are. No."

"I won't snoop! I'll just come hang out. Promise."

Birdie stared Alex down and then his face relaxed.

"Fine. Come with me."

Alex squealed and kissed Birdie on the cheek.

"I'll be on my best behavior."

Birdie looked down at his cell phone and checked a text message.

"That's Jen. She's bringing Tweet tonight," said Birdie.

Birdie's first marriage had ended in an ultra-messy divorce. Five years later, he and his ex-wife were finally able to be in the same room together without turning it into Armageddon. Unfortunately, her relationship with Alex had not yet thawed. Though Alex treated Birdie's daughter as if she were her own (something that made his heart swell with love for her), she wasn't a big fan of Jennifer.

"You okay with keeping an eye on Tweet?" Birdie asked. "I have a show tonight."

"Of course," said Alex. "We'll be fine."

"Alex . . . about the money," Birdie began.

"What money?"

"You haven't spent any of the money in your budget."

Alex ignored him.

"Where are you performing tonight?"

"I'm doing a one-off show in Stamford. Opening for Jake."

"What are they paying you?"

"Twenty-five."

"Nice."

"It's a living."

Alex did a half nod and went back to her computer. Bird watched her long, slim fingers move across the keyboard at lightning speed. If he had never actually sat next to her and watched her write, he'd never believe she was actually typing anything.

"Need anything?" he asked.

"Cup of coffee would be great."

Bird began to brew a pot and then searched for Alex's favorite creamer. When he saw there was none, he ran down to the bodega to pick some up and brought it right back. When he returned, he started the ritual of making his wife's coffee.

You couldn't just pour the coffee in a cup and keep it moving with Alex. Birdie always felt like he worked at Starbucks when he made her complicated cup. She liked the powdered creamer mixed with a teaspoon of sugar and a splash of milk. And she liked for Birdie to fill the cup with coffee halfway, stir it, and then add the rest of the coffee.

"Here you go, babe," said Birdie, rolling his eyes. "Exactly to your specifications."

Alex smiled and took a sip. "It's perfect," she said.

Birdie sat down at the table across from her.

"I'm not trying to say you shouldn't write, Alex," Birdie said. "I'm just saying you can do it when *you* feel like it. Don't treat it like a job."

"But it *is* my job! I'm not gonna just sit home all day and spend your money."

Bird stood up.

"Look, when you were making more than I was, is that how you thought of it? Was it *your* money?"

"No. But that was different. We needed that money to live. What you bring home now is bonus money."

Bird dug into the pockets of his jeans and took out a bank envelope stuffed with new, crisp one-hundred-dollar bills.

"Spend it. Today. I don't care on what. Buy a whole new wardrobe for Jamaica. Drop it all on one of those fancy bags you always salivate over. Start an account for yourself so you can leave me whenever you get ready. Or donate it to charity. I don't care. But you better show me some receipts when I get back from this show."

Bird couldn't quite make out what was beneath the surface of his wife's face as he pressed the envelope into her warm hand. Was it gratitude, fear, loathing, resentment? He had a sinking feeling that it was all the above.

4

Ras Bennett had a foolproof formula for figuring out his life's worth at any given moment. Every so often, he did a mental tally of the major categories in his life, from health to finances to relationships. Once, when he was twelve years old, he sat on a curb at the corner of South Orange Avenue and Twentieth Street in Newark and ticked off on his fingers what was right in his life. His asthma wasn't too bad and he hadn't been hospitalized for it in months. His mom had started letting him walk to the store by himself. He was going to the fireworks at Marten's stadium the next day. And he had three dollars folded up neatly in his back pocket. Of course, everything wasn't perfect. His father was still on a ventilator, his girlfriend of sixteen hours had just dumped him, and his brand-new bicycle had a nasty flat. Ras clearly remembered standing up, brushing the dust off the back of his pants, and walking his bike to a gas station, having decided that his life was firmly on the not-so-bad side of the scale.

Ras had noticed even way back then, long before he'd had any success, that when things were high off the charts in one category, they were usually lacking in another. Because of this, Ras never prayed for a financial windfall or six-pack abs. He craved balance over all.

On a warm and breezy night in his beloved Jamaica, over dinner with friends at Café Au Lait, Ras was having one of those rare moments when he realized that things in his life were as perfect as they could possibly be. That morning, his lawyer called to let him know that a $50,000 payment had been wired for his work with a Brazilian pop band. His daughter, Reina, was on the verge of taking her first steps, and his relationship with his wife was better than it had ever been.

"Ras? Did you hear me?'

Ras looked around the dinner table. His wife Josephine was staring at him with a smile on her face. Next to her sat Birdie and his wife Alex.

"Babe? Are you with us?" asked Josephine, leaning over and rubbing her husband's forearm.

"Zoning out," said Ras. He picked up his champagne glass and gestured to his guests to do the same.

"To love," Ras said, tipping his glass toward his wife's. Josephine smiled.

Birdie and Alex looked at each other and kissed. "To love," they all said in unison.

Ras hadn't been expecting Birdie to bring his wife to the island. They'd booked a few weeks of studio time, and although Alex hadn't been in the way, he still wasn't thrilled that she was there. A year ago, Alex had interviewed his wife for a story in *Vibe* about women married to rappers and producers. And Josephine had given her an earful. Worse yet, Alex had also ghost-written a book called *Platinum* for Cleo, a woman who detailed her affairs with dozens of musicians, including Ras.

The publicity explosion from the book forced Ras to make a hard choice. He packed up, put the house in New Jersey on the market, and moved his wife and newborn daughter to Jamaica. It was the only way Josephine could stop being reminded about all the stories in Cleo's book. And it was the only way Ras felt like he could actually stop messing with her.

"How's the music coming along?" Alex asked Birdie and Ras.

Birdie shook his head.

"This is not a business dinner. No talking about work."

"What are *you* working on right now, Alex?" Ras asked. "Any new books on the horizon?"

Josephine paused with a forkful of salmon halfway to her

mouth. She cut her eyes toward Ras without moving her head. Birdie coughed, and Alex looked down at her plate.

"Not right now," Alex said softly. "Maybe working on a memoir about trying to have a baby. But that's it."

Ras nodded. He was happy that she felt uncomfortable. He knew Josephine liked Alex. And he accepted that she was his wife's friend and Birdie's wife. But he still didn't have to like the fact that she had helped his mistress attempt to destroy his life.

Josephine touched Alex's arm and then sent a warning look to Ras.

"How do you like the hotel? The views are beautiful, right?" Josephine said.

Birdie began to speak, and Alex interrupted him.

"We might as well talk about it," Alex said. "All of us."

Josephine, Birdie, and Ras were all silent, each looking out at different parts of the restaurant.

"Look, I worked with Cleo on her book, and Ras has every right to hate me because of that," said Alex, her voice high-pitched and wavering.

"It's in the past, Alex," said Josephine. "We're moving on. Right, Ras?"

Ras looked at his wife. Her eyebrows were raised. He nodded and grabbed her hand.

"We're working on it."

Dessert and coffee were served, and the conversation turned to cheesecake and espresso and the beautiful sunset they could see from the porch of the open-air restaurant. But Ras's mind was still on Alex. He could not shake the feeling that Alex had ulterior motives for traveling with Birdie to Jamaica. And he just didn't like the idea of her spending too much time alone with his wife.

Ras took a deep breath and dismissed the feeling. The important thing was that he was doing the right thing now. It didn't matter what Alex said. It didn't matter if Cleo wrote ten more books. What mattered was that Ras had no secrets. He had been faithful to his wife for nearly a year and they were moving into a new chapter in their lives.

Ras felt his cell phone buzz in his pocket and tried desperately to ignore it. He'd promised his wife he would stop answering his phone and checking text messages during meals. The phone stopped ringing and then he heard a text message chirp. Alex and Josephine had their heads together, whispering about something. Ras took the opportunity to ease his cell phone out of his pocket and unlock it.

I like your hair like that. Did you cut it?

Ras's hand flew up to his head and then he whipped his neck around to see who else was in the restaurant.

"What's wrong?" Josephine asked.

Ras shook his head and kept looking around. Who would be texting him about his haircut? He looked down at the phone. The text message came from a number in Jamaica. Ras racked his brain to think of anyone in Jamaica who would text him and came up empty. It could have been a wrong number. Ras exhaled.

"I'll be right back," Ras said, excusing himself from the table. He walked quickly to the back of the restaurant, typing out a message on the way.

"I'm pretty sure you have the wrong number."

He hit SEND and then pushed in the door to the bathroom. He ran water over his face, wiped his face and hands with a paper towel, and then checked his face in the mirror. His heart was still racing and he couldn't seem to calm himself. *It was just a wrong number*, he said out loud. And what if it wasn't? What if it was . . . her?

The last time Ras saw Cleo, he didn't tell her it was over. He had no idea what she was capable of. So he went out of his way to make her think there was nothing unusual about the visit. For ninety minutes, he'd engaged in every twisted sexual fantasy he could possibly imagine and, as usual, Cleo didn't deny him anything. He kissed her on her forehead when he left, as always. She told him she loved him, as always.

And when he pulled up to his house, he jumped in the shower and was clean and dressed just as the movers arrived to pack up all of their belongings. He changed his cell number and instructed his bodyguards and drivers—anyone Cleo had access to—to do the same. Within forty-eight hours of their last sexual encounter, he was sitting on the front porch of the house on a former sugar plantation in Saint Catherine Parrish. Just as quickly, he'd put Cleo out of his mind. Or at least tried to.

Completely forgetting Cleo had been impossible. For the past year, as he repaired his relationship with his wife, he dreamt of his mistress nightly. He had orgasms in his dreams, waking up and quickly stripping the bed before Josephine could find out. One night several months ago, he broke down. He flew out to New Jersey and found out where Cleo lived. He was halfway to her house when he turned back around and headed to the airport. He Googled her often, tracking her whereabouts through the blogs that always posted items about her.

Lately, Ras had been wondering if he'd ever be completely free of her. Would she always cast a shadow over his life? And now, one year after he'd walked away from her and rededicated himself to his marriage, he felt like he might know the answer.

Ras left the bathroom and began walking back to the table. His breathing was controlled and he'd stopped sweating. Cleo had not won. He wasn't over her yet. But she had not—

Ras's cell phone chirped again.

"I can't believe you would have dinner with Alex but not with me . . ."

Ras clenched his teeth and marched through the dining room, his eyes trained on the table where his wife sat. If that bitch was anywhere near his wife . . .

He could see someone sitting in his seat, facing Alex, Birdie, and Josephine. He recognized the jet-black sheet of hair immediately. Ras saw his wife, frozen in her seat, her head held high.

She briefly caught Ras's eye and then looked back at the woman sitting in his seat.

The woman saw the three of them looking behind her so she turned around just as Ras reached the table.

"Ras!" Cleo said, smiling wide. "We were just talking about you. So good to see you. Have a seat."

Cleo gestured to a chair near Birdie.

"Get up," Ras said, through clenched teeth.

"Don't be rude, Ras," Cleo said. "We're all just having a little chat. Join in."

Ras grabbed Cleo's shoulder and pulled her out of her seat. A few patrons in the restaurant gasped, and one couple quickly exited the restaurant.

"Get out. Or I will hurt you."

Cleo wriggled out of his grasp and then looked down at her dress, a black strapless shift that hit the top of her thigh. She used both hands to smooth out the wrinkles and then picked up her bag off the table and put it on her shoulder.

"I was just in the neighborhood and I wanted to say hi," said Cleo.

Ras looked toward the manager and gestured for him to come over.

"There's no need for all of that, Ras," said Cleo. "I'm leaving."

The manager came over and stood next to Ras.

"Is everything okay here?"

"We have an unwanted guest," said Ras. "We need her to be removed."

Cleo laughed loud enough to get the attention of anyone in the restaurant who might have missed Ras grabbing her arm.

"I'm unwanted. Can you imagine that? This guy"—she pointed to Birdie—"He was more than happy to get a blow job from me in the studio last year. Right, Alex?"

The sounds of silverware hitting several plates filled the restaurant. Alex and Birdie looked at each other, but neither said a word or revealed any sort of emotion on their faces.

"And my beloved Ras . . ." Cleo continued. "For years, you came to me whenever I called you. And vice versa. And now I'm unwanted? I never thought I'd see the day."

Ras sat back down at his seat and took his wife's hand. Josephine's face was stone.

"I'm going to sit here with my wife and my friends and finish my dessert," Ras announced.

Cleo remained standing.

"It was good to see all of you," Cleo said. She looked over at Josephine. "Especially you, Josephine. You look amazing. Motherhood truly agrees with you." Josephine didn't move.

"I'm sure your little girl is absolutely gorgeous."

Ras felt his wife squeeze his hand so hard that his knuckles began to crack. He knew she was trying to refrain from standing up and punching Cleo out.

"Do not give her the satisfaction," Ras whispered to his wife. Josephine nodded but kept her eyes on Cleo.

"Please, Ras," Cleo said. "I'm very satisfied. Your wife knows exactly what we have. And she knows that it won't change no matter how far away you go. You can pack up and move to China. It doesn't change a thing."

Cleo tossed her hair back and turned to walk away.

"If you ever need me—and I think you might—Alex will know where to find me."

Cleo walked away, leaving the foursome in stunned silence. As soon as she was out of sight, Josephine stood up quickly and grabbed her shawl from the back of her chair.

"Wait, Josephine!" Ras yelled out as she half-ran toward the back entrance, where their driver was waiting.

"Go to hell, Ras!" Josephine yelled out. "Stay away from me!"

Ras turned around to Alex and Birdie. He pointed a finger in Alex's direction.

"Why did she say you would know where to find her?"

"I have no idea, Ras," Alex said. "I swear I don't."

Ras's eyes went from Birdie's to Alex's. Then he dashed off to catch up to his wife.

"Josephine! Would you just stop for a second so we can talk about this?!"

Ras's wife continued tossing clothes from her bureau into one of several suitcases opened on her bed.

"You keep talking," Josephine said. "I'm leaving."

Ras grabbed his wife's wrist and pulled her close to him.

"Please. Sit down."

Josephine flopped down on the bed and dropped her head into her hands. Ras rubbed her back.

"We are not going to let this woman run us off this island," Ras said.

"We? There is no 'we,' Ras." Josephine spat. "There is me. There is you. And there is her."

"You are my wife," said Ras.

"Tell that to Cleo."

"She knows."

"Yes, she does. And guess what? She doesn't care. She will fly to Jamaica, find out where we're having dinner, and torture us just for sport. I'm supposed to stay with you and deal with that? We moved here to get away from her. And she's just taken me back to day one."

"That's exactly what she wants to do," Ras said. "I have not seen her in a year, Josephine. She's pissed that I walked away forever and she doesn't want to see us happy."

"I've tried . . ." Josephine said, her eyes on the floor. "I've tried to put all of this behind us. But seeing her tonight . . ."

Josephine stopped talking. She looked as if she were suddenly gasping for breath. Ras eased her back on the bed and lay with her, holding her as she struggled to speak.

"I am so sorry I hurt you," Ras said. "I am so so sorry."

"She came to my office, Ras!" Josephine sobbed. "Don't you remember?"

Ras nodded, a lump in his throat.

"And you—you did such awful things with her. Dirty, nasty . . ."

"You said you were not going to read that book."

Josephine stood and lifted her suitcase to the floor.

"Can we get a restraining order?" she asked Ras.

"First thing in the morning."

"What if she comes here? What if she wants to hurt me or Reina?"

Ras shook his head.

"We have two full-time security guards here. No one is coming on this property unless we've invited them."

"I'm not always here. I go to the market. I take Reina out . . ." Josephine shook her head. "This bitch is going to have me be a prisoner in my own home."

"I will not let that happen."

"You're the one who brought this on us in the first place. If you could keep your dick in your pants, we wouldn't have to deal with this shit."

Ras kept his mouth shut. He wanted to protest. But there was nothing he could say.

"We're not just dealing with a random groupie here," Josephine said.

"I know."

"You were in a relationship with her. You were in *love* with her." Josephine looked away and shrugged her shoulders. "Sometimes I think you still are."

"I told you I haven't spoken to her in over a year."

"What does that mean? That your feelings for her magically evaporated? That's not how that works. God knows, if it did work that way, I would have left you a long time ago. Nothing's changed. Moving five hundred miles away doesn't end a relationship with someone."

Ras sighed heavily.

"Then what does?"

Josephine leaned against their bedroom door.

"I wouldn't know."

Ras watched his wife turn the knob and go out into the hall to check on the baby. He realized his jaw was throbbing from clenching his teeth so hard. He'd worked on his wife for a year. He'd catered to her every whim. He traveled rarely without her and the baby. He showered her with attention and affection, checked in with her hourly when he was in the studio. And now a five-minute visit from Cleo was threatening to ruin it all. Ras relived the scene in the restaurant and two things were going to bother him until he dealt with them. First, he needed to know why Cleo really came to Jamaica. And then he needed to figure out why on God's green earth he still desperately wanted to fuck her.

5

B e aware of your breathing," said the yoga instructor, her
voice a whisper.

Z did a headstand and balanced himself in the air. It had
taken months to get his body to adjust to being upside down.
Now it was simple. He felt every breath as if it were both his first
and his last. When he felt a burning sensation in his forearms, he
envisioned his children, their faces flashing before him like patterns in a kaleidoscope.

"Z, you can come down any time you're ready," the instructor
whispered.

Z brought his legs down gracefully and the class clapped
softly.

"This is exactly what we want to accomplish," said the instructor. "Your body will do what you ask of it."

On his mat, Z lay flat on his back, in the Savasana pose. The
instructor lit incense and turned the lights down.

"Feel every part of your body," the instructor said. "Be aware
of your toes, your ankles, knees, and thighs. Feel the top of your
head, the tips of your fingertips. If you focus, you can feel your
own vibration."

Z's breath came in shallow. The corpse pose was his favorite
part of yoga class. It was the only time he felt completely relaxed.

Z, a former crackhead and recovering alcoholic who once
wore the same underwear for two weeks, wasn't the yoga type.
But two months of in-patient rehab, followed by months of out-
patient meetings, had changed his world.

Soon after his daughter was born, his faith and sobriety were tested: Cleo had called him.

Z had cheated on his wife from the moment they married and long before. And Cleo was one of his repeat customers. He barely hid his affair with Cleo from his wife. They were photographed together often, and he regularly took her shopping and out to eat. Cleo knew two core things: how to get Z to come and how to get him high. Sometimes she did both at the same time.

Just the sound of Cleo's voice through the phone made Z forget all the tenets he'd been learning in AA. He was at her new home, in a gated community in central New Jersey, an hour after she told him to come over.

But something was different about Cleo that night. Z saw the coke ready on the table. The blunt was freshly rolled. But Z felt like he couldn't see her clearly. It was as if a haze covered her.

He stood in her living room and watched her slowly strip down to her bra and panties. She took the blunt, put it inside her, and then took it out. She lit it. Blew a smoke ring. And passed it over to Z.

Z took the blunt, looked at it for a long moment, and then pressed it out in the ashtray next to her sofa. He walked up to Cleo, held her shoulders, and kissed her forehead.

"You take care of yourself," he said.

He walked out of Cleo's house, closing the door softly behind him. And he got in the car and drove off without looking back. He went home to his wife Beth and their five children. And he stayed there.

Z had been introduced to yoga by one of his sponsors in AA. He thought it was New Age and hokey and absolutely ridiculous for a hard-core rapper from the Bronx who had sold millions of records. But he agreed to try it. And he immediately appreciated what yoga did for him. He came up with rhymes in the Downward Facing Dog position and beats came to him whenever he put the sole of one foot on his thigh and clasped his hands in front of him.

He tried to get everyone he knew to try yoga with him. There were no takers. His oldest son, Zander, was too busy in the studio. His boy Jake, head of the record label Z was signed to, told him in no uncertain terms that it would never happen. The look on his wife Beth's face was priceless. She didn't have to say a word.

It ended up working out better this way. He chose a studio far from his house, where he knew that no one would know that he was on their kid's iPods.

When the lights came up, Z stayed in place. He could hear the other students in the background begin to stand up and whisper "*namaste.*" The instructor knelt down next to Z.

"What are you thinking about?"

Z opened his eyes and blinked.

"I once smoked crack in front of my infant son."

"How long ago was this?" the instructor asked, her eyebrows wrinkled.

"He's nineteen now."

"Is he okay?"

"He's perfect."

"Are you okay?"

"I'm working on it."

The instructor smiled and patted his shoulder, leaving him on the floor.

Z stayed in place, eyes closed, for ten more minutes. He thought about the last time he saw Kipenzi, his wife's closest friend and his boy Jake's wife. Kipenzi had come to visit him in rehab in Anguilla and begged him to get it together for Beth and the kids. She physically got down on her knees and begged him. She even booked a photo shoot for Anguilla so that she could check on him. She was on her way to see him when her plane crashed just a mile away from his rehab center. No one could convince Z that it was not his fault that Kipenzi was dead. No one.

Z and Beth had named their last child, a girl, after Kipenzi. Beth had just given birth when they got the news of her death.

Z rolled over onto his stomach, lifted himself up, and did twenty-five push-ups in rapid secession. He felt better, as always. He jogged to the car.

The reentry into the real world after yoga always stunned Z. If it was just a bit sunny, it felt as if the sun were boring into his skull. If it was drizzling, it felt like a monsoon. Today, a mild winter chill felt like subzero temperatures to Z. He clomped through the crunchy gravel mixed with snow and walked to the front door of the house. He punched in the security code, opened the door slowly, and was instantly hit in the face by the smell of soiled diapers. In the distance of the home, a seven-bedroom on four levels, he could hear his daughter screaming, two of his sons fighting over a toy, and his oldest son working on music in the basement.

His wife Beth came down the steps, a garbage can in her hand.

"Just in time," she said, handing the garbage can over to Z.

The stench overpowered Z and he gagged.

"What the hell is this?"

"The baby threw up, she's got some kind of virus."

Z looked closely at his wife's face. There was dried mucus in the corner of one eye. Her dirty blond hair sat heavy and oily. A large angry pimple sat in the crevice of her nose.

"Did you get a chance to take a shower today?" he asked.

"Yeah. Why?"

"Just asking," Z said. "Let me throw this out, then I'll check on the baby."

"Don't go in Zeke's room; he's in time-out."

"When is he *not* in time-out?"

Z held the trash can out in front of him and took it to the garage to hose it out. Z had first met Beth when he was nine years old while visiting family in West Virginia. He'd fallen in love with her immediately and swore he'd marry her one day. He did. And after all they'd been through together, she'd stuck by him. He was in awe of her support. But after rehab, everyone—including Beth—started to look different. All the tiny flaws and tics he'd been too high to notice were now in sharp focus.

At the dinner table, Z noticed that Beth ate with her mouth open. She'd catch him looking at her and ask, "What?" And Z would go back to his food, using a fork and knife to cut his steak into small pieces. Even with full-time help, the house was always a mess. There was clean laundry in piles and dirty laundry in piles. The dishes piled up faster than the housekeeper could wash them.

Z finished with the hose and went back to the house. First stop: Zeke's room. His youngest son was on his back in bed, his tiny feet propped on the wall.

"Hi, Daddy."

"Why are you in time-out?"

"'Cause I said dammit."

"And why did you say dammit?"

"'Cause I hurt my toe. Mommy always says dammit when she hurts something."

"Mommy shouldn't say it either."

"So how come *she's* never in time-out?"

Z tried unsuccessfully not to laugh. Zeke rolled over and went to his father to be picked up and as Z obliged, the boy put his head on his dad's shoulder and his thumb in his mouth.

"You know you're too big to be sucking your thumb," Z said.

"I know," said Zeke, his words jumbled.

Z hugged his son tight against his chest. And he felt that familiar pull of intense guilt and shame. He'd barely spoken to his youngest son when he was high. And the idea that this little boy would forgive him and not seem to harbor any ill feelings was almost too much to take. Z wanted Zeke to hate him. He wanted to be forced to win him over, like he had to do with Beth and his oldest son Zander. But Zeke just wasn't that way. He barely remembered the old version of Z. And he was perfectly content to be held by his father all day.

The sound of something crashing and breaking sent Z hustling into the hallway, still holding Zeke. He went into Zakee's room, where he and Zach were standing over a broken lamp with wide eyes.

"Y'all were wrestling in here, weren't you?" Z asked.

The boys looked at the floor.

"Get this cleaned up. And make up the beds in here."

"Yes, Dad," they said in unison.

Z carried Zeke down the opposite end of the hallway, toward the bedroom he shared with his wife. She was on the bed, rocking their daughter back and forth, trying to quiet her cries.

"She just won't stop fucking crying," Beth whined.

Zeke looked up at his father. "See, she just cursed *again*," he whispered.

"Where's the sling?" Z asked.

"I don't know. I don't feel like dealing with that thing."

When their daughter was inconsolable, wrapping her up in a sling so that she was close to your chest was the only thing that calmed her. But Beth refused to use it. She said it made her feel claustrophobic. Z put Zeke down and started to dig through a pile of dirty laundry at the foot of the bed to find the sling. He jumped back when he saw a pair of panties inside out with a bloody pad still attached. He clenched his teeth and picked around the underwear until he found the sling.

He stood up, his eyes on his wife, who was still rocking the baby with a look of sheer fatigue on her face. He wrapped the fabric around his waist, over his shoulders, and back around his waist. Beth stood up and put the baby inside the sling. The little girl, brown like her father but with dirty blond hair like her mom, snuggled against her father's chest and stopped crying immediately.

"See, Beth? This works."

"Doesn't work when I use it."

"You never use it."

"How do you know what I do?"

"I know you don't use the sling. And it would help you."

"I need a lot more help than a goddamn sling."

Z felt a flash of something. Anger. And as fast as it came, it was gone. Ten years ago, he'd punched her in the mouth because she yelled at him when she caught him smoking crack in the nursery. Now Beth cursed him out nearly every day, and he just sighed and walked away.

Z took Zeke's hand and, with the baby on his chest in the sling, he made his way back to Zakee and Zachary's room. The boys were done cleaning up and followed their father downstairs. Z led them into the basement, where his oldest son Zander was sitting at a mixing board listening to a playback of himself singing.

"You ready for your party?" Z asked his oldest son.

"Yeah." Zander grinned. "You're coming, right?"

"Look, don't let yourself get gassed up," said Z, as he moved to sit on the floor, his knees in the air. He managed to cradle the baby and Zeke at the same time. Zach and Zakee put their chins in their hands, listening to their big brother's voice. Z leaned his head back and closed his eyes, losing himself in his son's strong voice as the song played.

"I heard this on the radio at least three times this morning," said Z. "You're doing well at pop radio. Not an easy thing to do with R&B."

Zander puffed up with pride.

"I still don't like the song," Z said, shrugging his shoulders. "But I guess it's working."

Zander's shoulders slumped. Z didn't want to be so hard on his oldest son. But he didn't know any other way to be. His son definitely had talent. He had just enough to either make it big or get his heart broken. Or both.

"Uncle Jake won't tell me how many albums they're gonna ship," said Zander. "That's the only way I'll know how I'm really going to do first week it's out."

"Why are you worrying about that?" asked Z. "You did your job. You handed in a good album. The rest is out of your hands."

"I know, but I can't help but think—"

"Don't think. And don't bet that this is going to last. Because it probably won't."

"You saying my music isn't good?"

"It's okay," said Z. "Not that much different from whatever else is on the radio right now." Zander winced, but Z continued. "I'm just saying you need more than that. You need luck and a lot of hard work. Do you hear me?"

"Yes, sir," Zander mumbled under his breath.

Z continued to rock Zeke on his lap while rubbing the baby's back. They both were minutes from falling asleep.

"It's not too late to go to Rutgers. You could start this semester or in the fall."

"I already told you I'm not going," Zander said softly.

"You got a full *academic* scholarship and you won't even consider it?" Z asked.

"I didn't turn it down yet," said Zander. "I just deferred. I have to get this music thing together first."

"And you need to get your personal life together too," said Z, sending Zander a pointed look.

A few months before, Zander ended up in jail for a night on a domestic violence charge. His girlfriend Bunny, a singer from Jamaica, goaded him into hitting her and then pressed charges. He'd gotten off with probation and anger management classes. But his father was still pissed.

"I know you're still running around with that girl," Z said, pointing at his son. "Even after she got you locked up. That's why I wish you would just go to school. Get some space from this chick."

Zander kept his eyes on the floor.

"Her career hasn't taken a hit at all," said Z. "She's on the cover of all those fashion magazines your mom reads. But they're having a hard time getting press for you because of what happened."

Zander looked up at his father. "Am I doing anything right?"

Z hesitated. He knew he went too hard on the boy. But no one else in the world would give it to Zander straighter than his own father.

"Of course, you're doing things right," said Z. "Let me hear what you're working on now."

Zander took his place at the piano. He started a backing track and began to play and sing a ballad. Z closed his eyes and settled down to listen. His son's voice was flawless and he hit the notes with ease. It was something Z and Beth had noticed when he was a very young child, back when they had nothing and lived with Z's grandmother in the Bronx. As Zander sang, Z's thoughts returned to his wife. She wasn't coping well, and he had no idea how to help her. Did she need therapy? Was she depressed? Z was so used to being the one who needed fixing that he'd never learned how to fix anyone else.

Z opened his eyes and happened to look up into the corner of the studio and see his wife on the baby monitor screen. She was in the same spot where he'd left her, staring out of their bedroom window.

There was something chilling about the way her hair laid flat on her cheeks and the way she sat with her back slumped, defeated and small. Beth had been the only person who had ever cared about him unconditionally. She was there for him when he had nothing. She was there when he was on top of the world. The drugs, the other women, and the other babies: she kept a stiff upper lip and forgave him.

But as he stared at his wife in the monitor, Z had a sinking feeling in his stomach. No matter how hard he tried to put the thought out of his mind, he couldn't help but admit to himself that he was growing apart from Beth. What he didn't know (and was afraid to know) was whether this feeling would be temporary or forever.

6

For some reason, Zander expected his *actual* friends to be at his big splashy record release party. The club was perfectly swanky with an ice-cold vibe, from the waitstaff to the owner who posted up in the VIP section. But none of his childhood friends and classmates were anywhere to be seen. Zander hadn't seen most of the guests a day in his life. Zander held his girlfriend Bunny's hand and led her in behind Boo, one of his dad and Uncle Jake's bodyguards that he was borrowing for the occasion.

"Zan! Zaaaaan, over here, sweetie!"

Zander kept holding Bunny's hand tight and turned toward the sound of his publicist's grating voice. Dylan was dragging a photographer toward Zander. He pulled Bunny next to his face and they both smiled.

The camera flashed and then Dylan ushered them into the back of the venue, while a few of the guests craned their necks to get a look at both of them.

"Why did you two come in together?" asked Dylan, under her breath.

"Zander is my boyfriend," Bunny said, ladling out her thick Jamaican accent. "I'm not hiding shit." Bunny turned to look Zander in the eye. "And he better not hide shit either."

"Dylan?" Zander asked, looking at the party guests. "Did you get my guest list for the party?"

"I did," said his publicist, her eyes on her clipboard. "I'm sure the people out front have the names. But look, this is more important. Your managers don't want you two seen at the same events together."

Bunny glared at Zander. He escaped her gaze and became extremely interested in a piece of lint on his jeans. Bunny turned to face Dylan.

"I'm going out there with *my* man to celebrate his new album. Anyone who doesn't like it can *fuck off.*"

Zander laughed. Dylan blushed. And they all walked out into the party, drinks in hand, though neither Zander nor Bunny were old enough to drink.

The DJ announced Zander's arrival as soon as they began making their way to the private VIP section on the second floor. Applause and cheers went up and Zander smiled.

Bunny squeezed his hand and he squeezed back.

It had all happened fast. Two years ago, Zander was making YouTube videos in his bedroom, playing piano and singing. He graduated from high school, deferred a full scholarship to Rutgers, and now Bunny and Zander were both signed to a major label and had released well-received albums. Zander was in awe. Not because he knew nothing about fame. On the contrary, he grew up in the spotlight as Z's oldest son. His father had become a platinum-certified artist by the time Zander was five years old. Though he had vague memories of living in a modest apartment in Fresh Meadows, he'd grown up in private schools with nannies and live-in housekeepers.

"Where's my dad?" he whispered to Bunny. She was waving at fans on the bottom level.

"Dude, are you seeing this right now?" Bunny asked, her face broken into a wide grin. "They're playing your song and people are singing along!"

Zander tried to focus on the music blaring out of the ten-foot-high speakers. He drank in the girls in skimpy outfits circling the floor with drinks and appetizers. His head started to thump as he saw more and more of his dad's industry friends:

rappers at the top of their game, R&B singers with number-one albums. But the one person who mattered wasn't—

"You think you bad now?" came a gruff voice from behind.

Zander swirled around and came face-to-face with his father. He wanted to play it cool but couldn't help breaking into a grin.

"Birdie is here," Zander said, pointing to a second VIP section on the other side of the club. "So is Drake. I heard Lil Wayne might come through."

Z nodded.

"But what did I tell you about all this?"

"Triumph and Disaster are both impostors," Zander said.

"Tonight is a triumph," said Z. "Your first album is dropping. Lots of good buzz. That's all great. But tomorrow could be a disaster. Then what?"

"I have to treat Triumph and Disaster exactly the same."

Z pointed at his son. "Don't forget that," he said. "Treat Triumph like it's unreliable and can disappear at any time. And treat Disaster exactly the same."

Zander turned back around to survey the crowd. He counted three more crews who'd sold millions of records between them. And they'd all come out in force to celebrate him. But was it really him? Or his famous dad? Or his famous girlfriend? Bunny's own album, gold-certified with several catchy hooks and choruses, was now blaring through the venue, and Zander noted that the crowd was considerably more hyped than they had been when his mellow, ballad-heavy collection played.

"I wonder if people came here to see me or you?" Zander said, holding Bunny tightly around the waist as cameras flashed.

"Probably me," Bunny said. Zander waited for her to laugh it off. She didn't. She was in her own zone, still waving at familiar faces in the crowd.

"Come on," Bunny said, pulling Zander into a corner. "Dance with me." Zander wanted to drink in more of his coming-out party, but he allowed Bunny to lead him away.

"Look," Zander said, pointing with his chin to the club entrance.

It was Jake, coming into the club flanked by two burly bodyguards. He had his head down as a collective swell of recognition swept through the club. Jake had on his uniform: baggy denim, button-up shirt, white Air Jordans, and a puffy nylon coat. In his left hand, he held a water bottle and swigged from it as he made away upstairs. His beard was thick and his hair was knotty and uncombed.

In addition to being his uncle, Jake was the head of his record label. So it was a huge show of support and confidence that Jake was there. Most of the partygoers hadn't seen much of him in public since Kipenzi's death. Zander knew he'd finally arrived when he saw his Uncle Jake bound up the stairs toward him and pulled him in for a bear hug.

"I feel like I was just teaching you how to tie your damn shoes," Jake said, as Zander beamed.

"You bought me my first keyboard. So you're responsible for a lot of this."

"Let's hope you catch up to your girl here," said Jake, jerking his head toward Bunny.

"He won't catch me," Bunny said. "I'm at half a million and I've only been out for six weeks. But he can stay in his lane, do half those numbers, and be happy with that." Zander saw the face Jake made and knew that once again, Bunny was making him look like a sucker in front of the only people that mattered. Jake said his good-byes, spotted Z sitting with a group of people from the label, and made his way over.

"Can you calm down, please?" Zander said to Bunny in a loud whisper.

"What are you talking about?" Bunny said, her eyes everywhere but on Zander. "I'm just playing with you."

"Try filtering what you say, instead of blurting out whatever pops into your brain."

"Jealous, much?"

Zander sighed and grabbed Bunny's wrist at the same time.

"And if I smack the shit out of you, I'm wrong."

Bunny licked her lips.

"Go for it, baby boy. Nice crowd here. Let's put on a show."

"This is supposed to be my—"

"Exactly," said Bunny. "It's your day. Don't pay me any mind. I'm just jealous because you have Jake at your party and he didn't come to mine."

"Bunny, I'm not putting my hands on you ever again. But I swear, you always try to—"

"I won't anymore," Bunny said. She stroked her chest with her finger. "Cross my heart and hope to die."

Zander saw his dad roll up to both of them as Bunny was talking. Her back was to him.

"I hope you mean that, little girl," Z said. "You got my son locked up because you want to play games. I told him to stay as far away from you as possible."

Bunny slowly turned around to face Z. Zander always marveled at how Bunny looked at his father as if he wasn't the incredibly imposing figure he actually was. She looked him up and down and didn't blink.

"Is that any way to talk to your label mate?" she asked, her voice drippy and sweet. "We're like family."

"Me, my son, and Jake are family," said Z. "You are not."

"DJ's calling me down," Zander said. "Let's go, Bunny."

"You go," Z said, pointing at Bunny. "Zander, let me talk to you."

Zander opened his mouth to protest and thought better of it. He stood with his hands on the balcony railing and watched Bunny make her way through the crowd, with Boo right behind her.

"Dad, I know what you're going to say."

"This girl got you locked *up*. On purpose. And you stroll in here with her like it's all good? Any chick in here would happily be on your arm. And 'cause Bunny's got some shine and some good pussy—you just follow along behind her like a lovesick puppy? I thought I taught you better than—"

Zander looked up at his father before he could finish his sentence. Z faltered and then cleared his throat and averted his eyes. For nearly twenty years, Z had been a less than stellar husband and father. When Zander could barely talk, he'd watched as Z knocked his mother's two front teeth clear out of her mouth. When he was seven, he saw his mother cowering in a corner, completely naked, while his father stood over her with a leather belt, bringing it down on her back over and over.

And then there was the drug use. Zander could identify cocaine, crack, heroin, and ecstasy by name by the time he was nine. Just a year ago, he was dragging his father from the hallway of their palatial home while he was in a drug-induced stupor and struggling to get him in bed before his little brothers woke up and saw him with vomit snaking through his afro.

"Okay, I haven't always shown you the best example," said Z. "But listen to what I'm saying *now*. Pussy makes the world go 'round Zan. And it also brings the world *down*."

Zander went to the DJ booth, his father's words echoing in his head. He used the DJ's mic to greet the crowd gathered, and he drank in the applause and adulation.

This is Triumph, he thought to himself. *Just an imposter. This is not real.*

Later that night, at the Parker Meridien, he pulled Bunny beneath him and moved deep inside her. Sweat made their stomachs glide across each other smoothly. Bunny used her own hands to pull her legs open wider and wider, squeezing her muscles to make it feel even tighter inside. Zander knew that no matter what Jake said, no matter what his mother said, no matter what his father said. No matter what Jesus Christ himself had to say about the matter: he was *never* going to voluntarily give up the inside of this woman's thighs.

This feels like Triumph, he thought to himself. *Please let this be real.*

W e specifically said No. Reality. Television!"
Birdie took off his Yankees cap, scratched his head, and then put it back.

"I know. And I wanted to honor that—"

"By signing a deal for a reality show? Please explain."

Birdie tried to lead his wife by the arm to get her to sit down. She snatched her arm away and crossed both arms over her chest.

"I want to know why you did this."

"Because I can't *not* do this. It's ten episodes. They're calling the show *Fistful of Dollars*, which is perfect promotion for my album. You don't ever have to appear on the show. Not ever."

"But they'll be in my house."

"Sometimes, yes. But mostly not. I won't let this affect you, I promise."

Alex's face softened. "It's not about how it's going to affect me," she said. "It's about how it's going to affect *you*."

Birdie stepped to his wife, put his arms around her waist, and kissed her neck.

"It's me, Alex," he said, starting up their favorite game.

"Me who?" Alex asked, trying not to smile.

"Peter Washington."

"I don't know anyone named Peter Washington."

"People call me Birdie."

"Oh. That's nice."

"And you and I are married."

"We are?"

"Yes. And we're very happy together. I run baths for you, paint your toenails, and all kinds of stuff I shouldn't be doing."

"And I give really good blow jobs," Alex said.

"The best."

"So I guess we sort of work well together," Alex said. She rested her head on his chest.

Birdie exhaled and squeezed his wife's waist a little tighter.

"I promise I won't change," he whispered in her ear. "I promise."

Alex pulled away just enough to look him in the face. Her eyes filled up.

"It's me," Birdie said.

Three weeks later, a television crew showed up at six a.m. Birdie let them into the brownstone and then went upstairs to let Alex know they were there. She wasn't in bed. He checked the bathroom, Tweet's room, and then went upstairs to her attic office. He tried the door. It was locked.

"Alex, you in there?"

"Yeah."

"Open the door."

"Are they here?"

"Yeah."

Alex was silent. And Birdie didn't hear her coming anywhere near the door to open it.

"I'll be downstairs," Birdie said. "They'll only be here for a few hours."

There was no response. Birdie went back downstairs and saw two men huddled in a corner of his kitchen, going over paperwork.

"So you're having a meeting today to discuss marketing for your album," said Alan, a producer with thin gray dreadlocks.

"Right."

"Jake is going to come to the meeting. But you're going to be really surprised."

"Got it."

"We're just going to have you talking to your friends about the album, how it's coming along, and how you're worried because you haven't heard anything from Jake yet."

As the producer continued to talk, three of Birdie's friends came in through the front door.

"What up, superstar," said Travis, leaning in to slap Birdie's hand. Travis had been Birdie's closest friend since fifth grade. In a lot of ways, Birdie felt like the tables had been turned in the wrong direction. Travis had taught Birdie everything he knew about hip-hop. And it was Travis's older brother who had taken them to the Fresh Fest in 1984. It was Travis who had shell-toed Adidas sneakers first, and he'd memorized all the verses to Run-DMC's *Rock Box* before anyone else. Truth be told, he was the strongest rapper in their whole crew. Everybody knew that. But Birdie had gotten the break . . .

"When you come over," said Alan, pointing to Travis, "you sit here. We're going to have camera one . . . *here* and a second camera right *there*."

A swarm of tecÿicians moved in, attaching microphones to Birdie, Travis, and his other boys, Daryl and Corey. Daryl was Birdie's manager, and Corey was Daryl's right-hand man. The three of them formed Birdie's inner circle, and as such, they also formed the cast of Birdie's "reality" show, though clearly, nothing was real about it.

"So we have a discussion here about what's going on with your album," said Alan.

"Then Jake comes in and you're going to be nervous about this conversation. And then you give us some cutaways talking about the new album."

"Got it," said Birdie, giving all his boys a pound.

"Where's your wife?" said Alan.

"She's not involved," Birdie said.

A cameraman stood close to Birdie while an assistant adjusted some overheard lighting.

"Can we talk about why? On camera?"

"Nah, I'm good on that."

"We know she's not on camera. But can you just tell the viewers that she's not involved."

"No, we're not even doing that."

Dylan came up to Birdie and put a hand on his shoulder. When Birdie was an underground rapper with a rabid cult following, Dylan ignored him at industry parties and never returned his calls when he tried to get tickets to events. Now, he was signed and officially blessed by his label mates Jake and Z. And suddenly Dylan made the oceans part anytime he walked into a room. Birdie had specifically asked for a different publicist. He even hated the sound of Dylan's voice. It was too throaty and scratchy, like she was a sixty-year-old smoker instead of a twenty-something blonde with jet-black roots.

"Can I talk to Alex?" Dylan asked, smiling. "I think I could get her to understand."

"We already discussed this when we put the show together," said Birdie. "Why is this even coming up now? There's nothing for her to understand. She's not involved. Period."

Dylan and the producer exchanged a quick glance and then nodded.

"No, it's your show," Dylan said. She closed her eyes and put a hand over her heart. "I'm just here to make sure we get the most bang for our buck. It's ten episodes. That's it. We have to make it count."

A Town Car pulled up and out of the living room window, Birdie saw Jake climb out of the back seat, his heavy denim jeans hanging low on his waist, a cell phone in the crook of his neck, and his hands clutching his ever-present water bottle. Instantly, the energy in Birdie's house changed. The biggest name in hip-hop was standing on DeKalb Avenue. Jake's handlers poured out of the car behind him, all on cell phones. Alan, the producer, went outside to talk with Jake's people.

"Let's go!" said Alan, when he came back inside. "Jake's

ready and he's only giving us ten minutes to get this right. Birdie, move."

Birdie walked toward the door, a cameraman keeping time with his every step. He opened the door and Jake threw out an arm and then pulled him in for an elaborate handshake.

"What the hell is going on here!" Jake said, laughing. "No cameras! I'm here to work!"

The crew tittered and stood back as Jake and Birdie made their way into the kitchen. Birdie felt awkward. All of a sudden he didn't know what to say. He wanted to know his promotional budget for *A Fistful of Dollars*. He wanted to know if they were doing print ads or internet marketing. And he wanted to know when he was getting the second part of his advance.

But none of that would be for the cameras. So he spent the next ten minutes talking to Jake about absolutely nothing. They trash talked sports and then freestyled for a few minutes. (Jake made a point to drop a verse from his new track with an R&B singer newly signed to the label.)

Jake leaned against Birdie's refrigerator. A cameraman panned close to his face.

"So, Bird," Jake said. "You ready to be famous?"

Birdie noticed that Jake knew the game. He threw out questions that were innocuous but might make for good TV. It made Bird slightly uncomfortable that the president of his label was so good at being fake.

"I don't need to be famous," Birdie said.

"You just want a fistful of dollars," Jake said, pointing at Birdie.

Birdie groaned. Jake threw up his hands and yelled out at the crew.

"Cut and print!" he said. "You see how I ended that scene? That's your promo spot right there! You're welcome."

The crew clapped and laughed out loud as Birdie smiled and shifted from one leg to the other. Wait. Was he acting now?

What part of the game was this? Why was it so easy for Jake to act while Birdie felt like a fraud?

Jake left in a blur, taking a bit of the air out of the room with him as he billowed out with his crew. He was his own little weather system, moving like a storm cloud.

"Let's get a little more random conversation between you and Travis," said the producer.

He motioned for a camera to start rolling and then Travis spoke up.

"Do you know when you're shooting your second video?"

"Nah, I haven't heard anything about it yet . . ."

"Wait," said Dylan, popping up behind a cameraman. "It sounds like you aren't being informed about things that are happening with the label. We can't have that. You should probably word that differently. Say something like, 'It should be soon. I'm waiting to hear back from the label.'"

Birdie signaled to the cameraman that he was ready. The cameraman nodded and Travis cleared his throat.

"Do you know when you're shooting your second video?"

Birdie caught Dylan's eye. She was nodding.

"It should be soon," Birdie said. "I'm waiting to hear back from the label."

Birdie saw Dylan give him the thumbs-up sign, then she wandered away to take a phone call.

After three hours of filming fake conversation throughout the house, the crew began wrapping cords and packing boxes of equipment.

"Where's Alex?" asked Daryl, looking around the house. "Is she even here?"

"She's in the office upstairs," said Birdie. "She's pissed off that I agreed to do this."

"Jess would have never let me do this shit either," said Travis. "It's fake and it's ridiculous."

"So why am I doing it?" Birdie asked.

"'Cause you'll be in millions of homes for ten weeks right before the release of your album. It's an infomercial. So say cheese and let's get this money."

Birdie and Travis slapped each other's palms three times, hard.

"Can we get one more scene before we go?" the producer asked.

Travis and Birdie took their usual places on either side of the kitchen and waited for instruction.

"This time just Birdie," said Alan.

Travis crossed the kitchen to the area in the living room where there was no filming taking place.

"It's all you, superstar," Travis said as he made his way out.

"You gonna get enough of calling me that, Travis," said Birdie. "I ain't nobody's superstar."

Alan had set up a space in the kitchen with a white backdrop for Bird to talk directly to the camera. Alan set himself up off camera, feeding him questions.

"Your first album is dropping in ten weeks," said Alan. "Are you nervous?"

Birdie had to concentrate and make sure his answer didn't reveal that he was being fed the question.

"Am I nervous about my first album?" he said, staring directly into the camera. "No. Not at all. Whatever happens is exactly what's supposed to happen."

After a few more questions, Alan gave him the all clear. Birdie looked over the man's shoulder and saw his wife standing on the steps, her arms crossed over her chest. She smiled on one side of her mouth, gave him a thumbs-up sign, and continued up the stairs.

"Next time we film, it'll be at the studio so you don't have to worry about—"

"Bird, I'm sorry I've been so bitchy about the reality show thing."

It was midnight and the house was empty. It was so quiet that they could hear little Tweet's soft snores in the next room. Birdie spread out Alex's fertility medications on the dresser and then dabbed alcohol on a cotton ball. Alex lifted her pajama top and Birdie wiped off an area near her belly button.

"It's okay," said Bird. He took out a syringe and filled it with the clear liquid. "I said I wouldn't do a reality show and now I'm doing one. I'm the one who should be apologizing."

"I want to be supportive. I really do. But . . ."

Birdie pinched Alex's skin between his thumb and forefinger and then sunk the syringe inside, pushed the medicine in, and pulled it out quickly.

"Ouch."

"All done," said Birdie, kissing his wife's belly. He cleared off the bed and guided his wife to it.

"You've been working for this moment for so long," said Alex, lying on her back. "I want you to do whatever you need to do to make this work. I mean that."

"So does this mean you'll be on the next episode of *Fistful of Dollars?*"

"Not on your life," Alex said, laughing.

"I was just checking," said Birdie. He moved in closer to Alex and wrapped both hands around her waist, pulling her closer to him. As soon as he got hard, she laughed and then wriggled out of his grasp.

"Don't start," Alex said. "Don't you have a party to host to-night?"

"What are you talking about? I'm not going anywhere to-night."

"Daryl said you're hosting a party at the 40/40 Club tonight. There are flyers in the kitchen with your picture on them."

Birdie rolled out of bed and grabbed the bathrobe hanging on the back of the door.

"Nah, something's not right."

Birdie took the stairs down two at a time with Alex padding along behind him.

"I don't see anything," Birdie said, his eyes sweeping the kitchen.

"Here," said Alex. "I put it on the fridge."

Alex peeled off the flyer and handed it to Birdie. He groaned.

"See, it says right there that you're hosting this party."

"Look closer, Alex."

Alex peered at the postcard.

"What? I don't get it."

"It doesn't say I'm hosting. It says it's in *honor* of me. Which means even if I don't show up, they kept their word. I'm gonna *kill* Daryl. Why would he do this?"

"Did you tell him you would do a party?"

"No!" Birdie said. "I mean Daryl told me he wanted to celebrate the reality show getting picked up and all that. I thought they were planning to take me out for drinks or something. Not promote a party with my name on it."

Birdie reached for the phone and dialed Daryl's number. There was no answer, and he trudged back up to his bedroom, mumbling and cursing under his breath. He threw on sweats and an old pair of Timberlands and shrugged into his heavy coat.

"Where are you going?" Alex asked.

"I gotta go down there and see what's going on."

Birdie drove across the Brooklyn Bridge into Manhattan. He parked on the street and watched the club. The line was long. He could see Daryl at the front door, next to the bouncer.

Birdie was stunned at how quickly his boys had gotten out of line. They'd joked about what would happen if one of them blew up. How the rest of them would find ways to make money at the expense of their newly famous friend. Just six months ago, they laughed hard at the idea of Travis getting a deal and Birdie making money by taking people on bus tours through Red Hook to see the house where he'd grown up. And now. Already. He had beef. And it wasn't a small thing that he could overlook or just mention in a offhand way. This was a major violation. He got the deal. Fine. But he'd sworn that he would take care of everyone.

And he was. Travis and Daryl were getting 5 percent of Birdie's performances as his road managers. And they were paying Corey to handle different odds and ends. So why promote a party and not even tell him about it? Birdie called Daryl, watching him from the car.

"Yo, what's up, Birdie."

"I'm across the street."

Daryl trotted over and got in the front seat of Birdie's truck.

"How are you gonna throw a party with my name on the flyer and not even tell me?"

"We told you we were going to put together a little something after the show. We were already having an after-party for the show and we figured you might come through."

"Are you selling tickets?"

"Yeah."

"So you're promoting a party."

"I guess. But it's not really—"

"Come on, man," said Birdie. "You can't put my name on stuff and not tell me."

"It's not that deep," said Daryl. "You don't even have to come inside."

"It *is* that deep. You got people thinking I'm going to be there. And then it makes me look bad when I'm not."

"I can't believe you're tripping over a party. It's cool, though."

Birdie sighed.

It's cool, though was code for "I see how you are, superstar." Daryl was trying to throw the fame card at Birdie, making him feel like he should cosign on their side projects since he was the one who got the deal.

"Wait," said Birdie. "You really don't see why—"

"I said it's cool, Birdie," Daryl said. "I hear you."

Daryl got out of the car and crossed the street back to the entrance to the club.

Birdie pulled off. It was too early for things to change like this. They had been on an equal playing field for so long, Birdie didn't know how to interact with them any other way. But he couldn't let them take advantage of his newfound fame either. He was looking out for them in every way he could—probably more than he should. How much did he have to change to prove he'd never change?

When am I going to see you?

Jake sat up in bed. He was soaked to the skin in a cold sweat. He turned and felt around the bed for Kipenzi. He always woke up feeling for his wife beside him. And every morning, he remembered again that she was somewhere else.

In his dream, she was sitting on a lilac settee that used to be in their bedroom. Her right eye was hanging by a bloody membrane. She didn't seem to be fazed by this at all. The hanging eye even blinked. And for some reason, it seemed perfectly normal for Jake to see Kipenzi as he imagined she looked at the site of the plane crash. Her face was bruised, her clothes burned. One finger on her left hand was missing.

Jake. When am I going to see you?

That's what she always asked him. Right before he woke up.

And in the shower, in his closet, in the car with his driver on the way to the studio, it's all he could hear in his head.

When am I going to see you?

Her voice was so crisp in his ear that for a moment, he thought he really was going crazy. Or that she was haunting him the way she jokingly promised she would if she died before him.

When am I going to see you?

Jake sipped from a water bottle filled with vodka on the way to the studio, wincing and shuddering as he choked the liquid down. He passed a billboard for Peter Luger's and thought about Lily, the waitress who had blown him off. He hadn't stopped thinking about her since that night. And he couldn't understand why. He'd had sex with at least a dozen women since his wife's death and could barely recall their names afterward. He'd had one brief conversation with Lily weeks ago and she was still on his mind. The only other time in his life that a woman had that effect on him, he married her. Jake thought about how that ended and drained his water bottle.

His driver pulled up on Eighth Street and he slipped into Electric Lady Studios and headed directly to Studio B.

Ten years, ten albums. All recorded in Studio B. He'd met Kipenzi here. He'd gotten head from groupies in the lounge. He'd eaten at least five hundred Chinese dinners on the black leather couch with the stuffing coming out. He'd coached Faith on a hook, wrote a track for Mary, ghostwrote an entire album for Puff. All in Studio B.

His engineer, a sixty-year-old man named Paul who'd been in the business since before hip-hop was invented, sat at the boards.

"Pull up what Jus sent over."

"It's not finished," said Paul.

Jake peeled out of his coat and dropped it onto a chair. He walked into the booth, slipped into his favorite headphones, and closed his eyes. The words *when am I going to see you* seemed to match up perfectly with the beat Just Blaze had sent over. It was a laconic track, almost as slow as screw music. He began to speak, slowly first, as his rhythm adjusted to the beat. Then faster. He nodded his head at a place in the song where he'd get someone to sing a hook. And then he dove into the second verse, weaving stories about his early days as a crack dealer and how he paid the price by losing his wife years after going straight.

When he finished, he was sweaty and spent. He sat in the booth alone for a few minutes until someone rapped on the glass to get his attention.

Jake looked up to see Z standing at the boards, talking to the engineer.

Jake came out of the booth and slapped hands with Z.

"I like that!" Z exclaimed.

"What's good with you, Yoga Boy?" Jake asked.

"Nothing. Just stopped by on my way to class."

"On your way to *what*?"

"You heard me. Class. Continuing education at Rutgers."

Jake shook his head. Z never ceased to amaze him. Ever since rehab, he'd transformed into more than just a reformed drug addict. He ate fruit and salads. He went home to have dinner with his family every night. He never cheated on Beth. He just did his music and hung out with his kids. And then he started doing yoga. And now he was in school.

"What class?"

"Poetry."

"You gotta be kidding me," Jake said.

"That's what we do, right? Ultimately, we're poets. You'd be surprised how similar some of the old-school poetry is to hip-hop. It's crazy."

Jake laughed. "I'm gonna need you to leave now."

"I'm leaving. Just wanted to know what Zander's first week sales look like."

"Are you asking me as the president of the label or as Zander's godfather?"

"Both."

"We shipped 250,000. It's looking like he'll bring in less than half."

"Not bad for a R&B record with only one or two rap hooks."

"The song with the most potential is the one with him and Bunny," said Jake.

"Don't start me up on that chick. Did you see her at Zander's party? She's nuts."

"Indeed," said Jake. "But if we can keep those two from killing each other, they can both be huge."

"My class is starting soon, I gotta get on the turnpike. You should come one day," said Z.

"Never that."

Z shook his head.

"You were always the one trying to get *me* to do different shit. Dinner with L.A. Reid. Going skiing. Eating sushi. Wearing shoes instead of Timberlands. All kinds of shit. But a poetry class is too much?" Z shook his head. "And everybody says *I'm* changing."

"I support you! It's great," said Jake. "But a poetry class? Not for me."

There was a lull in the conversation; both men pretended to send text messages. Without looking up from his phone, Z spoke.

"How you dealing with . . . everything?"

"I'm chilling," said Jake.

In two sentences, the two friends had done all the co-mourning they could do for Kipenzi. Two women would still be hugging each other, rocking back and forth at the gravesite. For the last year, Z and Jake had asked basic questions once a month and expected the same answers each time.

"Yo, Jake," Z said, his eyes still on his phone. "If I wasn't in Anguilla in rehab, Kipenzi would still be alive. We might as well put that out there."

Jake froze. With his eyes on the floor, he took in what Z was saying and thought about how to react.

"It was just her time," Jake said. "You didn't have anything to do with it."

"It was my fault," said Z.

Jake was silent, praying that Z would take the hint and shut up. What was talking about it going to do?

"I'm on my fourth step in recovery," Z said. "I have to take a moral inventory of who I am and what I've done wrong when I was using. Knowing Kipenzi was on her way to see me when she died . . ."

"Yo, I know you're on the Russell Simmons chanting trip now," Jake spat. "Drinking your wheat grass and folding your body into a pretzel and writing poetry in Central Park. Good for you. But you go that way with that."

The engineer felt the tension in the room and rose to leave.

"Stay right there," Jake said. "I'm going back in."

Jake slipped into the booth and put on his headphones. He saw Z leaving the studio. And on the video cameras he could see that he'd left the building completely.

"Ladies and gentleman," Jake said into the mic. "Z has left the building."

The engineer played back that one sentence, adjusting the speed to make it sound faster and then slower. He put it on a loop and the room filled with the sound of Jake's voice saying "Z has left the building," in his own voice, a Barry White version, an Alvin and the Chipmunks version, and everything in between.

Jake smiled. It was amazing how one offhand sentence could be turned into a hook, a beat, a lyric, a song.

He took a breath and recited, in one take, the lyrics he'd been writing in his head while talking to Z just ten minutes before. The hook came to him immediately:

Recovering now. But acting funny style.

When he was done, he lumbered out of the studio and pulled on his jacket.

"Thanks, Paul," he said. "I'll see you in the morning."

"I just sent you the track," Paul said.

"No hard copies."

"No hard copies," Paul said.

In his car, on his way back to the penthouse he once shared with his wife, Jake listened to the song "Z Has Left the Building" on repeat. This was his version of therapy. This was his way to cry it out. This was how he dealt with it all. He did blame Z. But not just for Kipenzi's death. He blamed him for *everything*. He blamed him for missing tour dates and album releases when he was still getting high and for treating Beth like crap and having Kipenzi stuck picking up the pieces.

Z had been a drain on Jake for years. And then suddenly, he wasn't. He was a productive member of society, working at a soup kitchen every week, and not using the word *nigga* in his rhymes. They had started out in the game together. But Z had been sidelined by his drug use, while Jake's career took off both as an artist and as an executive. Jake knew he should be proud of Z now that he was getting his life back on track. But he wasn't.

It was something about the fact that his transformation came on the heels of what happened to Kipenzi. Why did he have to get better after Kipenzi was dead?

Recovering now / But acting funny style
Recovering now / But acting funny style

Jake hummed along to the hook he'd created all the way to the parking garage beneath the penthouse. When he pulled up to the valet, he held up a finger to the attendant, asking him to wait.

He pushed a few buttons on the dashboard of his car. The song was deleted. Forever. Like a journal entry or a blog post, Jake needed to get his thoughts out. But unlike most forms of expression, Jake often deleted his most cathartic rhymes. The one he recorded after Kipenzi's plane went down still haunted him. It was the best writing he'd ever done. It was hard to delete. But he did. He reached inside his glove compartment, pulled out a half-empty bottle of Crown Royal, and drained it, tossing the empty bottle back into the compartment.

On the private elevator, Jake closed his eyes, feeling the car move up the shaft quickly. The lyrics to the song felt far away. But the hook stayed on repeat in his mind.

Recovering now / But acting funny style
Recovering now / But acting funny style

At home, Jake slipped into his favorite chair in the living room and took out his cell.

"Peter Luger Steakhouse, this is Anna speaking. How can I help you?"

Jake cleared his throat and sat up in the chair.

"Um. Yeah. Is Lily on duty tonight?"

"No, she's not. Can I leave a message for her?"

"No, thank you."

Jake turned off his phone and hummed the hook to the song he'd recorded while he flipped through the channels on the wall-mounted television. Ian stuck his head in the doorway.

Ian had been his wife's assistant for ten years. Jake had never liked him. But after the accident, they needed each other, for reasons both spoken and unspoken.

"On my way out for the night, sir," said Ian. "Anything I can do for you?"

Jake sat up. "One thing. Can you send some flowers to Peter Luger's Steakhouse in Brooklyn? Lilies. Only lilies."

Ian took out a notepad and a pen.

"Of course. To whom?"

"Have the card made out to Lily. Don't sign it."

Ian nodded.

"Anything else?"

Jake shook his head. When he heard the door close behind Ian, Jake got up and took a long shower. For the entire time, he thought about Lily and the flower tucked just so behind her ear.

9

Lily leaned over the vase on her kitchen counter and continued to arrange and rearrange the flowers. She plucked one flower out and then stuck it a few inches back and turned the whole container around.

"Are you nervous?" Corinne asked, her head inside Lily's refrigerator.

"No."

"I can't tell," Corinne said, using a soda bottle to point to the vase. "You've been organizing that bouquet for twenty minutes."

Lily stepped back from the counter.

"They're beautiful, right?"

Corinne nodded, draining the soda and burping out loud.

"Still no idea who's been sending them?"

Lily shook her head and avoided Corinne's eyes. If she looked at Corinne while she was lying, her friend would know right away. In reality, as soon as the delivery guy had walked into the restaurant that first time, Lily knew the flowers were for her and she knew they were from Jake. And every day that the flowers had arrived since then, she knew. She would have bet her very life on it. The card attached to the flowers was never signed. Clearly, he wanted her to know he was thinking about her, but he didn't want her to be sure it was him. God forbid, he actually admit that he liked her. That would make him way too vulnerable. Lily smiled. The idea that he was thinking of her made her feel tingly and short of breath. Sometimes, when she glanced at the flowers as she made her way around her tiny apartment, she would let her mind wander. She imagined sitting next to him in a park, her legs propped up in his lap, while he—

"I said it's time to go," said Corinne, waving her hand in Lily's face. "Are you awake over there?"

"Of course, I am," said Lily. "Let me just grab my coat."

As always, Corinne went to the living room window and looked outside just as they were about to leave.

"All clear?" Lily asked.

Corinne held up a finger. She stuck her head out of the window and turned to look both ways. The pesky teenage boys who hung outside the building weren't at their posts yet.

"Clear. Let's go."

Off the train and in the city, Lily and Corinne walked briskly up Seventh Avenue. They stopped to check out the vendors hawking limp Valentine's Day trinkets on the corners as they made their way up the street. They turned onto a side street and ran up the steps to the medical building.

"What would be worse?" Corinne asked. "Getting a stuffed animal from a street vendor for Valentine's Day or getting nothing at all?"

"Getting nothing because your man forgot? Or getting nothing because you don't have a man?"

"Because he forgot."

"I'd forgive him."

Corinne laughed.

"You say that now because you don't have a man. But the moment you land one, you'll be pissed off that he's not strewing a path to your tub with rose petals."

In the lobby of the building, Lily pressed for the elevator and then leaned against the wall.

"Do you really think I care about Valentine's Day gifts?"

Corinne hugged Lily. "You're going to be okay."

"You think so?"

"I have no doubts."

"And one day I'll have a man I can be pissed off at?"

"You will curse him out on a daily basis."

Lily and Corinne went to the doctor's suite on the top floor.

"You can go inside the first room on your right," said the nurse, pointing down the hallway.

Lily gave her bag to Corinne, who sat down in the reception area. She hesitated and looked at Corinne. Her friend gave her a stern look that said *buck up*. Lily exhaled and smiled. Corinne nodded.

Lily made her way to the examination room and sat down gingerly on the table. With her hands folded tightly in her lap, she closed her eyes and tried to be patient. This wasn't her first follow-up visit. The surgery had taken place a year ago. But for some reason, this time she was nervous.

"How are you?" said the doctor, bounding into the room after a few long minutes. He gave Lily a bright, fake smile that lasted for two seconds.

"I feel good," she said.

"Are you taking all the medications you've been prescribed?"

"Yes."

"Let's see how you're doing. Take off everything. Put on this robe, open at the front, and lie down. I'll be back."

Lily slowly peeled off her clothes, keeping her eyes closed in case she got a glimpse of her reflection in the shiny cabinets lining the walls. When she was fully naked, she instinctively put her hand between her legs. And as always, since the surgery, her heart leaped.

She climbed back on the table, her body shaking from sheer nervousness. She held her robe together tightly. She couldn't put her finger on why she was so terrified this time. She knew Dr. Alexander well and fully trusted him. He'd seen her naked at least a dozen times in the past year. And she'd never shaken like a leaf before a follow-up visit. Lily suspected it was somehow related to the flowers sitting on her kitchen counter and the man she knew had sent them. If he could see where she was right now . . .

When the doctor came back in, he stood with his back to her, entering data on a computer.

"Any pain?" the doctor asked.

"None"

The doctor nodded.

"Any secretions?"

"Some."

"It's been a year," the doctor said, turning around to face Lily. "How do you feel?"

Lily took a deep breath and considered the doctor's question.

"I feel like a woman."

The doctor smiled.

"Good. Because that's what you are."

The doctor wheeled himself up to Lily on a small stool and carefully put her feet inside the stirrups. Lily's legs locked up and she started to grit her teeth.

"You have to relax," said the doctor. "Take a deep breath."

Lily inhaled. And then exhaled. Her legs began to fall open.

"Mmmmhmmm," said the doctor. He opened the outer labia of the vagina he'd created from the inverted flap of the penis he'd removed in a three-hour procedure at Mount Sinai Hospital.

"Everything looks very good," said the doctor. "You've healed beautifully."

Lily stared at the ceiling, taking measured breaths.

"Do you feel sensation in the new clitoris?"

Lily nodded.

"Have you had an orgasm?"

"No. Not yet."

The doctor gently closed Lily's legs and stood up, going over to the sink to wash his hands.

"Remember, this new vagina is treated by your body as a wound," said the doctor. "Which means it's going to continue to try to close up. Are you dilating with the stents?"

"Yes, every week," Lily said.

"This is very important. You must insert the stents once every week for thirty minutes or the opening will start to close up."

"I know."

"Do you think you're ready to have intercourse?" the doctor asked.

"No," Lily said quickly.

"There's no rush. Is it because you're physically not ready or mentally not ready?"

"Mentally."

The doctor nodded.

"That's completely normal. Take your time."

"What if . . ."

The doctor looked up from his paperwork.

"What if what?"

Lily looked down at the floor.

"What if I never find someone to . . ."

"You tell me. What are you going to do if you don't find someone who will accept you?"

Lily shrugged, clutching the robe to her body.

"I don't know."

The doctor looked down at his paperwork.

"Do you feel like you made the right decision?"

"I made the *only* decision," said Lily. "But it's still scary."

"Understood," said the doctor. "You can get dressed now. I'd like to see you again in a few months."

Lily checked in with the receptionist, made an appointment, and then walked out with Corinne back out to the street, bundling herself up against the cold with a heavy wool scarf. Lily took comfort in the sounds of her stilettos clicking on the cement sidewalk as Corinne chatted away.

"What'd he say?" Corinne asked.

"Nothing really."

"Can you . . . y'know. Do it?"

"I told you yes! I could have done it months ago."

"So why haven't you? Don't you want to give that thing a test drive?"

Lily laughed out loud and then clapped her hand over her mouth.

"It doesn't work like that," Lily said. "At least not for me."

"Remember the rules," Corinne said, her face suddenly stern and serious.

Lily shook her head and walked a bit faster.

"Corinne, trust me. I know a lot of women who have done that. But I won't. I will tell the guy first."

"I would not want to have that conversation with anybody."

Lily stopped walking and turned to face Corinne.

"What would you do?" Lily asked. "You have sex with some dude and then he tells you he used to be a woman. You'd freak out, right?"

"Of course, I would. The problem is if he told me ahead of time, I would never have sex with him."

"Yeah," Lily said. "I know."

The two women stopped on the corner of Fourteenth Street and hugged. Lily took the F train to Delancey Street and then transferred to the J train to Brooklyn. She counted seven guys who let their eyes linger on her for longer than a second. And it wasn't her body that they stared at. She was bundled up in a heavy coat so they couldn't see her tiny waist and her 34C breasts. It was her face, the color of lightly creamed coffee and her jet-black eyes that captured them. Lily had been mesmerizing men for as long as she could remember. Long before the surgery, she'd had to keep her distance from men who didn't know better. (And a few who did know better and just didn't care.)

She quickened her step as she walked down Broadway toward the East River. Instinctively, she patted her bag to make sure she had everything. When she got to the restaurant, she slipped to the back to clock in.

"Mamacita, you're late. Again," said Manny.

Lily pulled off her heels and slipped into a pair of flats. She whipped out her apron and tied it around her waist.

"Manny, I told you I had a doctor's appointment today."

"It's always something with you," Manny said, waving a hand in her direction.

"Any large parties tonight?"

Manny passed Lily some papers.

"Here's everything you need to know. Engagement party at eight, so be ready."

Lily nodded and looked out into the dining room.

"You look different today," said Manny, peering at Lily's face.

"Yeah? How so?"

"I don't know. You pregnant or something?"

Lily stifled a laugh.

"I doubt that very seriously."

"So what are you always going to the doctor for?"

"Manny," Lily said, putting a hand on his shoulder. "Mind your business. Please. Thank you."

Manny sucked his teeth and walked away.

"Women," he muttered under his breath.

Lily smiled so hard that the sides of her mouth felt like they were going to crack.

"Indeed, Manny," she said to him as he walked away. "Women."

Ten hours later, Lily stumbled into the break room and sat down hard on the threadbare couch.

"You done?" Manny asked, wheeling in an empty dessert tray.

"I'm beyond done," said Lily. "I need sleep."

"Forgot to tell you earlier. You got something."

Manny went into the office and came back out with a huge bouquet of lilies in a square silver container.

"Whoa," said Lily, taking the vase out of Manny's hand and leaning in to smell them.

"What's up with all the flowers? You've been turning tricks behind the bar or something?"

"Whatever, Manny," Lily said. She set down the vase and looked for a card.

"Well?"

Lily frowned.

"No card."

"Whoever it is knows you love lilies."

She pulled one lily out of the vase and clipped the stem. She walked over to the mirror over the sink and tucked it into her bun.

The flower thing had started years ago. She couldn't even remember exactly when or why. But she never felt completely dressed for the day if she didn't have a flower tucked into her hair. The idea of being adorned by something alive made her feel special.

"They're from me," Manny said, walking closer to Lily.

Lily backed up.

"Down, boy."

Manny reached out in Lily's direction.

"You're not going to say thank you?"

Lily slapped Manny's hands away and grabbed her bag. She slipped into her heels and put her flats in the bag.

"I'm coming home with you," said Manny.

"Sorry. I have a date."

"With who? Your cat?"

Lily put her bag on her shoulder and picked up her vase.

"I'll have you know that my cat is quite the companion."

"I know exactly what kind of companion you need," Manny leered.

"You really need help," said Lily, walking out of the break room.

"No, *you* need help," yelled Manny. "And believe me, I could help you."

Lily turned around to see Manny with his hands in the air, pumping his pelvis in her direction. She shuddered and walked out of the restaurant and onto the street. As she walked to the subway, Lily counted all the couples arm in arm enjoying a Valentine's Day date night. The women looked so carefree and happy, some with their heads on their dates' shoulders.

On the L train, Lily dozed off and dreamt of walking hand in hand with Jake, her head on his shoulder. She woke up just in time to see the doors opening for her stop. She grabbed her bag and dashed off the train just as the doors were closing.

When she got closer to her apartment, she slowed down. The teenagers were out. Lily quickly went to the back of her building and used the service elevator.

Safely inside her apartment, Lily changed into sweats and a T-shirt and curled up on the sofa with her cat, a tabby she called Cat. She pressed the power button on the remote and let the sounds of a sitcom laugh track fill her tiny apartment.

10

The edges of the rope dug deep into Ras's wrists. He grimaced, trying to keep his hands still so that the fabric didn't cut him anymore. He looked over to his left; the rope attached to the headboard was tinged with blood. If it weren't for what was happening at the bottom half of the bed, all of his attention would have been focused on the pain in his arms. As it were, there were more pressing matters for Ras to attend to.

He tried desperately to catch his breath as his legs were pushed further and further apart. A pillow was slipped under him and he felt that familiar pull began to grow. The closer he came to coming, the more he strained against the ropes, which made him yelp in frustration.

She climbed on top of him and quieted him by kissing his lips. She sat up and began to bounce up and down on top of him, staring straight into his eyes and whispering obscenities. Ras felt his stomach clench and his head began to spin. He couldn't hold back any longer, and he felt a low, guttural groan escape his lips.

"Let it out, Ras," she whispered. "Let it out . . ."

Ras shut his eyes tight and jerked against the ropes, trying desperately to lift his body higher. Finally, he gave in, collapsing on his back and remaining still as the orgasm ripped through his body, forcing him to scream out loud.

Immediately after, Ras didn't move. He felt her untie him and then carefully roll the condom off as she always did and wrap it in tissue. He kept his eyes closed until he heard her go into the bathroom and begin running the shower. He threw his legs over the side of the bed and kicked aside the dildos and other sex toys on the floor. Ras's stomach retched. As soon as it was over, he was always disgusted by the things she wanted him to do to her. And the things he wanted her to do to him. He pulled on his jeans and went into her kitchen shirtless and barefoot. He grabbed a bottle of water out of the refrigerator as his cell phone began to ring. He slid his phone out of his back pocket and pressed TALK.

"My love," he said. "How are you?"

"I'm good. Tired. How are you? Are you getting a lot done?"

Ras looked out of the window to a well-landscaped backyard. A gardener was clipping bushes that dotted the perimeter of a heated swimming pool.

"It's going well. But I miss you. How's Reina?"

"She's good. Talk to her."

Before Ras could protest, he could hear his wife encouraging his daughter to speak into the phone. The little girl did nothing but laugh. Ras told her he loved her and kissed her through the phone.

"She just blew the phone a kiss," Josephine said.

"I'll be kissing you both in person very soon."

"When are you coming home?"

"Tomorrow morning."

Ras heard someone clearing their throat behind him and he turned around. Cleo stood in the doorway, wearing his shirt, which was completely unbuttoned. She put a finger to her lips and smiled.

"I have to go, Josephine. I'll call you when I'm done at the studio."

Ras hung up quickly and turned his back to Cleo.

"How come you can't look at me?"

"What are you talking about . . ." Ras said, brushing past Cleo and going back to the bedroom. Cleo followed him.

"You're always weird afterward . . . am I gross to you or something?"

"I need my shirt back."

"No," Cleo said quickly. "I'm keeping it. I want a souvenir. I might never see you again."

"Whatever," Ras said. He pulled on his undershirt and looked for his shoes.

"When are you going to just leave her?"

Ras stopped tying his shoelace and snapped his head up to look at Cleo.

"What did you just say?"

"You heard me. I said, when are you going to do the right thing and leave your wife?"

"Don't say anything about my wife," Ras said.

"If you really loved her, you'd let her go so she could find someone she deserves."

Ras tugged on his shoelace so hard that he snapped the string in half. Annoyed, he ripped the laces out and threw them in the trash.

"I'm not going to tell you again. Do not talk about my wife."

"What did she say about me showing up to the restaurant? Was she upset?"

Ras left the bedroom, with Cleo on his heels.

"How could you come back to me after that?" Cleo asked.

Ras ran a hand over his hair and sat down on the living room couch. It was an excellent question. And he would have paid very good money for an answer. Cleo climbed onto the sofa next to Ras and pulled her knees up underneath her body.

"Maybe you really do love me?"

"That's definitely not it."

Cleo smiled.

"So, then, what is it?"

Ras went inside his head and thought about a song he had been working on the night before. It was 99 percent finished. And the singer who wanted to use it begged him to just let it go and turn it over. But he could not do it. He kept tinkering with it. Layering one instrument and then another over the beat. Then he'd erase the changes and try again. There was a singular sound, somewhere in the universe, that was perfect for that song. One snatch of music that would complete the whole process. If it took him months, he would not let go until then. Whenever he was stressed out about anything, he felt his surroundings slip away as he played the song over and over in his mind, trying out the different sounds he had stored on his brain's hard drive.

When he opened his eyes, Cleo was still on the sofa staring at him.

"I need to go," he said, standing up.

"You're a horrible husband," Cleo said.

"I do the best I can."

"Is this what you call doing the best you can? You leave here and say you will never see me again. And two weeks later, I've got you hog-tied and squealing like a pig. When are you going to realize that you should just be with me?"

"If I was ever going to realize something like that, don't you think I would have by now?"

"You're holding on to Josephine because you feel sorry for her."

Ras stepped to Cleo and put a finger in her face.

"Don't let her name come out of your mouth again."

"Is she happy with the new baby?" Cleo asked. "Is she a good mother?"

"Do you have any idea what I would do to you if you went anywhere near my daughter?"

Cleo rubbed her hands down her belly.

"Your wife and I have something in common with the whole infertility thing. But I would find a way to give you a baby. Don't you think we'd make a beautiful baby, Ras?"

Ras wanted to run out of Cleo's apartment at breakneck speed. But his feet remained rooted to the floor. It was always this way when he came here. Ever since she popped up in Jamaica, his resolve had been shattered. He would fly up to go to the studio or take a meeting with an artist. And no matter how hard he fought against it, he would find himself driving to her home in Jersey.

A house she'd purchased with the funds she earned from a book that almost ended his marriage. The sheer insanity of it all dumbfounded him.

"You don't have to marry me," said Cleo. "But we should have a baby. You can have two families. One here in the States. And one in Jamaica with Josephine. What's the big deal? Aren't you related to Bob Marley? Josephine could be your Rita Marley. And turn a blind eye while you populate the world with your seed."

"I'm going now," Ras said, walking to the front door. At the door, Ras turned to face Cleo. He looked at her, but he saw his wife standing on their front porch with the baby on her hip, staring at the water, her hair blowing softly in the night breeze. No one had ever believed in him besides Josephine. And no one—not even his parents—had truly loved him like she had. Why couldn't he do right by her?

"I'm not doing this anymore," Ras said. His voice cracked at the end.

"Oh jeez, here we go again. Ras, just go. Don't give me this spiel."

"You're right. Josephine can do better. And maybe one day we will break up. And she will find someone else. But that doesn't matter. I will never, ever want to do anything but screw you. And you know what? I think you deserve better too."

For the first time since they met, Ras could tell that Cleo was speechless. She sputtered and her lips moved, but she didn't speak.

"Whatever this is that we've been doing?" Ras said. "It's not going anywhere good. The only thing we can try to do now is end this civilly."

"You can't just walk away from me, Ras."

"We can walk away from each other."

"I've kept all your secrets. Did you forget that?"

"Cleo, you wrote a book about every dude you had sex with. And you put me in it. How is that keeping my secrets?"

"I know stuff about you that you don't even know about

yourself," Cleo said defiantly. "And I'm still very close to Alex . . .
Maybe she could help me write a sequel."

"So what is this? You're going to blackmail me into keeping
you as my side piece?"

Ras laughed, although he thought it was more sad than funny.
He walked over to Cleo and stroked her chin with his thumb.
Cleo closed her eyes and leaned in for a kiss. Ras moved away.

"You take care of yourself," said Ras.

Cleo grabbed his arm and pulled him toward her.

"Wait," she whispered. "If you're really leaving forever . . ."
She dropped to her knees and began to unzip Ras's jeans. Before
she could do anything further, Ras leaned down and grabbed her
hands. He pushed her away and shook his head.

"No, Cleo."

And before she could say anything else, he was gone.

11

Z always stayed behind after class was dismissed. His professor, Dr. James, had a PhD in African American history from Harvard. How he ended up teaching African American Literature 101 in a continuing education program never came up. But Z could tell from the first day of class that Dr. James had seen some shit behind those wire-rimmed glasses. And once, when Z had stayed behind to talk about Claude Brown's *Manchild in the Promised Land*, Dr. James got animated and rolled up his shirtsleeves. He pulled them back down quickly. But Z still saw the ancient track mark scars.

On Mondays and Wednesdays, from seven-thirty to nine, Z stuffed himself into the wooden desk-chair combos in Scott Hall. He was amazed that he was often recognized but rarely approached. A few girls had giggled walking past him on campus. But for the most part, he went to class undisturbed. He wasn't officially matriculated and had not declared a major.

Z was just trying on a new skin to see what it felt like. School was one of those things that other people did. People who didn't smoke crack apparently paid people for the privilege of being told what to read and then be tested on it. And then, after a few years of that, they got a piece of paper that said they read a lot of books and did all their homework.

"You need to get your hands on a copy of *Howard Street*," Dr. James said. "I've been trying to get it back in print so I can make it required reading."

"It's something like *Manchild*?" Z asked.

"Yes. But more chilling."

"It seems . . ." Z often struggled to find a non-slang word to get his point out. "It seems crazy that people could live these lives and then write books about them. They used ghostwriters or something?"

"Did you use a ghostwriter to write any of your songs?"

"Hell, no," Z said.

"You do the same exact thing that Claude Brown and Nathan Heard did. They showed off the world—as they saw it—for people to experience."

"Yeah, but they wrote books. I just wrote and memorized some rhymes."

"Although it's not a popular opinion in my field," Dr. James said, "I've always thought rapping was actually harder than writing a book. You've got five minutes, sometimes less, to get your story across and make me feel it. When done right, it can be more insightful than a book."

Z nodded.

"There's a song my son loves by one of the members of Wu-Tang," Dr. James said, closing his eyes to think. "A very poignant song about growing up poor . . ."

"'All That I Got Is You,'" Z answered quickly.

Z knew the song forward and backward. He was on his first promo tour, crisscrossing the country in a dilapidated tour bus with no bathroom. Jake was there and Beth too. They listened to "All That I Got Is You" on repeat from New York to Columbus, Ohio. Jake and Z argued for hours on which Jackson 5 sample RZA used.

"So what's so special about that song?" Z asked. He knew it had peeled back a layer on him that he wanted scabbed over forever. But he couldn't imagine Dr. James's son, half-white and living in upper-crust Bergen County, relating to the lyrics.

"My son loves Wu-Tang. He's very disappointed that he wasn't born poor."

Z laughed.

"But there's a verse on that song," Dr. James said. "It's more powerful than some memoirs . . ." Dr. James began to recite the lyrics. His nasally, upper-class accent made Ghostface's lyrics sound more like poetry. It was weird for Z to hear them in plain English, with no Shaolin twang or hand gestures to illustrate.

Seven o'clock, plucking roaches out the cereal box
Some shared the same spoon, watching Saturday cartoons
Sugar water was our thing, every meal was no-frill
In the summer, free lunch held us down like steel

Z nodded. "Whole song was hot," he said.

"I believe it can be harder to do *that*," said Dr. James, "than to just get your story on the page start to finish."

"If you say so."

"Don't take my word for it, try it yourself."

Z looked up.

"Write a book?"

"You've probably told me only ten percent of your story," Dr. James said.

"One percent," Z said.

"Exactly. And I know you have a powerful story to tell. Think about getting it down."

"And then what?" Z asked. "You'll end up using it in this class as required reading?"

"Yes," said Dr. James. "I would leap at the chance."

Every single day for three weeks, Z woke up at six a.m., when the baby started crying. Instead of nudging his wife, who was usually in a Tylenol PM–induced coma, he slipped into the nursery himself, scooped up the baby, and soothed her. They would pad down to the kitchen, the house still and quiet. Baby Kipenzi would sit in her high chair, throwing back a bottle of milk. Z would sit at the island in the center of their expansive kitchen with a legal pad and a pencil.

There was a deep indentation on the side of his right pointer finger, where his pencil pressed while he was writing. First it bruised. But now a thick callous was developing. Z wrote more in three weeks than he had in his entire life, including every song he recorded. Throughout the day, whether he was at home or in the studio, he would sit at the island and write while the boys were at school and the baby was with the nanny.

"So what's all this scribbling you've been doing?" Beth asked one morning.

"Dr. James got it in my head that I should write a book," Z said, his eyes on his notebook.

Beth paused. Then turned to the refrigerator.

"A book about what?"

"My life."

"Why would you want to do that?"

"Why wouldn't I?"

Beth brought the cream over to the counter island where Z sat and dumped some into her coffee. Beth had never been thin. But she was never fat. And she was always conscious of what she ate. But ever since Kipenzi died and the baby was born, she was bringing home donuts and making brownies, marshmallow treats, and pecan pies. There was always something sweet in the house and Z saw a new chin begin to start peeking out from under her first one.

Z didn't care about her weight at all. She could have been three hundred pounds and he'd still love her. It was the behavior that was leading to the weight gain that bothered him.

Addiction in any form was now difficult to watch. He even stopped hanging out with some of his boys who smoked cigarettes. It was a constant reminder of the many times Z was somewhere he wasn't supposed to be, holding a glass pipe to his mouth and inhaling.

Beth slid a slice of pound cake in Z's direction and cut a larger slice for herself.

"Lot of things in your life I can't imagine you'd want to revisit."

"Like getting molested?"

Beth stopped chewing and nodded. He knew she'd never heard him actually say that word before.

"That's why people write books, Beth. To purge. To vent. It's therapy."

"You're already in therapy."

Z opened his mouth to explain how those things were different. But he stopped. It was just one of those things Beth was not going to get. When he went to rehab, she was ecstatic and supportive. But the real work came after he returned home. And Beth was overwhelmed in her own world of mourning her best friend's death, nursing a newborn, and raising four boys. Z did his best to help out. But he had to attend a twelve-step meeting every day. And he knew Beth resented that time away. She made a face when she saw him in bed reading *The Big Book* and other self-help books. He read voraciously. And when he was done, he would place the books on Beth's side of the bed and tell her she should read them too. The stack was two feet tall. And Z had finally started a new stack next to the old one.

Beth was having a hard time dealing with a sober Z—and he could feel it. He sometimes wondered if she'd rather he was back on drugs.

"I'm just trying to figure out how you're going to fit in writing a book with studio time," Beth said, slicing off another piece of cake.

"I'm taking it easy on the music for now," Z said.

Beth picked up the baby from the high chair and held her with one hand while wiping down the tray with the other.

"Does Jake know you're taking a break? I heard him on the radio saying you were coming out fourth quarter."

"I'm going to talk to Jake about it," said Z. "I think he'll understand if I'm not making music right now. I'll probably do a best-of or a compilation. I might do one song. Jake knows what's up. He'll support me."

Z let that last sentence hang in the air. Beth had her back to him, pulling down various boxes of cereal for the boys. She gathered cups, bowls, and spoons, arranging them at the island bar. The sentence hung in the air: *He'll support me.*

Z was quiet. Waiting for his wife to respond. Beth left the kitchen and yelled up the stairs for the boys to come down. Z went back to his notebook and continued to write.

That night in bed, Z sat up, with his reading glasses on, reading *Howard Street*, which he'd managed to find at a bookstore in the city called the Strand. The copy was even autographed by Nathan Heard. Made out to someone named Lumpy, which amused Z to no end.

"You just don't imagine a guy named Lumpy reading this kind of book. And getting it signed, y'know?"

Beth was spooned against Z.

"Maybe someone got it for him as a gift," said Beth.

"Why would you get it signed to Lumpy? I'm sure he had a real name."

Beth sat up straight and smoothed her hair out of her face. It had grown like crab grass while she was pregnant. And the locks now reached down to the small of her back.

"Z, I do support you."

Z took off his glasses and closed his book. But he didn't turn to face his wife's direction.

"I don't feel that way sometimes," he said.

"This is weird for me too. You're a completely different person than the boy I met in West Virginia."

"Is that a good thing or a bad thing?"

Beth put her hands on her husband's cheeks and turned him to face her.

"It's a glorious, miraculous thing. I thank God every single day. But I'm scared."

"That I'll relapse?"

Beth nodded. And they were both silent for a spell.

"Remember that book we had to read in ninth grade?" Beth asked. "About the dumb guy who takes some experimental drug that makes him a genius?"

"*Flowers for Algernon*," Z said.

"Remember what happened to Charlie?"

"He got super duper smart. Sort of started looking down at his people. And then the drug wore off and he started losing everything he knew."

"I feel like you're Charlie right now," Beth said, her voice breaking. "I see how you look at me and the kids. I know I need to get myself together. But seeing you in your self-help-guru phase is tough for me."

"So you prefer me in my crack-smoking phase?"

"Of course not. But I don't know what to do. I don't know how to act. I don't know my place and my role."

Beth dropped her head into her hands.

"I just feel like you don't need me anymore."

Z's heart flipped over twice, and he threw his arm around his wife's fleshy waist and kissed her forehead.

"I love you more now than I ever did," Z whispered into her ear. "I can never repay you for what you did for me."

"So now what? I just sit around watching you read books and stand on your head?"

Z chose his words carefully. In the early days of recovery, there was always the danger that everything you say could come out preachy.

"I think now you just chill out," Z said. "You'll find your place."

"How do I help you?" Beth asked.

"You help me every day. Just by being here."

"Are you serious about writing a book?"

"Yes. I've finished the outline. Everything from the foster home at age three to the last trip to rehab in Anguilla."

"Now what?"

"Now I find a collaborator. I won't be able to do this alone."

Beth reached over to her bedside table and handed Z a sheet of paper. It was a printout of several emails sent back and forth from two people.

BethieZ@aol.com
My husband's working on a book. He might need a co-writer. Would you be interested?

AlexWashington@gmail.com
I think I'm getting out of the collaboration business for a while. But tell him to call my agent. He can probably recommend someone.

BethieZ@aol.com
I want my husband to work with someone I trust. And I trust you. Will you just meet with him? For me?

AlexWashington@gmail.com
Sure. Name the time and place.

"Wait," said Z. "Isn't this the same chick who wrote Cleo's book?"

"She wrote most of it. Then she quit."

"I'm not working with her."

"Despite that," Beth said, "I respect her. She's fair. And she's diligent. Did you see the story she wrote for *Vibe* on Kipenzi's life and death?"

"It was good," Z said.

"So talk to her."

"Email her for me," Z said. "Tell her to meet me in room 210 at Scott Hall tomorrow at nine-thirty a.m."

Beth nodded and started texting.

Z turned over to curl up next to his wife.

"Thank you, Bethie," he said, kissing her on her neck. "Thank you for everything."

Alex was already sitting at a desk when Z strolled in to the classroom at 8:55.

"You're early," Z said, slipping into the chair next to her.

Alex stuck out her hand.

"Good to see you, Z."

"Same here," Z said, pumping her hand.

"So what kind of story do you have to tell?"

"A disturbing one."

"Can't be more disturbing than some of the things I've read about."

"So you know about the cigarette burns from my stepfather and getting kicked out of the house by my mother when I was ten because dude didn't like me?" Z looked Alex squarely in the eye.

"Oh. And you know about getting shipped off to live with my grandparents and being molested by my grandfather when I was eleven?"

Alex's lips parted and her eyes locked on Z's.

"And those were the good old days!" Z said with a laugh. "If you can believe it, things got worse."

Alex still didn't speak. Z moved his chair closer to hers.

"It's not a good sign when an eighth-grader comes to school high on crack cocaine and fall-down drunk. It's even worse when he was introduced to both by his own grandmother . . ."

"I can introduce you to my agent," Alex said. "You obviously have a story. He can help you find a writer."

"I thought I found one already," Z said. "Isn't this why we're meeting?"

"Well, no, I just told Beth I would talk to you, but I'm not sure I'm the best person for the job."

"Why wouldn't you be?"

"Z, you don't harbor any resentments toward me about Cleo's book? She put a lot of your business out there, and I'm the one who helped her write it."

"Please. I'm thanking Cleo in my own book. If she hadn't written that book, I might still be out there."

Alex nodded. She stood up, slipped into her jacket, and put her messenger bag across her chest.

"Let's both give it some thought," she said, extending a hand for a final shake.

"You think about it. I already know I want you," Z said. He ignored her hand and pulled her in for a hug.

"My wife says you're the one," said Z. "So that's it. You're the one."

Alex gave Z a weak smile and left the classroom. Z watched her go.

Z tried to suppress the connection he felt when he hugged her. He wasn't even sure why he'd hugged her. It wasn't his style at all. But after telling her about his past, saying things he'd never said outside of therapy, he felt vulnerable. Alex had been completely attentive. Z could have talked to her for five hours straight.

As his classmates began to file into class, he kept his eye on the window facing campus. Eventually, he saw Alex make her way to her car, walking quickly and stomping through the snow in high rubber boots. But she didn't get inside. She put her hands on the roof and put her head down. He stared at her until Dr. James asked him to bring up his paper. When he got back to his seat, Alex was gone.

A thin line of bright sunshine came through the bottom of the bedroom door at the Parker Meridien. And Zander dreamt of Bunny.

The penthouse suite in midtown Manhattan had been Zander's ad hoc home for nearly a year, ever since he and Bunny had gotten into their first serious fight. Although she'd started it by hitting him first, Zander ended it by punching her in the eye, regretting it as soon as he lifted his hand but too far gone to stop it.

As soon as his parents bailed him out of jail that night, he checked into the hotel, long his father's favorite, with nothing but the clothes on his back. Two months later, anything of importance that he owned had made its way from the house to the hotel. He hadn't planned on moving out at nineteen. He thought he'd live at home until he was legal. But once the music started to take off, he felt supremely out of place sharing space with a newborn baby and three annoying younger brothers.

As much as he'd hated to admit it, the fight had made him feel like a man. Not because he'd hit Bunny. (He'd decided ten years before that any man who could hit a woman was less than a punk.) But the whole incident made people take notice. Getting arrested had been his coming-out party. He'd had to face the judge, and it was the first time in his adult life he had to take admonishment from an authority figure other than his mother. That first fight with Bunny gave him purpose and direction. He now knew who he didn't want to be (his father) and what he needed to do to ensure that (control his temper). A better idea would have been to stop seeing Bunny altogether. But Zander wasn't strong enough for that.

This morning he turned to his left side and hugged the warm body close to him. Less than a half-second later, he remembered the night before and bolted out of the bed, whipping the sheets off and wrapping them around his waist.

"Yo, what are you still doing here?" Zander asked the woman he'd met in the hotel lobby bar the night before.

"Did you sleep well?"

Zander stood up and went to the door.

"You need to get up outta here—"

"Or what? You'll smack me around like you do that little girlfriend of yours?"

"Go."

"For the record," the woman said, "you did not cheat on Bunny. Not really anyway. You *definitely* wanted to. But I knew you'd regret it so I didn't let it happen." Zander had gotten up too suddenly. His head was swimming and spinning. Things slowly came back to him. Coming back from a studio session. Meeting his boys in the lobby bar. Throwing back drinks until three a.m. Paying off the paparazzi so they wouldn't publish pictures of him and his underage friends drinking. Then the girl. Zander remembered doing a double take at her neck. It was thin and long. And she held her head up so high it looked like she was being controlled by a string threaded through the top of her head. The neck mesmerized Zander. Soon the neck was in his hotel room. He was pulling his pants down and trying to push her back onto the bed. But something happened. He didn't have sex with her. She went down on him. But then what? He could vaguely remember coming so hard that his legs buckled beneath him. He fell asleep on the floor, his pants pooled around his ankles. She must have pulled him into bed.

"So you just get in the bed with me like I invited you?" Zander asked, his lip curled up in disgust.

"I had a great time with you, Zander," said the woman, tugging on a pair of jeans. "I programmed my number into your phone. Use it."

"You did what?"

The woman took a final look in the mirror, ran her tongue across her front teeth, and straightened her back.

"Call me."

As soon as she stepped to the front door, there was a sharp knock.

"Zander!" a woman's voice screamed. "Open the door before I break it down!"

Zander grabbed the girl by the shoulders and shoved her into the back bedroom. He opened the bathroom door and pushed her inside.

"Don't say a word," Zander whispered through his teeth.

The girl smiled. "You think I'm scared of Bunny?"

"You should be," said Zander.

"Zander!" Bunny screamed out again. "I'm not playing with you. Open the door now!"

Zander took a deep breath and opened the door a crack. He tried to look like he was just waking up.

"What's up, Bunny. Did you call me?"

"Move," Bunny said, smashing her way into the room. "You had some chick in here last night. And y'all both better pray to God she had enough sense to leave."

"Bunny," Zander said. "You need to calm down."

Bunny moved quickly throughout the suite, turning over couch cushions and opening and closing doors.

"Ooooh, this bitch better not be in this room . . ." Bunny whispered.

"There's no one here, Bunny," Zander said. "Your wilding out for no reason. Again."

Bunny didn't answer. Instead, she went into the back bedroom and tugged at the bathroom door.

"Who's in here, Zander?" Bunny asked, shaking the door

handle so hard that Zander was convinced she was going to break it off completely.

"Bunny, you need to—"

Bunny tugged harder at the door, grunting.

"I'm not leaving until this door opens up," said Bunny.

Zander moved Bunny to the side and stood in front of her. He grabbed her forearms and pulled her close to his face.

"Stop, Bunny," he said. "Just stop. Now."

Zander slowly backed Bunny away from the door and toward the front foyer. The bathroom doorknob clicked and the girl from last night sprinted out of the bathroom and ran barefoot, shoes in hand, to the front door of the suite.

"Oh hell, no!" Bunny said, breaking away from Zander's grasp and giving chase. She caught the girl by the ponytail as soon as she got one hand on the doorknob. Bunny got her arm around the girl's neck and brought her down to the floor quickly.

"Bunny, chill out!" Zander said, attempting to peel her off the girl who was trying to shield her head with both of her arms. Bunny got in two good punches to the side of the girl's head before Zander was able to pull her off. The girl screamed and finally scrambled to her feet and ran out of the room, leaving the door to the suite wide open. A cleaning woman rolled by with her cart and stopped, staring at Bunny and Zander, who were both out of breath and heaving.

"Should I call for help?" the cleaning woman asked.

"We're fine," Bunny said, slamming the door in her face. She turned to face Zander.

"You just can't keep your dick in your pants, can you?"

"I didn't touch her," Zander said.

"So what the hell was she doing hiding in the goddamn bathroom, Zander?!"

"She ended up here last night and fell asleep," said Zander. "Nothing happened. And now this chick will probably be calling the cops on both of us because you're an idiot."

Bunny rushed up to Zander, trying to slap at his face with her hands. Zander bobbed and weaved, blocking her hands with his forearms and ducking when she tried to punch him directly in the jaw.

"I'm an idiot?" Bunny screamed. "You have random girls in your hotel room all night and I'm an idiot?!"

Zander took all the strength he had left and slammed Bunny down on the couch in the front room of the hotel.

"Look at me, Bunny," he said softly. Bunny kept her eyes shut tight.

"I said look at me."

Bunny slowly opened her eyes and glared at Zander.

"I love you."

Bunny squirmed, struggling to get out of Zander's grasp.

"Just stop and listen to me," said Zander, still holding her arms down firmly.

Zander finally felt Bunny stop resisting and go limp in his arms. It always came to this. Zander did something to piss her off. Bunny went buck wild. And then he had to try to subdue her before he lost his temper and smacked the shit out of her (which she wanted) or she caused some kind of irreparable damage to something (or someone).

"I should not have had that chick up here," Zander said.

Bunny just glared at him.

"But you gotta meet me halfway, Bunny. You can't always try to kill someone when you get pissed off."

"Your problem is that now that you've dropped a record, you think you can do whatever you want," Bunny said.

"I grew up in this," Zander said. "You know I'm not fazed by any of this shit. If this don't work out for me, I'll be right at Rutgers getting a degree in communications."

"Girls want your autograph, your picture . . . you love that shit."

"What about you?" Zander asked, slowly letting his body cover hers on the couch. "You think I don't see how guys look at you?"

Zander thought he saw the slightest smile on Bunny's face and his body relaxed. Still holding her arms pinned above her head, he leaned in and kissed her on the lips. Bunny moved her hips beneath him and got him hard without even touching him with her hands.

"Did you have sex with that girl?" Bunny asked, between kisses.

"I swear to God, I didn't touch her."

"Don't lie to me, Zander."

Zander pulled away a bit to look at Bunny's face. When she was calm, soft, and vulnerable, he was in awe of how beautiful she was. Her eyes, dark brown and wide, drew him in. There was something angelic about her—when she wasn't trying to kill him.

"I will not lie to you, Bunny," said Zander, grinding himself slowly on top of her. He kissed her neck and finally let go of her arms. She wrapped them around his back and squeezed him hard. By the third time they'd climaxed together, all was forgiven. Again. Hours later, wrapped up in the hotel bedsheets, Zander pressed Bunny's small head to his chest and kissed the top of her head. He tried hard to remember the last time they'd had sex without fighting first. He couldn't think of a single time. He thought back to his childhood, when the sounds of his parents' screams and the heavy thump of bodies being slammed into walls and onto the floor would eventually segue into loud moans and groans as the night wore on.

"You see *Billboard* numbers this week," Zander asked, his hand winding through her hair.

"I dropped three spots . . ." said Bunny. "You moved up to eleven. Congratulations."

"Give me another month, I'll pass you right on by."

"Not with that crappy video you just shot," Bunny snapped.

Zander laughed.

"Look, when you learn how to dance, maybe you'll have a halfway decent video."

"When I learn how to *what?*" Bunny sat up and looked back at Zander. "You're insane."

"You dance like a wooden toy soldier."

Zander and Bunny collapsed into laughter until heavy knocks at the door interrupted them.

"Security," yelled out a deep voice.

Zander and Bunny looked at each other.

"You just had to punch that girl," Zander said, shaking his head. He pulled on a T-shirt and went to the door. He opened it with the chain still on.

"Yes, sir?" Zander asked.

"We had a call about a disturbance here a little while ago. A young woman in our lobby is filing a complaint with the NYPD."

"I see," said Zander. He kept the door half-closed. "I'm sure it was just a misunderstanding."

"I just thought you should know that the police may be up to question you."

"Thanks," said Zander. "Appreciate you letting me know."

Zander shut the door and turned to Bunny, who was still naked under the sheets on the sofa.

"You think she's gonna press charges?" Bunny asked.

"Wouldn't you?" said Zander. He pulled his legs through his oversized jeans and began lacing up his boots.

"Should I tell Robert?"

Robert was Bunny's manager. He had discovered her and guided her career since the very beginning. He was also a strict disciplinarian who was known for cursing Bunny out when she got out of hand—which was often.

"You have to tell him," said Zander. "And he's going to find a way to make this my fault. As usual."

"When I heard you came up here with a bunch of girls last night, I just . . ."

"I gotta go, Bunny," Zander said. "I've already missed three meetings today and you know our phones are blowing up."

Zander turned to Bunny and saw her sitting up straight on

the sofa, still naked, her perky breasts poking out of the top of the sheet wrapped around her. She pulled her bag into her lap and took out a small baggie of weed and rolling papers.

"When the hell did you start smoking?" said Zander, snatching the bag out of her lap.

"It's just left over from last night," Bunny said. "Would you stop freaking out? Since when did a little weed hurt anybody?"

Zander gave Bunny a look and tossed the weed back onto her lap.

"I just thought you knew better. That shit will destroy your voice."

Bunny blew Zander a kiss.

"I'll be fine, Daddy."

"What else did you do last night?"

"I had two drinks and I smoked a little," said Bunny. "That's it."

"Slow down, Bunny," Zander said. "Slow down."

Bunny stood up, letting the sheets fall around her feet. Zander threw her a towel, which she wrapped around her, and then she walked toward the bathroom.

"Don't worry about me," said Bunny, her hand on the bathroom door. "I got this."

13

"A fistful of dollars! A fistful of dollars! All I really need is a fistful of dollars!"

The chant from the crowd was so loud that it was hard to make out the individual words. The only word Birdie heard clearly was *dollars*. It was partly because he was at an open-air theater in Tel Aviv. And it was partly because his Israeli fans had accents that made his catchphrase sound a lot different than when he first performed the song to a crowd of fifty at SOB's in downtown Manhattan.

Will.I.Am had heard the single at the label offices. He immediately called Birdie and asked him to open for the Black Eyed Peas on an international tour. Prague. London. Paris. Rome. Birdie had seen more of the world in three months than he had in his entire life. It was thrilling. And more than a little bit scary. He hated not knowing the history of the major city he was landing in. And he found himself often sneaking in a call to Alex to ask the difference between Great Britain and the United Kingdom or whether Wales was a part of England or a separate country altogether.

Tel Aviv had been his favorite city so far. Birdie always thought of bombs, Jesus, and desert when he thought of Israel. But Tel Aviv turned out to be much more than that—it was bright and vibrant and reminded Birdie of Manhattan.

Onstage, throwing out the fake dollars with his name and photo on them, Birdie was running through his verses, Will.I.Am standing off stage, nodding his head vigorously.

Birdie stopped rapping abruptly and signaled for the sound tech to stop the music.

"Wait a minute, wait a minute," Birdie said, mopping his brow with a rag from his back pocket and pacing the stage.

"My song is called 'Fistful of Dollars' and y'all like that joint?"

The cheers went up in the open-air theater and crushed Birdie with the volume.

"But y'all ain't even messing with the dollar right now!"

Ripples of laughter from the audience.

"Y'all want a fistful of shekels up in this piece!"

Birdie signaled to the sound tech, Ras Bennett's beat dropped and Birdie went in.

A fistful of shekels! A fistful of shekels!
All I really want is a fistful of shekels!

Birdie tore through his last verse, coming back to the chorus one final time. Then he did something he'd dreamed of since he was four years old. He dropped the mic, raised both hands, and screamed "Thank you, Tel Aviv!"

From backstage, he watched the Black Eyed Peas run through their catalog while mainlining bottled water. Dylan moved around him like a butterfly. The crew from the reality show set up nearby and trained their cameras on both of them.

"I'm good, Dylan," Birdie said. "Just chill."

"You haven't eaten since you performed. We have baked chicken and lamb kebobs."

Birdie watched Fergie launch into "Big Girls Don't Cry."

"Dylan, I'm a grown man. I managed to feed myself for many years before I got signed."

"And if you pass out from exhaustion, I'll get fired. Just eat some chicken. Please."

Birdie laughed and accepted the plate of food. He patted the speaker he was sitting on, inviting Dylan to sit next to him. She climbed up with her clipboard and watched the show with

Birdie. After months of working together, Birdie was finally beginning to thaw out his icy feelings for the woman who controlled his daily schedule.

"It's the water that really does it for me," Birdie said.

"I know, it's beautiful," Dylan said. "What's it like to stand up there and perform, screaming crowds in front of you and a sea of blue water behind them?"

"No words," Birdie said.

The camera crew rotated to get a different view of Birdie. He'd already learned to ignore them. When they stepped to him and motioned that they would like to start shooting, he went into mode. The producer told Birdie they were done for the day and the crew began quietly packing up.

Dylan shielded her eyes with her hands and peered out toward the water.

"What body of water is that anyway?" Dylan asked.

"No clue," said Birdie. He slipped out his cell phone and held it up. "Let me call my atlas."

Dylan laughed.

"Your wife has to be tired of you calling her for a geography lesson five times a day."

Birdie shot a look to the producer of the television show. The producer nodded. No mention of Birdie's wife was to appear on the show. He didn't care if people knew he was married; he wore his wedding ring proudly. But their relationship was too delicate to be a plot on a television show.

Birdie shushed Dylan, covered one ear with his hands, and listened to Alex's phone ring. He'd called her from the hotel that morning, as soon as he woke up. And he got her voicemail. He called her once more from the tour bus. No answer. And now, again. Nothing.

Birdie thought back to their last conversation a few days ago. He'd only been half listening because he was in Amsterdam buying legal marijuana. Did she say she was immersed in a story? Was she on deadline? Alex was known to turn off her phone when she had to buckle down and write. Just before he left, she'd gone through the IVF procedure for the third time. So she could have been tired or not feeling well.

It came to Birdie suddenly. She had met with Z to talk about writing his memoirs.

Had she agreed to write the book? Or was she just in the negotiating phase? Birdie couldn't remember. But the realization that she could, at that very moment, be alone with Z, asking him personal questions about his entire life, made him uncomfortable.

Alex and Birdie were only together because she had broken a cardinal rule in journalism. She was sent to write a story on him. And she ended up sleeping with him.

Years later, Birdie and Alex had put their beginnings behind them. But now, halfway across the world and unable to get his wife on the phone, doubt crept in. Birdie had talked her into bed with ease. But that was years ago. Could Z do the same?

Birdie shook the thought out of his head and focused on the show. Alex had never given him a reason to doubt her fidelity. Ever. The distance was messing with his head.

"Alex, it's Birdie. Again. I'm saying, this is the fourth voicemail I'm leaving for you today. I hope you're okay. Call me back."

That night, Birdie lay across the bed in his hotel room. There was a knock at the door. He ambled over and looked through the peephole. A busty Israeli woman with too-red lipstick was standing with an equally voluptuous woman.

"I'm good, ladies," Birdie said.

"We know you're good," said one woman, in a thick accent. "We're good too. Can we show you?"

Birdie shook his head in disbelief. He was no stranger to American groupies in LA, Vegas, and Atlanta. But international pussy-throwing was a completely different variety. He called security and asked them to come up and deal with the girls, then he sat back on the bed and dialed Alex's number again.

"Hello?" Alex answered, out of breath.

"What the hell, Alex?"

"I'm sorry, baby," Alex said. "I lost my charger. I just bought another one. Is everything okay?"

"How's Tweet?"

"She's fine. She's with her mom."

"What happened with Z?"

"I haven't decided what to do. I met with him. He has a great story. But I just don't know if I want to go down that road."

"What road?"

"His story is freaking depressing."

"Did you meet with him in person or on the phone?"

"Both," said Alex. "Why do you sound like that?"

"Like what?"

"Like you think I had sex with him or something."

"Did you?"

"Birdie!" Alex yelled.

"Shit, I'm sorry," said Birdie. He ran his hands over his face and paced his room. "I don't know where that came from."

"Me either. But it's not cool."

"It's this trip. Being really far away. My mind starts tripping when your phone goes to voicemail for a whole day."

"My marriage vows are valid internationally, Birdie," Alex said.

"I know."

"No matter where you go, there I am."

There was another knock at the door. The groupies were back. *Jesus*. This time, he wasn't calling security.

"Hold on a sec, Alex."

Birdie threw open the door, curses ready to fly out of his mouth. And there was his wife, laden with bags.

"Baby!"

"I was on the flight, that's why you couldn't reach me." Alex smiled weakly.

"Get in here!" Birdie picked her up by the waist and hoisted.

"Wait, Birdie, I'm smelly. I need to shower."

"No," Birdie said, leaning her back onto the bed.

"Let me bring my bags in . . ." Alex said, in between kissing her husband.

"No," Birdie said.

"Let me take my shoes off at least, Birdie," Alex said with a laugh.

"No," Birdie said, peeling off her clothes and kissing every part of bare skin he could touch.

Birdie stopped suddenly and touched Alex's stomach.

"Are you—Did you . . . What happened with—"

Alex shook her head slowly from side to side and her eyes filled up quickly.

"Not this time," she said.

Birdie went back to kissing Alex's neck.

"It's okay, baby. Don't worry. It's going to happen."

Alex nodded, smiled, and then wiped her eyes. Birdie held her close and stroked her hair until she fell asleep.

Over breakfast the next morning, Alex and Birdie buried their heads in the news summaries sent up by the hotel.

"Where are you performing tonight?" Alex asked, between forkfuls of eggs.

"Off today. Going out on a date with my wife."

"Let's drive out to the Dead Sea! I've always wanted to go there!"

Birdie wiped his mouth with his napkin and placed it back in his lap. He clapped his hands together.

"Get the info. Let's go."

Alex got up to call the front desk and her cell phone rang.

"Told you not to get the international joint," Birdie said.

Alex spoke to someone for about ten minutes. Birdie tuned out, reading about a suicide bombing that had taken place just two miles away from where he'd performed the night before. He looked out of the tiny sliver of window in their hotel. People were already walking along the beach in Tel Aviv. It was bizarre. From one window, his view was a bright blue sea. From the other window, he could see a bustling city. Manhattan was surrounded by water too, but the Manhattan end of the Hudson River definitely didn't have any beautiful beaches.

"It's official," Alex said. "I'm doing Z's book." Alex flopped into the chair across from Birdie.

Before Birdie could respond, the camera crew was knocking at the door. Birdie opened the door a crack and told them to come back later. He went back to the breakfast table and looked at his wife.

"That's not a good idea."

"Why not?"

"He's a crackhead."

"A reformed crackhead."

"Why would he even want to work with you, after Cleo's book?"

"I asked him the same thing. He said I was an honest writer. And that's all he wanted."

"Heaped you with praise and that was it."

Alex's eyebrows knitted. She stood up and tied the hotel robe tight around her. "Wait. Birdie. You know this is what I do, right? This is my job. I write books for people."

"Yeah. But you don't have to write them for just anybody."

"Z has sold over fifty million records. He was an orphan when he got his first record deal. He was molested as a young boy. After twenty years of drugging, he's clean. It's a good story. And people are going to buy it. There's stuff he's never talked about publicly."

"Like what?" said Birdie.

"Kipenzi is the one who really pulled for him to go to rehab. They were really close."

"Alex, I can't tell you what to write. But the Z I know is not the kind of dude I want you meeting with three times a week for a book."

"What are you saying exactly?"

"I'm saying. Back in the day, I did a few tour dates with Z. He's got . . . issues."

"You're talking to the woman who wrote Cleo Wright's book."

Birdie made a face that said "touché." Alex walked over and wrapped her arms around her husband's waist.

"He got three hundred fifty thousand for his book," Alex said. "And I'm getting thirty percent."

"Nice. I'm getting three hundred fifty thousand for this tour. And half of it is yours."

Alex's face fell. He knew how sensitive she was about making her own money.

"I'm sorry," Birdie said, holding up a hand. "Out of line."

"Why are you blocking me? You really want me to stop working altogether now that the money is coming in from your music?"

"Truthfully? Yeah, I do."

"And I'm supposed to do what exactly," Alex said. "Sit on the couch and watch television until you get back?"

"You can come with me on tour—"

Before he could get the sentence out, Alex was shaking her head vigorously.

"I've seen those girls. Shopping in a different city each day. Backstage at the concert at night in their new outfits. And then doing it all again the next day. No lives."

"Remember when you interviewed Josephine Bennett. And you asked her why she designed wedding gowns when Ras made more than enough money?"

Alex nodded.

"You told her that if you were in her shoes, you'd find ways to fill your days without working."

"Birdie. What is this really about? For real."

"I don't like the idea of you spending time with this dude while I'm on tour. That's what this is about."

"Then you need to get over it. Because I don't care how big you get, I'm still a writer. Forever. And wherever that road takes me, I'm going. I love you. I'm loyal to you. And I'm proud of you. But I'm not going to lose myself in *your* world."

Birdie caught Alex's eye and stared her down. She lifted her chin in defiance and didn't blink.

A minute later, Birdie was still staring at Alex. And she still hadn't blinked.

"How long can you do that?" Birdie asked.

"Do what?" Alex said, her eyes welling up.

"Not blink."

"Until I get my point across."

"Eyes looking kinda dry over there."

Alex broke into laughter and rubbed her eyes. Birdie laughed with her and they ended up back in bed.

"One time," Birdie said, "I did a show with Z at Irving Plaza."

"Yes," Alex said.

"He was being interviewed at the same time by some chick from the *LA Times*. Real buttoned-up chick. Asked us to stop smoking. Real jumpy. Acted like she'd never been around rappers before."

"I know the type," Alex said.

"So, she's hanging with us for the whole night. Has a couple of drinks, loosens up a bit. But not much. I saw Z whisper into this chick's ear. And she put her hand up her skirt and took her panties off. Z put 'em in his pocket."

Alex covered her mouth with her hand.

"Whoa."

"She ended up hitting off Z, Damon, and Rodney."

"Birdie," Alex said, turning to face him. "That was the real her. The jumpy reporter was an act."

"I've seen Z operate. And I think he does have that ability to get under people's skin. He can be very manipulative. I want you to be careful."

"You think I'm gonna peel my panties off and give 'em to Z?"

"No. But I know how you get with your subjects. And I just want you to be careful. That's all I'm saying. Just report the story. Don't try to save his life."

"I don't do that," Alex said.

Birdie narrowed his eyes and twisted his lips.

"I don't!" said Alex.

Alex had written a story about a man who spent life in prison for a crime he didn't commit and she was still helping to pay his son's college tuition three years later. There was the high school student who got jumped into a gang. Alex spent three months writing a story on gang culture for the *New York Times*. And she still wired the kid money whenever he asked.

"Maybe once or twice," said Alex.

"Just stay focused."

Alex sat up and ran her hand over her head.

"Bird? I went to the hospital where Ras and Josephine's daughter was born."

Birdie got out of bed.

"Why would you do that?"

"I was just curious! I wanted to know who the young girl was."

"Didn't I ask you *not* to do that?"

Alex dropped her head to her chest and murmured "yes."

"We agreed. You're not going to try to find out whatever Cleo is trying to say. Leave it alone. You won't do anything but get someone hurt."

"You're right, Birdie."

Bird sat on the edge of the bed and turned his wife to face him.

"Promise me."

"Promise."

Birdie kissed his wife on the forehead and went into the bathroom to shower. He didn't know why he bothered to make his wife promise to leave it alone. If there was ever anything Alex would lie to him about without a second thought, it was a mystery she couldn't help but solve.

14

Jake lowered himself into his bathtub slowly, exhaling as he adjusted to the extra-hot water. It was the only way he could get moving in the morning, a long soak to loosen up his knees. It always reminded him of a photo of Michael Jordan he once saw in a magazine. It was taken at his house and he had his legs submerged in a huge bucket of ice. His back was slumped and he looked beat down.

That's how Jake felt every single morning. Except he wasn't a ballplayer; he was a rapper. A rapper who was getting old. There was a knock on the bathroom door.

"Yo," Jake said.

Ian opened the door and brought in warm towels, Bengay, and Ace bandages.

"Breakfast is served."

"Thanks."

Jake leaned back in the tub, a washcloth covering his eyes.

"Sir, ordinarily I wouldn't disturb you."

"Stop calling me 'sir'."

"Your wife . . ."

Jake took the washcloth off his face and looked at Ian. For some strange reason, he thought Ian was going to say she was alive. That she had survived the crash and was in a coma at a hospital. And she woke up this morning and asked for Jake. Jake had buried his wife's coffin with his own hands at the small, private funeral. He knew she was dead. But somehow, hearing Ian say the words *your wife* in the present tense scrambled his brain.

"What about her?"

Ian hesitated.

"What?" Jake said again.

"We need to talk about donating her things."

"No."

"Mr. Giles, it's not healthy to live here as if—"

"Since when is it your job to keep me healthy?"

"It's not. But I think it's time to—"

"I said no, Ian."

"Sir, your wife gave me *strict* instructions on every facet of her life."

"Ian, what's your fucking point?"

"She wanted certain items stored. Some things she wanted donated. And some things she wanted sold and the money disbursed to several charities. I think that we should honor her wishes."

"Leave me alone," Jake said, sinking deeper into the tub. "Please."

"And also," said Ian, his voice dropping to a whisper. "I found something you might want to keep. This was in a lockbox at the top of her closet . . ." Ian handed over a box wrapped in plain brown paper. On the top it said, *For Jake*. It was dated nineteen years in the future, which would have been their twentieth wedding anniversary. Only Kipenzi would have a gift ready twenty years in advance.

"Thanks," Jake said.

Ian left, closing the door behind him. Jake got out of the tub and bent his knees a few times. He toweled off, put on his robe, and sat on the teak bench with the box in his lap. Inside was a receipt, faded and ripped at the edges. It had been laminated. Jake was confused. Two orders of pancakes at the Brooklyn Diner ten years ago?

And then, a smile crept across his face. The first time he met Kipenzi, he took her out for a late-night breakfast at the Brooklyn Diner. She'd kept the receipt. It was definitely something Kipenzi would do.

Jake let out a chuckle and then turned the receipt over. There, in Kipenzi's signature pink, always perfect script: *I can't wait to be your wife.*

Jake clenched his teeth and felt something pinch his chest. On that first date, before he knew her last name or where she was from, Jake had asked Kipenzi to marry him. She'd laughed him off and said yes, not really seeming to mean it. But she knew. She'd accepted his proposal at that moment. Even though all this time, he didn't know it. He'd worked on getting her to marry him for years after that first date. And it was all completely unnecessary.

Jake allowed himself a quick crying jag: he pinched his nose, bent his forehead, and cried, heavy and loud, for ten seconds. Then, as always, he stopped himself abruptly and got back to preparing for his day.

He put the receipt in his top dresser drawer, with all of his other important papers. He filed the whole thing in his brain under Grief, in case he needed to access it later. And then he let it go.

Damon was already in Jake's living room, pacing the floor, when Jake came down for the day.

"What's the problem?" Jake asked, picking up a screwdriver, his first drink of the day, which Ian had brought in on a tray.

"Ciph and Rosenberg put out a podcast," Damon said. "They had Z on the radio this morning . . ."

"So?"

"I don't know, he just sounded like he had beef with you. He didn't say your name specifically but it was suspicious . . ."

Jake went to his office at the rear of the penthouse, Damon trailing behind him. He sat down at his desk and opened up his laptop. After a few keystrokes; he was downloading the podcast.

There was Z, talking to the DJs about his upcoming projects, including a book he was writing. He threw out some subtle lines about people not accepting that he wasn't a mess anymore.

It didn't have to be Jake he was talking about. But it definitely could be. When the interview ended, Jake exhaled hard and sat back in his chair.

"I can get you on the show tomorrow," said Damon.

"For what? I'm supposed to start a beef with Z?"

"I'm just saying . . . you can't let him get that."

"He's been my boy for damn near twenty years. If he wants to trip because he can't get over what happened to Kipenzi, so be it."

"The blogs are saying that you won't say anything about him since he's clean now—"

"The blogs. That's what I pay you to do? Read blogs?"

"You pay me to keep my ear to the street," said Damon. "And that's what I'm doing."

Damon left Jake alone in the office. Jake turned the podcast on again. And listened closely.

A week later, Damon slapped a magazine down on Jake's desk at the label.

"Check it." Damon said.

One of the hip-hop tabloids bore the splashy headline "Z Says Jake Is an Alcoholic!" There was a picture of Jake coming out of Zander's album release party, and he was definitely less than sober. He had one hand draped over the shoulder of his body-guard and the other side of his body looked like it was about to collapse.

Jake picked up the paper.

"We don't know that Z really said this, though," said Jake, scratching his beard.

Damon shrugged.

"Just don't look good."

"This is some bullshit," Jake said, tossing the magazine in the trash. "I've got other things to worry about. Where is every-body?"

Damon opened the door to Jake's office, and various employ-ees began streaming in with notebooks and coffee cups in hand.

They all sat down on the various chairs and sofas in the office and chatted with each other while Jake arranged paperwork on his desk.

"I know y'all saw this mess in the paper. I'm not speaking on it. And neither is anyone else at this label."

There were head nods and murmurs of agreement.

"And if I find out y'all are talking to the press, it's your last day in this office. I promise you that."

With that, Jake settled back in his chair.

"So what's going on this week?"

As his staff ran down the schedule for the week, including whose album was dropping, what videos were being shot, and who was getting signed to the label, Jake half-listened and nodded when it seemed appropriate. But he was really thinking about Z. Did he really talk to the press about him? It seemed completely out of character for the new Z. Wasn't he supposed to be self-actualized or something?

Jake felt for his cell phone in his pocket. He could call Z immediately. And say what? Ask him if it was true? Jake felt like it would be a punk move to call him and ask, *Did you really say that?*

For the rest of the afternoon, Jake's office hummed. His employees dropped their heads when he walked by. His publicists fielded calls from the press for the entire day. Jake stayed in his office, brooding.

When everyone was gone for the day, he called for his car, slipped out unnoticed, and directed his driver to Peter Luger's. There Jake looked around for Lily. There was no sign of her. Jake posted up at the bar and signaled for a drink. Within an hour, he was drunk enough to start thinking about how he was going to deal with Z.

Jake wasn't a stranger to corny rap beefs. He'd gone back and forth on wax with Ghostface, Ludicrous, and T-Pain. There was a straight-up hand-to-hand fight with Tupac back in the nineties.

But it was a new century. Was he really going to beef out publicly? Forty-one years old and trying to come up with words that rhymed with *bitch* and *wack*?

A tall, thin woman with a spiky jet-black haircut brought a drink over to Jake's table. Jake lifted up his head to thank her and did a double take. It was Samantha, a chick Z used to mess with years ago. They'd actually taken turns with her at first until Z caught feelings. And then she became an unofficial part of the crew. Z was foul back then. He'd take Samantha and his wife on the same tour bus, moving from the front, with Sam, to the back with Beth, whenever he felt like it.

"Hello, Jacob," Sam said, setting down the drink. She waited with her hands clasped behind her back. Jake gestured for her to sit and she did.

Samantha was the only person besides Kipenzi and his mother who called him Jacob. Years ago, she'd managed to get ahold of his driver's license and found out his real name. She called him nothing else. No matter how many times he said, *Don't call me that*, she would just laugh and say, *I do what I want*. Eventually, he stopped fighting it. Jake hadn't seen Samantha in years. He remembered Z crying in the studio after she came by to tell him she was getting married. He thought they would still see each other after that, but she disappeared. Jake couldn't understand how Z had that much love in his heart for women. Z would kill someone who even looked at his wife. And yet he was crushed when his jump-off got married?

"Jacob?" Samantha asked, leaning in close. "Are you okay?"

Jake tried to focus. There were two Samanthas weaving in and out of each other, wavy and distorted. Four ears, four eyes, four breasts . . .

"Let's go," said Jake, getting up from the table and walking quickly toward the back exit. Sam followed.

Jake's driver was in the employee parking lot. He came around and opened the door for Sam, who slipped into the back seat of the white Maybach. Jake pushed himself in behind her and collapsed on the back seat, throwing his head back on the headrest.

"You need a smoke break?" Jake asked the driver.

"I do," said the driver. "Thank you, Mr. Giles."

The driver didn't smoke. But in the past year, he'd learned what that question meant. As soon as the driver closed the door behind him, Jake unzipped his pants, grabbed Sam by the back of the neck, and forced himself into her mouth. Eyes closed, he waited to gauge her reaction. If she flinched or tried to pull back, he'd let her go. She didn't. She took him completely into her mouth, while somehow managing to use her tongue to lick him at the same time.

She came up for a breath and looked up at Jake.

"I never thought you were checking for me like that," she whispered.

"I'm not," Jake said.

Samantha went back to work, undressing herself and blowing Jake simultaneously. Somewhere, in a sober corner of his mind, Jake wondered if screwing Samantha was his (lame) way of lashing out at Z. While Z was a changed man and seemed to be happy with Beth, he definitely wouldn't have cosigned this random move.

When she was completely naked, Jake pushed her away and turned her over, her knees up in the back seat. He slid inside her easily. She was warm, wet, and tight. Jake's mind was still swirling from the Dewar's. For a second, he thought he was going to throw up on Sam's back. He caught himself and continued pushing, harder. Samantha started to whisper *Oww you're hurting me, Jacob,* which just made him go harder. He pulled out just before he came and Sam hurried to take him in her mouth and finish him off.

Jake looked down and saw his wife's face; that left eye hanging down by a bloody vessel. She held her husband in her mouth, her face bloody and bruised, her one good eye welling with tears.

"I love you, Jake," Kipenzi said.

Jake closed his eyes and fell back against the car cushion. He

opened them again slowly, praying he wouldn't see his wife's dis-
figured body again. There was Sam, struggling to find her clothes
strewn all over the back seat. Jake zipped himself up and waited.

"It was good seeing you, Jake," Samantha said. She leaned in
to kiss him, and Jake pulled away. He pointed at the door and
said nothing else.

"You're so rude," Samantha said, opening up the car door.
"I'm off for the next few days. But call me!" she said before slamming it shut.

Jake's driver came back to the car. "Are we ready for home,
sir?"

"No, not yet."

Jake stumbled back into the restaurant and sat down in the
chair he'd just left. His head was swimming, and he had to grasp
the bar to stay seated. Another waitress came over with a cocktail
napkin and beer nuts.

"Lily?" he asked, looking closer.

"Oh, hey."

"I didn't see you in here earlier," said Jake. He ran his hands
across his face, hoping to wipe the just-had-sex look away.

"I just got in," said Lily. "Jack and Coke?"

Jake nodded.

"And then come back and talk to me."

"I can't. I'm working."

"Take a break."

Lily turned her head toward the bar and then looked back at
Jake.

"A break . . ."

Jake nodded.

"Just for a minute."

Lily sighed.

"I'll go get your drink."

It had been years since Jake had to wait for a woman. He
honestly couldn't remember a woman ever making him wait for
more than three seconds. He checked his watch. It had been ex-

actly ten minutes since Lily left to get his drink. How long did it take to make a Jack and Coke? Sam approached Jake with a glass in hand.

"Back for more so soon?" She placed the beverage down and smiled.

"What happened to Lily?"

"Oh, her shift was over."

Jake smiled. He hadn't been played out by a woman in over ten years. It was actually refreshing. She wasn't getting another chance. But Jake was still impressed. He drained his drink, paid for it and went out to his car.

"Now," he said to the driver. "Home."

15

Lily could not relax. No matter how many times she did it, she couldn't begin using the stents without becoming incredibly tense, which made the whole thing even harder to do. It was getting to the point where she was tempted to take a shot of Patrón before she started the process.

She went into the bathroom and gathered the supplies: lubrication, plastic stents in various sizes, and a plastic sheet to lay over her bed.

She spread the plastic over the bed and then laid down on her back on top of it. She brought her knees up and opened her legs wide. *Inhale. Exhale. Inhale. Exhale.* For ten minutes, she just tried to control her breathing. Finally, she took one of the plastic stents and covered it in lubrication. She held the stent up to take a good look at it. The hard plastic tube could have been mistaken for a dildo with its rounded tip and thick length. But the doctor had made it clear that a stent and a dildo weren't the same thing and that she would have to use an actual stent for her weekly dilating.

Lily took the tip of the stent and leaned it against the top of her vaginal opening. She closed her eyes, exhaled, and pushed the stent inside. While holding it in place for a few minutes, Lily opened her eyes and looked up at the ceiling. After another minute, Lily pushed the stent in further, making sure not to move too quickly or push too deeply. Ten minutes later, she removed the stent and reached for the larger one. She lubricated it and laid back down. Again, she pressed the plastic inside her and held it in for as long as she could, pushing it in a small amount at a time. Her hands were shaking and sweaty as she struggled to keep the stent in without hurting herself. She could feel her muscles trying to force the stent out, and she tried again to relax her body and accept the foreign object inside her.

Lily tried to think about a man—a man who would accept her and love her and want to make love to her. The doctor told her that vaginal intercourse was not a substitute for using the stent. But Lily liked to think that being in a relationship with a man and having normal sex would have to help somehow.

She wanted to think about Idris Elba or Taye Diggs. But the only man who would come to mind was Jake. He always smelled like Ivory soap and brand-new leather. Even though he usually looked a hot mess, Lily still inhaled his scent and tried her best to hold on to it for moments like this.

Lily removed the second stent and inserted the last one, the largest of the three. It went in easier and she was able to hold it in longer.

Sex better be better than this . . . she mumbled to herself as she slowly pushed the stent inside her and held it firm. When the required thirty minutes of using the stents was done, Lily usually rushed up, eager to move on. But this time, for the first time since the surgery, she stayed put a little longer. She held the stent in place, imagining it wasn't a hard plastic object but a warm, real flesh-and-blood man.

Jake was there in her bedroom. His shirt was open and he was unzipping his pants. He climbed on top of Lily and kissed her. She held him, guided him inside . . .

Lily's nipples hardened and she felt her breath quicken. And then, she felt droplets of moisture leaking out of her vagina. For the first time, she'd lubricated herself. Her doctor had told her it would happen at some point, but she didn't believe him. She slowly took out the last stent and then lay in bed quietly.

Hours later, at work, Lily stood behind the bar and filled orders without even thinking about them. Her mind was somewhere else entirely. On the outside, she joked and made small talk with her customers and coworkers. But inside, she was reflective and meditative. Samantha was on duty, talking her ear off while making drinks, but Lily could barely hear her.

"I shouldn't have done it," Sam said, shrugging her shoulders. "But I couldn't pass up that opportunity."

"Right," Lily said.

"You weren't even listening to me."

"What?" Lily looked over at Sam. "You said you shouldn't have done it."

"I shouldn't have done *what*."

"Uh."

"Jake!" Sam whispered. "Right here in the parking lot. So hot!"

"The rapper guy? With the beard?" Lily asked, holding her breath.

"Who else?" Sam turned around and leaned against the bar. "He's such a whore."

"No, he's not," Lily said quickly. "He's just . . . hurt. Grieving. You know, his wife and all."

"I knew him long before he married that chick. Trust me, Jake is as slimy as they come. Great piece of ass. But a total sleaze."

Lily was just about to protest once again when Manny tugged her arm.

"Get in the break room," said Manny, as he walked by the bar.

"What's wrong?" Lily called out. Manny didn't answer. She waved Samantha over to cover her section of the bar and walked to the back of the restaurant.

"We had a large group in here yesterday," Manny said, not looking at Lily directly.

"I was off yesterday."

"Yeah, I know. But they've been in here before. They asked for you specifically."

Lily's nostrils flared and she struggled to remain composed.

"Asked for me . . . by name?" Lily choked out.

Manny continued to look away from Lily.

"That's the weird thing," said Manny. "They just described you. Didn't say your name."

"Oh."

"But they obviously know you. Very well."

"I gotta get back to the bar . . ." Lily said, backing out of the room.

"Don't move," Manny said, pointing a finger at Lily.

Lily froze. Manny walked toward her with a sneer on his face.

"One of the guys said he knew you from back home. I thought you told me you were from Brooklyn?"

"I've lived in Brooklyn for years," Lily said.

"But you're not *from* Brooklyn, are you?" Lily was silent. Manny walked up closer to Lily and looked her over from head to toe.

"I would have never guessed . . ."

Manny reached out a hand toward Lily's breast, and she smacked his hand away.

"Don't touch me!" Lily hissed.

"You nasty faggot," Manny said, grabbing Lily's hand and twisting it until she was on her knees.

"Get off me!" Lily screamed. "Somebody get back here, please!"

Manny crouched down and smacked his hand over Lily's mouth.

"Shut up."

Manny dragged Lily up to her feet and over to the break room door. He locked it and pushed Lily against the door.

"I knew something was weird about you."

"Look. Just let me go."

"Did you get your shit chopped off?" Manny asked, his eyes wide and spittle in the corners of his mouth.

"Manny."

He twisted Lily's arms harder around her back and tears squirted out of her eyes.

"Did you?"

Lily didn't answer.

"I thought you were a lesbian the way you act like you were scared of dick," Manny said.

"Let me go, Manny. Now."

A strange look came over Manny's face—a blend of disgust and curiosity. Lily's heart began to beat hard in her chest. *Not like this*, she thought to herself. *It cannot happen like this.* Manny used one of his beefy hands to hold both of Lily's hands together. With the other hand he slipped his hand under her skirt and began to move up her thigh.

"You got a hole in there?" Manny whispered, holding her arms tight. "I wanna see it."

Lily summoned up every bit of strength she had and brought her knee up directly into Manny's groin, connecting with his nuts with such force that she felt them flatten against her kneecaps.

"Oh god, oh god, oh god . . ." Manny sputtered as he dropped down to the ground. Lily threw open the door and sprinted through the break room and into the restaurant, nearly knocking over customers lined up three deep at the bar. At the front door, she pushed through and ran up Broadway, pumping her legs to move faster, faster, faster. She looked back just once and saw Samantha standing in the doorway of the restaurant, yelling out her name.

"Lily! What's wrong? Where are you going?!"

Lily didn't stop running until she got to the subway station. It was then that she realized that she'd left everything behind in the break room—her wallet, her shoes, everything. All she had was her cell phone, which she always kept in her back pocket.

Lily called Sam back at the restaurant and asked her to bring her bag to the subway station. Ten minutes later, Sam was there, out of breath.

"What the hell happened? And what did you do to Manny?"

"Thanks," Lily said, grabbing her bag. "I gotta go."

"Are you coming back?"

"No."

"We get paid tomorrow. You want me to get your check?"

"Yes, please. Just hold it for me. I'll call you."

"Lily," Sam said, reaching out to touch her arm. "Did Manny try to put his hands on you?"

Lily was silent.

"He tried that with another girl once and she smacked the shit out of him. You should really go to the owner. I'll back you up. Don't just walk away and let him get away with this again."

"I can't."

"Why not?"

Lily shook her head vigorously.

"I just can't. Look, I gotta go. I'll call you. And thank you. I mean it."

Lily was in the station before Sam could protest. She took the flower out of her hair and picked off the petals, tossing them to the ground as she waited for the train. She took the L to Union Square and then walked across the park to the W Hotel. In two hours, she had a new job and a new boss—a woman. She got her schedule for the new gig and treated herself to a taxi ride back to Brooklyn. At home, she took an extra-long shower, climbed onto her bed, and cried until her eyes had swollen up so badly that she couldn't see.

16

On a balmy Monday morning, a strong breeze coming off the Blue Mountains, Ras awakened to an empty bed. His wife had left a note: *At work. Come say hello*. Before he got out of bed, Ras murmured a prayer. He rolled over and took out a small journal he kept near his bed and jotted down a few quick thoughts. Then he closed his eyes again to determine where his mind might take him today.

The feeling was still there. And it was even stronger than it was yesterday. He was perfectly happy at home in Jamaica, making beats and spending time with his wife and daughter. But he kept dreaming about flying to Newark Airport and driving to that gated community in New Jersey. He made love to his wife and felt ashamed at how little she turned him on. She was breathtakingly beautiful. But her soft kisses may as well have been from his mother. Two weeks before, he'd flipped his wife on her stomach, spread her legs roughly, and entered her. He grabbed her hair and squeezed her tight. She began to cry and Ras released her, petrified that he'd hurt her. She ran into the living room and slept on the couch, refusing to return to the bedroom.

Ras felt like a werewolf a few days from the next full moon, desperately not wanting to change but depressingly sure he wouldn't be able to stop it. Ras grabbed the personalized cigarette lighter Josephine had bought him for their anniversary. He held the flame to his hand, as close as he could without burning himself. He'd read somewhere that Muhammad Ali held a lighter to his hand every time he felt the urge to be unfaithful. The heat was to remind him that hell would be the end result of doing his wife dirty. Ras closed the lighter and tossed it back to the nightstand. He went next door to the bedroom he had converted into an office. At the computer, he logged on to a travel website and booked two tickets to Miami and two nights at a hotel. As soon as he got the e-ticket numbers sent to his cell phone, he closed the laptop and breathed a sigh of relief. Ras showered, dressed, and went to the kitchen. He shooed away the housekeeper and cook who started fussing over him, muttering in heavily accented English. Ras made himself a slice of toast and found himself locked in a stare-down with the cook as he waited for it to pop up. The cook, a seventy-six-year-old woman from Cuba they all just called Cook, was fanatical about what she called *her* kitchen. It was Ras's house, but it was somehow *her* kitchen. She liked everything just so, without a single cloth napkin or fork out of place. It was cute. But sometimes Ras just wanted to get a handful of pistachios without someone hovering nearby, waiting to pick up the shells. The bread popped up, fully out of the toaster, and in the air. Ras made a grab for it but too late. Cook caught the toast in midair and placed it on their finest china. She garnished the plate with perfectly formed roses made of butter, a few fresh strawberries, and orange slices.

"Thank you," Ras said, a smile playing on his lips.

He went out of the sliding glass doors that opened to the backyard. Down the path, he could see women bustling around Josephine's annex, shouting orders and drawing patterns out on large white tables.

Ras stood to the side, watching his wife. She was peering over the shoulder of a seamstress, giving feedback. And on her hip was baby Reina, laughing at nothing in particular and making raspberry sounds with her mouth. Occasionally, Josephine would notice the baby's antics and tickle her under the chin or give her a kiss before going back to checking on her work.

The baby had really changed her. She grew taller, it seemed. There was a brightness in her eyes that he'd never seen before. The baby had made her whole in a way Ras never could.

Ras knew that Josephine was still self-conscious about being the adoptive mother. Little Reina looked nothing like either of her parents. She didn't have Josephine's pale skin and jet-black hair. And she didn't have her father's coal-black skin and broad nose. Everything on baby Reina was a kneaded mixture of features, all softened, like a sculptor smoothed out all her skin before she was born.

Today, as she stood barefoot on their property, her heavy hair tied back with a bright red scarf, Ras's wife looked absolutely perfect.

"Good morning," Ras said, stepping into Josephine's view.

Josephine smiled and gave Ras the baby. "You're just in time, I have to return a call. Buyer from Nordstrom's Bridal."

"What else is on your agenda today?"

Josephine's face broke out into a wide grin.

"Ras, what are you planning . . ."

"We have a flight leaving in five hours."

"Where are we going?"

"Miami. We'll be back Sunday night. Just a quick getaway."

Josephine moved close to Ras and kissed him.

"Thank you," she said. "That's just what we needed."

Josephine started mumbling under her breath about what she would need to pack for herself and the baby.

"Oh, I'm sorry," Ras said. "This little one is not invited."

"I've never been apart from her overnight!" said Josephine.

"Exactly. And she's a year old; it's time."

"I . . . I'm not sure if I'm ready for that."

"You still feel like you could lose her . . ."

Josephine hesitated.

"It's not that . . . It's just . . ."

Ras put the baby back in his wife's arms.

"The car will be here to take us to the airport at four. Grand-mére will be here at two."

Ras kissed Josephine on the cheek and left her to her work.

* * *

It turned out to be one of those trips that Ras wanted to hold on to and replay over and over in his mind with total recall. They rented the triplex penthouse at the Shore Club, their favorite hotel in Miami. The residence included a private elevator, indoor pool and sauna, and Josephine's favorite detail: 360 degrees of water views.

For two days, they didn't leave the room. They dipped strawberries in chocolate, made love, caught up on reading, sat out on the balcony for a bit of sun, made love again, ordered up steak and lobster for dinner.

And then, for long stretches of time, they simply sprawled out on the sofa in the main room, holding hands and watching reruns of *Will and Grace* and *Reba* on Lifetime. Occasionally, Ras would try to reclaim the remote control and Josephine would keep it just out of reach, giggling and tucking the remote into various areas on her body. When it was time to go home, Ras and Josephine were relaxed and loose. They slumped back in the taxi. Ras didn't try to tell the driver the fastest route to the airport. Josephine didn't sit up, watching every other car for near-accidents. They simply lounged, smiling at each other and the memories they were leaving behind in Miami.

When they returned home, Josephine fell in step with the housekeeper and the cook, finalizing plans for an upcoming dinner party. Their soft chatter buzzed in Ras's head as he headed upstairs to his bedroom to unpack.

He sat down on their bed and exhaled. He pinched the bridge of his nose with his hand. The feeling was still there. Even two days alone with his beautiful wife was not enough to wipe Cleo from his mind.

Ras closed his eyes tight and put his head in his hands. He mumbled a few quick prayers and tried to force his thoughts to focus on his wife and daughter. He had everything he wanted. Josephine was happy. Reina was healthy. Business was booming. He was in his beloved home country.

But it was still there. That feeling in the pit of his stomach, an empty pang that he needed to fill. From downstairs, Ras could hear his grandmother bringing Reina back and Josephine squealing with delight. Ras picked up his cell phone and turned it around and around in his hand. He dropped it on his bed and went downstairs to play with the baby.

The next morning, his wife was still in bed when he woke up. She was sipping coffee and reading the newspaper.

Ras checked his cell phone and then put it down.

"I have to go to New York for a few days for a session with Jake," Ras said.

"Okay, sweetie," Josephine said. "You want me to come up too?"

"It's up to you," said Ras. "I'll be doing twelve-hour days at the studio. But if you want to come, you should. And bring the baby too if you'd like."

Josephine got out of bed and shrugged into her bathrobe. Ras held his breath.

"I'll stay," she said. "I've got work to do. You go."

Ras shrugged.

"Let me know if you change your mind," said Ras. He kissed his wife on the cheek and walked into their closet to pack a bag.

During the entire time that Ras packed a bag, made travel arrangements, and packed the equipment he would need, he prayed to God for the strength to stay put. He put the lighter to his palm and accidentally burned his hand. He begged himself over and over to stay put, to fight the itch.

The next morning, at the airport, he stopped trying to fight it. Josephine sent him a text message: "Love you. Be safe." Ras read the text three times and then turned his phone off and put it in his carry-on bag.

17

Z sat in a booth at the Brooklyn Diner, flipping through the first few chapters of his book. He was stunned at how well Alex captured much of what he felt and went through as a young child. It was scary to see some of that stuff in print. But in a way it was freeing as well. He was writing notes in the margins of one page when Alex breezed into the restaurant and flopped down next to him.

"You know I hate meeting here," Alex said, tossing her bag next to her in the booth.

"What's the big deal?" Z said. "They make great coffee."

"I met Cleo here to write *Platinum*," said Alex. "Not a lot of good memories for me."

"Might bring us good luck," Z said, smiling and then gesturing to a waitress for more coffee.

"I just think it's kind of creepy."

"I read what you have so far . . ." Z said.

"And?"

"I like it. A lot."

Alex nodded.

"Good. I'm glad. We should keep going. There's lots more I need to know."

Alex fumbled with a recorder and a notebook and Z watched, slightly amused. He'd always gotten the impression that Alex was one of those mega-professional writers who only asked questions and follow-up questions, never giving up any part of themselves. But he'd realized when they first started working together that

Alex was unhinged. Nervous. Not on her game. She was a great writer. But there was obviously something going on in her personal life.

She constantly used her hands to sweep her hair out of her face. She was always digging in her bag for a pen. Today, she found one and scribbled on a napkin with it. It didn't work. She dug around her mammoth bag for another pen. That one didn't work either.

"Are you okay?" Z asked. He took a sip of his coffee and continued watching Alex empty her bag.

"I'm fine," Alex snapped. Then she caught herself. "I don't have the batteries for my recorder and I've somehow become a writer who can't find a working pen. Nice." Z dug into the inside pocket of his peacoat and pulled out a pen, a brand-new reporter's notebook, and a mini digital recorder.

"Here, use these. I use them to write rhymes. But you need them more than I do right now."

Alex seemed to hesitate for a brief moment. Then she exhaled and swiped Z's supplies to her side of the table. She turned on the recorder and flipped to a new page in the notebook.

"Are you ready?" Alex asked.

Z only smiled.

"Who are you today?" Alex asked.

"I'm a junkie. I'm a father. I'm a husband. I'm a rapper."

"In that order?"

"Today? Yes," said Z. "But it changes day to day."

"You've been clean for a year now. Biggest regret?"

"Too many to count. Right now, I really regret telling a reporter that Jake is an alcoholic. Dumb move. Make sure you put that in the book."

"Did you talk to him about it?"

"I didn't. But I will. I have a question for you, Alex. Are you an alcoholic?"

Z watched Alex's mouth open, close, and then open again.

"Why would you ask me that?"

"Beth might have mentioned something . . . Is that part of the reason why you agreed to work with me? Because you can relate to my story?"

"It was more about paying my mortgage."

"What are you talking about? Birdie has the number-one song in the country right now."

"I'm aware of my husband's success."

"So why are you acting like you need to make money?"

"Z, I'm supposed to be interviewing you."

Z reached across the table and turned off her recorder.

"You have been," Z said. "And you're doing a great job."

Alex looked up and leveled her eyes at Z.

"Thank you."

"When's the last time you've been to a meeting?" Z asked.

"Years."

"Come on," Z said, standing up and motioning for Alex to follow.

The church basement had folding chairs arranged in a semicircle with an ancient teacher's desk at the middle of the circle.

A white man with a heavily pockmarked face and no front teeth was talking with a young black man wearing sagging jeans and construction boots.

Z led Alex to a seat and went over to help make the coffee. No matter how hard they tried, the coffee always tasted like swill. They tried those fancy little creamers, fancy beans someone brought back from Brazil. No matter, the coffee was always just a half-step above dishwater.

But it wasn't about the coffee in the meetings. It was about being of service. After three months of sitting in the back of a variety of church basements, saying nothing, and counting down the minutes until the meeting was over, Z had begun sharing. He would open with the traditional: "Hello, my name is Z. And I'm a drug addict and an alcoholic." He heard stories worse than his, which he'd never considered a possibility. There was the man in need of a liver transplant who'd run over his own wife while she was gardening. There was the woman who drove her daughter to day care while drunk and ran into a tree, killing her child. There were people with no family and no friends. He attended funerals monthly and sometimes the bereaved consisted of just people from twelve-step meetings who didn't even know the dead person's last name.

Like most people new to recovery, once he got used to sharing in meetings, Z felt like he needed to share his experiences with everyone. He tried to get Beth to come on Family Night, but she refused. He'd even asked Jake to come through. But he said he wasn't trying to deal with all the rumors that would come from him going to an AA meeting. Jake was close to sealing a deal with Seagram's for his own lifestyle brand: wine, clothing, food, cars—everything. He couldn't have a paparazzo catching him slipping into one of Z's church basements.

Z knew Alex would come. He saw something in her. Something familiar. She wasn't drinking. But she wasn't sober either. Z was just learning the difference. Just because you didn't pick up a drink or a drug, it didn't mean you were mentally on your game. Binge eating, smoking cigarettes, irritability, restlessness— all signs that you weren't in control of your sobriety. It was a warning sign that you could slip. Z didn't know what Alex was doing in her personal life. But he could tell from the way she continuously ran her hands through her hair, nibbled at the cuticles on her thumb, and constantly bit the inside of her cheek that she was a nervous wreck.

Z snuck a few looks at Alex while he set up the coffee. Her hair hung down her face and she kept tucking it behind her ear. She had her legs crossed and tucked beneath the chair. She knew better than to take out her pen and notebook, so she just sat there, looking monumentally uncomfortable. Occasionally, she reached into her bag, took out a small container of lotion, and rubbed a bit between her hands.

Z slipped into the seat next to hers once the leader of the

meeting began speaking. Z stared straight ahead. Alex kept her eyes on the floor.

As people began to share their triumphs, defeats, and all the tiny moments in between, Z noticed Alex slowly opening up. She smiled when a woman talked about faking a cough so she could justify taking NyQuil. And her eyes welled up when a sixteen-year-old got up to receive his one-year sobriety chip.

Z raised his hand. The leader nodded in his direction.

"My name is Z. And I'm a drug addict and an alcoholic."

"Hi, Z," said the group. Alex remained silent.

"I'm glad to be here. I'm glad to be sober. But I'm anxious about what being sober is going to do to my career. I feel like I need the edge of drugs and alcohol to make me relevant. What am I supposed to rap about now? Doing yoga and going to twelve-step meetings?"

There was a smattering of laughter and Z smiled.

"Rappers ain't known to be a sensitive bunch," Z continued. "But maybe I can start a new genre. Thanks for letting me share."

"Thanks for sharing," the group chorused.

The leader scanned the room, checking to see if anyone else had a hand raised to be acknowledged. A half-minute passed before Alex raised her hand, just up to her shoulder.

"My name is Alex," she said, her voice barely above a whisper. "And I'm . . ." Alex stopped. And looked over at Z. He nodded his head.

"And I'm an alcoholic," she said, letting out a loud sigh afterward.

"Hi, Alex," the group said.

"Um. It's been a few years since I said those words. Not sure why it was so hard to say. I've been sober for five years, and my life has changed a lot since my drinking days. Real grateful for that. I have a wonderful husband who is doing well. I have my own career that I love. But I haven't been to meetings. I rarely read *The Big Book*. I'm disconnected from actively realizing that I'm an alcoholic. I can't say I'm going to start going to meetings again. But I am glad to be here today. Thanks for letting me share."

Z squeezed Alex's shoulder. She turned to face him, shrugged, and smiled.

After the meeting, Z and Alex sat on a bench outside the church. The sun was now shining through, turning a blustery day into a tolerably cold one. Alex wrapped her scarf tighter around her neck and zipped her jacket all the way up.

Z spoke freely while Alex nodded and took notes, occasionally checking to make sure the recorder was working. Z sat stiff, his back against the benches, his hands folded in his lap. Most of the time he kept his eyes closed tight. When Alex asked certain questions, his eyes popped open.

"Who is your closest friend?"

"I thought we were talking about summer camp in seventy-nine?"

"I made a sharp left."

Z drummed his fingers on his lap for a few seconds. He finally looked up at Alex.

"Probably Jake."

"So why did you tell a reporter that he's a drunk now? Is that how you treat your friends?"

Z looked down at the ground and then back up at Alex.

"Have you seen him lately?" asked Z. "He looks a mess. He's drinking way too much."

"You and Jake have always been very close . . ." Alex said.

"And we always will be. But that doesn't mean I can't call him out on his shit."

"The same way he called you out on yours."

Z nodded.

"Jake didn't make it easy for me when I was using," Z said. "There was talk that he was going to drop me from the label. And he probably would have if the song I did with Kipenzi hadn't blown up."

"Why aren't you speaking about this with him directly?"

"Me and Jake are very similar. We're hotheaded and hard-headed. This ain't the first time we beefed out. And it won't be the last. It'll pass."

"Technically, since he's the head of the label you both record for, he's sort of your boss, right?"

"I guess so. Doesn't really work like that in the real world. I don't work for anyone."

Z watched Alex scribble in her notepad, eyebrows in a V-shape. What was she thinking? Was she judging him? Could she tell that he was a completely different person than he used to be? He thought about how somber she was at the meeting. What was she going through? She knew Birdie was on tour. Was the absence already messing things up for them? It had taken Beth years to get sick of Z's traveling. But then again, she always had a small child or a pregnancy to deal with.

"You want to have kids one day?" Z asked.

The look on Alex's face made Z instantly regret the question.

"Sorry," he said.

Alex just smiled.

"How are you handling Birdie being halfway across the world?"

"I miss him. A lot."

"You don't have to be here doing this," Z said, pointing to the notebook. "You could be with him."

"I caught up with him in Israel for a few days and that was fun. But other than that, I can't. I have to work."

"They don't have paper and pens around the world? You need to write? So write. You don't have to be in Brooklyn ghost-writing an aging rapper's memoir."

"Did you just refer to yourself as aging?" Alex smiled.

"We're all aging. Even the young cats."

"Maybe I'll stop writing for a bit after we turn this book in."

"Alex, I know you're the one who's supposed to be asking the questions. But at the meeting today . . ."

Alex turned her recorder off.

"What?" Alex asked.

"Do you think you'll ever pick up a drink again?"

Z expected Alex to tell him to mind his own business. But Alex looked up at the bright sky.

"I've been a little stressed lately," said Alex. "And I can't front. A drink has crossed my mind a few times."

"What's stressing you?"

Alex twisted a straw wrapper around her pinkie.

"I've been thinking about losing my husband to some groupie like Cleo. I'm scared we'll grow apart or he'll start changing because we have a little paper now. Things are moving too fast. The last time I saw him, there was a line of people waiting to get his autograph. And he signed each and every one. How long until we're trying to avoid the autograph seekers?"

Z laughed. "Not long at all."

"I think we're done for today," Alex said, shoving things into her bag.

"Where are you off to now?" Z asked.

Z detected a whiff of something from her and put up both his hands.

"Too personal?"

Alex stood up.

"A little."

"Is it weird to hear all the minute details of your subjects' lives? Does it ever weigh you down?"

"Sometimes."

"You ever cry when you work with someone on their book?"

"Rarely."

"I'll try to keep you from crying," Z said, standing up.

"Don't worry about it," Alex said. "I don't cry easily."

They walked away from the church, Z on his way back to the diner to get his car, Alex on the way to the subway back to Brooklyn. Z stopped to check his cell phone. Alex marched toward the subway. Z noted that she never looked back.

18

Birdie held his breath as the plane dipped while preparing to touch down at Newark Airport. Normally, he said a silent prayer when he landed, thanking God that the plane didn't crash. But this time, he was thankful that he managed to complete the first leg of his tour without being unfaithful. Birdie knew that his first international tour might have temptations. But he never would have expected all the drugs and women that were shoved into his face at every opportunity. Birdie turned it all down on two different continents, sticking with the (very) occasional beer and a nightly blunt.

Birdie flipped through his iPod, looking for a song that wouldn't make him feel restless.

"Ready to go home?"

Gerald, a label representative, had upgraded his ticket to first class and was sitting next to Birdie. Bird felt weird about this dude being in first class while his friends were in coach. But when Birdie offered to upgrade his friends, they'd all refused.

"I'm definitely ready," Birdie said, closing his eyes.

Birdie and Alex had bought a spacious but not over-the-top five-thousand-square-foot colonial in Teaneck, New Jersey. Birdie had signed all the paperwork from the tour bus driving through Europe. When the tour was extended beyond the date they were closing on the house, Birdie could tell that Alex was pissed. She'd have to do all the heavy lifting. But she just told him she would take care of everything and not to worry about it. At baggage claim, Birdie stood at the carousel with his friends, waiting for the luggage to come down the chute.

"Birdie? What are you doing?" Dylan asked.

Birdie turned around and saw Dylan, standing with Gerald and his driver, all of his luggage neatly arranged. No matter how many flights he got on, he never remembered that Dylan and Gerald always arranged for his things to come off the plane first, so that he wouldn't have to wait.

"Aiight fellas," Birdie said, "I'll see y'all tonight at the studio."

There was a momentary awkwardness. Birdie's luggage had already been pulled and he had a driver waiting to take him to his new digs. Gerald was nearby, about to hop into his own car service to take him back to the label offices. And Travis, Daryl, and Corey had to wait for their luggage and then share a $75 cab back to their tiny apartments in Brooklyn.

"Y'all good with the cab and stuff?" Birdie asked. "You need me to—"

"Nah, we're good," said Travis. "Go see your new crib, superstar. We'll see you tonight."

Travis smiled, but it looked forced and strained. Everything had changed after Birdie went off about the party they promoted with his name. Now things were weird wherever they went. Birdie felt a strange vibe when he picked up the tab at expensive restaurants. And he felt something even more strange when he didn't reach for the bill right away. Travis, Daryl, and Corey were his aces. There was nothing they didn't know about each other. So why was it so hard to adjust to the new normal?

Travis and the guys got their luggage and left the terminal for the taxi line. Birdie walked over to Dylan and noticed the commotion back at the carousel. People were pointing and whispering. Some women were smiling. Some men were glaring. *They're looking at me?* Birdie thought to himself. *No way.*

Birdie nodded while Dylan ran down his press schedule for the next two days. He promised to keep his cell phone nearby and to check his text messages. He raised a hand and swore not to miss his interview with *Rolling Stone* the next morning. Birdie closed his eyes and shifted from one foot to the other while Dylan droned. Finally, she said her good-byes and got into her own waiting Town Car and pulled off.

"To New Jersey, Mr. Washington?" the driver asked, picking up Birdie's bags. Birdie looked behind him at the New York skyline he'd always stared at from Alex's brownstone.

"To New Jersey," he said.

The driver pulled into the cul-de-sac of the new house, and Birdie's mouth dropped. The house was much bigger than it had looked on the paperwork he and Alex had faxed and emailed back and forth. None of the pictures had done it justice. The stones laid out on the driveway were so neat and clean that Birdie felt like he could sit down and eat a meal prepared right on the pavers.

The driver took his bags out of the car and brought them to the front door, as Birdie followed, his eyes wide and his head moving slowly, taking in the property.

"Long time since you've been home, Mr. Washington?" the driver asked.

"First time I've been home," Birdie said.

He tipped the driver and then stood at the front door, confused. How was he supposed to get into his own house? Maybe Alex had left keys in the mailbox. He looked around and couldn't find the mailbox. He turned and looked down the driveway. The mailbox was at the start of the cul-de-sac, at least five hundred feet away.

Birdie turned back around and knocked on the heavy oak door. The door was double his height, reminding him of the Wizard's palace in *The Wizard of Oz*. From far away, he could hear Alex's voice: "*I'm coming!*"

A full minute later, the door creaked open and Alex pulled it back, her face broken into the widest smile Birdie had ever seen.

"Baby," Birdie said, wrapping his arms around his wife's waist and lifting her off the floor. "I missed you."

Alex had on Birdie's favorite outfit, the tank top and basketball shorts. It was comforting to see her in an outfit he was used to seeing on her back in Brooklyn. The strangeness of coming home to a brand-new house definitely needed a shot of familiarity.

"Well," Alex said, shrugging her shoulders and gesturing to the house. "Welcome home. What do you think?"

Birdie's eyes swept across the rooms he could see. To his left, there was a huge room with a mammoth plasma television mounted on the wall. Straight ahead, there was a carved mahogany staircase. At the top of the stairs, the second floor was open, so that you could look down into the foyer where he stood. To his right, he saw a kitchen that looked like it was ripped right out of a Martha Stewart magazine, down to the copper pots hanging from the ceiling over the stove.

"We have pots," Birdie said, realizing immediately how stupid that sounded.

Alex laughed and put her hands on her hips. "Yes. We have pots. And not just any pots," she said, taking Birdie's hand and leading him into the kitchen. "We have the finest pots and pans in all the land." Alex reached up and took down one of the frying pans from the rack.

"These are Mauviel pans," Alex said. She closed her eyes and raised her chin. "Preferred by professional chefs."

"Like yourself," Birdie said.

"Ha ha," Alex said. "Very funny. So? What do you think?"

Birdie blinked. "Everything is so . . . white."

It was true. The house had an all-white theme. There were touches of cream and tan in certain places. But for the most part, the house was white white white. Walls, sofas, carpeting, picture frames, artwork—their house looked like it had been blanketed in snow.

"Where's all our stuff?" Birdie asked, wandering around the house with Alex close behind.

"What stuff?"

"You know, *our* stuff. Like that picture we used to have over the fireplace in Brooklyn."

It was Birdie's favorite picture—the three of them in the judge's chambers on their wedding day. Birdie had his arm bent into an *L* shape over his stomach with his head held comically high and his eyes shut. Alex's mouth was wide open; she didn't know how to laugh any other way. And all you could see of Tweet was her chin—her head was thrown back so far that she was facing the ceiling and obviously laughing.

"It's still here," Alex said. "Come."

"And why do we have two living rooms?" Birdie asked, passing by an all-white room with a plasma television that looked identical to the one at the front of the house.

"The first one is a living room, for formal entertaining. The one back here is the family room. For hanging out. See, here's the picture."

Birdie frowned. The photo had been blown up to poster size, converted to black and white, and matted and framed in an over-sized white frame.

"What happened to the old picture?" Birdie asked. "And the frame made out of sticks that Tweet made at summer camp?"

"It's in the basement," Alex said. "With the rest of our embarrassing furnishings that have no place here."

"My recliner?"

Alex scrunched up her nose.

"That smelly tweed thing? Basement."

"Our mini golf set?"

"Basement."

Birdie nodded and flopped down on the overstuffed sofa in white slipcovers.

"So this is where we live."

Alex nodded and sat down next to him.

"I thought I would miss Brooklyn," Alex said. "But I could get used to this."

"You don't say?" Birdie asked, pulling his wife closer to him.

"It reminds me of Ras and Josephine's place. So grand and formal. I never thought I'd live in a house like this."

"Alex. Please. You grew up in a house like this."

Alex shook her head.

"No. We were in Manhattan. Not the same."

"Yes, in Manhattan. In a converted church that was featured in a bunch of magazines."

"Still. It was quirky and unique with small bedrooms. This is traditional. And huge."

"Did you have fun doing all this decorating?"

Alex hesitated and then laughed out loud.

"I totally did, Bird," she said. "At first, I felt weird about buying stuff. Everything was so expensive. And then I just thought, *what the hell* and I went for it. You like it?"

Birdie looked around the family room. In the corner was a basket of books. All had been covered with white book covers and the titles were written on the spine.

"It's *different*."

"I just went along with whatever the designer suggested," Alex said.

"I like it. It's gonna take some getting used to. I'm used to a little more dust. I'm scared to walk around here. Feel like I might break something."

"Come on," Alex said, pulling Birdie off the sofa and dragging him out of the room. "Let me show you the bedrooms."

Birdie followed his wife up the winding staircase, looking back to see the view from the top of the stairs.

"This is a guest room," Alex said, pointing to another all-white room with a mounted plasma. "There's a guest bath in there."

"Nice," Birdie said.

"Across the hall is another guest bedroom and bathroom," said Alex. "And here's Tweet's room . . ."

Alex opened a door in the center of the hallway and Birdie was nearly blinded by the sudden burst of color. There were hot-pink walls, yellow window treatments, and colorful vinyl circles behind her four-poster canopy bed.

"Tweet wasn't going with the all-white thing," Alex said plopping onto the little girl's bed.

"Obviously," Birdie said. He chuckled and poked around the room. "When is Jen bringing her over?"

"Tonight," Alex said. "Birdie, are you okay?"

Birdie went out into the hallway and looked both ways.

"Where's our bedroom?"

The bed was way too high. That was the first problem. Birdie liked the extra-thick mattress. Comfortable. But he was certain he could nearly touch the ceiling from their bed. It looked and felt like there were at least eight mattresses piled up.

"If I fall off this bed, I could break a limb," Birdie said, as he climbed onto the bed and lay on his back.

"You're being silly," Alex said. "It's not that high. Maybe it's the thick carpet that makes it feel like that."

"Are you sure this is just one mattress?"

Alex laughed out loud.

"Yes, Birdie. And a mattress pad for extra comfort."

Birdie stared at the white ceiling and tried to gather his thoughts. He was jet-lagged. So he knew anything he felt would be amplified. What was nagging him? The weirdness of being in his own home for the first time and his clothes already being hung up in closets and folded into drawers? In Birdie's closet, all two hundred pairs of his sneakers were encased in see-through plastic boxes, stored on an angle so he could see them all clearly. But the only room he really liked was Tweet's. It had personality. You could tell what kind of child lived there. Every other room felt sterile, like a nursing home or a hospital room.

"We need to hang our pictures up downstairs. My parents, your parents. That will make this feel more like home . . ."

Alex shook her head.

"We can't do that. Leslie said family photos on the first floor are tacky."

"Who's Leslie?"

"The designer."

"Well, what does she—"

"He. This Leslie is a he."

"Well, what does he know about tacky?"

"Lots," Alex said, her eyes wide. "It's considered grandiose and nouveau riche to have family photos in common areas of the house. Unless you're descended from royalty or something. Family photos go in personal spaces, like bedrooms."

Birdie blinked. He took a long look at his wife and waited for her to break out laughing and tell him how dumb Leslie's ideas were and help him start hanging the pictures. But Alex just kept staring at Birdie, eyebrows raised.

"Okay," Birdie said, turning his body back so that he faced the ceiling. "No photos. What about all of our books?"

Alex and Birdie had a sick book collection. Signed rare editions of Octavia Butler. First-edition books by Alice Walker and even an original copy of Zora Neale Hurston's *Their Eyes Were Watching God,* a gift from Alex's agent after *Platinum* made the best-sellers list.

"Books are in the basement," Alex said, her face solemn. "Until we get a library hooked up, maybe in one of the guest bedrooms, they stay there."

"Why?" Birdie asked. "We like our books."

"Leslie says showing off books anywhere but a library is ostentatious and presumptuous. Like you just want everyone to know what books you've read."

"It could also mean you like looking at books."

Alex shrugged.

"We're going for a bare, minimalist theme. Leslie said you would like to come off tour to a house that whispered instead of roared."

"Please stop saying 'Leslie said.'"

"Sorry."

Alex used the footstool to climb onto the bed with Birdie. He heard her breathing deep, until her breaths measured his.

"What did you get into while I was gone?" Birdie asked.

"Still working with Z on the book . . ."

Birdie stiffened and then forced himself to relax.

"What else?"

"I've been poking myself full of hormones every day."

Birdie squeezed Alex's hand.

"I know it sucks."

"Oh. I went down to Jamaica last weekend to see Josephine," Alex said, rolling off the bed and walking toward the bedroom.

"Freeze," Birdie said.

Alex kept walking into the bathroom and closed the door.

"I gotta pee!" she said.

"Come out here, Alex!"

"In a minute."

"Did you look for Reina's parents? And don't lie to me."

There was silence from the other side of the door.

"Alex! Get out here now."

Alex slowly opened the bathroom door and slinked out. She sat on the bed and clasped her hands in her lap.

"I found them. Really young girl from Trelawny Parish."

Birdie shook his head.

"And? Did you find out what Cleo was talking about?"

"You were right. Cleo was just manufacturing some drama. The girl got pregnant by her boyfriend. I met them both. They decided to put the baby up for adoption and someone told them about Ras and Josephine. They were excited to have their child raised by a celebrity in the States. I even talked to the midwife who was there when the baby was born."

Alex shrugged.

"No mystery there."

"Are you happy now?"

Alex looked over at Birdie as if she'd just realized he was finally home. She climbed onto the bed. And then climbed onto her husband.

"I'm not completely happy yet. But I'm about to be."

19

Everything about the day felt like it had been done before. Jake woke up early, turned on CNN. Ian brought in the newspaper. He drank a glass of fresh-squeezed orange juice (the only nonalcoholic drink he would have for the day) and then he allowed himself to think about Kipenzi for five sober minutes. He showered, dressed, and sat on the edge of his bed, checking his phone for appointments and tasks.

Someone had sent him a few songs via email from a rap duo named Trip & Step. On a song called "That's Not Hip-Hop," they were clowning him for living in TriBeCa with a manservant and wearing flip-flops on the beach. He entertained the idea of heading into the booth and then let it go. Going after them on wax would be a dream come true for their careers.

It was the exact same thing he'd done the day before that. (Including a dis song from Trip & Step.) Each day ended the same as well. Jake in a hotel lobby, drunk as a skunk, bringing some random chick home. If he was too drunk to kick her out, she stayed the night, getting pushed out of the bed the next morning. If he was somewhat sober, he was kicking her out literally minutes after peeling off the condom and throwing it away. Jake replayed last night. Which girl was it? Was it Sam again? Was he doubling up now? There was a chick who was singing in his ear at one point . . .

"Good morning, Jake!"

An Asian woman with a short haircut peeked around the door of Jake's bedroom. The memories flooded back and Jake nodded his head and mumbled something neither of them could understand. But he hoped she knew it translated to *get out*.

"Nice meeting you," said the woman. She actually came all the way inside the room with her arm outstretched for a handshake. He'd had her up against the bathroom wall last night. She'd given him a blow job on the stairs. And now she wanted to shake his hand? Jake sighed and extended his hand.

"Hope to see you again," she said, a smile on her lips.

Jake smiled with his mouth closed and leaned back down to look at his phone. He heard Ian ushering the woman out and then coming back up to Jake's room.

"Dude," Jake said, a pained expression on his face. "Why is this chick up in my fucking house? Nobody is supposed to break night up in here. Nobody."

"First of all, don't use profanities with me. I never endured that with Mrs. Giles, and I won't accept it from you either."

Jake stared at the floor for a few seconds. Ian knew that was his version of an apology.

"Second, if I don't know you have brought a woman into the house, I cannot dispose of her. I was shocked to see Ms. Liu exiting the guest bedroom this morning."

"Right, right."

"Sir, not that you asked . . ." Ian said.

Jake set his jaw and looked up.

"Your behavior is troubling," said Ian. "Someone of your stature . . . I would just imagine you'd be more careful. I'm sure a hotel would be just as convenient for a . . . tryst."

"Does it bother you?" Jake asked. He turned to let his back hit the headboard and then stretched his feet out on the bed.

"Does what bother me?"

"Knowing that I'm messing with other women. You think I'm betraying Kipenzi?"

Ian looked at a spot on the wall, somewhere behind Jake's head.

"I only know that if you had met an untimely demise, Mrs.

Giles would *not* have been having sex with other men in the bed she once shared with you."

"How come you never said anything?"

"You didn't ask my opinion."

The buzzer went off and Ian picked up the intercom phone.

"Your driver is here," Ian said, turning to leave.

"You don't have anything else to say?" Jake asked.

"No," said Ian, slipping into the room that used to be Kipenzi's office and closing the door. As Jake filled his water bottle before leaving for the day, there was an audible click.

"What does he need to lock the door for?" Jake mumbled under his breath.

The same roads, to the same studio. To spit new lyrics to new beats. The same label. Jake thought about the Digital Underground song "Same Song."

And wasn't it?

Jake took the steps down two at a time to Studio B and ran into Dylan, who had her head down in paperwork as she charged up the stairs and walked directly into Jake.

"Oooh, sorry, Jake," Dylan said, leaning down to pick up the papers she dropped.

"Who's in here today?" Jake asked.

"Zander's in Studio A. His dad just left . . ."

Dylan let her eyes drop to the floor for just a second. Jake wondered how much she knew about his falling-out with Z.

"What else?"

"Studio B's all ready for you. I'll be at the office if you need anything."

"Cool. Did you find Lily?"

Dylan shook her head.

"She doesn't work at Peter Luger's anymore. Samantha said she's tending bar at a hotel downtown, but she didn't know which one."

Jake nodded and turned to walk away.

"Jake?"

Jake turned but didn't speak.

"The tribute album?"

Dylan cowered, as if she thought Jake would hit her for asking.

"No," Jake said. "I'm not doing it."

"Z's on it," Dylan whispered. "And just about everyone else who ever worked with Kipenzi . . ."

"Cool. Then you don't need me."

Jake went into Studio B and closed the door. Kipenzi would not have wanted a tribute album. Jake was sure of it. As the executor of her estate, he could have put a stop to it, but he knew her father would be crushed. He needed to push his child. Even in death, he had her working. She'd retired! Why didn't people understand that? She didn't want news stories, magazine covers, and music videos. And now, she was looming larger in the media than she ever did when she was alive.

Jake played around with a few buttons on the mixing board, waiting for the engineer to arrive. Although the walls were practically 100 percent soundproof, he could hear a high note being hit somewhere in the distance. It was Mariah Carey–high. The kind of note that broke glass on those old Memorex commercials.

Jake stuck his head out of the studio door and listened. The note was still being held. And the singer was having fun with it, moving the note around, scatting and adibbing. Jake followed the voice, peeking into rooms as he made his way down the hallway. Zander was in one room, sitting at a piano, alone, playing the same melody over and over.

"Hey, Unc," said Zander.

Jake nodded and kept walking. In the last room, near the rear entrance to the studio, Jake heard it again. The angelic voice was laughing and hitting an even higher note than the first one he heard.

Jake stood at the doorway and slowly lifted his head up to the glass window in the door. A young woman had her back to the door. She had one hand on her stomach and the other hand pressed into her ear. Jake drained the last of his drink and peered inside. Jake didn't recognize the woman. But his eyes lingered on her ass, firm and tight. In tight jeans, he could see the outline of her body clearly, from her tiny waist to her slim thighs and the ankles both covered in gold anklets. He opened the door to the room and jumped when the young woman turned and he realized it was Bunny.

"Yo," he said, trying to maintain his composure. "I didn't recognize you." Jake made an awkward gesture to his head. "Your hair's short."

Bunny gave Jake a wicked smile.

"Do you like it? My manager hates it. But he said if you're okay with it, he'd let it go."

Jake could hardly hear her. How did he not know that was Bunny? He'd signed her to the label just after Kipenzi's death. And he'd been guiding her career as best as he could ever since. Every so often, she'd bring a few songs she worked on and he would yay or nay them. But she'd never actually registered on his radar as a woman. She was just Bunny Clifton, the girl from Jamaica with the charming accent and the immaculate voice. She was Zander's girl. And that was about it as far as he was concerned.

"It's different," Jake said. "You colored it or something too?"

Bunny nodded.

"That blond shit is so played," Bunny said, rolling her eyes.

Jake thought about his wife's blond mane. Bunny sighed.

"I want to do things my way. I'll take everyone's suggestions into consideration. But I need y'all to fucking trust me."

"Watch the mouth," Jake said, pointing at Bunny and then sliding onto a fake leather sofa in the corner of the studio.

"I'm eighteen years old. We curse sometimes. It's normal."

"If you don't rein it in now, you won't be able to rein it in when you're being interviewed by *Seventeen*. We don't need you to get the bad-girl rep."

"Even if I deserve it?" Bunny asked, leveling her eyes at Jake.

Jake opened his mouth, although he had no idea what he was about to say, just as Zander came into the studio.

"I think I got it, Bunny," Zander said, trotting over to the keyboard.

"You think you got what, baby?" Bunny asked, still looking at Jake.

"The melody. For the lyrics you wrote. Check it."

Zander put his head down and began playing the keyboard. An intricate melody, filled with those high notes Jake had heard Bunny practicing, filled the room. Bunny hummed at first, her eyes closed tight. Jake knew she could sing. The whole world knew she could. But this was something different. Bunny pursed her lips and started in with a few random *ooohs* and *ahhhs*.

Instantly, Jake's dick was hard. It was just a biological fact. He wasn't happy about it, but there it was. He was half lying on the couch, the same one he'd screwed his first groupie on fifteen years ago, and he had to adjust himself to make sure this child didn't see what she had done to him.

She was a teenager. She was his artist. She was Zander's girl. Jake put those three sentences on repeat in his head, hoping it would deflate him. Bunny launched into the lyrics of her song and turned to face Zander, giving Jake another view of her ass. He was not deflated. Just the opposite.

Should he stand up, gesture to his watch, and get out of there? Stay still and think of something like how much he loved his wife, even in death? Take a chance and get up and get some water?

Jake felt choppy and unnerved, as if he were controlling his body from somewhere else. And he wasn't sure which lever moved which limb.

"What do you think? Do we have something here?" Bunny asked Jake, turning around to face him.

Yes. We have something here, Jake said to himself. *We have a big fucking problem.*

*   *   *

Despite his allegiance to his wife, his common sense, and his sense of morality, Jake found himself drafting a text message to Bunny—and then quickly erasing it and moving on to the next task of the day. After a business meeting or a studio session, he'd find himself drafting again. Twenty times, he wrote out a text message to her number and then shook his head, knowing it was an insane thing to do.

"HEY, YOU SOUNDED GOOD IN THE STUDIO TODAY. KEEP IT UP.
"HEY, THE HAIR LOOKS GOOD. KEEP IT.
"HEY, I'M GONNA JUMP ON THE REMIX TO THE SONG YOU WORKED ON TODAY."

No matter what he said, he sounded like a dirty old man. Partly because he was. Somehow, Bunny had turned off a commonsense switch inside of Jake. And after she turned it off, he felt like she ripped it out permanently. There would be no going back. He knew that immediately.

When Kipenzi died, Jake had actually thought about killing himself. He dismissed that within the first week. Then the drinking started. And continued. And got out of control. And continued some more. And Jake walked through life in a buzzed haze. The alcohol helped him do whatever he wanted to do without thinking twice. And the alcohol told him it made all the sense in the world to text Bunny and ask a crazy question.

"Why were you looking at me like that?" He typed out, feeling like a thirteen-year-old scribbling a note with checkboxes.

Bunny responded immediately.

"I think I felt something coming from you. Not sure what. Let's talk about it later."

Just like that. No mind games. No fake doe-eyed innocence. No *who-me?* bullshit. She felt what he felt and she told him so without hesitation. She sent him another text message, simply asking where to meet. He gave her the room number of one of the penthouses at the W Hotel in Union Square and then told her where she could pick up a key.

She was already there when he arrived. Naked, on the bed, hands behind her head.

"Please don't say anything to me," Bunny said, spreading her legs wide. "Let's do this first. Then we can talk."

Bunny was thinner than any woman Jake had ever been with. Kipenzi's thick thighs and full breasts were still imprinted in his mind and his body. He remembered exactly how he had to hold her to mold them both together. And it didn't work with Bunny. One of his arms went entirely around her waist and looped around her stomach. She was a slippery, tiny eel, moving easily into complicated positions that made sure Jake was hitting her exactly where she needed him to. She moved to her side, sliding Jake back inside her with her hand. She didn't moan or make any noises. Her breathing was shallow and smooth. She sounded like she could have been doing yoga poses or writing a poem. Jake came inside of her. Wearing protection hadn't even dawned on him until after they were a sweaty, entwined mess, tangled in the W's fabled fluffy bedding.

When Jake recovered, he sobered up immediately. He jumped up from the bed and pulled on his boxers and then his jeans.

"This never happened," said Jake.

Bunny smiled.

"Oh, but it did." Bunny closed her eyes and spread her arms out wide. "It definitely did."

Jake stood at the mirror over the bureau, adjusted his hat, and then rubbed his beard. Over the past year, he'd bed-hopped nonstop. But now he had to admit that things were officially out of control. Bunny Clifton was an artist signed to his label and the girlfriend of a young man he considered his nephew. He'd gone from being trifling to just plain foul.

"This is never going to happen again," Jake said to Bunny.

"Yeah, it will," said Bunny. She rolled over and dressed quietly.

"No. It won't."

"I love Zander," said Bunny. "And what happened today doesn't change that. But there's something here. I'm not going to try to define it, excuse it, or explain it. It's hella messy. But it is what it is. And it's not over."

Jake reached for his water bottle on the nightstand. It was empty. He groaned inwardly and sat back down on the bed.

Bunny moved to the minibar and yanked it open.

"From what I can smell, vodka's your drink of choice," she said, tossing a mini-bottle from across the room. Jake opened it while staring at Bunny and finished it in two swallows.

"You need to switch to something else," Bunny said, fluffing up her super-short haircut in the mirror.

"Why?"

Bunny picked up her purse and walked to the door.

"Maybe you'd last a little longer."

Bunny let the door slam behind her. Jake considered her words. Then he burped, waved the smell away from his face, laid back on the bed, and stared at the door.

20

So where are you from originally?" asked the man with the too-small feet.

"Born and raised here in New York," Lily lied.

She'd planned to go on this date and be rigorously honest. But then she took a look at the man's tiny feet, encased in a pair of sad, dusty penny loafers, and she changed her mind. She would say just enough to be sociable, skip dessert, and hopefully get home in time for *Jeopardy*.

"I'm from Dallas. You ever been?"

Lily peered at her menu.

"I think once," she said, not looking up.

"Look, if you'd rather be somewhere else, we can end this early."

Lily looked up at Shawn and then put her head in her hands.

"Shawn, I am so sorry."

"It's okay. You want to go?"

Lily sat up straight in her seat. Shawn looked at her directly and waited for an answer.

"No, I don't want to go," said Lily. "I want to have dinner with you." She lightly tapped her fist on the table. "We are going to exchange awkward jokes and tell funny family stories and then I'm going to wonder if you're ever going to call me again."

Shawn smiled. And Lily noticed that he had two deep dimples. So what his feet were too small? He had a beautiful smile, he was clean, and had dimples, for God's sake. Two of 'em.

After an hour and three glasses of wine, Lily felt her shoulders relaxing. She was laughing more and had slipped out of her shoes under the table. Shawn put his hands on top of Lily's.

"Do you feel more comfortable now?" Shawn asked. He looked so sincere that Lily had to look away.

"I do. Thank you."

"Are you ready to talk about—"

"No, I'm not," Lily answered quickly. She tried to move her hands away, but Shawn held them tighter.

"You know Corinne told me."

Lily swallowed hard and nodded, keeping her eyes in her lap. She was wearing her favorite dress: a wool wraparound with a self-tie that she'd gotten on sale at Anthropologie for forty bucks. It had flowers embroidered all over the hem, and she kept her head down, counting the flowers repeatedly while Shawn held her hand tight.

"Lily, we have to talk about it. I mean, we don't *have* to. But we should at least acknowledge it so we can move on."

Lily's breath was coming in shallow, and she felt sweaty and shaky. She had never discussed her former self with any man except her doctor and her father. She'd never even dreamed about how she would discuss it with a man she might be interested in. When Corinne told her about Shawn, whom she'd met at a conference for addiction counselors, Lily blew her off. But Corinne continued to bug Lily about going out with him. Finally, one day Lily blurted out that if Corinne told Shawn the truth about her, and he was okay with it, she would go out with him. Two days later, she got a text message from Corinne: "I told him. He's fine with it. I gave him your number." Lily read the text and had to steady herself on the back of her sofa to keep from keeling over. A straight man who was okay with someone like her? Nope, she couldn't believe it. And now she was sitting across from Shawn, who was holding her hands tightly and asking her to talk about it.

Lily tugged, but Shawn wouldn't let go of her hands and he didn't stop looking at her directly.

"So what exactly did Corinne tell you?" Lily whispered.

"That you were born a boy."

Lily peeked up at Shawn.

"And?"

"Is there more? Are you an alien too?"

"Would you be okay with that?"

Shawn laughed.

"That's a stretch."

Lily bit her lip and held in a smile.

"I would really like to see you smile. Without covering up your face with your hand," Shawn said.

Lily looked up and beamed.

"You are beautiful."

Lily sunk lower into her chair and felt a warmth spreading across her face.

"Thank you, Shawn."

Shawn finally let go of her hands and she folded them into her lap. Suddenly she had no idea what to do with them. She was so flustered and confused that she could barely remember what her hands were used for.

"So when did you know?" Shawn asked.

Lily picked up her wineglass and took a gulp.

"I was probably four. Maybe five."

"And when did you know you were going to do something about it?"

"As soon as I found out on the internet that I could."

"Can I say something really crass without you thinking I'm a jerk?"

"Take a chance."

"I don't care where you got them from, you have the best rack I have ever seen in my entire life."

"Thanks. I think."

Shawn peered closer at Lily.

"There is no way in the world I would have ever thought you were—"

"Shawn," Lily said, leaning away from him. "You're sort of creeping me out now."

"I mean, I work with people in recovery with different addictions and I've treated a number of trannies, so I—"

"Did you just say trannies?" Lily asked.

"Is that politically incorrect?" said Shawn.

Lily sighed.

"Can we just change the subject?"

Shawn gave Lily a look of irritation and then seemed to catch himself.

"Now it's my turn to apologize," he said. "I got a little carried away."

"I just want to make sure you're getting to know me as a person and not as a fetish," said Lily.

"Does this mean I'm supposed to pretend like I don't want to have sex with you?"

Lily choked on her wine and coughed so hard that a waiter came over and patted her on the back. Lily patted her mouth with her white cloth napkin and thanked the waiter.

"Shawn, are you this forward on all your first dates?"

"If I know what I want, yes, I am."

Lily nodded and went back to picking at her salad. This was too much, too fast. She did not imagine that her first date with a man who knew her background would go this far. She thought about Rick, her first serious crush. One weekend, the summer she turned sixteen, she went fishing with him and his two older brothers in upstate New York. That whole weekend, she'd wanted so desperately to tell him. But at sixteen, she just didn't have the words. She'd already been taking hormones that she bought illegally online. And her body, always slight and feminine even without hormones, didn't give her away at all. At least not the parts Rick could see.

She knew Rick was crazy about her. His arm was permanently attached to her shoulders and he had this adorable habit of looking for her whenever they were separated for a bit and saying, "I just wanted to make sure you're okay." She let him kiss her for the first time that weekend at the dock, their legs hanging over the side. His brothers whooped and hollered from the other side of the lake. He caressed her face with his hand and then slowly brought his hand down to the side of her breast. Rick was so sweet and tender with her, it was physically painful to pull away from him. But she had no choice. This was presurgery. And there was no way she was going to be able to explain away that appendage when the time came. Rick went away to school. Lily waited. He returned and came to her job at the Waffle House before he even dropped off his luggage at his parents' house. By then, she'd found the words.

She honestly thought that Rick was going to hit her right there in the break room of the restaurant. She'd prepared for it. What happened instead was much worse. Lily was shocked when Rick dropped to his knees and covered his face with his hands. He didn't lash out at her. He didn't scream or ask her why she deceived him. He just cried. Hard. "I knew you were too good to be true," he said, crying. "Why couldn't you be real?"

Lily wished he'd hit her instead.

"I need to take things really slow," she said to Shawn.

"Are you at least glad that I know?"

"I don't know. This is all very new to me. I just have to absorb it and try to deal with all these weird things I'm feeling."

"This isn't my first time . . . in this situation," Shawn said.

Lily raised her eyebrows.

"It's not?"

"No. I thought you should know that. So you can see why I'm not freaking out about it. Lily, I don't care who you were when you were born. And I don't care who you were five years ago. I'm interested in who you are now. That's it."

"In the other relationship," Lily began, "did you . . . did you guys ever . . ."

Shawn closed his eyes and held up a hand to stop her from speaking.

"Yes. And I enjoyed myself very much."

Lily let out a breath she didn't know she'd been holding in. He was more experienced in her world than she was! And she had been about to write him off because of his tiny penny loafers.

"Okay. Well, that's . . . good to know."

"And I don't care what anybody says, it doesn't make me gay."

Lily looked up from her plate. *Who said anything about being gay?*

"Well. Yeah. That's kind of the point of reassignment surgery," said Lily. "You're not having sex with a man. You're having sex with a woman."

"Some people think that just because you're dating a woman with male genitals that you must be—"

Lily gently placed her fork down on the table.

"Wait. Shawn. I don't have any male genitals. I'm a woman. Last year, I had my male genitals removed. And I now have a vagina."

Lily had no idea she'd ever be able to say that sentence so plainly. But when she realized that Shawn was mistaken about who she was, she knew she had no choice. She watched as Shawn's eyes widened and wondered if there would still be time to catch the last round of *Jeopardy.* She'd been having a winning streak all week against all the contestants.

"You mean . . . you got it taken off?"

"Yes, Shawn. I have girl bits. On the top and the bottom."

Shawn took his napkin out of his lap and put it over his unfinished plate. He drained his wineglass, poured another glass, and drained that one as well.

"I think there's been a misunderstanding," he said, not making eye contact.

"Ya think?"

"I thought you were . . . Corinne said . . ."

"So you don't like women," Lily said, leaning back in her

chair. "You like chicks with dicks. Well. Sorry. I'm just a boring old girl."

"I'm not gay," Shawn said.

"Of course you're not . . ."

Shawn stood up and placed several twenty-dollar bills on the table. Lily looked around the restaurant to see if anyone was paying attention to how fast he was trying to get away from her.

"It was nice meeting you," Lily said.

Shawn was looking behind her toward the exit. She was shocked at how quickly he'd checked out.

"Right," Shawn said, pulling on his coat. "Same here."

Shawn walked quickly out of the restaurant, never looking back.

"If I get a penis tacked back on I'll be sure to give you a call," Lily mumbled to herself as she stood up, slipped into her coat, and buttoned it all the way up.

"I swear to God I told him everything!" Corinne said.

Lily had gone straight from the restaurant to Corinne's job at the bar.

"Well, somehow you left out something important. Or rather left it in. Or something . . ."

Lily laughed—a little too loudly—at her own joke and Corinne looked nervous.

"Lily, are you okay?"

Lily shrugged and accepted the glass of wine Corinne offered.

"I spend my whole life refusing to get close to any guy because I've got a dick. And the first guy I'm interested in after the fact doesn't want me because I *don't* have a dick. I think this would actually be considered ironic."

"Would it? I'm not sure if . . ."

"Corinne, I don't care if it's ironic or not!"

Corinne went back to washing out the dirty glasses lining the back of the bar and kept quiet until she heard Lily crying softly.

"I am so sorry, honey," said Corinne. "This is totally my fault."

"No it's not your fault," Lily sniffed. "This is just the way it is. This is what I'm going to have to deal with. Dating guys who don't know what to make of me."

On the way home, Corinne kept up a steady stream of conversation and didn't bother waiting for Lily to respond or join in. Lily knew she was chatting nonstop on purpose, and she appreciated not having to make conversation. All the way home, she thought about Shawn and his tiny penny loafers. She had actually envisioned them tucked under her bed. She'd already made plans to get them buffed and shined. On the train, Lily nodded as Corinne babbled. She kept her eyes on the shoes of every man on the train. None of them were wearing loafers.

Just before Ras grabbed the handle to the door of the studio, he glanced at the Starbucks next door. Birdie's wife Alex was sitting in the window, typing furiously on her laptop. He could hear his wife urging him to leave Alex be. But he also heard Cleo's voice, hinting about talking to Alex. Ras looked around and then slipped into the café and sat in the seat next to Alex. She didn't notice him and he didn't say a word. He looked out of the window and occasionally glanced at her screen. He couldn't read whole sentences but he saw words like *in vitro, needles*, and *fertility*. He glanced once more and Alex finally noticed and looked up at him.

"Hey," Ras said. He didn't look at Alex, instead continuing to look out the window.

"Hey, Ras . . ." Alex said. She closed her laptop and put her chin in her hand. "What's up?"

"Just saying hello."

"Bullshit," Alex said softly.

Ras turned to face Alex.

"I want you to mind your business and stop talking to my wife."

"Your wife happens to be my friend."

"She's not your friend. You interviewed her for a story. That doesn't make you friends."

"That was a year ago. We're friends now. And what do you care if I'm friendly with Josephine?"

"I just don't like it."

"Well, I don't know what to tell you," said Alex. "If Josephine says she doesn't want to talk to me anymore, fine. But she's an adult. She can decide who she wants to be friends with."

Ras wanted to choke Alex. Knowing that Birdie was right upstairs in the studio waiting for him was the only thing that kept him from wrapping his hands around her neck. He could actually feel his fingers flexing and he forced himself to keep his hands at his side.

"Fine," Ras said. "But don't get yourself hurt talking about shit you don't know anything about."

"Are you still messing with Cleo?"

A flash of scenes played in Ras's head. He stood up and leaned in close to Alex's ear.

"This is exactly what I'm talking about," Ras whispered. "You have *no* right to ask me that. None!"

"And what about Reina?" Alex asked. "Is there something Cleo knows about her that Josephine doesn't?"

"Where the *hell* are you getting this bullshit from?" Ras said, his face contorted.

Alex pulled her bag onto the counter and pulled out the copy of *Platinum* that Cleo had sent her when the book was published. Ras recoiled in horror.

"Get that thing away from me," Ras said, pushing the book away.

"It's a book," Alex said. "Not a bomb."

Ras sat back down next to Alex and picked up the book.

"That's what you don't understand," Ras said. "This book *is* like a bomb. It almost blew my marriage and my life to bits. You wrote this, Alex. And it almost destroyed me. To see you sitting across from my wife chatting her up . . ."

"I understand all that," Alex said. "But did Cleo make this stuff up? Or did it all really happen?"

Ras felt like that was beside the point so he kept quiet.

"Exactly," Alex said. "I know what Cleo did was wrong. But you gave her the ammunition. You're guilty as hell and you need to check yourself. Not me."

"Before you came around interviewing my wife, she didn't pay attention to what was going on in the industry. You ruined all of that."

"Read what Cleo wrote to me," Alex said, pointing at the first page of the book. Ras sat up and read, moving his lips quickly as he did: "'You should ask Ras about that baby he adopted. There's a good story there. And if I know you the way I think you do, you won't be able to resist finding out the truth. You can thank me later.'"

He slammed the book shut and slid it in Alex's direction.

"That bitch is *insane*," Ras said. "Completely out of her mind."

"So why would she tell me this?" Alex asked. "She said there's a good story there. What's the story?"

"You *know* the story," Ras said. "You were at my house the day Josephine met Reina for the first time. A young lady from Trelawny contacted my grandmother and let her know she was having a baby and planned to give it up for adoption. She knew Josephine and I had been trying for a child. She wanted her baby to have a better life with us. You know this, Alex. There's no hidden agenda here."

"So what is Cleo talking about?"

"She's sending you off to chase a nonexistent story just to mess with me."

"Is the baby . . . is it really someone you were . . . involved with?"

"What are you asking me?"

Alex looked around the café and then leaned closer to Ras and whispered.

"I mean, is Reina really *your* baby? Were you involved with the girl from Trelawney?

"You really think I could do something like that? Have a baby by someone else and pass her off to my *wife*? That's sick, Alex."

"So your answer is no."

"My answer is no. A thousand times no. I swear to God, I do not know who Reina's biological parents are. I never met the young girl. I don't know anything about her except what my grandmother told me. Which was not much."

Ras could tell that Alex's mind was moving a mile in a minute.

"Look, Alex. Do this. Find out who the mother is. Find her. I'm sure Reina will want to know one day. Find out the story with this girl. I'll send you what information I have. When you find out, you will see that I'm telling you the truth. Reina is my daughter. And I love her dearly. She is the only pure and innocent thing in my marriage. I put this on my life. My story is the truth."

Ras saw Alex's face soften. She nodded.

"I don't need to find out anything," she whispered.

"No. Do your reporter thing. Find the girl. Get the truth. You'll never believe me until you do."

Alex shook her head, but Ras knew better. He had a feeling she'd already started looking into Reina's biological parents.

"Did you tell my wife what Cleo wrote in that book?" Ras asked.

"No. She would have been devastated. And I wasn't sure if Cleo was telling the truth. That's why I wanted to ask you."

Ras stood up.

"I'm going to talk to my wife about all of this. We'll straighten it out. But right now, I need to make some hit records for your husband."

Ras extended his hand and Alex leaned over and shook it. On the elevator up to the studio, he rubbed his hands together, the way he always did when he was nervous or deep in thought. What the hell was Cleo trying to do? She'd always been vindictive and spiteful. But this was different. Making things up out of thin air? If Josephine suspected for a moment that Cleo knew something about her baby that she didn't, Ras didn't have a chance in hell of saving his marriage. Or his life for that matter.

Josephine was silent. Her eyes were closed and she had her legs tucked under the swing, cradling the baby as she rocked back and forth. Ras sat on the steps leading from the back porch to the backyard. He turned around to face his wife and waited for her to speak.

"Why would she make up something like that?" Josephine finally asked.

"I don't know."

"Does she know Reina's biological parents?"

"No."

"Do you?"

"No."

"Are you still . . . ?"

Ras's heart pumped hard and he felt the sweat glands under his arms explode.

"No."

Josephine opened her eyes and glared at Ras.

"I said no."

"I hear what's coming out of your mouth. But I don't know if it matches what's in your heart."

Ras climbed up the steps and sat next to Josephine on the swing. Reina had fallen asleep on Josephine's chest, and she laid her on her lap. Ras leaned over and stroked the baby's back.

They were quiet for a long time, listening to the sound of the waves crashing against the beach just a few hundred feet away.

"Would you stay with me if I cheated on you?" Josephine asked.

Ras thought about Josephine on her back, spreading her legs for a nameless, faceless man. He felt his stomach retch and a pounding sensation begin in his temple.

"That would not happen."

"But what if it did?"

"We would deal with it."

"You would forgive me?"

Ras got up and walked into the house. Josephine followed, walking slowly so that she would not wake the baby.

"I'm just curious," said Josephine. "How would you deal with it? How would you get over it?"

Ras took the steps two at a time to their bedroom and sat down on the bed. He heard Josephine put the baby down in her room and then he saw her standing in the doorway.

"It's different when a woman does it, isn't it?" Josephine said.

Hell, yeah, it's different. Ras thought to himself. But he knew better than to admit it. Josephine wanted to fight. And Ras was too weary to take it there.

"It's a fucked-up thing to do," said Ras. "No matter who's doing it."

Josephine shrugged and turned down the bed. She climbed in and rolled over to her side. She was asleep almost immediately. Ras stayed up, flicking through channels on the television but finding nothing that would hold his attention for more than thirty seconds. On one channel, he saw nothing but Josephine spread-eagled on their marriage bed, a naked man on top of her. Then on the next channel, there was Josephine, on her knees in their bathroom, taking the man into her mouth, moaning with delight. Ras closed his eyes tight and saw another image of Josephine, tied to the bed the way he always tied Cleo up. She was being slapped across the face and smiling through it, wriggling and groaning in ecstasy. After a few more minutes of the images flashing through his head, Ras stood up and felt his head start to spin.

Ras flew into the bathroom and made it just in time. He threw up for ten minutes, until nothing came up but blood.

Breathless and weakened, he turned away from the toilet and sat on the floor. He looked up and saw his wife standing above him. She tossed a towel into his lap.

"Welcome to my world," she said, before returning to bed.

22

The thrill of discussing his entire sordid life story had gotten old very quickly. A rap song lasted five minutes. And Z knew how to cram twenty years of history into sixteen bars. But talking in full sentences with Alex each week was draining. Now that they were finally getting to the end of the book, Z thought things would get easier. He was wrong. No matter how deep he went into the details of an event, Alex went deeper, twisting the knife. Even when he stopped to cry, her eyes remained dry. She waited patiently for him to compose himself. And then she'd pick up exactly where she left off.

"What did your stepfather smell like?"

Z brought his head up and dried his eyes with the back of his hand. He grabbed a napkin and noisily blew his nose.

"Shit, Alex, I don't remember."

"Yes, you do. Think about it."

Z closed his eyes and allowed himself to go back to the tiny apartment in the Bronx. His mother away at work. His stepfather standing behind the sofa where Z pretended to be asleep.

"Flowers," Z said. "He smelled like a funeral home. I guess it was some kind of cologne. But it smelled like a sickly sweet perfume."

Alex nodded, scribbling.

"Can't stand flowers to this day. Didn't let Beth have any at our wedding. Never go to funerals. Except for Kipenzi's."

Z shuddered and then leaned back against the booth, closing his eyes and putting a hand up to his forehead.

"Where's your stepfather now?"

"Dead."

"What happened to him?" Alex asked.

The waitress appeared with omelets, turkey sausage, and toast. Z pulled a plate closer to him, leaned his head down, and mumbled a prayer. Z and Alex chewed in silence.

"So what happened to your stepfather?" Alex asked again.

"You're like a rabid animal," Z said. "You lock on to something and just don't let go."

"That's my job."

"You do realize that this is hard for me . . ." Z asked.

"Yes," Alex said.

"I can't tell. I tell you the most horrible details of my life. And you just nod your head and write."

Alex pushed her plate aside and slid her notebook back in front of her.

"My job is to get a book out of you. Not help you deal with your demons."

Z nodded and went back to his omelet. Alex closed her notebook.

"Z, I'm sorry."

"For what?"

"You're right. I could be more sensitive about this. It's just that in order for me to do this right, I have to sort of detach myself from it. I have to get the facts out of you, all of them. Even the painful ones. But I can do better."

Z smiled, his mouth packed with food.

"Thanks," he said, opening his mouth just enough to speak. He swallowed and wiped his mouth with his napkin. "I'm assuming you're going through your own shit too."

"What are you talking about?" Alex asked.

Z pulled out a copy of *Rolling Stone*. Birdie was on the cover, holding two fistfuls of cash. His mouth was wide, in a half-grimace, half-smile. Alex shrieked and yanked the magazine out of Z's hand. She scrambled out of the booth and turned around in a circle.

"Oh my gosh! Did you see this?!" Alex asked Z, turning the magazine around.

Z laughed out loud.

"Yes, Alex. I just handed it to you."

Alex looked around the diner as if she wanted to dash over to someone else's table and show them the magazine. Then she seemed to catch herself and slid back into the booth, clutching the magazine to her chest. She peeled it back and stared at the cover of the magazine.

"Did you know he was doing *Rolling Stone?*" Z asked.

"I knew he did a shoot and an interview. Didn't know it would be a cover," Alex said, digging into her purse.

"You need to call him right now?"

Alex looked up at Z.

"I'm sorry. So unprofessional of me. But my husband is on the freaking cover of *Rolling Stone!* I gotta tell him I'm holding it in my hand."

"Why didn't he call you and tell you? I'm sure he's seen it . . ."

As soon as the words came out of his mouth, he realized he'd said aloud what he meant to say to himself. Alex gave him a look and excused herself from the table.

Z mentally kicked himself. All his self-help work still went out the window when the green-eyed monster reared his ugly head. Z had done a double take at the newsstand when he was walking from his parking spot to the diner to meet Alex. He almost choked on his own spit when he saw Birdie on the cover. Z did a quick calculation and realized it had been ten years since his first (and last) *Rolling Stone* cover. Not counting being part of a montage of criminal-minded musicians. Dylan had actually included that cover on her list of press she'd secured for him that year.

Z thought Birdie was cool. The "Fistful of Dollars" song was infectious. He'd even done a few freestyles to the beat as an interlude on Zander's mixed tape. And he'd met Birdie a few times. Seemed like a cool dude. There was not a single thing Z could draw on to rightfully hate on Birdie. But he hated on him anyway. Especially when he slid into the booth across from Alex every week and watched her brush her hair out of her face. And when she cleared her throat and turned on her recorder with a certain grace that made his stomach knot up.

It was cool for Birdie to have a hit song, magazine covers, and all of the trappings of fame Z had enjoyed for over a decade. But he had Alex too? Z watched Alex in the corner of the diner talking into her cell phone. He'd never seen her face look so alive. She was listening, throwing her head back and laughing, and then nodding her head vigorously.

Alex returned to the booth and exhaled.

"Sorry about that."

"I'm sorry about what I said. About Birdie not telling you. That wasn't called for."

"It's cool."

"Is he excited?"

Alex shrugged.

"Dunno."

"Didn't you just speak to him?"

Alex shook her head.

"He's at a sound check. I was talking to his manager."

"Ah."

"What does that mean?"

Z looked up. "What? Ah?"

"Yes," Alex said, her lips set in a straight line. "What do you mean by 'Ah.'"

"Don't be insecure," Z said. "It's not good for your marriage."

"What can you tell me about marriage?" Alex asked.

Z threw up his hands.

"Hey, don't get mad at me because I know what's going on at your husband's 'sound check.' Some chick is sound checking his nuts."

Alex gasped. Z tried to pull back the urge to be petty. But it was too late. He was going in, whether he wanted to or not.

"Now don't get me wrong," Z said, a sneer spreading across his face. "He's probably not the mess I was. Unless he's on crack. But please believe your husband is getting all kinds of ass thrown at him right now. And he's catching some of it. And if he's not right now. He will. Soon."

Alex narrowed her eyes, and Z saw her working her jaw and grinding her teeth. A certain level of numbness had washed over him, and suddenly he didn't care that he was pissing Alex off. Or worse, hurting her feelings. He just felt like being brutally honest. He'd never come across an artist who remained faithful on the road. Not ever. And yet here was Alex, week after week, sitting across from him, assuming somehow that her husband was different.

"Thank you, Z," Alex said. "I'll definitely take that into consideration."

Z expected her to sound teary and defeated. Instead, she was steely and determined. She wasn't going to let him get under her skin. Which made Z feel worse than if she had burst into tears. Z dropped his head into his hands and lowered both to the diner table.

"What is *wrong* with me?"

"You're jealous," Alex spat.

Z looked up.

"You're right."

"I know I am," said Alex. "You're on the tail end of your career and Birdie's on the come-up. You're hating."

"The main issue is that on top of all that he has you."

Alex slid out of the booth and took her jacket off the hook. She didn't bother to put it on. She grabbed her bag and walked out. Z lumbered out of the booth and followed her.

"Yo, Alex," he yelled out. He was walking slowly up Atlantic. She was nearly sprinting.

"Alex! Wait up!" Z yelled out, cupping his hands around his mouth.

Out of the corner of his eye, he saw a photographer across the street training a lens on him. Z broke into a jog and caught up to Alex easily. She was standing at the top of the subway steps and Z caught her by the arm just as she was about to run down. When he yanked her, she whipped around and jerked her arm out of his hand.

"Wait," Z said. He dropped his voice to a whisper. "I'm attracted to you. I'm just going to put that out there. You're gorgeous and smart and funny."

Alex glared at Z, her nostrils flaring.

"And now that I've admitted it," said Z, "I can let it go. I can assure you that I am very committed to my wife. It doesn't make me a robot. And I would imagine it would be normal for a subject to feel an attraction to their cowriter. It's an intimate relationship."

Alex's face softened, just the tiniest bit. Z fought against touching her and lost. He grabbed both her wrists. She didn't pull away.

"Birdie and I have been trying to have a baby," Alex whispered, her eyes on her feet. "It's been really hard . . ."

Z nodded and waited for Alex to continue.

"I think I'm finally pregnant."

"Wow. Did you tell Birdie yet?"

"No. I'm waiting until he comes home. I don't want him to worry about me while he's on the road. And plus . . . who knows what could happen . . ."

Z lifted her chin with one hand, slipped it around to the back of her head, and pulled her close to his face. He kissed her on the forehead.

"You'll be fine," Z said. "You should tell him. He would want to know."

Alex pulled back.

"You really think Birdie's cheating on me?" she asked.

Why on earth did he say that to her? Z struggled to come up with something to say to smooth it all over.

"Not necessarily, I just—"

"Do you know any rapper who has remained faithful while out on tour? Please name me one, Z. Just one."

Z locked eyes with Alex.

"Define faithful . . ."

Alex closed her eyes. She pulled her wrists away from Z's arms and turned to walk down the subway steps. Z followed her all the way to the train platform. He stood a few feet away from her, watching as she stood alone on the platform. She was still staring straight ahead when the train roared up and the doors opened.

Z heard the recorded message: "Stand clear of the closing doors, please." And he watched Alex fling herself into an empty seat. She looked up and saw Z standing there. They held each other's gaze until the train was gone.

23

I haven't seen you in three weeks and I can't even get a hug?"
Zander didn't actually want to hug Bunny. He was dead tired and ready to pass out after a near month out of town trying to write and produce in a few different studios with new producers. But the fact that Bunny was physically distant was a red flag.

"I'm tired, Zan . . ." Bunny said. She yawned for emphasis and even threw in a halfhearted stretch. "Tomorrow I'll give you all the—"

"It's not about what I want from your body," Zan said in a sharp voice. "A hug and a kiss after a month apart just doesn't seem like too much to ask."

Zander stopped speaking and waited. Bunny finally gave in. She walked over to Zander and threw her arms around his neck. She made sure to keep her body completely distant. A whole person could have stood between them in the space she made.

Zander let her go and Bunny sat cross-legged on the bed. She took out weed and rolling papers and began making a joint.

"You're still smoking?" Zander asked.

"When did you become my dad?" she said, offering the joint to him.

Zander shook his head and pulled Bunny off the bed and to her feet.

"Why are you acting like this?" Zander asked, pulling Bunny close.

"I'm tired. I've been running around cross-country just like you have."

"You're up to something," said Zander. He leaned in closer to her face and grabbed her arm. "And you're *on* something too."

"I don't need this shit from you, Zander. I left my parents in Jamaica. Now let me go."

"You sure you don't have something to tell me?"

Zander watched anger flash in Bunny's eyes. He knew what was going to happen, but he was two seconds too late to stop it.

Bunny's knee came up hard, landing right in Zander's crotch. A tear spilled from his left eye. The throbbing pain was so intense that he immediately crumpled to the floor. He looked up and saw a pair of pointy-toed pumps near his face. She tapped him on the nose with one shoe.

"Stop trying to control me, Zander," she yelled. "And that didn't even hurt, get up, you little—"

Zander sprang to his feet and Bunny sprinted away, jumping over sofas and throwing pillows behind her to stop him from reaching her.

"I'ma kill you, Bunny," Zander said, still limping across the room, trying to catch up to her. "I've told you a million times. Don't put your hands on me. If I hit you back, I'm wrong. And I go to jail."

"So don't hit me back," Bunny said plainly. She even had the nerve to shrug her shoulders when she said it. They faced each other, both breathing heavily. Zander grabbed both of her hands with one of his own and yanked hard.

"You do *not* kick me in the nuts and think it's okay," said Zander. He yanked Bunny's arms harder with each syllable he spit in her face: "That. Shit. Is. Not. O. Kay." Zander glowered. Bunny smiled.

"I'm done," Bunny said. "I swear."

"I don't believe you."

"Let me go and you'll find out."

"No."

"Let go of me, Zander. Now."

The air in the room got thick, tight, and tense. Zander refused to let go, holding on so tight that red welts formed on her wrists.

"You're putting marks on me, Zan . . . You know we can't have that."

Zander still refused to let go, and Bunny twisted and pulled away, grunting and swearing.

"Let. Me—"

Zander released her arms. But she was pulling away so hard that when he finally let go, she ended up falling backward on the coffee table, rolling over it, and then hitting the ground facedown with a sickening thud.

"Bunny!" Zander yelled out, rushing to where she lay, her face in a pool of blood. Bunny sat up and put her head in her hands, rocking back and forth very slowly.

"Shit," she whispered. "Get a doctor. Get somebody. My mouth. Damn, Zander."

"I'm calling 911," Zander said reaching for his cell.

"No!" Bunny yelled.

"Why the hell not?!"

"Are you crazy?" Bunny said, bringing herself to her feet while keeping her hands over her nose and mouth. She moaned and then sat down on the bed.

"My face! Rob is gonna kill you! I have a show tonight, Zander."

Zander dashed into the bathroom, drenched a towel in hot water and went back to Bunny.

"Hold your head back," he said.

"Shit, that hurts. Owwwww!"

After mopping up blood spurting from her nose and mouth, Zander had a better idea of what was going on. Her upper lip was busted. And her nose was swollen to twice its size. Bunny grabbed the towel from Zander and spit into it. A blood-covered tooth landed in the middle of the red-stained cloth.

Bunny and Zander looked up at each other in horror.

"You knocked my tooth out," Bunny said.

"Are you kidding me?!" Zander yelled. "I let you go and you fell over! You know I didn't do that on purpose."

"You should have just let me go like I said!"

"You attacked *me*. As usual."

"Call somebody. Find a dentist. I have to get this fixed."

Bunny ran her lip around the gums where her front tooth used to be.

"I don't believe this shit."

"Stay right here," said Zander. "I'll be right back."

"Where are you going? Who are you going to call? Don't call my manager."

Zander dashed into the hallway, filled up an ice bucket, and came back inside. He wrapped up ice in a clean towel and held it up to Bunny's face.

"Just shut the hell up and keep this on your nose," he said.

Zander picked up his phone, closed his eyes, and pressed a speed dial number.

"Yeah, it's Zander. I need help. Bunny had . . ."

Zander looked up at Bunny, who was scowling at him.

"Bunny had an accident. We need a dentist to get up here quick."

"Yeah, Bunny had an accident!" she screamed toward the phone. "Zander beat me up. Again!"

"No!" Zander said into the phone. "I didn't touch her, I swear. It was an accident. Just please send someone. You're on your way now? Okay."

Zander was visibly relieved and he sat at the desk on the far side of the hotel room. Bunny propped herself up on the bed, a rolled-up towel behind her head for support.

"What did your mom say?"

Zander sucked his teeth.

"I did not call my mother."

Bunny's eyes widened.

"You called your dad?! He's gonna kill you."

"I did not call my father. Just chill."

Twenty minutes later, there was a knock on the door. Zander and Bunny traded a long look. Bunny stood up and tried to make it to the door before Zander could. He grabbed her by the shoulders and pushed her back down on the bed.

"Chill out," he said.

Zander opened the door, while still looking behind at Bunny. Her face froze when she saw Jake walk through the door and for the briefest of seconds, Zander wondered why. Who else did she think he would have called?

Zander sat on one side of the room, watching the dentist intently. Bunny clenched the sides of the armchair as the dentist inserted a needle full of novocaine. Jake stood up, his back against the door of the hotel suite, staring at Zander. Zander noticed that Jake was making a point not to even look in Bunny's direction. He was completely focused on him.

"Did you put your hands on her?" Jake asked, his voice weary and tired.

"I swear to God, I did not—"

"Never mind, Zander. It doesn't matter. I don't think the chick punched her own self in the face and knocked her tooth out. Something happened. And there were only two of you in the room."

"I was holding on to her arms to keep her from hitting me and I let go and she—" Zander stopped talking abruptly. There was no point explaining. The story sounded convoluted and Jake wouldn't believe him anyway. Zander had already been worried about his relationship with Jake. He didn't hear from him nearly as much as he had when he first got signed. And he'd been closer to this man than his own father at times, especially when his father was using heavily. Jake Giles was just a half-step under God in Zander's world. And his eyes burned with shame and embarrassment that Jake was getting him out of a scrape like this.

"Unc," Zander started.

"Don't, Zander," Jake said, not looking up from his phone. "It doesn't matter now."

The dentist held up Bunny's tooth and moved it back and forth.

"I can implant this back in," he said. "It's in good condition. But I can't do it here. You'll have to get her to my office. It's only three blocks from here. I'll meet you there in ten minutes."

"How are we getting her out of here?" Zander mumbled.

Jake went to the window and looked down at the street.

"Jackson's down there," Jake said, motioning to Jackson Figueroa, the paparazzo who had assigned himself to Jake, Bunny, Zander, and Z. Ninety percent of all photos that appeared on the blogs and in gossip magazines of the four of them came from one photographer who had an uncanny ability to know exactly where they were at any given moment.

"Zander, me and you are going right through the front door. My car is waiting outside. Bunny, put Zander's baseball cap on. Keep your head low. Boo's in the hallway. He's going to take you down to the kitchen, go out the service entrance, and get in the car. Move, people."

Zander followed Jake out of the room and into the elevator.

"This is not cool, Zan," Jake said, shaking his head. "We can't have this. Bunny's the biggest thing we have going on this label. I can't have her performing with a missing tooth."

"This was not my fault, Unc, she's always—"

"Did you ever think that maybe—just maybe—your dad is right about Bunny? If y'all can't stop trying to kill each other, why bother with this bullshit?"

"I'm cutting her off," Zander said.

"No, you're not," said Jake. "But you should. Now, when are you going to tell your father what happened?"

"Never."

"He's gonna find out. Might as well get it over with."

The two were silent for the ride to the dentist's office.

"Stay with her," said Jake to Zander. "And make sure she's okay. Then get to the studio and write."

Zander nodded his head and climbed out of the truck. Normally, he would case the area as soon as he stepped out of any car. But this time, he was preoccupied.

Jackson Figueroa sat in a coffee shop right across the street from the dentist's office. He trained his lens on Zander and shot a few pictures in rapid succession. Ten minutes later, he brought his camera up once again and got a few grainy shots of a young girl with a baseball cap pulled low over her head. Jackson took his head away from the viewfinder for a brief second. Her hands were covering the bottom of her face. Jackson zoomed in as far as he could and snapped. She was gone in an instant. He looked down and saw what he captured. The picture was grainy, but clearly, she was headed into a doctor's office for a reason. A clear cut on her bottom lip sealed the deal. And sealed Jackson's paycheck for the next month.

Zander came to Bunny's house as soon as she came home.

"Look," said Bunny, opening her mouth wide. "He did a good job, right?"

"Yeah," said Zander. "I guess."

"It still hurts like crazy and my nose is still swollen."

Bunny shook out a few pills from a tiny canister.

"What are those?"

"Percocet. Thanks to you, I'll be on pain pills for a few days."

"Bunny, this wasn't my fault. You love to start shit with me and then put it back on me."

"You pushed me."

"You fell. And none of this would have happened if you hadn't kneed me in the nuts."

"I'm sorry, Zan," she whispered.

"No, you're not. Everybody and their mother keeps telling me to leave your crazy ass alone. And here I am."

Bunny walked over to Zan and kissed his neck softly.

"Because you know I love you very much."

"That won't mean anything when you get me locked up over some dumb shit."

Bunny backed away to look Zander in the eye.

"I'm done, Zan. Tonight was really scary. I actually lost a *tooth*. I'm not gonna play around like that anymore. No more kneeing you in the groin, no more hitting you to see if you'll hit me back. I swear, I'm done with all that."

"I wish I could believe you," Zander said, trying not to be affected by how close Bunny was to him.

"You can believe me," said Bunny. "I would never lie to you."

Zander leaned in and kissed Bunny, feeling tiny explosions from his mouth to his feet. Within minutes, Bunny was naked before him, getting down on her knees, and slowly taking him into her mouth. She had been the first woman to give him a blow job and she still hadn't been topped by anyone else.

Zander came violently and collapsed onto the bed. She stood up and climbed into bed with him.

"You okay?" she asked.

"I can't believe you did that with a busted mouth."

"I'm hopped up on drugs," said Bunny. "I didn't feel a thing."

Zander turned over to take Bunny into his arms. She fit perfectly.

"You got me ready to go write a song or something," Zander said.

"Yeah, you better start writing something."

Zander leaned back.

"Why'd you say that?"

"I'm just saying. Your album is moving slow. It might be time to move on to the next album before Jake . . ."

"Before Jake *what*?" Zander said. "He would never drop me from the label. We're practically family."

"I just know he's pissed at you for this tooth drama. And they spent a *lot* of money marketing and promoting your album. Just be on the lookout."

Zander held Bunny tighter and smelled the inside of her neck. He rolled her over on her back, spread her legs wide, and pushed inside her roughly. She pushed back and they rocked the bed until their bodies were half on and half off.

Afterward, as he held Bunny in his arms, Zander thought about what his father said about treating Triumph and Disaster just the same. And he finally knew exactly which category Bunny fell into.

24

It all started with the towels. Birdie had never been particular about what he used to dry himself off. If it was clean, or clean enough, he'd whisk it over his body after a shower and throw it in a hamper.

But then, at a show in Miami, Birdie saw the production assistants grabbing dirty towels from a laundry bag, folding them, and then passing them off as clean towels in his dressing room to use after the show. If he hadn't seen them with his own eyes, he would have never believed it. From then on, he asked Dylan if he could have white towels in his dressing room. At least then he might be able to see the dirt if they were used. Then came the soda. Whenever Birdie performed, he came off stage with the worst pain in his chest. It felt like he had a massive burp that just wouldn't come up. A hit of an extremely icy Coke always helped him. Dylan started to make sure that as soon as he got off stage, she had one waiting for him.

"What's next, superstar," said Travis, as he watched Birdie gulp down his postshow soda in Los Angeles.

"Are you going to make Dylan take out all the blue M&Ms from the candy dish?"

Birdie laughed.

"A white towel and a soda! Is that too much to ask?"

Travis and Daryl began to shuffle and bow down to Birdie.

"Naw suh, we just here to please you, superstah, suh."

They all laughed. But Birdie still felt uncomfortable. He did want certain things. There were certain hotels he didn't want to stay in and certain tour bus companies that he didn't like. Did that make him an obnoxious entertainer? Birdie decided he was still safely in the normal zone. Except when it came to women. They were getting harder and harder to resist.

Birdie had been unfaithful to Alex in the past. There were a few one-offs when he was on bootleg college tours with other unsigned acts. He'd never felt guilty. It seemed like a natural part of a man's life. As long as he wasn't disrespectful and he didn't get caught, he was always able to justify it in his mind. It wasn't love. Nowhere near it. It was lust, pure and simple. He knew it was wrong. But he liked to pretend he wasn't hurting Alex if she didn't know.

But the blow job from Cleo changed all of that. A year later, the intense shame was still there. And the pain in Alex's eyes when she confronted him had never fully melted away. She forgave him. That much was clear. But he knew she hadn't forgotten. And never would.

He vowed, not just to Alex but himself, that once he said "I do," that would be it. He'd be 100 percent faithful to Alex for the rest of their time together on Earth.

So why'd he get the itch as soon as he went on tour? It was the distance, first of all. Alex was in New Jersey. There was (almost) no way she could find out if he did stray. And then, it was the sheer headiness of realizing that women actually *wanted* to have sex with him—with no strings attached. Travis, Daryl, and Corey were getting more ass than they could handle just from being af-filiated with Birdie. And as the tour progressed, Birdie came to a sad conclusion. It was going to happen. He didn't know when or with whom. But his resolve had weakened. He was now one of *them*: a predictable rap artist who couldn't resist free pussy—es-pecially on the road. He hadn't given up entirely. But he knew the possibility was there.

Years ago, slipping into something new and different was thrilling. The circumstances were always more exotic. A hotel shower instead of the same bedroom where he slept night after night; loud and rowdy sex, instead of the rushed, furtive, don't-wake-the-baby episodes at home. And of course, there was always alcohol involved with groupie sex. Something that never happened at home.

Although Birdie knew cheating with a groupie could be pleasurable, he'd avoided it throughout the Black Eyed Peas tour. There were girls everywhere, of every possible nationality. There were thick girls, thin girls, and straight-up fat girls. Girls with freckles and red hair, girls with blond hair and blue eyes, jet-black hair and dark brown eyes. Small breasts, oversized implants, firm butts, sloppy asses. Each city brought more girls backstage, until they began to blur into one Girl in Birdie's eyes. They all had the same body language. *I'm available. To you. Because you just performed before a sold-out crowd, and I want to be close to that.*

When word got around that Birdie didn't mess with groupies, the women became even bolder.

After a show in Brisbane, Birdie came backstage, peeled off his sweaty T-shirt, slipped into the clean one Dylan held out, and then went back to his dressing room. Daryl was already there with the promoter, who was peeling off bills from a huge roll of cash. The promoter had two people with him. And there were two women sitting together on the couch, speaking to each other in hushed tones.

Birdie did hand slaps with his manager and then flopped into the closest chair and guzzled a bottle of ice cold soda. One knock and the door opened; Dylan peeked her head in and Birdie waved her over.

"Just need you to sign these release forms," Dylan said, handing over a clipboard. "And here's the rest of your itinerary."

"When do we wrap up?"

"Two more weeks. Then you're home for a week. Then we go back out again."

Dylan moved her head closer to Birdie and whispered. "Who are the two girls?"

"Don't know," Birdie said, stealing a glance in their direction. "Think they came with the promoter."

"Find out," Dylan said. "You should never have anyone you don't know up in your space."

Dylan walked to the door, raised an eyebrow, and then raised a pointer finger in warning.

Birdie crossed the room to where the women sat. He saw the first girl turn around. Her face was round, pale, and plain. She was obviously the Friend. Which meant that the other chick was probably . . .

"Hi, Birdie. I'm Cheka."

She was tall. Almost as tall as Birdie. And the first thing he noticed was that she wasn't dressed like a groupie. No Lycra, cleavage or skin. She had on jeans. They were low rise but not too much. And she was wearing a plain, heather-gray henley with white Chuck Taylors and no socks. Birdie knew in that split second that he was going to have sex with her. The same way he knew he was going to have sex with Alex the night they met at the House of Blues. He pushed his guilt to the back of his mind and envisioned himself inside this woman. She would be on her stomach, he would be behind her, holding her up. She would arch her back—she looked like the back-arching type—and she would moan. Then, right before he came, she would . . .

"Hi, Cheka. It's nice to meet you," Birdie said, trying to think of something to keep his dick from getting hard. "Are you with the promoter?"

"He's my brother," said the woman. "I come along as protection."

Birdie laughed, but Cheka did not.

"And you are," Birdie asked, gesturing to her friend.

"There's no need to know my name," the woman said, standing up. "I'm not the one you're taking home tonight."

Birdie made a face.

"Excuse me?"

The friend turned to Cheka.

"Enjoy," she said, bending down to kiss Cheka on the cheek and then standing up straight again. "He looks delicious."

The friend left the room before Birdie could say anything else. He sat down next to Cheka.

"What is she talking about?"

"I came to the show at the very end. You had already performed."

"So you didn't see my show."

"I saw you in London. But no, I didn't see you tonight. I just brought the money straight from the bank for my brother."

Birdie nodded.

"When you walked in, I told my friend that it was on."

Birdie laughed.

"How did you know that?"

"The same way you did."

Birdie glanced over at his manager. He was leading the promoter out of the dressing room. He looked back at Birdie, nodded once, and followed the promoter and his two assistants out of the room, closing the door behind him.

"How does your manager know I'm not a murderer?" the woman asked. "Why would he leave me alone with you?"

"Are you?"

"No."

"How long are we gonna do this back-and-forth talking thing?" Birdie asked.

"Birdie, are you involved?"

"Excuse me?"

"At home, in the States, are you involved with someone?"

Birdie hesitated for only the briefest of seconds. He would never deny his wife to get some ass. That would be worse than cheating.

"Yes, I am," Birdie said. "I'm married."

Cheka stood up.

"That's too bad," she said, pulling her purse onto her shoulder. "I don't mess with married men. And I definitely saw myself being very naughty with you tonight."

Birdie felt himself straining against the zipper of his pants. She wasn't wearing a bra and her nipples were clearly outlined in her shirt. Birdie stood up, held Cheka by the waist, and pushed her up against the wall of the dressing room.

"Don't worry about what I got at home," Birdie said, slipping his hands inside the back of Cheka's jeans. Cheka put her arms around Birdie's shoulders and then pushed him back just enough to look him in the eye.

"Here?" she asked. "I can't even get a proper bed?"

Birdie answered by unbuttoning her jeans, yanking them down to her ankles, turning her around, and bending her over the sofa.

He was right. She was a back archer.

The whole thing was over in ten minutes. Cheka scribbled her number on the back of an envelope and slipped out of the door. Birdie zipped up, went into the bathroom, washed his face and hands, and then brushed his teeth. It almost felt like it never happened. An intense pang of guilt shot through him. Alex was at home. Worrying about him cheating. And he hadn't been. Until today. He mentally folded up the guilt and placed it in the far recesses of his mind. Alex would never have to know. Never. And if she didn't know, then it didn't really happen.

There were only two people in the room who could say they saw them talking together before the room cleared out. Cheka's friend could call *Life and Style*. The promoter could tell his friends. Even if he and his manager started beefing and he ratted Birdie out in revenge, no one would be able to definitively say what happened in that room with Cheka. He could and would deny until he was six feet under.

And yet Birdie still couldn't sleep that night. In his hotel room, he stared at the ceiling for an hour, replaying the episode with

Cheka. Except in his imagination, Alex was somehow watching the whole thing on television. She was at the house in Jersey. She had just put Tweet to bed. And she sat on the couch, turned on the television, and saw Birdie hitting Cheka from the back.

Knowing that this was impossible did not help Birdie get to sleep. He forced himself to shut his eyes tight. They popped open again and he flopped onto his stomach. Then he rolled over to his back. He got up and looked for something to put him to sleep. The alcohol in the minibar was the only option. He washed down two Tylenol PMs with a mini bottle of vodka. Within minutes, his heart had stopped pounding and he felt at ease. Alex wouldn't know. That's all there was to it. She would not see him on television with Cheka. Birdie smiled at the silly thought. She'd never find out. And that was okay. Alex would never believe that having sex with Cheka did not change that one iota. She would think Cheka represented everything she wasn't. And maybe she did. But that didn't change the fact that Birdie believed Alex was perfect.

Birdie stretched out in the bed, his hands folded behind his head. His eyes were now closed gently, and his breathing was calm and measured. As soon as he felt himself drifting to sleep, a heavy rap on the door forced him up quickly. His head was swimming. He flung his feet over to the side of the bed and then reached over to steady himself on the headboard. He took one step, stumbled, and then steadied himself. He burped, the heavy smell of the vodka filling the air. He took a few more steps, leaned into the door and looked through the peephole.

It was Cheka.

Birdie slid the lock off and opened the door a crack.

"How'd you know where I was staying?" he asked.

"That's Groupie 101," she said. "Now let me in."

Birdie pulled the door open and Cheka closed it and then pushed him back onto the bed. Before he could even process what was happening, he was inside her, his hands on her tiny waist.

"Wait, hold up," Birdie said, pulling out and rolling over to the side of the bed. He pulled a condom out of the back pocket of his jeans and fumbled with the wrapper. Cheka took it from him, eased it onto him, and then lowered herself on top of him. *If I hadn't taken those Tylenol PMs, I'd be putting in serious work right now*, Birdie thought to himself. Instead, she was in control, grinding on Birdie and leaning down to kiss his neck occasionally. Somewhere, he heard an alarm clock. No, it was the television. Or the radio. A fire alarm? Birdie tried to open his eyes but when he did, the room was spinning. He closed them and listened again.

"Hello?" Cheka said.

Birdie opened his eyes a crack. She was still on top of him, bobbing. With a cell phone pressed to her ear.

"He's busy right now," Cheka said, panting. "You might want to give him a call later."

He's busy?

Birdie sobered up immediately, throwing Cheka off him and sitting up straight. Cheka rolled over to the side of the bed, still holding the phone and giggling.

"Okay, you want to speak to Birdie," she said into the phone. "Here he is." Cheka tossed the cell phone over to Birdie, who moved away from it like it was a coiled rattlesnake.

"It's some girl named Alex," Cheka said, wriggling back into her jeans. "Next time you're in Australia, give me a call."

Birdie stood up and then leaned over the bed, placing his palms down. Through the phone, which was still a few feet away on the bed, where Cheka had thrown it, he could hear Alex's voice. *"Birdie? Bird? Are you there? BIRDIE?"*

Birdie closed his eyes and reached for the phone. Then he turned the ringer off and covered his face with his hands.

The next morning, Birdie checked his phone. Alex had sent him a text message before she called him:

"WE'RE HAVING A BABY . . ."

25

On the first warm day in spring, a day Jake had been waiting for desperately, he let the sun pour in from the windows as he went over the numbers with the A&R department a dozen times. He redid Zander's P&L statement himself by hand. Twice. It wasn't adding up. Zander's popularity on YouTube was just not translating into sales. When Zander's album dropped, there was initial buzz and press because he was Z's son. (And because he was dating Bunny, whose album had dropped two months before and was already platinum.)

But the PR rush ended with a thud. He slipped out of the *Billboard* Top 200 within two weeks and continued free-falling. Jake allowed more singles and gave him a budget for more extravagant videos.

Nothing was working. It seemed clear that Zander's chance had passed. And it was Jake's responsibility to tell him. He could have sent word from attorneys or executives. But this was Zander. He was family. Jake had come to the hospital when Zander was born. He saw Z smoking a crack-laced blunt in the parking lot as he made his way inside. But was it just the record sales? Was that really why Jake was releasing Zander from his contract? Was it Bunny? Was it Z?

Jake drummed his fingers on his desk. The guilt he felt for the Bunny situation was overwhelming. He couldn't even imagine Zander's reaction if he knew. Jake covered his eyes with his hand.

Jake could only marvel at how wrong he'd been. A feeling

took hold in his chest. He thought about his wife, his beautiful, flawless wife. He thought about how much she loved Zander, Z, Beth, and Jake. They had formed an ad hoc family, for better or for worse. He thought about how Kipenzi disliked Bunny. He thought about how Bunny had gotten Zander locked up last year after goading him into hitting her. He thought about Z, brand new in his drug-free world but still vulnerable.

Self-loathing, disgust, and shame ballooned in his heart. He reached into the locked cabinet under his desk and pulled out his flask. Into the water bottle went his liquid courage. Jake guzzled instead of sipped, waiting for that moment when he didn't care about anything anymore.

A knock at the office door jerked Jake to attention. He spun his chair around and saw Zander standing in the doorway.

"What up, Unc."

Jake didn't make eye contact.

"Sit down, Zander."

"I already know what you're going to say."

"No, you don't."

"Yes, I do. Bunny told me."

"Bunny told you what."

"That you're thinking about dropping me from the label."

Jake swallowed hard.

"Where'd she get that from?"

Zander shrugged.

"She just heard rumblings around the office."

Zander looked up at Jake. "Is it true?"

For a week, Jake had mentally rehearsed what he'd planned to say: *We're going to try a different way to do this. Sign you to an independent label and see what happens there. In the meantime, go to college. I'll pay for it.*

But that didn't come out. Instead: "You're not getting dropped."

Zander slumped in his chair in relief.

"Unc, I really appreciate that. I'm in the studio now. I'm focused. Album two. I got this."

"Zander," Jake said, standing up, "as long as I'm at this label, you'll be signed here."

Zander smiled.

"Does that go for my dad too?"

"Me and your pops got some shit to work out. We'll be alright."

"Yeah. Y'all need to talk," Zander said, eyebrows raised.

"Why do you say it like that?"

"You got my dad punching walls," Zander said, chuckling.

"For what?"

Zander looked beyond Jake, out of the windows lining the back wall of his office.

"You didn't hear it from me. But I heard him telling someone over the phone that you were messing around with the wrong girl."

Jake blinked. But he did not allow his eyes to reveal anything.

"What girl?"

"I have no idea. Y'all sharing girls lately?"

Jake had to close his eyes to keep from groaning.

"Not that I know of."

"Well, he's heated about whoever you're hitting off right now."

Jake walked Zander to his office door.

"Focus on your music. I'm booking Studio B at Electric Lady for a straight month. One month from today I wanna hear what you've got."

"No doubt, Unc," Zander said.

Zander opened the door. Z was standing on the other side. He looked as if he had not been listening but rather waiting. The women in the few cubicles near Jake's office were peeking out to see what was going on.

"Dad?" Zander asked, looking back at Jake, who looked weary.

"Car's downstairs," said Z. "I'll be right down."

Jake waved Z in and closed the door behind him. Before Jake turned around, he collected himself and thought about where he'd punch Z if he came at him. Z was shorter. But he was stouter and stronger. Especially after his new yoga lifestyle and vegan diet. He decided that if he had to, he'd go for the tender area just at Z's jawbone.

"What's up?" Jake said, turning around to face Z.

"Why you gotta mess with her, Jake? Her? Of all people? That shit is disgusting."

Jake crossed his arms over his chest and said nothing. Z put his forehead in one hand shook his head.

"I mean, I haven't touched her in years," said Z. "And I won't. I'm committed to Beth. But still. I don't need to know hear that you are sleeping with her. That's crossing a line."

"Did you say it's been years?!" Jake asked. "But she just turned—"

"Oh now, you don't remember when she came out on tour with us?"

An audible whoosh of breath escaped Jake's nose and mouth at the same time.

"Sam?" Jake said. "You're talking about Samantha?"

"Who else would I be talking about?" Z asked.

"I was drunk," said Jake. "Sam stepped to me in the bar. I wasn't in my right frame of mind. That was foul. My bad."

"And what about the other times?" said Z. "After that."

"Well shit, Z, the girl gives a hell of a blow job."

"I'm ashamed to say it, but I still have feelings for her," Z said.

"I don't," Jake said, "No worries there. But you need to forget about Sam and focus on your marriage."

"So do you."

Jake furrowed his eyebrows.

"What are you talking about?

"What would Kipenzi think?" Z asked. "A year after her death and you're messing with Sam? Sam, of all people?" Zander shook his head. "She deserves better than that. Even in death."

Jake didn't hear or see Z leave his office or close the door behind him. His words about Kipenzi deserving more in death shook him to the core. But not because of Sam. Jake knew Kipenzi wouldn't have cared about Sam. She'd approve, happy that he could get a sexual release from someone who would never replace her in his heart. Sam was a blow-up doll. And Kipenzi would recognize that.

But Bunny was different. And it was the thought of Kipenzi's reaction to his feelings for Bunny that kept him frozen in his office for thirty minutes, standing at the window. It took another knock at the door to wake him up once again. He popped a mint in his mouth and tried to look alert.

His assistant came in with a concerned look on her face. "You have some fires to put out, Jake," Sydney said, adjusting her glasses. "You want them all at once or one at a time?"

"Out with it."

"Staff at Jake's are filing a suit. They say they haven't been paid overtime in months and the working conditions are less than satisfactory."

"Have Jeff get up here immediately," Jake said. "And tell my business manager we need to find a replacement ASAP. Put out a statement. I'm on top of this situation and it will be resolved immediately."

"Got it," said Sydney, nodding her head and scribbling in a notepad.

"Anything else?"

"I got a call from someone I know pretty well at *Life and Style*. Jackson is peddling a picture of Bunny with a split lip to all of the tabloids."

Jake gave Sydney a long look, wondering what she knew.

"So? She hurt her lip and went to the doctor."

"He has pictures of Zander going into the same building. It looks bad."

"That's her boyfriend," said Jake. "She hurt herself, went to the doctor. He went with her. End of story."

"Jake, everyone knows that Zander hit Bunny last year and got locked up for it. This will only fuel more rumors."

"Ignore it. No statements. Nothing. What else?"

"That's it for now. Unless you want to talk about the tribute concert for Kipenzi."

"Absolutely not."

"Okay, last thing. I have Bunny in the conference room waiting to see you. Management says she wants to talk to you about the last leg of her tour. She wants a live band for the last few shows."

"You can bring her back. Thanks, Sydney."

Sydney bowed her head and left the office, closing the door softly behind her.

Once upon a time, Kipenzi came to visit Jake at the office. She wore a full-length white chinchilla coat and oversized sunglasses. Her body, full and thick, had been outlined in a body-hugging dress beneath the coat, capped off with thigh-high boots.

He'd never had sex with his wife in the office, but he came close to it that day, moving her up against the closed door of his office and pressing himself against her for a long second.

If he had been sober, he would have remembered this when Bunny came into his office, in an outfit freakishly similar to the one his wife wore the last time she'd been in that very executive suite.

If he had been sober, he would have never let Bunny into the sanctity of his office. The hotel was one thing. But his private space was something else. Kipenzi's soul lived in that room. She spent many afternoons napping, reading, or writing on the chaise. This was as much her space as it was Jake's. Bunny did not belong there.

But alas, Jake hadn't been sober for more than a day since his wife died. So when Bunny walked in, his first thought was that he wanted to hoist her up by the waist and wrap her legs around his back.

Jake shook his head to get the thoughts out.

"What's going on?" Jake asked.

Bunny sat down on the couch.

"I feel like you've been avoiding me since . . ."

Jake looked at Bunny with a blank expression.

"Since when?"

"Since the hotel."

Jake leaned up against his desk.

"I don't know what you're talking about."

Bunny raised her eyebrows.

"Don't remember?"

"Bunny," Jake said. "I have a lot going on today. How can I help you?"

Bunny stepped closer to Jake and unbuttoned her belted spring jacket. She let it fall open just enough for Jake to see that she wasn't wearing much underneath. Jake felt himself straining against the zipper of his pants. But he held fast.

"I want a repeat performance," said Bunny.

"Bunny, I need you to go."

Jake took a swig from his bottle and prayed she'd listen. He wasn't sure how much resolve he actually had.

"Jake. I'm really very spoiled," Bunny said. "I'm used to getting what I want."

"I can't help you."

Bunny closed her coat and cinched the belt.

"I guess you haven't had enough to drink yet today."

"I don't care how drunk I get," said Jake. "That's not going to happen again."

Bunny smiled and walked to the door.

"We'll see about that," she said, before closing the door behind her.

26

Ras pressed harder and harder on the gas pedal of his ancient Alfa Romeo until he got the car up to 75. The car protested, roaring and threatening to sputter out completely. But Ras kept going, his eyes darting back and forth from his cell phone to the road.

This bitch must be crazy.

He turned the steering wheel hard to the left when he got to the front of the hotel and threw the car into park. Leaving the keys inside, he jumped out of the car, motioned to the valet, and jogged into the lobby.

A few hotel guests whispered and pointed at Ras as he made his way to the elevator bank. He couldn't tell if they recognized him for his celebrity or were taking in his disheveled sweatsuit and his uncombed afro. At the elevator, he pressed the up button constantly, even though he could see that the elevator was on the twentieth floor and making its way down. He turned and took the stairs instead, taking three and four stairs in a single leap until he got to the fourth floor. He looked both ways, darted down the hall to room 412, and knocked once.

As soon as the door opened a half-inch, Ras pushed it all the way open and grabbed at Cleo, who was standing behind it.

"Are you crazy?" Ras asked, squeezing his hands around Cleo's neck until she fell to her knees.

"What the hell are you doing here?" he asked, not taking his hands off her neck. Cleo pointed to his hands, indicating that she couldn't speak since he was choking off her air supply.

Ras let go and pushed her to the floor.

"I did *not* tell you to come here," said Ras. "You're supposed to tell me if you end up in Jamaica for any reason."

"I'm not here to see you!" Cleo sputtered, her hands at her neck as she tried to stand. "I came here to take care of some business."

"So why are you texting me and telling me where you're staying?" Ras snapped. "Why would you call my house and tell me you're here?"

"I wanted to see you."

Ras pulled his hand back as far as he could and slapped Cleo across the face.

"You see me when I want to see you," Ras hissed. "And that's the *only* time you see me. I told you when you showed up at that restaurant that you are not to come within a mile of my house again or I will kill you. Did I not?"

Cleo stared at him.

"I just thought if you knew I was here . . ."

"I'd come running out here, happy to see you and lay up in the bed with you all night? Are you an idiot?"

"I missed you, Ras. That's the only reason why I called you."

"This is what you *don't* do," said Ras. "You don't have any business missing me. This right here?" Ras quickly gestured to himself and then back at Cleo. "This is *over*. Get a life."

Cleo seemed as if she were about to speak but thought better about it. Ras slunk down into one of the club chairs and threw his head back.

"I have a few things I need to take care of here," Cleo said. "And then I'm going back to the States."

"Think twice before coming to this island," Ras said. "And don't you ever stay anywhere near my house. You got that?"

Cleo nodded.

If Josephine hadn't been at the market, all hell could have broken loose when that phone rang. Ras rubbed his eyes absentmindedly, still slumped in the chair.

"When are you leaving?" Ras asked, without opening his eyes.

"Tonight."

"I'm sorry I hit you," Ras mumbled.

Cleo walked to the bathroom.

"I'm sorry I called you."

Ras stepped into the bathroom and stood behind her.

"I meant it when I said you deserve better than this, Cleo . . ."

Cleo turned around. Her left eye was swollen and her cheek was still red where Ras had hit her.

"I know what I deserve," said Cleo, as she slipped on a pair of sunglasses.

"I have a car downstairs waiting for me," she said. "Do you want me to leave first? Or should you?"

"I'm going first," Ras said. "Wait at least twenty minutes."

"Ras, wait," Cleo said. "Take this. Just in case."

Ras looked back and saw a business card in Cleo's hand. He looked at it without touching it.

"I don't need to know how to contact you."

"Take it anyway," Cleo said, pushing it into a pocket of Ras's jeans. "In case of an emergency."

Ras walked to the doors of the hotel suite.

"Do not contact me," Ras said, as he turned the locks on the door. "Do not call me. Do not text me. *Nothing.*"

Someone turned the lock on the door and Ras stepped to the door and looked through the peephole. A housekeeper stood there. Ras opened the door and someone immediately pushed her away.

"Well, hello there, you two!" said Josephine, sweeping into the suite. "Fancy seeing you here!"

Ras was always under the impression that Josephine was just slightly afraid of Cleo. But it was Cleo who crept backward. She kept moving back until her entire body was pressed against the window. She turned her head and saw the busy streets of Kingston below.

"Don't worry," said Josephine, still smiling. "I'm not going to hurt you."

"I-I-I . . ." Cleo sputtered.

"Why the shades?" asked Josephine. "I hope my husband hasn't been violent. He does tend to have quite the temper when it comes to his other women. Thankfully, I've never seen that side of him."

"Let's go, Josephine," said Ras, taking his wife by the elbow. Josephine snatched herself away.

"I'm not going anywhere with you," she said. "I just came here so you could stop hiding. I know you've been seeing Cleo in New York when you're supposed to be working. And I'm sure this isn't the first time you two have *liaisoned* here on the island."

Cleo kept her back against the window, her palms pressed against the glass. It was as if she thought Josephine could push her out of the window and into the street below with just one light breath.

Ras's mind raced. How could he get Josephine home and clean this up? Just the fact that he was there with Cleo didn't mean anything had happened. *Deny 'til you die,* his boys always said.

"Nothing happened here, Josephine," said Ras.

Josephine laughed.

"Right. And I'm the Queen of England."

"I'm telling you the truth."

Josephine's face twisted quickly into a snarl.

"You wouldn't know the truth if it hit you in the back of the head like a two-by-four. Don't talk to me about truth. Ever. You don't know shit about it."

Josephine took a step close to Cleo, who managed to press herself even harder into the glass.

"I'll bet Cleo here knows a little about truth. Don't you?"

Cleo was silent, her eyes invisible behind the shades.

"The truth is, my marriage is over. And it has been for some time. You won, Cleo. You can have him. He is all yours."

"Josephine," Ras said, his voice a near whine. "Don't do this. It's not necessary."

Josephine took another step toward Cleo cowering in the corner.

"You were not the first woman my husband screwed behind my back. But you have the honor of being the last."

Ras made one last attempt to grab at Josephine's arms as she walked toward the door. But Josephine snatched her entire body away before he could reach her. She pulled a sheaf of paperwork out of her bag and thrust it into Ras's chest.

"You've been served," Josephine said.

Ras looked at the paperwork and then threw it to the ground and raced out of the room behind Josephine. He got to the elevator just as the doors were closing. He slammed his shoulder into the tiny opening and stopped the elevator from moving. The elevator opened back up and Ras saw a group of cleaning women in uniform staring at him in fear.

He stepped out of the elevator just in time to see the door at the exit stairwell slam shut. Ras raced to the door and took the steps back down to the lobby. He saw no sign of his wife. He checked the elevator. It was coming down slowly, stopping at what seemed like every floor. Ras waited. He had no magic words. He just had to pray that seeing him standing there would at least buy him a few seconds.

The door opened and a bustling group of English businessmen in suits hurried out. No Josephine.

Ras went to retrieve his car from the valet and gunned it all the way home.

He knew before he walked in that she was gone. Before he walked up the steps. Before he turned the key in the lock, he could feel the emptiness and lack of warmth. Before he noticed her bare closets and little Reina's missing luggage set, he knew his wife was gone.

So you don't know for sure that he cheated," Z said to Alex, over breakfast at the Brooklyn Diner.

"A woman answered his phone in the middle of the night," said Alex, rolling her eyes. "He calls me back, *the next morning*, with some bullshit story about one of his boys having his phone. He cheated."

Z nodded. He didn't agree with Alex's logic. But he didn't want to upset her.

"Until you know the whole story, maybe you should just—"

"Z, let's get started."

Alex's eyes were red, and her hair was a knotty mess pulled back into a fuzzy ponytail. Z found himself feeling guilty and ashamed for all the times he'd made Beth feel this way: alone, betrayed, and vulnerable.

"I'm sorry," Z said.

"What are you sorry for?" Alex asked, her eyes on the table.

"For telling you not to trust him."

Alex sat up straight in her seat and clasped her hands together on the table.

"You were just honest with me," said Alex. "And I appreciate that."

"What are you going to do now?"

"Get a divorce."

"No way.

"Do you know for a fact that Birdie loves me?"

"Yes. I know that for a fact."

"Then why would he cheat on me? Why?"

Z couldn't think of a single word to say. So he didn't say anything. Alex continued to glare at him.

"Can we start over?" Z finally asked. "We've gotten way off course from what we're supposed to be doing with this book. I promise to stay out of your personal life. Interview me for this book. And let's get it done."

Alex's face softened.

"Deal."

Z sat back and closed his eyes.

"Where did we leave off?"

Alex dug a notebook out of her bag and flipped through some pages.

"You were telling me about being a father."

"I'm still learning how to be a father. Haven't been so good at it for the past nineteen years."

"What's your relationship like with Zander?"

"Zander's the only child who knew me before I blew up. He remembers having a regular father. So we have a different connection than I do with the younger ones. It's like Beth. She's been there since day one—composition notebooks and nursery rhymes."

"Zander's a celebrity now . . ."

Z exhaled.

"He is . . . and I'm watching him make some of the same mistakes I made."

"Like what?"

An image of Zander throwing a punch at Bunny flashed before his eyes. But he held his tongue.

"He's just young and feeling things out. I worry about him. He's put a lot into his music and if it doesn't jump off the way he wants it to . . ."

"What will you do if your career never jumps off again?"

Z sat up and cleared his throat.

"Listen. I'm healthy. I'm drug free. I'm alive. My kids are

healthy and safe. My career . . . well, I'm not on fire like I was five years ago. But I'm doing okay for myself. I'm sitting here with you, writing a book about my life. Sometimes I'm in awe of how far I've come."

"I'm really happy for you, Z."

"I want you to think about me before you file for divorce from Birdie."

Alex narrowed her eyes.

"I thought we were going to stick with the book."

"Men are animals," said Z. "We think with our dicks."

"Please don't make excuses for Birdie."

"I won't. I'm just telling you facts. He's hot shit right now. And yes, he's messing up. But it doesn't mean that's the man he'll be forever. This could have been a onetime lapse in judgment. It doesn't mean he'll go as far as I did—having babies by other women and all that."

"So if he cheated me, that's supposed to be okay because he didn't cheat *too* much."

Alex sucked her teeth and stood up.

"I think we're done for today."

"We can't end a session without you being pissed off, can we?"

"I don't know? Can we?" Alex asked.

"What are you about to do now?"

Alex held up her recorder.

"Go back to Jersey, transcribe today's interview."

"I'll walk you to your car."

They left the diner, drinking in the bright sunshine that warmed them up. They both took their jackets off as they walked and talked. They chatted about the weather as they reached the parking garage where Alex parked her car.

"I tried yoga a few times," said Alex, reaching for her keys. "I'm too out of shape."

"No such thing," said Z. "You just have to—"

Alex and Z both stopped abruptly. Beth was standing in the

driveway of the garage, her face frozen and her teeth clenched. She had the baby on her hip.

"Beth?" Z asked, taking a step toward his wife.

"I know you've been fucking her," Beth said flatly.

"Who? Alex?" Z exclaimed, pointing to where she stood. "No!"

"Beth, that is not true," Alex said, one hand over her heart. "I swear to you, nothing—"

"Whatever!" Beth screamed. "I've been dealing with Z's shit long enough. I know when he's messing around."

"Bethie," said Z. "You know that's not me anymore."

"You roll up to this diner with Miss Priss every other day. And then a few weeks ago, y'all went to church together. I saw you."

"We went to a twelve-step meeting," said Z. "That's all."

"What the hell does that have to do with writing a book?" said Beth.

Alex stepped back from both of them.

"I'm gonna go."

"You're not going anywhere until you tell me what's been going on with my husband."

Alex opened her mouth to speak, but Z interrupted.

"Beth, I said nothing's going on! Now, let's talk about this at home."

"I've been coming here every week. Watching the both of you."

Beth hoisted the baby up higher on her hip and pointed at Z.

"You know I always know."

"Beth, can I please say something?" Alex asked. Beth just stared at her.

"I am not involved with Z in any way," said Alex. "We got cool while working on this book. I've confided in him about stuff. But I would never disrespect you like that. I swear. Nothing happened."

Beth stared at Alex. The baby began to whimper and struggle

in her arms. Z, Alex, and Beth looked at each other for a long, uncomfortable moment. Beth turned to get into her car.

"Bullshit," she spat. "And you both know it."

Z and Alex stood there silently, while Beth strapped the baby into her car seat, climbed up to the driver's side of the Land Cruiser, and slammed the door. Z and Alex stood stock-still and watched Beth speed out of the garage and down Atlantic Avenue.

"I'm sorry," Alex said to Z when they couldn't see Beth's car anymore.

"I can't believe this," Z said, shaking his head. "All these years, she's never said a word. Never confronted me about anything. And now, the first time she decides to stand up for herself and step to me—she's wrong. And she won't believe me."

"Let's take a few days off. Call me when things settle down," Alex said, handing her ticket to the valet.

Z nodded and walked away. His mind raced, thinking of all the women. All the affairs. All the babies. Beth kept a stiff upper lip, complained to Kipenzi, and hardly ever said a word to Z. As long as he came home at some point, she was cool. And now that he was sober, she was seeing things where there was nothing.

Z got to his own car and jumped inside. His car roared down the street, toward the Manhattan Bridge to find his wife.

28

Birdie barely waited for the driver to stop before he jumped out of the car, leaving his luggage inside and the car door wide open.

"Alex!" he yelled out as soon as he pushed the front door open. "Where are you?" His voice echoed through the house, scaring him. He hated the oversized mansion. It was way too big for two people. He could never find Alex when he came home. If she were in the attic working or in the basement doing the laundry, she couldn't hear him until he was practically in her line of vision.

"Alex? Are you here?"

Birdie whipped through the front foyer, past the living room and the family room. He stopped in each doorway, scanning for his wife.

The morning after the episode with Cheka, Birdie woke up with a splitting headache, and the reality of what had happened the night before crashed down on him. Did that woman really have the nerve to answer his phone and talk to his *wife*?

He'd called Alex nonstop from one end of Europe to the other. He got her on the phone just once. He made up a quick lie about Travis having his phone. She hung up on him and refused to take any more of his calls. He even resorted to calling one of Travis's girlfriends, Jess, and begging her to get a message to Alex. Nothing had worked.

Immediately after his show in Prague, he flew back to New York, his knee jumping up and down for the entire flight. He'd gotten a second chance with Alex. Last year, after she found out about the blow job from Cleo, she could have left forever. But she didn't. She forgave him and moved on with him. She married him. She was helping him to raise his daughter. She dealt with his ex-wife. She stood back and let him enjoy his newfound fame. And this is how he paid her back. By deciding that cheating wouldn't hurt as long as he didn't get caught. The problem with that stupid-ass theory was that there was always the possibility that you *could* get caught. And he did.

"Alex!"

Birdie went up the third flight of stairs to the office. It was empty. He doubled back and went into the bedroom to make sure she hadn't actually packed up and left. In her walk-in closet, the size of their old guest room in Brooklyn, her luggage was lined up neatly, and it didn't look like any of her clothes were missing.

Birdie's cell rang and he fumbled to answer right away.

"Yo."

"You talk to Alex yet?" asked Travis.

"She's not here," Birdie said, walking to the window and looking out at the cul-de-sac at the front of the house. "Her car is here. But she's not."

"Yo, Jess told me the chick in Australia talked to some British newspaper about you."

Birdie froze.

"What?"

"Yeah. It's pretty bad. She talks about . . . stuff she would only know if . . ."

"Let me call you back."

Birdie hung up the phone before Travis could respond. He sat down hard on the too-high bed and rubbed his temples.

Birdie thought of something. He snapped his fingers and ran downstairs to the kitchen. In one of the cupboards, they kept the key cup. It had random keys to everything—the garage, the tool shed, extra sets of car keys, and various other spares. Birdie shook out all the keys. And he immediately realized which set was missing. It was so obvious he didn't know how it hadn't come to him sooner. He picked up a set of keys and dashed out of the house.

Although he had the key, Birdie rang the doorbell to the old house in Brooklyn and waited for his wife to answer the door. She'd never wanted to leave the brownstone and so he knew, in this time of crisis, she'd come back to the first home they shared together. This was the place that represented life without the fame, the money, and the groupies that were threatening to end it all.

Alex opened the door and stepped back to let Birdie into the foyer. He expected her to be red-eyed and weepy. Instead she looked radiant, though she wore a weak, pained smile.

"I figured you'd find me eventually."

"Alex. Baby."

Birdie reached out for his wife and she pulled back.

"Don't," she said, running her hands through her hair. "Don't touch me. Please."

"Are you okay? Is everything—"

Birdie put his hands to his wife's belly and looked at her. Tears streamed down Alex's face as she shook her head back and forth. "I lost the baby," Alex said.

Birdie sunk down to his knees and wrapped his arms around Alex's legs.

"Oh no. Oh baby, I'm so sorry. *Shit.*"

"While I'm here, trying to hold it together, you're out—" Alex cried harder.

"I didn't touch that girl, I swear to God. Travis borrowed my phone and he was with some—"

Alex raised up a hand to stop Birdie from speaking.

"You think I didn't go over all the possibilities?" Alex said. "You don't think I tried to make myself believe that story was true? You don't think I cried over it? Wanting to believe it? I saw the story. She said your dick curves to the left. How on earth would she know that?"

"Believe me," Birdie said. "Please."

"I asked you not to do a reality show," Alex said. "You did one."

Birdie lowered his head.

"I should have known then that you were going to become one of them. I know these people, Birdie! I've been reporting on them for ten years. They are entitled. They get whatever they want. As long as they're selling records, the world is theirs. And now, that's you. It's your turn. Enjoy it."

"Alex, we can work through—"

"I'm not working through *shit*," Alex spat. "You can work through whatever you want in that house by yourself. I'm staying here, in Brooklyn, where I belong."

"Can we talk about it. Please? *Please.*"

Alex turned and walked toward the kitchen. Birdie followed. She sat down at the kitchen table and folded her hands.

"I just want you to leave."

"We are building a life together," Birdie said.

"Past tense," Alex said.

"I'm not leaving until we talk this out."

"What is there to talk about?! You cheated. *Again.*" Alex paused. "I was carrying your *baby*. A baby we fought tooth and nail for. While you . . ."

Alex put her hand to her mouth and closed her eyes. She shook her head back and forth and began to cry.

Birdie couldn't go to her. He couldn't even look in her direction. He felt hot tears of shame streaming down his face as he held Alex's gaze.

"And you stand here," Alex said, "and you still lie to me to my *face*. I thought maybe when you saw me you'd be honest and tell me what happened. But you—"

"It happened, Alex," Birdie said. "I did it."

Alex looked up at Birdie.

"What happened, Bird?" she asked, her voice small. "Tell me."

"I . . . after the show . . . I had sex with—"

Alex continued to stare at him.

"I had sex with some girl I met after the show," Birdie said. Breath rushed out of his body and his shoulders slumped.

"Was it worth it?"

"You know it wasn't worth—"

Alex held up a hand.

"I'll have my stuff out of the house by the end of the week. I'll be staying here."

"Can we talk about this? Go to counseling? Get therapy? You can't just walk away like this."

"Birdie, I could forgive you. I really could. I just don't *want* to. I've seen what this world does to relationships. And I should have known that you would be no different. I need to walk away now, with some shred of dignity and self-respect. I can't be like Beth, letting Z cheat on her. And Josephine, accepting Ras's affairs. I can't do it and I won't do it. I need you to go."

On the ride back to New Jersey, Birdie clutched the steering wheel tight and fought back tears. He knew that all the money in the world wouldn't make up for having that one person in the world who had his back unconditionally. And he knew he'd never have that again. No woman who came along after Alex would ever be on her level. No one would have been there when he had nothing but a few underground hits and a college tour under his belt.

When he got back to the house, Travis, Daryl, and Corey were playing ball out back. Although he'd only let a few tears escape, his friends noticed right away. This not-so-small fact was ignored by all.

"What happened with Alex?" Daryl asked.

Birdie shrugged.

"She's bugging out. Said she's not coming back."

"Word?"

"I told her the truth and she went off."

"Why would you do that?!" Daryl said. "Deny 'til you die!"

"She's not stupid. The chick is talking to the press."

Daryl shrugged.

"You deny anyway. Then she can forgive you based on the lie. Now that you've admitted it, she'll never take you back."

"Maybe we're not supposed to be together anyway."

"Why would you say that?"

"I messed up . . ." said Birdie. "Once. With one stupid chick. And now it's over forever? I even offered to do some counseling or something. And she's just like, *no*. It's a wrap."

Daryl palmed the basketball and then stood behind the three-point line and let it go. *Swoosh.*

"So she should leave you if you have sex with *lots* of chicks," said Corey. "But not if you just have sex with one?"

"Whose side are you on?" Birdie asked, snatching the basketball out of his hands. Corey threw up his hands.

"I'm not on any side," said Corey. "I just know that if it were the other way around, you wouldn't have taken her back either."

"I'm going inside," Birdie said.

"Yo, Bird," said Corey.

Birdie stopped walking and turned around.

"What's up?"

"You can't stop trying to get her back."

Birdie moved the sliding doors back and stepped into the den.

"How long am I supposed to try?"

Corey shrugged.

"I can't tell you that," he said. "I just know that I gave up on Dana and now she's married to someone else. If I could go back, I'd stay in her face until she had no choice but to give in."

Birdie nodded and went back to his bedroom. From the window he could see Travis, Daryl, and Corey playing horse, loudly jostling each other and laughing.

The next morning Birdie realized he was actually mad at Alex. Pissed off, even. After everything he'd put her through, he was actually angry that she wasn't going to give him another chance. He thought about all the pussy he *didn't* take and felt like it should have earned him some points. He knew it didn't make sense to think of fidelity that way. But it didn't change how he felt. The doorbell rang and Birdie went downstairs to answer it. Jen and Tweet rushed in, laden with balloons, goodie bags, and shopping bags.

"Daddy!" Tweet shrieked.

Birdie groaned inwardly. How was he going to tell Tweet about Alex?

"Hey, Birdie," said Jennifer, kissing him on the cheek. "Where's Alex?"

"How's my baby girl?" Birdie said, hoisting Tweet up and kissing her on the cheek. "I missed you."

"You're back from far away?" Tweet asked.

"I'm back."

"I went to a birthday party," Tweet said. "And we made balloon animals. But mine popped and I cried a whole lot and then they made me another one and then I asked them to make one for Alex because she likes balloon animals too!"

"You take your things upstairs," Birdie said to Tweet. "I'll be right up."

Jennifer walked into the family room and sat down on the couch. Birdie walked behind her and stayed in the doorway.

"So where's Alex?"

"She's not here."

"I see that, Birdie. *Why* isn't she here?"

"She's just not here, what's the big deal?"

"That chick . . . on the blogs. The one from Australia. Is she telling the truth?"

"No."

"Birdie, do you know why we got divorced?"

"We got married too young."

"That's part of it. But the real reason we broke up is because you didn't want to fight for me when things got tough."

Birdie folded his arms across his chest and listened.

"I'm seeing you on television now," said Jen. "I'm hearing you on the radio. People are"—Jen paused—"lying about having sex with you. And I know your life is changing in ways I can't even imagine. If I were still married to you, I don't know how I would take it."

Birdie just nodded.

"If you want things to work with your wife, you're going to have to fight for her."

"And what if she doesn't want me to fight for her?" Birdie asked.

Jen stood up and walked past Birdie toward the front door.

"Fight harder."

29

As soon as Jake dropped the microphone, he jogged off stage and headed to his dressing room. He could still hear the roar of the crowd. They were chanting his name and singing the chorus to the last song he performed.

This time, for the first time, Jake was not moved.

Normally, the first moments after the end of a show were like being high. Having ten thousand people yelling out your name could do wonders for a man's ego. But this time, he felt nothing. He just wanted to go home and go to bed. Reality hit him: Jake was done. Not just for tonight. But forever.

Crowded outside his dressing room were a gaggle of people: two of his usual bodyguards, a few reporters, a girl he'd slept with the night before who sometimes cut his hair, and some people from his label who came out to support him.

He opened the dressing room and saw his assistant Sydney and his publicist Dylan going over his schedule. Damon and Joey were throwing back beers and watching television on the mounted plasma.

"He can't be there for the boat christening," said Dylan. "He's doing *Good Morning America*."

"I'm not doing *Good Morning America*," Jake whispered, realizing as he said it that he actually meant it.

"What if we move *GMA* to the following Thursday?"

"No good. Diane Sawyer will be on vacation."

"Don't matter," Jake said under his breath. "I won't be there..."

"When is Jake's opening up in AC?"

"Saturday the twenty-second. Everyone needs to be on board for that."

"I'm selling Jake's," Jake mumbled under his breath.

Jake took a seat on a black leather couch and mopped his face with a brand new-white T-shirt.

"Ladies?"

The two women ignored him and continued going over their calendars.

"I can have him in Sweden for the *Forbes* shoot."

"And then it's Australia for the rest of the month."

"Can we squeeze him into Birdie's next video shoot?"

"When is it?"

"Saturday."

Sydney looked over at Jake.

"Can you do Birdie's video?"

"Oh, now you see me?"

"Sorry, Jake. I'm trying to make sure your schedule isn't so packed that you're cursing me out."

"I appreciate that. And no, I'm not doing Birdie's video. Or the *Forbes* shoot. And I'm not spending the rest of the month in Australia."

Sydney and Dylan stopped talking. Jake watched them fidget and then he took a sip from his water bottle. Sydney grimaced.

"What's the problem?" he said, daring her to mention the smell of alcohol permeating the room.

Damon and Joey picked up on the tension and they both stopped talking, their beer bottles in mid-air.

"Nothing," Sydney said. She turned back to Dylan and they exchanged a quick look that didn't escape Jake. Damon and Joey went back to watching television.

"Yo, I sent two tickets to someone named Lily. Did she come to the show?"

Sydney shook her head.

"Those tickets were never scanned."

Jake nodded slowly.

Jake had finally found out that Lily was working at the bar at the W Hotel in Union Square. He went in several times looking for her and she was never there. She was always off-duty or on a break. But Jake got the distinct impression that she was hiding from him. One night, he was almost positive he saw a woman who looked just like her coming out of the kitchen with her head down. And then just as quickly, the woman turned back around and the kitchen doors swung shut behind her. Jake asked the bartender where she was and he said she was off that night.

Tonight, he had sent Damon over to the hotel with tickets and VIP passes to the show. Damon said she wasn't there but that the manager attached the tickets to her paycheck, which she was on her way to pick up.

Jake wasn't even sure exactly *why* he wanted to see her. He just knew he did. He wanted to see those liquid pools in her eyes. He wanted to hear her voice, honey smooth and clipped with an accent he couldn't place. And of course, he desperately wanted whatever he couldn't have on demand.

Jake continued drinking while Sydney and Dylan kept their heads down, pretending to be engrossed in their notepads, calendars, and PDAs.

The best part of Jake's celebrity was also the worst: no one stood up to him. Jake stood up, crossed the room, and opened a fresh bottle of gin that sat on a mobile bar. He poured the clear liquid into his water bottle and went back to the couch.

"We're gonna go, Jake," Dylan said. "Do you need anything?"

"I'm telling you," said Jake. "You need to completely clear my schedule. I'm not doing anything right now."

"Anything else?"

"Is there a car ready?"

"It's at the back, ready whenever you are."

Jake nodded and leaned his head back on the sofa.

"I'll see y'all in the morning."

Jake hiccoughed and then swigged from his bottle again.

"Be careful, Jake," said Dylan. "Jackson Figueroa is hanging out by your car tonight. He's definitely going to get some flicks of you when you leave. So you might want to—"

Dylan let her eyes linger on his water bottle.

"I'll be fine," Jake said. "Thanks. Good night."

As soon as the two women opened the door, Jake could see that the number of people outside his room had tripled and a few bodyguards were aggressively holding people back from coming too close to the door.

"Not going out tonight, Jake?" Damon asked.

"Nah. I'm going home."

Damon and Joey each slapped palms with Jake and left the room, fighting back the small crowd gathered at the door. Tonight, Jake wasn't taking anyone home. No groupies. None of his boys. No one. He was going to have Boo clear the hallway, grab his stuff, and head for home—alone. Jake had some things he needed to work out in his head. And he needed some peace and quiet to do it.

The door opened and Boo's massive face was in the room.

"You ready, Boss?" he asked.

"Yep."

"Let's go."

Boo led the way for Jake, walking him down the hallway. When they reached the exit, Boo opened the heavy door first and peered out.

"Small crowd. Wanna try a different exit? I can have the driver come around."

"Nah, let's go."

Boo pushed through a dozen or so kids holding cameras and phones. Jake slapped hands with a few and took a picture with one young girl who looked like she might faint. Boo opened the door of the Suburban and closed it after Jake climbed in.

"It's about time," said Bunny.

Jake nearly jumped out of his skin.

"What the hell are you doing in here?"

"Waiting for you."

Boo heard Jake yell out and he opened the car door. He looked inside, saw Bunny, and pointed at her.

"Yo!" Boo barked. "Out of the car."

Jake waved Boo off, closed the car door, and then pressed his face against the car window and peered outside.

"Who saw you get in this car?!"

"Would you calm down," Bunny said. "No one saw me."

Jake didn't take his face away from the car window.

"Jackson is out there right now snapping away. How do you know he didn't see you?"

"Because I was in this car long before he got there. I've been in here practically since the show started."

"Now tell me *why*."

Bunny sat up in her seat across from Jake.

"You haven't returned any of my calls or my text messages. I don't like that shit."

"Who the hell are you?" Jake asked, his top lip curled up. "I don't care what you don't *like*."

Bunny's mouth dropped.

"Why are you talking to me like that? Have you been drinking?"

"Yeah, I have been drinking." Jake held up his water bottle; the liquid swished around inside of it. "But that has nothing to do with why you don't belong in the back seat of my car."

"I wanted to talk to you. And you've been blowing me off."

"Mr. Giles, should we go?" asked the driver.

"Not to my house," Jake said. "Just drive."

The driver pulled out of the stadium parking lot and headed onto the turnpike.

"How come you've never taken me back to your place?"

"Because you don't belong there."

"But Sam does?"

"How do you know about her?"

"Everyone knows about her. She used to mess with Z. And now you're knocking her down every once in a while. Common knowledge."

"What else do you know?"

"I know you're catching feelings for me and you don't know what to do about it."

"It's over."

"No it's not."

Jake looked up and leveled his eyes at the young girl staring at him.

"It should have never happened. But it did."

Bunny crossed her leg, letting her thigh slip between the split in her skirt.

"Yup, it did."

"It was wrong from the door. And I'll pay the price for it. But it ends now. Where do you want me to drop you off?"

"Drop me off?" Bunny said, her eyes locked onto Jake's face. "You can't just drop me off somewhere."

"Do you want to go home?"

"Take me to the Parker Meridien. So I can tell Zander what happened between his girlfriend and his beloved uncle."

Jake sighed. And this is why you didn't have sex with your nephew's teenaged girlfriend. He opened his water bottle, took a heavy swallow, and forced it down.

"Do what you gotta do," he said.

"You don't care if I tell Zander?"

Jake leaned up to the driver.

"The Parker Meridien," Jake said. "Fifty-sixth and Seventh."

The driver nodded and Jake looked back at Bunny.

"You do whatever you need to do. Just don't contact me anymore."

"I'm signed to your label. How do we handle that?"

"If I have to drop you from the label to get the point across, I will."

"Picture that!" Bunny said. "And keep Zander? You'd lose your job by the close of business day."

"Test me."

It was dead quiet in the car for the entire twenty-minute

ride through the Lincoln Tunnel and across town to Zander's hotel.

"You told Zander to break up with me," Bunny finally said.

"You're a psycho."

"He's the one who knocked my tooth out!"

"Don't care."

"So you screw my brains out and then just—"

The driver pulled up to the front entrance of the hotel and eased behind a taxi parked ahead.

"Out."

Bunny stared at Jake, and he thought for a second that her eyes were filling up with tears. Crying would not be good. He'd rather fight her hand-to-hand right there in the back of the car than deal with her sniveling and crying.

"Bunny," Jake said. "I should have never touched you. If you feel like you need to tell Zander, do that."

Bunny nodded and picked up her oversized bag. She climbed over to the door and Jake pressed back to make sure he could not be seen from the street.

The driver opened the door and grabbed her hand, guiding her out. Teetering on impossibly high heels, Bunny let the driver guide her into the lobby of the hotel. He returned to the car.

"Home, sir?"

"Hold up," said Jake. He watched Bunny. She pressed the button for the elevator and then walked away before it came down. She came back outside and slipped into the back of the taxi sitting in front of the Suburban. Jake watched her lean up and speak to the driver and then sit back in her seat. The taxi pulled off.

"Home, sir?"

"Yeah. Home," said Jake, his head down. He took his cell out of his pocket and dialed a number from memory.

"Yo," said Z. "What's up?"

"I need to talk to you," said Jake. "And Zander, too. Immediately."

30

Lily sat on her sofa with her legs tucked beneath her. Her hair, usually in a tight bun at the back of her neck, was hanging loosely, covering one side of her face. She swatted it back occasionally when she reached for a different colored crayon. Her left hand twisted and turned as she sketched, erased, and redrew lines and whipped the pencil back and forth to shade certain areas. She stopped for a moment, leaned back, and squinted at the paper. She looked at her aquarium for reference and bent down again, shading, drawing, and coloring.

Since she was five years old and watched her father illustrate his never-published children's books, Lily had been fascinated with what colored pencils could do to a blank page. Some of her friends meditated, some did yoga, some went to church. Lily lugged out a sketch pad and a fresh pack of colored pencils when she wanted to commune with God.

She started out trying to drawing whatever her dad was working on. Once she started school, she made a habit of freeze-framing images in her mind and then attempting to re-create them later. In third grade, she drew a picture of her teacher snoring in her chair, her eyeglasses falling off her face. Her father was convinced she'd traced it from somewhere. She proudly said *nope* and shook her head until she was dizzy. By eighth grade, she scribbled so she had an excuse to keep her head down. By then, she'd learned that no matter what she wore, no matter how short her hair was, no matter how much her clothes screamed *boy,* she still looked into a person's face and they just knew something was off. She'd seen guys jump back when they looked at her in the face, realizing that she'd manage to trick them into thinking about her in the wrong way. Even though she did nothing but blink her eyes. The safest thing to escape the wrath from confused prepubescent boys was to keep her head in her sketch pad at all times. A few days before the promotion exercises from eighth grade to high school, Lily sat in class, ignoring the teacher's drone. She was pointing to different forms of animal and plant life in the aquarium next to her desk while most of the class was passing notes and flirting.

Lily kept her eyes on the fish for a second and then back down to her notepad, where she was re-creating the entire aquarium in rich, vibrant colors. She'd decided that the fish tank was the only thing worth remembering at the school. She planned to tack this piece on her bedroom wall and leave it there indefinitely. She was trying to figure out what color to use for the sea life that looked more like a flower when she realized the teacher had said something that sounded weird. She put her pencil down and listened.

"It's one of the only plants that will change gender depending on what other gender is nearby," she said, peeking through the top of the aquarium. "It's really incredible the way it works."

Lily put her sketch pad down and picked up her black-and-white composition book, the one her father bought at the beginning of the school year to take notes. It was completely empty. As the teacher listed all the different types of plant and sea life that were capable of switching from male to female, Lily scribbled down every word she said. After class, she went straight to the library and printed up images of all the species listed on her paper. Her father did not bother to ask why the bedroom wall was suddenly plastered with pictures of clownfish, wrasses, and moray eels. He was relieved to see that his child was settling on an appropriately boyish nautical theme. He decided to ignore the lilies that had started appearing in his child's hair.

Ten years later, Lily lived alone in a one-bedroom apartment, waiting tables, teaching art classes, and still drawing fish found in the coral reef when her mind raced.

Lily ignored Corinne's knock at her apartment door. As expected, Corinne barely waited thirty seconds before she used her spare key to open the door. On the few occasions when Lily really didn't want company, she put the chain lock on the door. Which didn't mean Corinne went away. It just meant she'd have a few minutes before Corinne started yelling for Lily to let her in.

"You have my key in case of *emergencies*," Lily said, not looking up from her notebook.

"This was an emergency. You weren't answering the door."

"You didn't even—"

Lily stopped herself.

"Never mind. Hello, Corinne."

Corinne looked around the apartment and shook her head.

"All you need is twenty more cats and you're ready for middle age."

"Maybe by then I'll find someone to share my life with."

"You're still on that?"

"If you haven't noticed, I've been having a tough time in the whole relationship department."

Corinne gave Lily a look and then walked into the kitchen.

"Get over yourself."

Lily scrambled off the couch and followed her.

"What's that supposed to mean? You saw what happened with Shawn. I have no idea when I will ever be able to—"

"Lily, we've been friends since you got to New York, same time I did. What do you know about my dating history?"

"You dated Luke. Who was gorgeous."

"And married. Who else?"

"That guy from the bodega."

"The one we only know as that-guy-from-the-bodega?"

Lily chuckled.

"At least you've dated. You know what it feels like to be held in someone's arms and feel loved and protected. Even if it didn't last. I don't know if I'm ever going to have even that. And I'm scared."

"Well, for starters, I had a bit of a head start on you with the whole being-a-woman thing."

Lily raised one eyebrow and shrugged. She was right on that point.

"And I don't know what makes you think you're special. Why do you deserve a man more than any other woman? Because you paid to become a woman? That was your choice."

Lily opened her mouth to protest. Corinne waved her hand in her face.

"No, Lily. That's not the way it works. You wanted to be a woman? Welcome. It's slim pickings for all of us. We're all out here, putting in work, meeting guys, meeting more guys, drinking endless cups of coffee at these horrible ten-minute Starbucks runs that serve as dates these days. We're speed-dating and creating profiles for dating sites and asking our friends to set us up. It's sad. And it's pathetic. And it's fun. So get over it. You chose this shit. You *wanted* it. Buck up. Getting a vagina does not automatically earn you a relationship."

"Are you done?" Lily asked.

"No. You're more of a woman than every woman I know, myself included. You'll be fine."

"As long as I lie about my past."

"I wouldn't recommend that."

Lily opened a drawer under her kitchen sink and took out a scrapbook overflowing with pictures, ticket stubs, pressed flowers, notes, and mementos. She placed it on the kitchen table and opened it carefully. Papers fluttered to the floor and spilled onto the table, as Lily rummaged through the pile.

"Look," she said, pressing two tickets into Corinne's hands.

"A Jake concert?"

"I went to pick up my check the other day and these were stapled to the envelope."

"No way."

"My boss said some guy came and dropped them off."

"And you didn't go?"

"Why would I do that?"

"Because you *like* him?"

"You said it yourself. I'm special. And guys like Jake do *not* do special."

"At least not publicly," Corinne said. "Who knows what he likes behind closed doors."

"See that's what I don't want. I'm *not* going to be some guy's fantasy blow-up doll. I *don't* want to be a delicacy or an experiment or any of that shit. I'm *not* advertising in the back of the *Village Voice*. I'm just a regular person! Kinda."

"Calm down."

Lily didn't realize she was breathing heavily until Corinne told her to calm down.

"I *am* calm," Lily said She ripped the tickets in half and then in half again. She continued ripping and ripping until the bits were flying out of her hands and onto the floor like confetti. She grabbed the broom from behind the refrigerator and furiously swept the tiny kitchen, stabbing the bristles behind the fridge and the stove with such force that Cat came out to see what was going on.

"Lily. Listen . . ." Corinne said.

"I really want to be alone right now," Lily said.

"Are you sure you don't want to—"

Lily threw her head back and screamed with her mouth shut.

"I'll call you later," Corinne said, walking quickly to the front door and letting herself out. Lily went to the door and threw all the locks into place, including the deadbolt. She picked up her sketch pad and ripped out her latest drawing. She crumpled it in her fists and put it in a black trash bag. She threw the bag into the foyer and threw herself onto the couch, her arms crossed over her chest and hot tears stinging her eyes. Her phone rang. It was

Corinne. She pressed ignore and then turned her phone off. She kept her eyes on the foyer, staring at the black garbage bag. She finally took it downstairs, to the side of the building.

On the way back inside, she noticed the crew of teenagers, but it was too late to turn around and go in the back way.

"What up, mama?" said the leader of the crew.

Lily smiled with her mouth shut and quickly walked past the boys and into the lobby. The boy grabbed her arm and yanked her back into the middle of the group.

"Why are you always in such a hurry?"

Lily couldn't speak. Her heart was pumping hard and she felt like she could feel the rush of blood in her ears.

"Leave her alone," said one of the taller boys. He was sitting on the bottom step of the stairwell. The leader turned to face him, letting Lily's arm go in the process.

"What does this have to do with you?"

"Come over here and find out," the boy said, not even bothering to stand up.

The leader and his minions seemed to think it over and decide to continue heading out the building. As soon as they were out the door, the elevator finally opened and Lily stepped inside.

"Thank you," she said to the boy on the bottom step.

He looked up at Lily and shook his head.

"Whatever."

Lily went back up and flopped facedown on her bed, trying to figure out why the boy on the bottom step looked at her like . . . like he *knew*. Cat hopped up and curled up next to her, licking her salty tears. Lily turned away and covered her head with her hands.

31

Belles Montagnes was a small, remote village seven thousand feet above sea level in the Blue Mountains of Jamaica. Ras always lost his breath when he stood at the base of the mountains, straining his neck to see the top. Years ago, settlers had turned Belles Montagnes into a luxurious playground for American tourists. The kind who would never step foot in Kingston. It was even accessible by helicopter; a helipad was perched at the peak of the mountain.

At the base, there was full-time security, private armed guards, and military. The president of Jamaica, as well as most of the aristocratic class, kept a home in Belles Montagnes. Ras was at the base of the mountain every morning at five a.m. He looked at the guard at the front gate and said nothing. The guard peeled back the heavy iron gates, signaling to the others with his eyes that it was okay to let him in though he did not have an access card.

A five-minute taxi ride would take him to where he needed to be. Every single morning. By five-thirty.

Another guard, outside an interior gated community would buzz him in each morning, though he knew full well that Ras did not live there. And by five-forty, every morning except Sunday when he went to her church instead, Ras sat down at the front door of his wife's condo. And waited.

The first few weeks, it caused a bit of commotion. People who lived nearby would look over their balconies and point and whisper. Ras Bennett! Unshaven and looking unkempt! Sitting outside that door every morning!

After a while, Ras became part of the fabric of the neighborhood, like the delivery truck that brought essentials from the outside world or the gaggle of uniformed schoolchildren picking their way down the mountain to school each morning.

The door to 295 Windmere Place, number 3B, opened slowly, at precisely six a.m. Ras glanced up and saw his wife, their infant daughter in her arms.

"Good morning, Ras," said Josephine, stepping over her husband's legs, which were stretched out in front of her doorway.

"Please come back to me, Josephine," Ras whispered. "Please."

For the first three weeks, Josephine answered by hurling epithets. After a month, she calmed down considerably and would simply say no and keep walking. Today, a new reaction. She smiled.

"You look unwell, Ras," Josephine said, walking past him with the baby at a fast pace in five-inch stilettos. "You should get some rest."

Ras watched his wife walk away. She was wearing a navy skirt suit. It was much too warm on the island for a suit. But she wore one every day. Except on Sunday. At church, she always blew in, bright colors and fabrics sweeping around her and the baby as she took her seat in the first pew, smiling and waving to friends.

She was gaining weight. Ras noticed her rear was just slightly more plump than before she left. When Marie Josef ran away with the baby they were planning to adopt, she'd dropped twenty pounds in less than a month. This time, though Ras knew she had to be devastated to learn that he had cheated again, she was *gaining* weight. Her eyes were clear. She looked strong and in control. Ras thought about what she always said: "I don't care what you do now. I have my baby . . ."

Ras pulled his knees up to his chest and put his hands behind his head. Would she file for sole custody of Baby Reina? Was there any hope? Ras could see the future and he wasn't having it—he was determined to reunite with his wife at any cost. Ras's mind began to drift, thinking about several things at once. A random thought drifted into his mind and settled there. Bits and pieces of body language from Josephine made him think even harder about the random thought. Why did Josephine seem so rested and relaxed? Suddenly, Ras scrambled up to his feet and ran down the stairwell in the direction of the parking garage where he knew Josephine kept her car.

He saw his wife, bending over to buckle the baby into her car seat. Ras sprinted. He didn't stop when he got close to the car. Josephine saw the blur coming toward her and stood up straight, her arms outstretched and her mouth wide. Ras ran directly into Josephine and pushed her against the car.

"Who is it?!" Ras screamed.

Josephine's eyes widened, but she said nothing. Ras held her wrists above her shoulders, against the car. He squeezed. When she still didn't respond, he sank his nails into the delicate skin of her wrists.

"Who?" Ras said, through gritted teeth. "When?"

"I don't know what you're talking about," Josephine said calmly. "But I do know my wrists are bleeding."

Ras didn't take his eyes off his wife's face to see if it were true.

"You're having sex with another man. Who is it?"

She closed her eyes and sighed. "What makes you think that?"

"I can tell. You're gaining weight. You're. . . . everything about you is . . . I just know. Now tell me who it is."

"How many women have you been with during our marriage?" Josephine asked.

Ras was silent, still squeezing her wrists.

"Dozens? Hundreds?" Josephine asked, her eyes still closed. "You were my first, Ras. Remember? Right in Peu de Ville. I cried. It hurt so bad. I kept saying, it's not going to fit! And you laughed and said, 'We'll go slow.' And we did. Do you remember, Ras?"

Ras was silent. He stopped digging his nails into her wrists but still held them tight. Josephine kept her eyes closed.

"You took your time. You were so patient with me. You would try to go in. And then I would stop you. And then you'd try a bit more. For an hour, until I bled. And I was no longer a virgin anymore. Then you bathed me and took me back to bed and made love to me with ease. There was no pain. Did you know I had never had an orgasm in my entire life until that night?"

Ras bit his lip to keep from speaking. He did know that. He also knew she'd never been completely nude in front of a man and had never given a blow job. Ras wasn't even sure she'd actually seen a penis up close before they had sex that first time.

Everything he did to her was brand new, which made it feel brand new to him as well. He remembered that first night. The second time, when he was able to move inside her, she asked, "How will I know when I'm coming?" and Ras had laughed. Five minutes later, Josephine was shaking and whimpering in his arms. "That's how you'll know," he'd said, before rolling her over for round three.

"You were my first," Josephine said, a slight smile playing on her lips. When she opened her eyes, the depth of the hatred inside them almost made Ras jump.

"But you won't be my last," she said.

Ras dropped her wrists, pulled back his hand, and slapped his wife's face before he could think twice. The baby heard the loud noise and began to cry.

Josephine kept her head down and rubbed her cheek with her hand. She tossed her hair back, stood up straight, and looked at her husband.

"You want to do that again? I'm sure the baby would love to have that burned in her memory. Go ahead. Smack me again."

Ras saw the red handprint clearly across the right side of his wife's face. Every finger was outlined, the pinkie finger right underneath her ear. A tiny line of blood began to drip out of her ear and onto the shoulder of her suit. Ras was in disbelief. His wife, the only woman he'd ever loved in this world besides his own mother, was standing before him, bloodied by his own hand.

"I'm going to get in the car and go to my office now," Josephine said. "Are you sure you don't want to hit me again?"

"Who was he?" Ras asked.

"He was a man. A man who said that this right here, this part of me?" Josephine motioned between her legs. "He said this was like an orchid, waiting to bloom. And Ras? He opened it up. And now I've got a fucking bouquet up in this piece."

Ras grabbed Josephine's face and squeezed hard. More blood dribbled from her ear.

"And tonight, I will see him and he will tend to my cuts and my bruises from you. And he will make me well and tell me that everything will be okay. And it will be." Josephine smiled again. And Ras noticed that the gums under her cheek were also bleeding. Yet she didn't look like she was in any pain at all. His wife walked around to the driver's side of her car, got inside, and settled the baby with a cup of juice and a few soft words. She turned around, looked at herself in the rearview mirror. She looked at Ras and mouthed the words "Thank you" before pulling off.

For weeks, Z had tried to get his wife to talk to him. And for weeks, he got barely more than a one-word response to anything he said. Every time he tried to bring up Alex, Beth lifted a hand and stopped him, whispering, "I don't want to talk about it."

"We have to talk about it," Z would say, "because you're wrong."

And Beth would just walk away.

"What did you do?" Zakee asked Z one morning, as he drove the kids to school.

"What do you mean, what did I do?"

"Mom's mad at you."

"Doesn't mean I did something."

Z looked in the rearview mirror and saw Zakee and his brother Zach exchange a quick glance. Z pulled over to the side of the road, threw the car in park, and turned around to face his children.

"Y'all know I am not perfect. I haven't always made the right choices. But I've never tried to hide anything. I am *not* the man I used to be. I'm getting better every single day. I would never put my hands on your mother—"

"Again," Zakee mumbled under his breath.

"I will never put my hands on her *again*. Anything else?"

"Yeah," said Zakee. "How many other children do you have besides us?"

Z exhaled loudly through his mouth. He knew this day was

coming. He just hadn't prepared for it. In fifteen years of marriage, he'd cheated on Beth more times than he could count. He was fairly certain that he'd had sex more with other women than he'd had sex with his own wife. And the kids? Beth had a better idea on a head count than he did. The women always came to her when it was time to talk lawyers and child support.

There were many things Z had done in his life that made him look back and shudder. None more so than the number of outside children he'd inflicted on Beth. Z turned around, put the car in drive, and pulled back onto the street.

"I have a daughter in Seattle," Z began, his eyes on the road. "And a set of twins in Virginia who are four. We never did a paternity test so I don't know for sure. And I have two boys in Miami."

"And that's it?" Zach asked.

"All he knows about," said Zakee. He sucked his teeth and kept his head turned toward the window.

"Look," Z said, "This is not easy for me. But I want to be honest with both of you. Same way I want you to be honest with me—about anything."

"Mommy's been crying a lot. Again."

"Your mom's going through some things right now."

"She's *always* going through something," Zakee yelled out. "Because of you!"

Z kept one hand on the steering wheel and turned back slightly with his other hand raised to slap Zakee in the face. He stopped himself and turned back around quickly, just in time to slam hard on the brakes to avoid hitting the car in front of him.

"Zakee, leave him alone before you get us all killed!" Zach said to his older brother.

"No, you leave *me* alone," Zakee said. "He's never here. Mommy's always crying. We have to end up taking care of the baby. Zander's off doing his own thing. It's not fair."

"Life's not fair," said Zach.

Z stayed quiet. He pulled up in front of the school, parked the car, and got out. He went over to the passenger side and opened the door.

"Boo's picking you all up at three o'clock," said Z. "Be ready."

"I don't want him picking us up," said Zakee.

Z visibly struggled to keep his composure.

"Don't tell me what you want," he said, his teeth clenched. "I didn't ask you what you wanted."

"I don't want Boo picking us up!" Zakee said, his voice raised.

Z exhaled. Having his son raising his voice at him in broad daylight was worthy of an ass beating. But he felt too guilty to discipline his son for anything.

It had been going on for months. As soon as Z got his act together and started being more involved in the boys' day-to-day lives, Zakee had become the lippy one, mouthing off about everything and constantly giving Z the stink eye. *It's just a phase,* Z continually reminded himself. It was his punishment for being nonexistent for most of Zakee's life. Z realized that he was like a brand-new parent to him. Much like a stepparent you don't ask for. Or some new guy your mom is dating that you don't want telling you what to do.

Z got back in the car. His youngest son, Zeke, was still sleeping in the back seat, oblivious to all the drama. When Z closed the door and restarted the car, Zeke woke up and began to whimper and whine.

He raised his head and rubbed his eyes with his fist.

"Where's Zakee and Zachary?"

"They went to school."

"Now where are we going?"

"Zeke, you know Daddy loves you, right?" said Z, pulling into a K-turn.

"Daddy, you always say that!"

"Listen to me," Z said. "I want you to know that no matter what, I love you very much. Do you hear me?"

"Daddy, are you mad at me?"

"Do you hear me?" Z said again, his voice booming loud enough to make Zeke jump in his car seat.

"Yes, Daddy," Zeke said. He stuck his thumb in his mouth and let his head fall over to rest on his shoulder.

Back at home, Z pulled Zeke out of his car seat and carried him into the house. As soon as he opened the door, he saw Beth in the kitchen, feeding the baby, who was sitting in her high chair, blowing food playfully out of her mouth.

"Go upstairs to your room for a little bit."

Zeke vanished and Z stood in the doorway of the kitchen, watching Beth attempt to keep most of the food in the baby's mouth.

"What's going on with Zakee?" Z asked. Beth kept her back to him.

"Nothing," she said.

"He told me you've been crying a lot lately and it's my fault."

Beth said nothing.

"Beth," Z whispered, "can you please fucking talk to me?"

"Don't curse in front of the baby," Beth said, still keeping her back to Z.

Z walked out into the hallway and called out for the nanny. From far away, Z heard the nanny's voice.

"I'm here," she said.

Z went into the kitchen and scooped the baby out of her high chair over Beth's protests.

"She's not done eating," said Beth. "Put her down."

Z walked out of the kitchen with the baby. The nanny came to the top of the steps holding Zeke's hand.

"Mr. Saddlebrook, you called me?" she said.

"Can you keep an eye on Kipenzi for a minute?" he asked. He walked up the stairs and put the baby in the nanny's arms.

"Let's go," he said to Beth, pointing to the kitchen.

"I don't want to talk."

Z grabbed her arm and pushed her into the kitchen.

"We're talking anyway."

"What are you going to do? Knock my teeth out because I don't want to talk to you?"

"I'm not going to touch you."

"You just grabbed my arm," Beth said.

Z sat at the kitchen table and pointed to the chair next to him.

"Sit," he said.

"Say whatever you have to say."

"What's wrong, Beth? Please tell me. I can't change anything if you won't tell me what's wrong."

"You can't change anything anyway."

Z ran his hands over his face.

"Why do you say that?"

Tears began to stream down Beth's face. Z stood up and took her into his arms. She leaned into him—finally giving in—and cried hard.

"What is it, Beth?"

His wife just cried harder, her back shaking as she tried to catch her breath.

"I don't know. It's just . . . I'm so sorry about accusing you of messing with Alex. My head has just been all over the place. I want to trust you but . . ."

Z pulled away from Beth and lifted her chin up so that he could look her in the eye.

"I'm different now, Beth," said Z. "But I swear to God, I don't love you any less. If anything, I love you more."

Beth's knees buckled and Z had to grab her and hold her by the waist to keep her from falling.

"Baby! Look at me!"

"I can't."

Something in the way Beth said this chilled Z.

"Why can't you?"

Beth kept her head down and fought against Z as he tried to lift her head up to face him.

"I just can't, Z," Beth said, through tears. "Just leave me alone. Please."

Z let go of Beth and moved back.

"I'll be in the studio if you want to talk."

Beth nodded, her head down. She walked out of the kitchen and up the stairs, following the direction of the kids' laughter.

In the studio, Z attempted to stay focused on the song he was trying to write for Kipenzi's tribute album. But all he could think about was how Zakee acted in the car that morning. And why Beth couldn't look him in the face. His mind kept racing between both moments. Zakee cursing him out; Beth falling apart.

He put aside his lyrics notebook and grabbed the pull-up bar near the mixing boards. *One. Two. Three.* Z got into a groove and felt beads of sweat begin to pour down his forehead. Physical movement always helped him think straight. He discovered that in rehab. One thing Z knew for certain: if Beth couldn't get it together, they weren't going to make it. He racked his brain, trying to figure out how he could help. He could stop working on the book with Alex. But he didn't want Beth to think she could wild out on any situation and he would just drop it. He'd signed a book deal to deliver a book and he planned to honor that. They could go to counseling. Z was already seeing a therapist once a week. And his daily twelve-step meetings were a form of counseling. But he'd see a marriage counselor too if it meant he could get to the root of Beth's issues.

"Pop, what's up?" said Zander, coming down the steps to the studio.

Z dropped down from the push-up bar and turned to face his son.

"I thought you were in LA?"

"Just got back. What's going on?'"

"Working on this song for Kipenzi's tribute album. How are you?"

"Just finished a track that is *fire,* Dad. I'm serious."

"I believe you."

"Jake hit me up," said Zander. "He said he wanted to talk to both of us. What's that about?"

Z shrugged.

"I told him you were out of town. We can get with him this week. So you've been working on music?"

Zander beamed.

"Yeah. And I want you on one song."

"Send it to me," said Z, smiling. "I'll see what I can do."

"I'm about to break it off with Bunny."

Z exhaled and sat down at the mixing console. Zander sat next to him and leaned back as far as he could in the chair.

"What made you come to your senses?"

"I think she's cheating on me."

"Why would you think that?"

"Just lately, she's been acting weird. Not looking me in the eye. Crying all the time. Never—"

Z jumped up so fast he tripped and nearly fell on top of Zander.

"Dad, what's wrong?"

"I'll be back," said Z. He ran up the stairs into the kitchen and then up the second flight of stairs. He walked down the hallway, throwing open bedroom doors. They were all empty. He came back down the stairs and walked through the foyer to the family room. Zeke was playing with toys on the floor. Beth was sleeping on the couch. Z stopped. This morning's words kept flooding his mind: *Look at me. I can't. Look at me. I can't.*

In nearly twenty years, it had never dawned on Z that Beth could be unfaithful to him. He would have bet money that it just wasn't possible. Her love for him was so overwhelming that she seemed to barely have time for herself, much less another man. Z's grandmother always told him that in a relationship, the grass might be greener on the other side—but only if you weren't watering your own lawn.

Z sat down next to Beth on the couch, moving slowly so he would not wake her. As far as he knew, she'd never lied to him. If he woke her up right then and asked her if she'd cheated, he knew for sure she'd tell him the truth. The question was did he want to know? Z sat back and closed his eyes. A parade of women danced before him. Groupies giving him blow jobs backstage at concerts. Women he brought back to this very house, into the basement. Women he'd had sex with while his wife was right upstairs sleeping. Outside babies born, at least one every other year.

Z leaned over and kissed Beth on the forehead. Did he have to ask? Did he already know? Was there anything *to* know? Z pulled a small blanket over her and then sat down on the floor with Zeke and played with him for the rest of the morning.

33

Zander raced into his hotel room, throwing the door open and looking all around.

"Bunny!" he yelled out. There was no reply and he ran into the bedroom and looked in the closets, the bathroom, and the minikitchen.

Back in the front room, he turned around and around, running his hands over his mouth. Where would she be? He dropped his head into his hands and rubbed his hair. The day before, he'd been texting back and forth with Bunny on his cell. He'd broken up with her—finally. She was pissed off but seemed ready to move on. And then this morning, one of her friends called and said that she was worried because Bunny had stayed up all night drinking and smoking weed.

Zander knew Bunny just wanted him to call and he refused to give in. He called his father instead, who told him he was doing the right thing and not to let her manipulate him. And then he got a text message from Bunny. She asked if she could come to the hotel. Her text messages were garbled and incoherent. Zander did not respond.

It wasn't until her girlfriend called again that Zander got worried. She asked him if he was with Bunny. He said no and she groaned. She said Bunny had gone outside, saying that Zander was sending a car to pick her up and bring her to the Parker Meridien. No one had seen her since. Reluctantly, Zander agreed to go to the hotel and see if he could find her.

In the lobby, there were two police officers talking to a receptionist. Zander walked by slowly and listened in. The woman behind the desk was talking about an intoxicated woman wandering around the lobby, half-dressed and babbling. "I've seen her on television," the woman said. Zander took the stairs up to his suite.

He just wanted to find her before the police did. He decided he would get her cleaned up—at least a bit. And then call her manager Robert to pick her up. But he'd come into the room and saw no signs of her. Someone banged on the door and Zander rushed over to open it. It was Robert.

"What have you done *now?*" he said in his stilted British accent.

"I didn't do anything. We're not even together anymore."

"You could have waited until we shot this video to dump her. We're losing money every hour she's not on set."

"I'm sorry that my life decisions are inconvenient for you."

Robert pushed Zander's shoulder hard enough that he fell back a few steps but caught himself from falling on the floor.

"Look here, you little pisser," Robert hissed. "You're the one who kept her in tears when you started cheating on her with your little groupies. And then you punched her in the face last year and that still wasn't enough."

"You don't even know what happened!" Zander protested. "She started—"

"*And* you knocked her front tooth out? You need to be locked up. If Bunny were my daughter, I'd kick your ass all around this hotel room right now."

"Bunny's just your meal ticket. You don't really give a shit about her."

"Neither one of you care about me."

Robert and Zander spun around to see Bunny slumped in the doorway that led out to the balcony, the one place Zander had not looked. Zander raced over and grabbed her by the arm before she completely fell over. Robert moved clothing and extra pillows off the couch just before Zander helped her lie down.

"I just want to take a nap . . ." Bunny said, turning her head to the side.

"Are you still taking Percocets?" Zander asked. He used his fingers to open her eyes. Her pupils were completely dilated.

"Zan," Bunny mumbled. "I just drank too much. Need to sleep it off." Bunny tried to wriggle out of Zander's arms and curl up on the couch.

"Let her be," Robert said. "I'll stay here until she sobers up."

"How come I don't smell alcohol on her breath?" Zander asked, standing up and looking around the room. "And there's no bottles here."

"She was probably already drunk when she got here."

Zander went out onto the balcony and stopped short. He saw a small plastic bag underneath a recliner. There was a small, thin rubber hose sticking out. Zander grabbed the bag and went back into the room, slamming the sliding glass door shut behind him.

"Wake her up!" Zander yelled out, throwing the plastic bag in Robert's direction.

"What the hell is this?" Robert whispered, dumping the contents on the floor.

"Bunny, get up. Bunny! Get. *Up*."

Zander snatched Bunny up to her feet. Her knees buckled, and he struggled to keep her upright. She began to open her eyes and tried to stand up on her own.

"*Ohmygod* . . ." Robert said. He was still sifting through the contents of the bag. There were handfuls of syringes, vials, and glassine packages.

Zander pulled up one of Bunny's arms and pushed her sleeve back.

"We can't let her fall asleep."

Within minutes, Zander knew there was no way he could keep Bunny up. Her eyes were rolling back in her head and she'd completely stopped communicating. He leaned in near her chest and listened to her breathing. He looked at his watch, waited for a full minute and counted her breaths. In sixty seconds, he'd counted ten deep breaths. When he pulled away, he heard a gurgling sound coming from Bunny's throat and her lips were starting to turn blue.

"She's ODing."

Robert's eyes widened as he fumbled for his cell phone.

"*No*," Zander said. "Wait a second."

Zander bent down and massaged Bunny's breastbone with a heavy hand. He kept leaning down, listening to her breaths and then rubbing harder. He switched from rubbing her breastbone to rubbing her lips with his thumb and then back to her chest again.

"What the hell are you doing?!" Robert screamed.

Zander ignored him and listened again to her breathing. Twelve breaths in a minute. Better. But not good enough. He tilted Bunny's head back, used his hand to purse her lips, and pressed his lips firm against her and blew three short, hard breaths into her lungs. He sat up, watched her for a moment. And then leaned in and did it again. He listened to her breathe. Thirteen breaths per minute.

Zander put Bunny back down on the sofa and ran into the bedroom. He pulled down the duffel bag he always brought with him when he traveled with his father on tour. He'd learned to always be ready to hit the ground running when his dad gave him the opportunity to travel with him. Many times, his father would come home and give him five minutes to get on the tour bus. He started having a bag packed at all times after he got left behind more than once. The red and white canvas duffel bag hadn't been used in so long that the clean clothes and underwear packed inside were three sizes too small. But it wasn't clothing that Zander was looking for.

He threw the bag on the bed, unzipped a side pocket, and took out a small sealed plastic bag. He tore it open with his teeth, dumped out the contents, and grabbed a small nasal spray pump. He ran back into the living area and knelt down next to Bunny. He twisted the top off the pump and squeezed a mist of spray into the air before easing the nozzle into Bunny's nostril. He squeezed lightly, waited, and then squeezed again. He didn't realize until he put the spray bottle down that his shirt was soaked and his breathing was coming in shallow.

"What the hell was that?" Robert asked.

"Narcan. It's for—"

There were a few short knocks on the door. Robert and Zander froze in place. Robert snuck to the door, looked through the peephole, and then put his finger to his lips and mouthed the word *police*. Zander dragged Bunny into the bedroom while Robert stuffed the paraphernalia back into the bag and threw it in the shower stall.

Zander sat on the bed, petrified, waiting to get some kind of response from Bunny. He whispered her name and gently shook her shoulders. He patted her face with his hands softly and then with more force. She remained as still as a corpse. He looked at his watch. It had been ninety seconds since he gave her the Narcan. She should have been conscious by now. Zander had watched his mother bring his father back from an overdose dozens of times by the time he was sixteen. He'd done it enough times on his own to remember to always bring Narcan in his travel bag. But Z always came to almost immediately. Maybe Bunny needed more. Was he supposed to give her three pumps or two? Zander searched the room for the spray bottle and remembered that it was in the front room. Zander came back out and saw the two officers in the living area of the suite.

"And you're sure she's okay?"

"She's gonna have a hell of a hangover," Robert said. "But yes, she's fine."

"Do you mind if we take a look at her? Just to be sure."

The officers looked at Zander, who still had his hands on the doorknob to the bedroom.

"She's right back here," Zander said, waving them over to the bedroom.

Robert looked at Zander, questioning him with his eyes. Zander looked away and turned to lead the officers into the bedroom.

"Ma'am? Are you okay?"

Zander held his breath.

"Ma'am?"

Bunny opened her eyes a quarter of an inch. She looked at each of the four people, then blinked. Zander saw Robert close his eyes and murmur the words *oh thank God* under his breath.

"Do you know where you are?" one of the officers asked.

Bunny opened and closed her mouth and ran her tongue across her lips. Robert grabbed a bottled water off the bureau and tipped it into her mouth. Bunny leaned up, took several gulps of water, and then exhaled and fell back against the pillows. Bunny's mouth moved, but no one could hear anything.

"Can you repeat that, ma'am?"

Bunny cleared her throat and tried to sit up.

"I'm at the Parker Meridien," Bunny whispered, her eyes closed.

"And can you tell us who these two gentlemen are?"

Bunny kept her eyes closed, raised her hand, and pointed in Zander's general direction.

"That's Zander. He's my boyfriend. I mean, my ex-boyfriend. The other one's my manager. His name is Robert."

The officers looked at each other and then over at Zander and Robert.

"You should probably keep an eye on her for a few days," said one of the officers.

"Of course," Robert said. "Thank you so much for stopping by."

As soon as he closed the door and locked it, Robert sunk to the floor. Zander flopped into a chair and threw his head back. He tried to take deep breaths, but his heart was beating too quickly.

"What did you give her?" Robert asked.

"Narcan. Brings you back from a heroin overdose."

"You got her hooked on *heroin?*"

"Hell, no," Zander said. "I would never touch that shit."

"I see," said Robert. "But you just travel with Narcan just in case. *Right.*"

Robert shook his head and got to his feet. He pulled out his cell phone, walked out onto the balcony, and started making phone calls. He could hear him reassuring someone on the video set that Bunny was fine and that she would be on-set in a few hours. Zander stood in the doorway of the bedroom and watched Bunny. She looked like she was sleeping. But Zander knew she just had her eyes closed.

"Hey," said Zander.

Bunny opened her eyes and focused on Zander.

"Hey," she said. Her voice was scratchy and weak.

"I love you," Zander said.

Zander stared at Bunny for a few more minutes and then turned around, closing the door behind him. He heard Bunny calling his name as he walked toward the door of the suite. He hesitated just a few seconds before he grabbed his bag and walked out.

34

Birdie was in that halfway place. The sun was pouring in from the window because he hadn't drawn the shades the night before. So he was awake, but only barely. Without opening his eyes, Birdie stretched out his arm, knowing Alex wasn't there. His arms moved across the empty space in the bed his wife had picked out.

Birdie sat up in bed, still not opening his eyes. There was a crippling headache spreading across his temples. He forced himself out of bed, pulling the curtains to block the sun and then limping back to bed.

Something was wrong with his hip. Birdie laid back down gently to assess all the damage. There was a raging headache, courtesy of a fifth of vodka straight from the bottle and six shots of Patrón at the impromptu party in his basement eight hours ago. His left hip was aching. He vaguely remembered pinning Travis to the ground in an ill-advised wrestling match. At some point, Travis was able to overturn Birdie and ended up flipping him onto the hardwood floor. There were various cuts and scratches that didn't come with any kind of memory. In general, it was just another Tuesday. Birdie rolled over onto his stomach at the same time there was a knock on the bedroom door.

"Who is it?" Birdie asked.

The door opened and Dylan poked her head inside.

"You got a meeting in thirty minutes."

"I said who is it. Not come inside."

Dylan slammed the door and knocked again.

"Who is it?" Birdie asked.

"The only person who gives a damn about your career, obviously."

Birdie swung his legs over to the side of his bed and planted his feet on the floor. Dylan opened the door and walked directly to the window and swiped the drapes open.

"Damn, Dylan," Birdie said, shielding his eyes with his hands. "Chill out. I'm up."

"Looks like you had a good time last night," said Dylan. She snapped open a garbage bag and began dumping ashtrays, empty beer bottles, and fast-food wrappers into it.

"I don't need you to clean up after me," Birdie said, making a grab for the bag. Dylan moved away and kept it just out of his reach.

"You go take a shower. I'll finish up in here."

Birdie dragged himself to his bathroom and pulled open the shower door.

"Oh shit!" Birdie yelled out, jumping back a full foot. There was Corey, in a crumpled heap, curled up in a ball inside the shower stall. Dylan rushed in.

"Oh my God, is he dead?"

"No," said Birdie, nudging him with his toe. "He's asleep."

Dylan knelt down and shook Corey, who began to wake up.

"Dude, you can't be falling asleep in my damn shower! Get the hell up!" Corey pulled himself up to his knees, leaned over, and threw up all over Dylan's feet.

"Ohmygod, eeeeeewwww!" Dylan said. She froze in place, her eyes wide.

"Birdie, get this off of me!!"

Birdie tried not to laugh and went into the hallway to find towels. On his way to the linen closet, he looked over the railing and got a glimpse of the first floor.

His house was trashed. Top to bottom.

There was a roll of toilet paper inexplicably threaded around all the furniture, from the couch to the lamps and the side tables, all the way into the kitchen. The empty cardboard insert was stuffed into a half-eaten cake. Birdie remembered singing (or rather screaming) "Happy Birthday" to someone he didn't know at some point in the night. He even vaguely remembered driving to go get the birthday cake.

There was something that looked like frosting all over the television screen and a pile of coats were on the floor. Birdie could make out Daryl on the sofa, in nothing but a pair of boxers. A girl Birdie had never seen before was curled up next to Daryl, in a bra and panties. There were two girls sharing a pallet on the floor. One had a mustache drawn on her face with a marker.

Birdie shook his head and continued down the hall. The only thing he could think was: *Better than last weekend.*

"Birdie!!" Dylan screamed.

"I'm coming, I'm coming . . ." Birdie muttered to himself.

After Dylan's shoes were cleaned off, she and Birdie hoisted Corey onto a bed in one of the guest rooms. Corey burped, groaned, and then immediately went back to sleep. Birdie went downstairs and began cleaning up. Dylan was on his heels with her head buried in her BlackBerry.

"I need you to get on the phone with an editor at *Vibe* at three. They need a quick quote about the Kipenzi tribute album."

"You told me," said Birdie. He stopped and gently shook the shoulder of one of the two girls sleeping on his sofa. The woman roused and then sat up abruptly.

"Where's my shirt?" the girl said. Her voice was low and sleepy.

"I'm not sure," Birdie said. "But you need to go."

The girl rooted around the sofa, pulling clothes out of the sofa cushions. She woke up the girl who had been sleeping next to her and they both began whispering to each other while they got dressed.

"You have a photo shoot for *Men's Health* tomorrow," Dylan said. "And I can't reschedule it, so please don't ask me to."

"Dylan, can't we do this over the phone?"

"Do you know where your phone is right now?"

Birdie looked around the living room and then patted the pockets of his robe.

"That's what I thought," said Dylan. "I can never get you on the phone. That's why I end up just coming over here."

"I just think you should let me—"

Before Birdie could finish his sentence, the doorbell rang.

"Oh, and your daughter's coming over today."

"What are you talking about?" Bird whispered. "Why isn't she in school?"

"No school today," Dylan said. "I guess you don't remember talking to her mom about this last night?"

Birdie's eyes widened and he held a finger up to his lips as he crept to the door. He looked through the peephole and saw Jen holding Tweet on her hip. Jen's face was stone. She rang the doorbell again and then knocked hard on the door.

"Birdie! Can you open the door, please?"

Birdie tightened his robe and tried to think. There was no way he could let them in right now. He'd have to stall them somehow. He ran upstairs, pulled on jeans and a T-shirt and dashed back downstairs, going outside through the back patio. He walked down the driveway and came around to the front of the house.

"Daddy!" Tweet said, scrambling down from her mom and making a beeline for Birdie.

"Hey, sweets," Birdie said. "How's my little girl?"

"Birdie, why are you outside?"

Birdie pretended he didn't hear his ex-wife. If he could just get Tweet inside from the kitchen, he could take her upstairs through the back staircase and get Dylan to keep her in the bedroom until he got the house cleaned up and kicked everyone out.

"Let's go, Tweet," Birdie said, picking up the little girl. He waved to Jen and turned around to make his way back up the driveway.

"Don't even think about it, Birdie," Jen said, walking close behind him. "What's going on?"

"What do you mean, what's going on? I'm taking Tweet inside. I'll see you when you pick her up."

Jennifer walked up, passed Birdie, and then turned around to face him.

"What's going on?" Jen asked.

Birdie cleared his throat.

"Nothing. Why?"

"I need to come inside."

"For what?"

"Bathroom."

"Place is a mess," Birdie said.

He tried to step out of her way, but Jennifer continued to step directly in front of him.

"I lived with you for three years," she said. "I don't care about your dirty bathroom."

Before Birdie could stop her, Jennifer dashed ahead and went into the house through the kitchen patio.

"Jen," Birdie yelled out. "Don't go in the—"

Birdie heard Jen gasp and closed his eyes.

"Daddy," Tweet said. "Are you in trouble?"

"Yeah, Tweet," Birdie said. "I'm in big trouble."

Birdie took Tweet up to her room, turned on *Princess and the Frog*, and closed the door tight behind him. As soon as he stepped into the living room, still strewn with garbage and random people, he saw Jennifer standing in the hallway, surveying the scene. She shook her head from side to side when she saw Birdie walking up to her.

"I can't believe you're living like this," Jen said.

"I had a little get-together last night and it got a little out of hand."

"A little?"

"Jen, I left my mother in Brooklyn. I don't need another one."

"Well, you obviously need something."

"I need you to go."

"Do you honestly think I'm leaving Tweet in this house with you? You've gotta be insane."

"Look, I'm gonna get this place cleaned up and it'll be fine."

"That's not the point, Bird."

Birdie exhaled. He knew Jennifer was right. But he wasn't in the mood for trying to placate her. He still needed to take a shower, get all these fools out of his house, and start the day.

"It's gonna be fine," Bird said. "You go."

Jen crossed her arms tight over her chest and set her lips in a thin line.

"Please bring Tweet back down here."

Birdie opened his mouth to speak and then changed his mind. There was nothing he could say and he knew it. If he'd taken Tweet to Jen's house and saw this scene, he wouldn't have left her either. He glanced around the house through Jen's eyes and rubbed his face. Birdie brought Tweet back down, making sure to use the back staircase leading into the kitchen.

"Daddy, I thought I was staying here with you today?"

"I'm going to pick you up tonight," Birdie said, kissing his daughter on the top of her head. "I promise."

Birdie transferred Tweet into Jen's arms.

"I'll call you tonight and pick her up."

Birdie walked them to the car and watched as Jen strapped Tweet into her car seat. She closed the car door and walked to where Birdie stood.

"I don't think you should pick Tweet up tonight," Jen said.

"What are you talking about? I just told her I would."

"Bird, I don't know what you're going through right now. But I don't want Tweet to be any part of it. You want to go all Animal House? That's fine. But I'm not going to subject our child to this kind of lifestyle."

"We have a custody agreement, Jennifer. And it's my weekend."

"So take me to court."

"Wait," Birdie said, holding up a hand. "Time out. We've never gotten down like this. We always work things out on our own."

"Here's how we work this out," Jen said. "Stop being a loser."

"One crazy party doesn't mean I'm a—"

The front door opened and the two girls from the sofa came outside, blinking in the bright rays of sunshine. One girl, a tiny blonde with wide hazel eyes, teetered over to where Birdie stood.

"It was nice meeting you, Birdie," she said. She hiccupped and then walked with her friend down the driveway.

Jennifer shook her head, got in the car, and pulled away, passing the two women as they got into a car parked at the foot of the driveway.

Bird stood there, watching the smoke from Jennifer's sedan billowing out of the tailpipe. When she turned left, Birdie saw Tweet turn around in her car seat and wave.

35

J ake felt someone taking off his shoes. He wanted to protest but knew if he moved he'd throw up.

"Sit up and drink this," said a woman's voice.

Without protesting, he slowly sat up in bed. He didn't open his eyes, but he opened his mouth and sipped. Alka-Seltzer. He took a hard gulp and sat back.

Who could it be? He didn't recognize the voice. How on earth did he end up bringing back a nameless, faceless girl *again*? And this one was taking care of him. He tried desperately to think about who the woman could be and nothing came up. He couldn't even remember where he'd ended up the night before.

No matter who it was, he was grateful for the cool side of the pillow and the Alka-Seltzer to settle his bubbling stomach. He opened one eye and squinted the other. The woman was in the bathroom, humming something random and running water over a washcloth. She squeezed out the water, folded the cloth, and came back into the bedroom. Jake shut his eyes tight as she placed the cool fabric on his forehead.

"You have a fever from the infection," she said.

"What infection?" Jake mumbled.

"I'm guessing kidney," said the woman. "You've been hard on it lately."

Jake opened his eyes. It was Lily. She leaned over Jake and looked him in the eyes, her face soft and full of concern. She had her long black hair pulled back in a bun with a lily tucked inside. She was dressed modestly in a V-neck T-shirt and jeans. She looked like a nurse—or a nun—compared to the women he usually woke up next to. Jake sat up in bed as much as he could.

"How'd you end up here?"

"You came by the bar last night," said Lily, wiping down Jake's face. "You were already drunk when you got there and I wouldn't serve you."

"So how'd you end up *here*?" Jake asked again.

"You asked me to come home with you."

"So all I have to do is be fall-down sloppy drunk for you to pay attention to me?"

"You were doing really bad," said Lily. She picked up a pillow and put it behind Jake's head.

Jake got a visual. He was swigging from his ever-present bottle and . . . *crying?* He looked over quickly at Lily, who was sitting at the foot of his bed.

"You didn't come to my show," Jake said. "I left you tickets."

"I don't like concerts," said Lily.

"I left you messages at the bar. More than once."

"I know. It's just that I'm not interested in . . . anything."

"Then why are you here?"

"If you saw what you looked like last night, you'd know. You begged me to come up here and I did, against my better judgment. And now I'm leaving. You're welcome."

"Did you eat breakfast?" Jake asked.

"Ian made me some toast."

"He's a little overly nice to company."

Lily smiled and shrugged.

"You know your lifestyle could be a little dangerous," she said. "I'd imagine a camera phone shot of you passed out in bed would go for a lot of money."

"Is that what you did?"

"You know I didn't."

"I don't know at all."

"If you suspected as much, we wouldn't be having a conversation in your bedroom right now."

"Let's go," said Jake, pointing toward the bedroom door. "Breakfast."

At the kitchen table, Lily and Jake sat, sipping coffee and picking at eggs.

"You're a decent cook," said Lily, holding up her coffee cup to toast.

Jake clinked her cup and set his down on a saucer.

"I'm not used to being turned down by women."

"Rejection is healthy," Lily said.

Jake smiled.

"I would imagine you wouldn't know anything about rejection. Something tells me you can have any guy you want."

Jake saw something like terror flash across Lily's face.

"What's wrong?" he asked. He put his hand on top of Lily's, but she snatched it away.

"Nothing. I gotta get to work."

"You're not gonna keep running away from me like you're Cinderella," said Jake. "Come here."

Jake grabbed Lily by the wrists and pulled her into the living room. Lily struggled to get away. She stopped short, planted her feet, and refused to move.

"Let go, Jake," Lily said. "Please."

Jake tugged until she tripped and had to take a few steps forward to avoid falling. He pulled her until they were standing in front of the couch. Jake sat down, still holding her wrists and dragged her to the couch with him.

Lily immediately began trying to wrestle her way off the couch, but Jake held her shoulders and turned her to face him.

"Stop it," he said. He shook her shoulders. "I'm not going to hurt you."

Jake slowly let go of Lily, watching her carefully to see if she would try to bolt. Instead, she turned around and leaned back in the sofa. She crossed her arms over her chest and stared straight ahead at the television.

Jake leaned over, grabbed the remote from an end table, and turned the television on.

"What do you want to watch?"

"I have choices? I thought I was being held captive."

"You are. But you can still choose what you want to watch."

Jake looked over at Lily. He could tell she was deciding whether she was going to give in or try to leave again. Watching her body slowly sink into the couch, he smiled.

Lily checked the time on her cell phone.

"I want to watch *Jeopardy*," she said.

Jake turned to ABC and put his feet up on the coffee table.

"What's your best category?"

Lily didn't take her eyes off the television.

"All of them."

"What do you want to put on that?"

"Anything you want."

Jake sat up.

"If I win, we're going to Atlantic City tonight. Play some slots. Catch a show. I'll take you to my spot down there. We come home in the morning."

"Fine," Lily said. She didn't take her eyes off the television.

"I'm serious," Jake said. "Don't let your mouth make a bet that your ass can't cover."

Lily didn't respond. She took the remote out of Jake's hand and turned the volume up on the television just as Alex Trebek began introducing the contestants. Jake called out for Ian to come and keep score. He sat behind the sofa, with a pen and pad in his hand. Thirty minutes later, Jake jumped up from the sofa, muted the television, and threw the remote down in mock frustration. From the first round until Final Jeopardy, Lily had maintained a triple-digit lead over Jake. She cleared out entire categories on obscure topics like the Balkans and Classic Kids' Poems. If there hadn't been a category called NFL Coaches of the Year and a few other sports categories, Jake would have been shut out. And Lily had beat out all three contestants on the show. As the credits rolled, Lily turned to Ian, a huge smile on her face.

"Can we get the final tally?" she asked.

Ian tapped his phone and then scribbled a few more numbers. "Jake. 2,300. Lily. 37,800."

"What the *hell,*" Jake said, laughing.

Lily smiled and stood up. "I guess that's that."

"Wait. Why are you so happy that I lost? You really don't want to go out with me, do you?"

Lily didn't answer. Jake got up and walked her to the back foyer of the penthouse. Lily stopped and looked at the platinum plaques that were lining the foyer walls. Kipenzi's solo plaques were in the studio, and Jake kept his at his mother's house. But the ones they'd earned together were hung along the corridor that led to the exit. Jake kept his hands clasped behind his back because he felt a strong urge to hug Lily. And she seemed like she would sock him in the jaw. He noticed that she was vibrant and giddy during the *Jeopardy* game, trash talking and making faces after she got another correct answer. At one point, she even slapped Jake on the back when she got a particularly difficult answer and then she seemed to catch herself and dial it down. But now she was stiff and wooden again.

Jake tried to remember how he actually courted women. He hadn't done it in so long that he had no idea how to make a woman feel relaxed and comfortable. Lily didn't seem like she wanted a compliment. And she definitely wasn't looking for anything material. Jake decided to try honesty.

"How long would it take for me to wear you down?"

"What do you mean?"

"What if I continued to pursue you? Even though I lost the bet."

"I guess I'd have to get a restraining order."

Jake laughed and after a few seconds, Lily joined in.

"I don't mean hanging outside your house or coming to your

job. I mean just letting you know I'm interested. How much time would I have to invest before you gave me a chance?"

Lily rubbed her temples like she was in pain. Jake moved back so that he wouldn't throw his arms around her and squeeze her tight.

"Do you realize that you have a drinking problem?"

Jake clenched his jaw. He liked her. But not that much.

"I'm not trying to tell you to stop," said Lily. "I'm just saying that it might be something you want to take a look at."

"You're an addiction counselor too?"

"Most bartenders are. By default."

"I'll let you know if I feel like I need help in that area."

Lily quickly shook her head.

"You don't have to let me know. I can't help you. But I would like to see you get some help."

Jake stared at Lily, and she held his gaze.

"I'm gonna go," Lily finally said.

"Cool," said Jake, opening the back door. He held it open and then just as Lily began walking past him out the door, he grabbed her forearm, pulled her back, and gently pressed her against the door. He wrapped his arm around her waist and kissed her hard on the mouth. He felt her muscles tensing up, trying to pull away. He kissed her again and then once more. Finally, she exhaled and kissed him back, running her hands down his back. She pulled away from him abruptly and shook her head as if to wake herself from a nightmare.

"Do you want to stay?" Jake asked, his arm still around her waist and his body pressed against her.

"Yes," Lily said. Then she pulled away and rushed out the door. Jake watched as Lily practically ran out into the hallway where someone from his twenty-four-hour security team waited near the service elevator.

Jake closed the door and watched from the peephole as Lily stepped onto the elevator and the doors closed in front of her. He ambled back through the kitchen, their conversation—and that kiss—swirling through his head.

"Did you see me last night, Ian?" Jake asked.

"More intoxicated than usual, sir."

"And this chick . . ."

"Helped you to bed. And then slept on the living room sofa."

"What's her deal?"

"I don't know, sir," said Ian.

Jake dismissed Ian early and stretched out on the living room sofa. His stomach still rumbled, but he had it under control. It was his mind that was swimming. All the women who had come in and out of his home in the past year, it was the one he didn't have sex with who got under his skin. Jake wanted to believe that she had a secret motive. That she was on her way to meet a reporter and tell them everything she saw at Jake's house. But for whatever reason, Jake knew that was not true. And he also knew he had to see her again.

Lily grunted as she stuffed the petals and stems down the garbage disposal in the restaurant's kitchen. She turned it on and the motor whirred and then stopped abruptly. She yanked the flowers out, went over to the cutting board, and grabbed a butcher knife from the wooden block. She hacked until she had several handfuls of a sweet-smelling colorful pulp.

She used the edge of the blade to swipe the chopped flowers off the cutting board and into her hand, just the way the chef did when he scraped the onions and mushrooms into the hot frying pan. The flowers went into the disposal and this time, when she turned it on, they disappeared down the drain.

She leaned over the sink and tried to catch her breath. For the fifth week in a row, she came to work and found a group of employees huddled over a huge bouquet of flowers, *oohing* and *ahhing* at a floral arrangement and holding the card up to the fluorescent lights to try and read the message.

Each arrangement was completely different than the last. All were bursting in vibrant colors and textures and shipped in from exotic locations like Holland and Japan. Her boss had refused to let her toss last week's delivery—three dozen bright white lilies from Hong Kong. She said they were too beautiful. So for two days, every time Lily walked past them, she swiped one flower and threw it out. Eventually, the arrangement had only a half dozen flowers left and her boss wondered aloud what happened to them. Then, on a Wednesday afternoon, Lily came in just to pick up her check and caught one of the bartenders trying to steam open the envelope addressed to her that was tucked into a mammoth arrangement of Stargazer lilies from Honolulu.

"Don't you want to know who they're from?" a bartender asked, as Lily snatched the card out of her hand.

"No, I don't," Lily said. She stuffed the card in the bottom of her bag, under her emergency flat shoes and her coffee mug.

"Well, why don't you let me read it, and then I'll throw it away for you."

"Absolutely not," Lily said, pushing back on the swinging doors back to the main dining room.

Every week, sometimes every day, Lily had to deal with the ever-changing arrangements that became increasingly elaborate. Finally, one day she'd had enough. As soon as she walked in the restaurant, she smelled the flowers. She choked down a scream, marched into the kitchen, snatched them out of the vase, and started stuffing them down the disposal.

Lily sat down at the counter where the chef always let her have a taste test of a new menu item while it was still being developed and sobbed.

Never in her life had one man paid so much attention to her. Not since Rick had she felt so special and loved. She'd kissed Jake just once. (And she didn't kiss him, she reminded herself daily, she just kissed him *back*, which wasn't quite as bad.) But it didn't matter. He didn't know what he was dealing with. He was smitten and interested, and he was having a great time pouring it on thick. But didn't he know something had to be wrong? Couldn't he tell that Lily was crazy about him? If things had been different, Lily would have jumped his bones the day he kissed her.

Lily stood up and splashed water from the sink over her face and dried her face and hands with a paper towel. She rubbed her lips with the paper, remembering how soft Jake's lips were on her own. Her pulse quickened again when she relived the feeling of his arms around her waist.

Lily screamed and then slammed both of her fists down on the counter. The spice rack popped up an inch off the counter and some of the small canisters popped out of the container, some falling onto the floor.

Beverley, her boss, pushed through the double doors, a tray of empty wineglasses in her hands.

"Go," said Beverley. She placed her tray on the counter and then jerked a thumb toward the service entrance. "Outta here."

"I'm okay. I'm sorry I yelled out."

"I'm giving you the night off. Get yourself together. Come back tomorrow ready to work or I'm going to have to let you go."

Lily nodded and took off her apron and her tennis shoes. She went into her bag and slowly put her shoes on while Beverley rinsed out the glasses and glared at her.

"You got another delivery," Beverley said.

Lily looked up from adjusting her shoes and groaned.

"I told the guy to take them back."

"Thank you."

Beverley sat down on a stool near the counter.

"Do you want to talk about whoever is sending you the flowers?"

Lily shook her head.

"Are you in trouble, Lily? Is someone hurting you?"

"No. It's not that. It's just someone who . . . likes me. Or thinks they do. Or something."

"Approximately five thousand flowers over the course of a few months . . . yeah. Sounds like they might be at least slightly interested."

"Thanks for the time off."

"Can I give you a suggestion?"

Lily stopped buttoning her sweater but didn't speak.

"Don't just go home to your cat and cry yourself to sleep," said Beverley. "Talk to somebody. Try to work this shit out. I don't know what's going on, but I know you need help."

Lily left. She didn't give two thoughts to anything Beverley said about talking to someone. She had two episodes of *Jeopardy* waiting for her at home. And she was in the middle of two online crossword games with some random people she met online. So she was shocked when she heard her own voice telling the taxi driver to take her to Penn Station.

The screen door still had a long, jagged rip right in the middle. Lily wondered how much it would cost to replace it. Was it still ripped because he couldn't afford to fix it? Or because he just didn't care? Lily opened the door and looked for a doorbell. To the right, a buzzer was hanging by a wire. She tried to stuff it back in the fixture and press it, but nothing happened.

She walked back to the curb and looked up at the house. There was a naked bulb hanging down in a room with no blinds or curtains. She could clearly see a closet door, half open, with several men's dress shirts hung up neatly inside. As she looked around to see if she could make out anything else, the front door opened. A young woman with a heavy round belly opened the door fully and looked Lily up and down.

"Is James here?" Lily asked.

"Yeah." The woman didn't move.

"Can I come inside?"

"Who are you?"

"I'm his . . ." Lily looked up and then back at the woman. "I'm his child."

The woman put her hands on her belly and glared at Lily.

"James don't have a daughter."

"I didn't say I was his daughter. I said I am his child."

The woman stood in the doorway, not moving. Lily pushed past her and started up the stairs.

"He doesn't like to be disturbed while he's eating!" the woman yelled from the bottom of the steps.

Lily held her breath when she walked past the bedroom that used to belong to her. For five awful seconds, scenes flashed through her head that she worked every single day of her life to suppress. She got to the last bedroom in the hallway and opened the door without knocking.

The man was sitting on the side of his bed, a plate of food settled on a rickety card table pulled up to him. He was using his fork to mash lumps out of what looked like potatoes. The smell of whatever was on his plate made Lily gag. Lily walked over to the tray and took the fork out of his hands and picked up the plate.

"What is this shit, Daddy?" Lily said, sliding the paper plate into an empty trashcan and setting the whole thing outside the room.

"It *was* my dinner."

"Who's the pregnant chick?"

Lily's father pretended he didn't hear her and walked over to the window.

"I didn't hear you drive up."

"I took a cab."

He turned around and looked at Lily for the first time.

"You don't have a car?"

"I live in Brooklyn."

"They don't have streets in Brooklyn?"

Lily sat down in a wooden chair near the door. She reached into her bag and pulled out a white plastic bag.

"Here. Brought you something."

Lily's father held up his hands and Lily threw the bag in his direction. She threw it overhand and it sailed past her father's head and landed on top of his bureau. Her father stood up and shook his head as he went to pick up the bag.

"You throw like a girl."

Lily dropped her head and laughed quietly.

"Well."

Lily's father sat back down on the bed and pulled out the oversized pretzels in the bag. He put one on his tray and bit into the other, closing his eyes and moaning with pleasure.

"Extra butter, no salt . . ." he said, his eyes still closed.

"The other one's extra salt no butter," Lily said.

The two were quiet for several minutes. The only sound was

Lily's father chomping on his pretzel and occasionally grunting his approval.

"Be even better if it was still warm," he said.

"How are you?" Lily asked.

Her father worked a piece of the doughy pretzel out of his teeth and glared at her.

"That's not why you're here."

"Why isn't it?"

"You only come here when you need something. I guess you'll come when I'm dead. But that will only be out of obligation."

Lily inspected her shoes.

"I'm not dead. So what do you want?"

"I'm not sure."

Her father picked up the other half of the pretzel, peeled off a piece and bit it, chewing carefully.

"If I had to guess, I'd think you were having some problems with your . . . situation."

"And what if it was that? What would you say?"

Lily's father shrugged. "Hell if I know."

He shook his head for a few seconds. As if he were reliving some tricky moments in his child's life that he'd rather forget.

"When did you know?" Lily asked. "About me."

Lily's father peeled off another piece of pretzel but didn't eat it.

"You know why pretzels are shaped like this?" he asked, laying out the bread on a napkin on his bed.

Lily shook her head.

"Came from leftover dough at a monastery. The monks baked bread. And they didn't want to waste the dough left over from a loaf of bread. So they rolled it out and then they folded it over. They decided to cross the ends of the dough over, so that it would look like a person praying with their arms folded across their chest. See that?" He held up the pretzel to show Lily and she nodded. He tossed the pretzel back on the bed and scratched the back of his head.

"I prayed a lot when your mother was pregnant with you. After

James Junior died, I thought having another baby right away made sense. I wouldn't leave your mother alone. She was still a mess. Walking around blubbering. Crying out for Junior in the middle of the night. Last thing she needed was me trying to mess with her. But I thought it would help settle her. She didn't even know she was pregnant with you until she was five months along."

Lily felt a chill. She knew the room was warm, but she still felt like she was being slowly submerged in ice water.

"I knew she was gone the minute she started calling you Junie. That was our special name for Junior. You popped out and just like that, she started calling you Junie like James had never died. Like he just regressed back to a newborn baby and she gave birth to him again. I think your mother really, truly thought we had somehow traveled back in time four years."

Lily's father stood up and went to the window. He kept his back to Lily and she could see only the side of his jaw working on the last bit of his pretzel.

"I came home early from work one day and your mother was sitting in the kitchen, sipping an empty coffee cup. A pot of coffee was burning and the smoke alarm was going off. After I waved the smoke away and it stopped ringing, I heard you. You were in the back bedroom *screaming*. You hadn't been changed or fed since I did both that morning before I left for work."

He slipped his hands into the back pockets of his pants and let his shoulders slump.

"I quit my job that day. Had to stay home until you were old enough to go to a sitter."

"How'd you know what to do with a newborn baby?" Lily asked.

"I didn't."

There was more quiet. Lily began to get restless. She didn't want to pressure her father to speak. But the quiet was becoming thick and uncomfortable. Now that he was done with both pretzels, he was just standing at the window, still and stiff.

"Daddy?"

"I knew right away," he said. "You were probably eighteen months old. Maybe less. We were at ShopRite and I had you in the cart. Every time I pulled up to a section, you would grab at something and I'd have to take it away. We got to the floral area. I wanted to get something nice for your mother. You grabbed a flower and held it up to your face." Lily's father turned around and his face was ashen.

"You smiled at me," he said. "With that flower held up to the side of your head. It was like you were imitating something a girl might do. Except you weren't imitating . . . You just . . ."

"I just what?"

"I've never thought of you as my son," he said. "Not since that day. I *know* women. And no matter how low I kept your hair cut. No matter how many times I took you out to tee-ball or flag football . . . you just. It was like . . ."

"I know . . ." Lily said.

"Your mother always said it was her fault. She wasn't in the right frame of mind when she got pregnant. She didn't take care of herself while she was pregnant. And she wasn't there mentally when you were born."

"That has nothing to do with—"

"And then when you were about eleven or twelve, I took you to a pediatrician for a checkup and he said he wanted me to get some bloodwork done for you."

Lily felt his father's demeanor change. What had been a light, conversational tone became halting. Like he wanted to purge but was afraid to.

"Why?"

"He just said there were some parts of your body that seemed . . . feminine."

"What?"

"They did this test. Brought me in and told me about Klinefelter syndrome."

Lily felt like she had been punched in the gut. She'd read about the chromosome disorder, where men had an extra X chromosome that resulted in infertility and sometimes a softer, rounder physique. But she never thought it applied to her. At thirteen, Lily already had small, round breasts, the same size as the thirteen-year-old-girls in her class. And years later, when she transitioned, she noticed that every man in the plastic surgeon's portfolio had to get huge breast implants. Lily went up exactly one cup size.

"How come I don't remember you telling me this?" Lily asked.

"Because I didn't."

"Why not?"

"I knew years before then that you were going to turn out to be a woman. What difference did some test make?"

"Do you hear yourself? What *difference* would it make? I was down the hall in that dingy-ass bedroom, trying to figure out how to get up the nerve to slice my wrists because I felt like a freak, and you're sitting on a medical explanation because *you* already knew?"

Lily pushed her chair back roughly and it hit the wall and then fell over.

"I didn't say I did the right thing," Lily's father said. "And looking back, I will admit that I never really considered what you might be going through. You just always seemed so certain of who you were. Even when you still had . . . your parts. It didn't matter. You were who you were from the very beginning."

"It would have been very helpful to hear this from you ten years ago. You could have saved me a lot of pain."

"Joseph?"

Lily looked up, despite herself.

"Here's what I do know. You were born a girl. You just happened to have some boy parts. I spent your entire life wishing you'd hurry up and get yourself fixed so you could just be who you were supposed to be in the first place."

Lily picked up the chair and set it upright before slumping into it.

"So you think I'm normal."

"Hell no. You're a freak of nature. But you're still a girl."

Lily scratched her head and absorbed her father's words. He came back to his bed and sat on the edge, this time on the side facing Lily.

"Sorry about the whole no-grandkids thing," Lily muttered.

"Eh. I'm having a kid in a few weeks. I'm old enough to be his great-grandfather."

"That's kind of gross, Dad."

"I know you brought me another pretzel. Let's have it."

Lily dug inside her bag, pulled out the last pretzel, and broke it in half. She handed one praying monk's arm to her father. Then she shrugged her shoulders and sunk her teeth into her own.

37

Ras refused to live at the house in Jamaica without his wife and daughter, so he wandered the country for weeks, staying at hotels and then flying back and forth to New York whenever the feeling struck him, which was often. His hair was beginning to become overgrown, like an untended lawn. And his beard was rivaling Jake's in thickness and in unkemptness.

Cleo called him daily. He either ignored the call or answered it and cursed her out until she hung up. He in turn called his wife daily. She just ignored the calls.

In New York at the beginning of June, Ras took a car service from his hotel to the Midtown studio he'd been working in for several weeks. He was having a hot streak. A few remixes he'd done had some chart success and suddenly his phone was ringing more than usual. Sometimes the artists would come down to the studio in Jamaica. But ever since Josephine left, he was just as likely to come to New York instead. The engineer and a few assistants came into the studio talking nonstop.

"Bunny in today?" Ras asked the engineer.

"Supposed to be."

"But?"

"Heard she's been missing a lot of days in the studio. Having some . . . issues."

Ras shook his head. He hated to see someone so young falling prey to the temptations in the music industry. Ras just hoped Zander wasn't following too close behind her.

Ras went to the console to cue up some music for he and

Bunny to write to. An hour later, Bunny rushed into the studio, flustered and unkempt.

"I'm sorry, Ras," she said, peeling out of a light jacket.

Ras noticed immediately that Bunny kept rubbing her nose. *Coke? Already?*

"You alright?" asked Ras.

"I'm fine," Bunny snapped.

"Are you sure . . ."

"I came here to work," said Bunny. "Can we make some music?"

For the next three hours, Ras and Bunny worked on two songs, completing one of them entirely. Every twenty minutes, Bunny disappeared into the bathroom and came back out as high as a kite. Ras said nothing and just focused on the music. As she sat with her back hunched over the table writing, Ras glanced at her face a few times. She was gone. Ras knew the signs well.

"Okay, I'm done," said Bunny. "I need to get out of here."

"I think we had a good session," said Ras.

Bunny nodded and avoided looking directly at Ras.

"Bunny, can I talk to you for a second?" Ras said, pointing to a chair. Bunny hesitated. And then sat.

"I don't want to get into your business . . ." he began.

"So don't."

"Z is a really good friend of mine," said Ras. "We've worked on a lot of music together over the years."

Bunny nodded.

"And Zander is a good kid. He has his issues. But he's a good kid for the most part."

Bunny's face was stony.

"I just want you to think about the influence you're having on him."

"Are you serious?" Bunny asked.

"Very."

Bunny stood up.

"You? You're trying to tell me about being a good influence

on someone? Your side chick wrote a book about your relationship. You cheat on your wife in front of the whole world and
you're trying to tell *me* about being a good influence on someone.
That is hilarious."

"You don't have to listen to a thing I say," said Ras. "Just think
about it. That's all I'm asking you to do."

"With all due respect, Ras. Stay in your lane."

Bunny left the studio and Ras stayed behind, adding some
extra elements to the work they'd done. He wished he hadn't said
anything to Bunny. Who was he to counsel anyone about anything? If Bunny wanted to flame out when her career was at its
height, so be it. But it would be a shame if she had to take Zander
down with her.

Ras went back to his hotel to get his luggage and prepare
to go back to Kingston. He stuffed clothes into his duffel bag
and thought about what hotel he would stay at when he got
home. Eventually, he was going to have to sell the house and
find a permanent place to stay. But for now, the nomadic life
suited him.

His cell phone began ringing nonstop while he took a quick
shower; he ignored it. When he got out and cinched a towel
around his waist, he checked the phone. Josephine had called him
eight times in a row.

Reina.

That was his first thought. There was no way Josephine
would call him like this unless there was something wrong with
the baby. Actually, he thought, as he stabbed the numbers on the
phone, there was no way she would call him at *all* unless there
was something wrong with the baby.

Josephine picked up on the first ring.

"Ras, you need to come."

"What's wrong?"

"The baby . . ."

Ras heard Josephine choking back tears, trying to keep herself
composed.

"What's wrong!" Ras yelled. "Where are you?!"

"I'm at the hospital. I can't explain everything right now. You just need to get here."

"Josephine," Ras pleaded. "Tell me Reina is okay."

"She will be," said Josephine. "She needs a blood transfusion and I'm not a match. She has a rare blood type. We're going to have to get in touch with her biological parents right away."

Ras sat down hard on the bed.

"A transfusion . . ."

"Do you know how to get in touch with . . . you know . . . them."

Ras stared at his reflection in the mirror of the hotel bathroom.

"I don't," said Ras. "But I know who does."

Ras hung up the phone and went downstairs to get a taxi to the airport. As soon as he was settled in the back seat he took out his phone. He dialed Alex's number and waited. He started speaking before she could even say hello.

"Did you look for Reina's mother?"

There was silence on the line.

"Alex!"

"Yes, Ras."

"I said did you look for Reina's mother?"

"I . . . I wasn't gonna . . . I just . . ."

"It's okay, Alex. Please tell me. Did you find Reina's parents?"

"They live in Saint James Parish now. Her name is Amelia. His name is David."

"What's the address?" Ras said, digging in his bag for a pad of paper.

"I don't know. I didn't write it down. I went to this part of town where some people knew her. And I asked around and they led me to her house. I know it when I see it. But I don't know the—"

"I'm booking a flight for you," said Ras. "Right now. I need you to come to JFK. You have to take me to her."

"I can't do that! Not right now. I'm—"

"Josephine just called me. Something's wrong with the baby. She needs a transfusion."

Ras heard Alex take in a sharp breath.

"I'm on my way."

38

Jake kept his eyes glued to the therapist. At every appointment, there was usually a few moments of dead space. She would just stare at him until it was uncomfortable. Jake would usually say something—anything—to break the silence. This time he was determined to see how long she would go without saying anything.

"So it only happened once with this young lady Bunny . . ." the doctor said.

Jake smiled, amused that he'd gotten her to speak first.

"Yes. And it will never happen again."

"And how do you feel about that?"

Jake looked up at the ceiling. How did he feel about that? He still felt guilty, first of all. If Kipenzi knew that he'd messed with Bunny, of all people, she'd be crushed. Bunny was trying hard to be Kipenzi's major competitor when she was alive. And now in death, of all the people in the world he could have, he let himself get mixed up in someone like Bunny.

"I'm fine with it," said Jake. "Now that it's over."

"How are you doing with the drinking?"

Jake held up his water bottle.

"Same."

"Do you think this is something you should deal with?"

Jake stood up. "I'm done."

"With our session? We still have twenty minutes to—"

"Nah, I'm out. For good. There's nothing else you can help me with."

"Do you feel like you've worked through your—"

"No," said Jake, his teeth clenched. "I haven't worked through shit. My wife is still dead. I'm an alcoholic, and I'm about to be the oldest rapper in recorded history."

"I'm here if you ever want to schedule an appointment," said the doctor. She stood up and put her notebook on her chair.

Before he could think twice about it, Jake squeezed his water bottle, hoisted it up, and threw it across the wall opposite where the doctor stood. It exploded and the smell of alcohol quickly filled the air.

The doctor jumped and then moved to stand behind her chair.

"I'm calling the police," she said.

Jake realized he was breathing heavily and still felt he needed to throw something else. He needed to release. He needed to turn that sofa over and hurl it out of the window and onto the street. He needed something to make him *feel*. He was suddenly the person from the Brevoort projects who never missed an opportunity to lose his temper and destroy anything in his path. But he'd left that man behind long ago. Until that moment.

The therapist reached behind her to pick up the phone without taking her eyes off Jake.

"You can leave now," said the doctor. "Or you can be escorted out. And I will press charges if you're here when the cops get here."

Jake moved to the wall where he'd thrown the bottle and picked it up.

"I'm sorry."

The doctor's face softened and she hung up the phone.

"Please leave," she said, pointing to the door.

"Back to the house?" said his driver when Jake climbed into the back seat.

"Yeah."

His driver turned onto Seventh Avenue toward the Holland Tunnel while Jake stared at the skateboarders zipping down the street, twisting their bodies from left to right. Jake was used to things moving fast. That was the main reason why he couldn't see the therapist anymore. He wanted her to just cure him in a session or two and be done with it. None of this drawn-out conversing with no real solutions.

Jake dug his phone out of his pocket and checked for messages. There was one. From Z.

"Me and Zander are on our way."

Jake took a deep breath, put his chin in his hands, and watched the city speed by.

Jake remained standing as the door creaked open and the young man he considered his nephew walked in with his father, Jake's best friend.

Jake sat on the sofa and Zander and Z sat in chairs positioned on either side of him.

"What's up?" Z asked. "You dropping both of us from the label or something?"

Jake grimaced.

"Never that."

"So?" Z asked. "What's going on?"

"I had a situation," he said. He looked from Zander to Z and back again. "With Bunny. It's over now. But I needed y'all to know about it. I was out of line and it got completely out of control before I could—"

Zander took a few steps toward where Jake sat on the sofa.

"For real, Uncle Jake? Word? That's how you get down?"

"There's a lot of things you don't understand," Jake said, standing up but making sure to keep his voice low and even.

"What is there to understand?" Zander screamed. "You fucked my girl?! What else is there to understand?"

Z didn't speak. He just sat in his chair, his eyes darting back and forth between Jake and Zander.

Jake looked down at the floor for just a second. And that was all the time it took for Zander to catch him off guard and punch him squarely in the face.

"Yo, are you crazy?" Jake said, grabbing Zander by his shirt and shaking him. Jake threw Zander to the floor and held him down with his forearm bearing down on his chest. Z jumped up and grabbed Jake from behind, trying to peel him off Zander. Even though Jake had Zander completely pinned from the waist up, Zander still struggled to get up, kicking his legs in the air.

"Calm down, Zander," Jake said, pressing his arm harder on Zander's chest. "Let me talk to you for a second."

"Jake, get off him," said Z. "Y'all gotta talk this shit out."

Jake felt Zander's body go limp underneath his arm. He let go of Zander and gave him a look. Nephew or no nephew, he would hurt him if he hit him again.

Zander sat up but stayed seated on the floor.

"I've known you all my life," Zander said. "You were the only person I trusted when my dad was—" Zander stopped and glanced at his father and then back at Jake. "And you do this?"

"Zander, what I did was foul," said Jake. "I'm man enough to admit that. But I want you to think about who you're trying to fight. We're bigger than this."

"Oh, so because you're family, I'm supposed to let this go? Is that what you're saying?"

"Yeah," said Jake. "I know it's gonna take some time. But you're going to get over this."

"Stay away from Bunny," Zander said.

Z spoke up.

"Don't tell me you're gonna stay with this broad," said Z. "You heard what Jake just told you and you're going to keep messing with this chick? If she'll do this to you, she'll do any-thing. *Anything.*"

Zander stood up and brushed himself off.

"Don't worry about what I'm doing with Bunny. I just want Jake to leave her alone."

Jake sighed.

"Fine, Zander. Whatever."

"And I want to get released from my contract," said Zander, making direct eye contact with Jake.

"Now that's something we gotta talk about at another time."

"You can get the lawyers on it today," Zander said. "I don't want anything to do with you or your label."

Jake rubbed his face.

"You want off the label? I'll let you off the label. What else?"

Zander's response was to storm out the front door and slam it behind him. Z and Jake stared at each other.

"I'm going to go talk to Zander," said Z. "You need to get your shit together."

"Look, I came clean with this shit," said Jake. "Bunny is toxic. He shouldn't be messing with her anyway."

"So what are you saying? You think you did him a favor?" asked Z.

"I'm not saying that," said Jake. "But he needs to know the type of chick she is."

"The only thing you did was show Zander who *you* are," said Z.

An hour later, Jake was at the W Hotel, sitting at the bar. He watched Lily out of the corner of his eye. She was just coming on duty, chatting with a friend. He turned his head slightly and watched her walk into the kitchen. She came out and took her place behind the bar, then looked up and saw Jake staring directly at her.

"Hey," Jake said.

Lily moved back a step, her eyes darting back and forth.

"Hey, Jake," Lily said. "I'm actually on my way out. Just finishing up for the night."

"You're lying," said Jake. "You just got here."

"No, I was coming off break. Now I'm off."

"Why do you keep lying to me?" Jake asked. "What did I ever do to you?"

"Nothing," Lily said. "I'm just really busy."

"A while back . . . you took care of me."

"You needed someone to take care of you. I happened to be here."

"I need someone to take care of me right *now*."

"I can't help you."

Jake picked up his drink and watched Lily carefully while he drank it. He set the empty glass down and Lily took it away and came back with a refill.

"What time do you get off? And don't lie."

"Jake," Lily pleaded. "Can you please just leave me alone?"

"What do you think I'm going to do to you?"

Lily leaned over the bar and wiped down the surface in front of Jake.

"Look," she whispered. "I made a mistake by coming to your house that day. I should not have done that. Totally inappropriate. Now please. *Go*."

Jake stared at Lily. Lily sighed and came around the bar and led Jake to a seat in the back of the bar area.

"What do you want?" Lily said.

"I just want to talk," said Jake, his words beginning to slur.

"So talk, then."

"I messed around with Bunny," Jake said.

Lily's eyebrows creased.

"Bunny who? The singer?"

"Yeah."

Lily nodded.

"Okay."

"Not okay. She's dating Zander, who is signed to my label. And he's my best friend's son. They're pissed."

"As well they should be."

"I'm closer to Z than anyone else in this world. And Zander is like my son," said Jake.

"So why would you do it?" Lily asked.

"That's what I was hoping you could tell me."

Lily shook her head slowly.

"I can't help you with this one, Jake."

Lily stood up and Jake stepped close to her. A few people in the bar craned their necks to see what Jake was doing. Lily slipped away and began to walk back toward the bar, with Jake right behind her.

"Come to my spot when you get off," said Jake. "I'll send a car to get you."

"No."

"I'm not accepting no."

Lily looked up at the ceiling.

"Fine. I get off at midnight."

"Perfect. A car will be here for you."

"Fine," said Lily. She went back behind the bar and kept her back to Jake.

"I'll see you later."

Lily grunted. Jake went back to the penthouse and showered. At midnight, he came out of his bedroom and went into the living room to wait for security to let him know Lily was on her way up. An hour later, his driver called his cell phone.

"I went inside to find her, but they said she was gone for the night," he said to Jake.

"No problem. Thanks."

Jake took out his cell phone and sent Lily a text message.

"I'll leave you alone."

Then he deleted her number from his phone and tossed the phone on to his couch. He actually convinced himself, for an hour or so at least, that he was never going to contact her again.

39

Z waited patiently for Beth to start snoring softly. It seemed as if it had taken forever for her to drift into a deep sleep. But he knew it only felt that way because of the task at hand. Z stayed on his back, breathing in and out. He practiced his corpse pose from yoga to pass the time before he had to act.

This was going to test his sobriety and his faith, two things he'd worked on considerably since he got clean. He'd known there would be obstacles. He was expecting the boys to hate him. He was expecting Zander to behave like a fatherless child. He expected his boys not to understand the new him and just stay away. He even expected his music to suffer, which it had.

Zander turned to face his wife. Not her. He never thought she would betray him. But he had every reason to believe she had. Her demeanor for the past few months had not just been about adjusting to Z's life—it was guilt. Z knew it when he saw it.

Z leaned in close to his wife's face. Her eyes were moving back and forth quickly. She was in as deep a sleep as she was going to get. Zander got up, went into the master bathroom, and dug out a box underneath the sink. He quickly skimmed the instructions and took out a cotton swab.

It was easier than he thought to get Beth's mouth open. He turned her over slowly onto her back and her mouth fell open. He swabbed the inside of her cheek, pulling away and sinking down to the floor as soon as Beth moaned and turned over to her other side. Z stayed put on the floor, holding the swab carefully in the air. When he was sure she was asleep, he crept back into the bedroom and sealed the swab. He quickly swabbed his own cheek and placed it in the container. He took the last swab and went out into the hallway. He was reading the label on the box and didn't see Zakee until he ran right into him.

"What are you doing up?" he whispered.

"Getting something to drink. What's that?" said Zakee, pointing to the box in Z's hand.

"Nothing. Go back to bed."

Zakee glared at his father. Z thought there was going to be a showdown and he was ready. His son had had more than enough chances to be disrespectful. Now it was time to start disciplining his ass when he got out of line. He could continue to hate his father if he wanted to. But he was going to have to respect him.

"I said go back to bed," said Z.

"I'm getting something to—"

"Don't talk back to me," Z spat. "Get your ass back in the bed and go to sleep."

Zakee skulked away and slipped into his bedroom, shutting the door behind him. As soon as his father walked past his room, he opened the door a crack and watched him. As Zakee watched, trying to see where his father was going, he saw something out of the corner of his eye. Right in front of his door was a folded sheet of paper. It looked like something that came out of the box his father had been carrying.

Zakee crept out into the hallway, snatched the pamphlet, and went back into his room, closing the door extra softly and not exhaling until he heard the click. Zakee scanned the paper and his heart started to pound. He went back to his door and flung it open, not caring about making noise. Which bedroom had his father gone into? He didn't know and he wouldn't be able to figure it out without getting caught.

Zakee went back to his bed and sat down. He slowly ripped the paper into tiny bits and then dropped them into the wastebasket next to his bed. He stayed in bed but didn't fall asleep.

Back in his bedroom, Z gathered all three cotton swabs and

placed them in the envelope. Z put the envelope into the minisafe that he kept under his bed and locked it. He wanted to read the directions once more but couldn't find the sheet of paper that had come inside the box.

Three days and he'd have an answer. He'd know if his wife had committed the ultimate betrayal. If his instincts were right, what would he do? Z had no idea. Part of him thought he might lose control and attack her, physically and mentally. Part of him thought he'd drop to his knees and cry. He had three days to prepare either way.

The next morning, Z got a text from Jake. "Let's meet up at the studio. 3PM." Z sighed. He knew he wouldn't be able to avoid the tension with Jake forever. After the dustup with Zander over Bunny, they'd avoided each other. But Z knew that the man who'd had his back since he was a teenager wasn't going to just disappear.

A part of Z wished that he'd been the one to reach out first. The whole situation with Jake and Bunny was ridiculous, and he really didn't know how to deal with it. He wasn't sure he could look Jake in the eye after this one. And he couldn't help but think of Kipenzi and how she would have felt about the whole thing.

"I'm going to the studio," Z told Beth over breakfast.

Beth just nodded and got up from the table, not looking at Z.

"And after that I'm going to the moon."

"Okay," Beth said.

Z shook his head, threw on his coat, and walked out.

At the studio, Z was buzzed in and headed down to the basement where Jake always recorded. And there he was, decked out in a sweatsuit from his own line, brand-new Air Force 1s on his feet.

They slapped palms three times and Z sat down hard in a nearby chair.

"What's going on?"

"That's what I was about to ask you."

A silence hung in the air as they each waited for the other to speak.

"How's Zander?" Jake finally asked.

"Heartbroken. Pissed off. Hurt."

Z looked his friend in the face.

"How could you do that to him?" Z asked.

"I don't know."

"Is this what you wanted to talk to me about? Because I'm done with the whole thing."

"No. I'm selling my stake in the label."

"Where'd this come from?"

"It's been coming for a while. I'm tired of this life. I see why Kipenzi wanted to retire. I thought she was crazy and that I would want to do this forever. But I don't."

"So why are you telling me?"

"I just wanted to tell all the artists on the label personally. Don't want you to hear it in the press."

Z nodded.

"I'm about to be put out to pasture myself," said Z. "I think I got one or two albums left before I apply for Social Security."

Jake tried to smile.

"Okay, so you're bailing on the label and I'll probably get dropped," said Z.

"It doesn't have to work out that way," said Jake, his eyes focused somewhere on the wall behind where Z sat.

"But it will work out that way and that's fine. I'm okay with that. Moving right along."

"What else?" Jake asked, his eyebrows raised high.

"You know what else," said Z. "Zander wants your head on a platter. And I don't blame him."

Jake just looked at Z blankly.

"Yo, that's your nephew!" Z said when Jake didn't speak up quickly enough.

"You think I don't know that!" Jake said, standing up. "I know the shit was wrong. It happened once. Now it's over."

"It's not over for my son."

"He'll get over it," Jake said.

"I gotta go," said Z. "I'll get at you later."

"What else is good with you, Yoga Boy?" Jake asked.

Z thought about what to say. There were a million things he would have talked about with Jake in another space and time. How deep his disappointment was for Jake, how much he wanted him to stop drinking, his crumbling relationship with Beth, the test results he was waiting for that could change his life . . .

"I'm good," Z said.

Z left the building feeling empty. He knew his relationship with Jake, his lifelong friend, was changed forever. They'd always be cool. But as far as Z was concerned, Jake wasn't the man he once was. Like most men, Z compartmentalized his feelings and never gave too much power to his emotions. He wasn't going to bemoan the end of his friendship with Jake like some lovesick girl. But he had to admit—at least to himself—that it hurt.

Bunny did a thirty-day stay in rehab and called Zander from the car before she even got back home. He came out to the house in Connecticut immediately and stayed there for the weekend. They weren't back together. But Zander couldn't exactly walk away from her when she was so vulnerable. The plan was to help her get used to being sober and then move on.

And then he found out about Jake. And instead of wanting to kill her, he wanted to possess her. He wanted to prove to Jake that he could hold on to Bunny. When he confronted her about Jake and she melted into tears, Zander was satisfied.

He knew all the reasons why he stayed. The sex was good. He'd never been in love before. Her stubborn, dangerous side turned him on in ways he couldn't explain. Zander was embarrassed by his love for Bunny. It was wholly consuming and without reservation. She could have slept with his father and he would have forgiven her. The relationship reminded him of his parents'. His mother had endured countless affairs and kept a stiff upper lip. Because Z always (eventually) came home to her. Zander had often ridiculed his mother for letting Z run all over her. And now, here he was, letting Bunny make a complete fool out of him.

Zander never actually said they were back together, but it was just understood. Bunny started coming by the hotel almost every night when she wasn't performing. And Zander had started traveling with her again for out-of-town gigs. A few weeks after they reunited, Zander was in Los Angeles with Bunny for a show.

"Slow down," Zander said, holding on tight to the door handle as Bunny sped down the Pacific Coast Highway.

"Relax," Bunny said. She took one hand off the steering wheel and squeezed Zander's leg.

"I'll be relaxing in a graveyard if you don't keep your eyes on the road."

"After the show tonight, we should drive up to Napa Valley," said Bunny. "It'll be fun."

"I need to get back to New York."

"Forget about New York. Why are you in such a hurry to get back there?"

"Because that's where I live."

Bunny took her eyes off the road again and glanced at Zander.

"I'm moving, Zander," Bunny said quietly. "And I want you to come with me."

"Moving where?"

"Here. LA. We're here all the time anyway."

"I'm not moving," Zander said, as he watched the highway soar by outside his window.

"Can you just think about it? I feel like we need a new beginning. You're still living in a hotel, for God's sake."

"This is because of Jake. You want to start over because of him."

Bunny kept her eyes on the road and gripped the wheel tight. Whenever Zander mentioned Jake, which was often, Bunny tensed up.

"You didn't have to take me back," said Bunny. "You could have dumped me and kept it moving."

"Is that why you want to move to LA? To get away from Jake?"

"It's all of that. It's Jake. It's your dad. It's the label. I just want to shed all the bullshit. It's summer. I'm clean. I'm sober. And I want to go into the new season with a fresh start."

Zander wasn't mad at the idea of a fresh start. But LA? What would he do out there? Follow behind Bunny like a lovesick puppy? He could always record in LA. But it didn't feel the same as being in New York.

"I'll think about it," Zander said.

Bunny put her right hand on top of Zander's and pushed on the gas. As soon as she passed a rest stop, the whirring lights of a police car came up fast behind them.

"Shit," Zander said. "You see what I'm talking about?"

Bunny put her hand to her chest and tears welled up in her eyes.

"Zander, oh my God."

"It's not that deep. You'll get a speeding ticket and keep it moving."

Bunny faced forward, keeping her head stiff as she waited for the officer to approach.

"License and registration please," said the officer.

Bunny reached over and popped open the glove compartment. She took out her registration and handed it over.

"License?"

Bunny turned to the back seat of the car and rooted around for her purse. Zander exhaled. She had so much stuff in the back seat of the rental that it looked like she lived in there. It was no wonder she couldn't find her license.

"Here you go, officer," said Bunny, her voice breaking.

"Are you okay, young lady?" the officer asked.

Zander had been wondering the same thing. Bunny was sweating bullets and her hands were shaking. Zander noticed her jaw was clenched tight too. And she looked like she was about to burst into tears. All this for a speeding ticket? Zander sighed.

"I'm . . . I'm fine, officer."

"I'm going to have to ask you to step out of the car," the officer said. "Both of you."

"Bunny, what the hell is wrong with you?" Zander whispered as he opened his car door.

In minutes, three squad cars had squealed up to where Zander and Bunny sat. The officers joined the first cop in searching the car thoroughly.

"Whose bag is this?" said one officer. He held up the Louis Vuitton bag Zander took on every trip as his carry-on.

"It's mine," said Zander.

"Does this bag belong to him?" the officer asked Bunny.

"Yes," said Bunny, nodding.

The officer stepped to Zander.

"Please turn around."

"What?!"

One of the officers turned the duffel bag over and dumped it out. On top of the underwear and tube socks was a small plastic baggie.

"Oxycotin, marijuana, heroin, ecstasy, Percocets, and a gram of coke."

Zander's jaw dropped and he turned to look at Bunny. She had her head down, her eyes on the ground.

"You're under arrest," said the office, clicking the handcuffs onto his wrists. "For possession of controlled dangerous substances."

"That's not mine," Zander said.

"I know, son," said the officer. "It's your bag, but it's not your drugs."

"Ma'am, we're transporting him to central booking," the officer said to Bunny.

"His bail will be set by ten p.m. if you want to bail him out."

Zander's heart beat wildly in his chest. He'd had a chance. He'd had a chance to leave Bunny. To be rid of her forever. His father had told him to get rid of her. Uncle Jake had warned him. Even his little brother told him that she wasn't to be trusted. But Zander went back every single time.

The first officer who arrived was the one who put his hand on Zander's head and guided him into the car. A bright bulb flashed and Bunny ran back to the car so she couldn't be seen.

The photographer got a shot of Bunny's leg. But the real money shot was Zander, the R&B star, son of one the greatest rappers alive, with his head just visible above the car window. It was

306 ALIYA S. KING

a crystal-clear shot and Zander knew with no uncertainty that those pictures would be published before he could even make it to the station.

As the police car began to cruise down the highway, the car approached Bunny's car. Bunny was talking to another officer and nodding her head slowly. The cop driving Zander slowed down to talk to the officer standing next to Bunny's car. Zander and Bunny could see each other clearly.

Bunny opened her mouth to speak. But she only mouthed a few words.

I'm so sorry.

Before he could even process what she said, Bunny was gone, driving down the Pacific Coast Highway without him.

At the station, a throng of photographers waited and the officer who arrested him put a jacket over his head and slipped him in through a side door.

"Thanks," Zander said.

"No problem," said the officer. "Have a seat."

They started to process Zander and he felt numb. All he could think about was what exactly happened in that car. He played everything in slow motion from the moment they got pulled over.

Bunny had been a nervous wreck and Zander didn't know why. She went into her glove compartment and got her registration. She reached back into the back seat to get her bag . . .

It all finally dawned on him. Zander shook his head and smiled. She'd taken her baggie out of her own bag and put it in his. It had only taken her three seconds while she was pretending to root around for her purse.

Zander instantly thought of Marion Barry. Years before Zander was born, Marion Barry, the mayor of Washington DC, had been caught smoking crack in a hotel room with a prostitute. The grainy video had an image of the man running down a hallway, pipe in hand, screaming, "That bitch set me up!"

Jake and Z had shown the video to Zander when he got older

and the three of them would fall out laughing every time they got to the part when he shouted out, "That bitch set me up!"

Sometimes, for no good reason, they would say it at odd times for laughs. Like in a bathroom stall at a restaurant or while waiting on a ride at an adventure park. It got old quickly, but they never stopped doing it.

Zander shook off the memories as the officer pulled him up by the arm and led him to a cell.

Zander surveyed the other guys in the cell, figured out the hierarchy, and took his place on the floor in a corner. He fixed his face tight. His mind instantly went back to something his father told him in Jake's apartment.

If she'll do this. She'll do anything.

41

Birdie put one hand on his forehead and tried to explain himself one more time.

"I know my wife hired you to decorate the tree," said Birdie. "But Christmas is still six months away."

Leslie flittered around the living room, throwing white tinsel on a twenty-foot tree in the corner of his living room.

"Your wife paid in advance for my services, Mr. Washington. And she had strict instructions. She wanted a full dress rehearsal for Christmas in summer. And then, no matter what, she wanted the tree up before Thanksgiving."

Birdie slumped on the sofa and threw his head back.

"That's because she thought we would be spending the holidays *together*," said Birdie, his eyes closed.

"I'm just following orders," said the designer, setting up a ladder to get up to the top of the tree to place the star.

"Look at that," said Leslie, from the top of the ladder. "I must say, I do good work."

Birdie opened his eyes.

"It's . . ."

Leslie came down the ladder and looked over at Birdie.

"You like?"

Birdie's eyes wandered up to the top of the tree. Every single ornament was white. It looked as if there had been a massive snowstorm right there in his living room.

"It's . . . interesting."

"I'll be back tomorrow to dismantle it. I need to take pictures first and make sure everything is in place. Live with it for a night. Let it marinate. Tell me if you want any changes in the morning."

Leslie packed up and left Birdie alone in the house with the tree. Birdie felt like it was mocking him and letting him know just how lonely he would be when the holidays finally did roll around. It was easy to be single in the summer. It was warm outside and he hung out at the pool in his backyard all day. But who was he going to celebrate Christmas with? His parents would be in the Caribbean, where they went every year. His siblings were scattered throughout the country. And he was married. He was supposed to be with his wife and daughter. Alex was still in Brooklyn and it didn't seem likely that she would magically forgive him and come back before Christmas. Birdie shuffled up the stairs and went into the bathroom to shower and get dressed. No matter how melancholy he was feeling, he had to get to work.

Birdie was antsy. The studio was the one place where he always felt at peace. But this time it wasn't happening. In fact, *nothing* was happening. He'd come into the studio with all kinds of ideas for songs he wanted to write. But now that he was in the booth and the engineer was playing the beats, nothing was coming out.

"Turn up the beat again," said Birdie. He flipped his notebook to a fresh page. He tapped his feet and nodded his head with his eyes closed. The beat was fast-paced, he'd have to rhyme twice as fast as he usually did to catch it. But what to rhyme about: His wife leaving him? Not seeing his daughter in weeks because Jen was bugging out? The all-white Christmas tree the interior designer had just trimmed? The checks getting larger and larger with the more albums his debut sold? None of that felt right. It was the first time in his life that what he was experiencing in the real world didn't feel like it would make a decent record.

Birdie saw Travis, Daryl, and Corey through the glass and waved them in.

"Let's hear some new shit, superstar," said Travis, rolling a thick blunt packed with weed.

"There is no new shit," said Birdie. "I'm blocked."

Travis clapped him hard on the back.

"There's no room for being blocked," he said. "You've got one album under your belt. You can't wait to get started on the next one. And then the one after that . . ."

"Thanks," Birdie said, rolling his eyes. "That's exactly what I need to hear right now."

"This happens all the time on that second album," said Corey, taking a drag on the blunt. "You don't have the same hunger you had the first time around. And don't forget, you worked on the first album for years. A lot of time to get your material together."

Corey leaned over to pass the blunt to Daryl, skipping Birdie, who didn't smoke when he was working.

"Let me hit that," Birdie said suddenly.

Travis and Daryl exchanged a glance. Corey shrugged and passed it over. As soon as he inhaled, Birdie's eyes dropped to slits and he felt a warm tingling sensation spread out from his lungs to his hands and feet.

"I gotta get my wife back," Birdie said, his words slurred.

The guys exchanged another look.

"I don't see that happening," said Travis.

"I don't see me finishing this album if it doesn't happen."

"Since when you need a woman to write rhymes?"

Birdie shrugged.

"Besides y'all, Alex is really the only person that's been down since day one. With her out of the picture, it just feels weird. I don't need her to write rhymes. But the fact that she's gone feels like a sign that I'm off track. Next thing you know, the four of us we'll be going our separate ways."

Travis blinked.

"You just need a break, superstar. Take some time off and it'll come back to you."

The blunt came back around to Birdie and he inhaled again.

He closed his eyes to steady himself and not end up falling over onto the floor.

"You better take it easy, Birdie . . ."

"I'm good," he said, keeping his eyes closed.

Travis leaned over the mixing board with a notebook in hand.

"I wrote a rhyme about all the women we met on tour. Something light. Maybe you can build off this and add on to it."

Birdie tried to focus on the writing on the paper. He read it through twice. It was good. Better than anything he'd been able to come up with in weeks.

"This could help," Birdie said, holding on to the notebook. "Thanks."

Birdie stood up and threw his headphones on the mixing board. He packed up his knapsack and headed toward the door.

"I still feel like I need something to *happen* in order to write," said Birdie. "My life is stale right now. I've never been into lyrics that talk about how much money I got or the cars I drive or any of that."

The weed made Birdie cough hard until Travis had to clap him on the back.

"So what has to happen?" asked Travis.

"I don't know," said Birdie. "I'll know when it happens."

Travis and Daryl looked at each other, and even though he was high, Birdie caught it.

"What's going on?"

"Nothing," said Daryl. "We can talk about it later. You got shit on your mind."

Birdie sat down. "Come on."

Travis cleared his throat.

"It's not that deep," he said. "You know I always wanted to start my own management company. Well, I'm branching out. I'm taking on some new clients."

Birdie nodded. "Good for you." He turned around to face Daryl.

"And you?"

"I'm taking an A&R gig at Interscope."

Birdie lifted an eyebrow. If he hadn't smoked, he might have felt something.

"Oh, so we're really splitting up."

"Hell, no," said Travis. "We just all trying to get on your level."

"Well, that's what I want for y'all too. It's all good. You're finally giving me something to write about. My whole crew is falling apart."

Birdie laughed and the guys chuckled nervously.

"It's all good," said Birdie. "It's allll good."

Birdie threw up a peace sign and left the studio.

On the ride back home, Birdie kept thinking about this ridiculous Chips Ahoy commercial that always made Tweet laugh. The cookies were alive, singing along to a song while speeding along in a convertible. Then, out of nowhere, a hand comes from the sky and plucks the cookies out, one at a time. That's how Birdie felt. Like he was a cookie in a convertible, about to be plucked up by some higher power.

"I really am high," Birdie whispered to himself as he pulled into the cul-de-sac. Back at home, Birdie threw his backpack on the white sofa in the family room and slumped on the sofa. The house was too big without Alex and Tweet in it. Without them, it was stale. Just what was he supposed to—

A smooth, thin arm locked around Birdie's neck and squeezed.

"Don't move, sweetie," said a squeaky voice behind Birdie's head. "This will be quick."

Birdie heard some rustling and whispering behind him. It was a woman. And there were at least two other women with her in the house. Did they just break in? Had they gotten into the house and waited for him? What the *hell*, Birdie thought to himself. I'm getting robbed by a *woman*?

For a half-second, Birdie thought of trying to overpower her. He could tell from the grip around his neck that she was tiny. He felt like he could flip her right over his head and onto the floor. The woman must've felt his body clench up because Birdie felt the cool touch of gunmetal at his temple.

"I said this would be quick," the woman said.

Birdie closed his eyes. *Thank God, Tweet's not here,* he thought. In minutes, the arm was lifting him to his feet and walking him into the kitchen.

Birdie started counting in his head for no good reason. It just seemed like the thing to do. He couldn't imagine she would shoot him. For what?

Birdie waited for whatever would happen next. And as he waited, he got more and more angry. He'd told Alex he wanted to get a gun for protection and she'd put her foot down. The fact that a gun would not have stopped him from getting robbed didn't change his mind. Maybe when they left, he could have chased after them and squeezed off a few shots.

I'm getting a gun as soon as this is over.

The butt of the gun hit the back of Birdie's head as soon as he completed the thought. He fell in a lump to the ground; three women stepped over his crumpled body and made their way out of the back door.

42

The moment Zander's flight landed from Los Angeles, he slipped his hand into his bag and turned his cell phone on. Hiding it from the flight attendant, he obsessively checked his text messages until he saw one from his father:

"I'm at baggage claim."

Zander exhaled and sat back in his seat and closed his eyes as the plane taxied to the gate. Even though he'd only spent a single night in jail, he could still feel it all over him. His father's attorney in LA had bailed him out, and a court date was set. Z and Beth flew out the very next morning and stood next to him as he pled not guilty. A month later, thanks to his father's relentless attorneys and a healthy dose of good luck, Zander was semifree. Five years of probation and a year of mandatory drug counseling and he was free to return to New Jersey—under one condition that he was more than happy to agree to. When the plane finally pulled to a stop, Zander didn't jump up to get his luggage out of the overhead compartment the way he usually did. He stayed in his seat as the other passengers struggled to get a head start on the bottleneck toward the exit.

"You plan on staying for a while?" a flight attendant said with a smile.

"I'm not in a hurry," said Zander.

When the last passenger began walking down the aisle, Zander stood up and got his bags. He walked slowly, deliberately, looking out of the windows of the plane where a torrential rain was coming down. At the front of the plane, the pilot stood in the doorway of the cockpit and smiled at Zander.

"Pleasure having you aboard," said the pilot.

"You don't know the half," mumbled Zander.

In the terminal, Zander walked slowly. Every few steps, he'd feel eyes on him. A group of girls at a fast-food restaurant pointed and took camera pics. A woman manning the cash register at a newsstand did a double take as he walked by.

Zander felt like he was shedding a second skin as he made his way to the escalator. People would always stare. For a long time, people would recognize him, for a variety of reasons. But he knew he'd be able to control how he felt about it.

The driver of his dad's Suburban came around to take his bags and put them in the trunk. Zander climbed into the back seat.

"Hey, Dad," he said, shaking his father's hand.

Z nodded and gestured to the driver to leave. For thirty minutes, father and son sat in absolute silence. The driver was on the New Jersey Turnpike, at exit 11 before Z cleared his throat.

"You think you're doing the right thing?" he said to Zander.

Zander nodded.

"You don't have to do what *I* want you to do, Zan," said Z.

"I know."

Father and son remained on opposite sides of the back seat, each staring out of his own window.

"Have you spoken to Bunny?" Z asked.

"She called," said Zander. "I haven't spoken to her."

"Are you going to?"

"No."

Z turned to face Zander.

"I'm sorry you had to go through all of this to see her for who she really was."

Zander shrugged.

"Everybody warned me. Don't have anyone to blame but myself."

"Jake's attorneys sent the paperwork releasing you from the label."

Zander nodded.

"And you know you'll be able to get another deal whenever you get ready."

"Nah, I'm done."

"I'm just saying you don't have to be. You're still young. You can do whatever you want to do."

"I know."

More silence. The driver turned off at exit 9 on the turnpike and drove onto Route 18.

"I've been a mess for just about your entire life, Zander," Z said. "That feeling of failure never goes away for me."

Zander held his breath, praying his father wouldn't start crying. Everything was too intense anyway. He couldn't deal.

"I feel like I let you down in a lot of ways too," said Zander.

"Fresh starts all around."

The driver pulled up to a large building set back from the street and stopped directly in front of the door.

"You ready?" Z said.

Zander nodded and climbed out.

It was intensely quiet and the air was cleaner. The soft crunch of gravel under Zander's feet was the only thing he focused on as he followed his father to the front door.

The door opened before Z could knock or ring the doorbell and a tall black man with gray streaks on either side of his jet-black hair ushered him inside.

"Good to see you, Z," said the man, pumping his hands.

"Dr. James," said Z, smiling. "Always good to see you. This is my son, Zander."

"It's nice to meet you, Zander," said Dr. James. "I've heard a lot of good things about you."

Zander looked down at the floor and mumbled a thank you.

"Your father was my star pupil. I'm sure you'll follow in his footsteps here at Rutgers."

"I plan to."

Dr. James handed over a package to Zander stuffed with paperwork.

"I'm the dean of student life here. If you have any questions about anything, come see me. You don't have a lot of time to prepare. Summer session starts in two weeks and you need to choose your courses and register."

Zander accepted the package and nodded.

"Your father told me you wanted to stay on campus . . ."

"Yessir."

Dr. James handed over a magnetic card reader and a key.

"We'll see how this works out. I have you in Campbell Hall. Most freshmen share a room or a suite. But I finagled a single room for you. I thought it would be better that way."

Zander felt his heart beating harder in his chest. The campus of Rutgers University was only thirty miles away from his home. An hour away from the Parker Meridien, where he'd lived for almost a year. He'd criss-crossed the country, performed for crowds, released an album. And nothing had scared him as much as being on a college campus.

"You can walk to the dorm from here," said Dr. James. "Follow the trail at the back of the house until you come to the courtyard. You'll see signs."

Z and Zander walked in silence from the back of Dr. James's home toward the courtyard.

"Your mom is going to send all of your stuff this week," said Z.

"Cool."

At the entryway to the dorm, a group of young kids stood around talking. They fell silent when Z and Zander walked up to the door.

"This is Campbell?" Zander asked, looking up at the building.

One of the guys, who obviously recognized both of them, nodded his head without speaking. They moved to the side so that Zander could open the front door. Before the door closed behind him, Zander turned back around.

"I'm Zander," he said, offering his hand to one of the guys staring at him.

"Ethan," the young man said.

"I'll check y'all later," Zander said.

The group exchanged looks and went back to talking, this time softly, barely above a whisper.

"This is *not* the Parker Meredien," Zander said with a laugh, as soon as he opened the door to the musty room on the second floor overlooking the courtyard. Z sat down on the hard bed and bounced on it a few times.

"You want me to ship you a new bed?"

Zander laughed.

"Nah, I'm good. It'll be a constant reminder of where I could be. In jail."

Z stood up and looked around the barren room. The walls were made out of white cinder blocks and there were stray marks where taped posters once hung.

"I've been in jail cells that looked better," Z mumbled.

Zander smiled and thumbed through the course catalog.

"I'm going to get back on the road," Z said.

Zander stood up.

"Thanks, Dad."

"You can come home whenever you need to. I hear college food is horrible."

"I'll live."

Zander took a step toward his father and quickly hugged him, clapping him once on the back and then stepping back, looking away. For an awkward moment, they mumbled "good-byes" and "see-you-soons."

Zander offered to walk his father back downstairs, but he brushed him off gently.

"Get yourself settled," said Z. "Here, take this."

Z pulled a small box out of his bag and Zander took it, turning it around in his hands.

"What's this?"

"I think you might need it."

The first thing Zander did when his father left was sit down on the bed and open the box. It was a cell phone. Zander's eyebrows knitted. Why would he need a new cell phone? As he turned it around in his hands, his own cell phone rang. He picked it up to check the Caller ID: *Bunny.*

Zander stared at the phone as it rang. Her photo came up. She had her knees drawn up to her chest with her head hanging to one side. Zander had taken the picture of her at the beach last summer. The strap to her bathing suit was hanging off one shoulder, showing a deep tan line.

When the phone stopped ringing, Zander turned it off. He opened the new phone and called his father.

"Yup," Z answered.

"Who has the number to this new phone?"

"Just me and your mother."

"I need this."

"I thought you might."

Zander hung up and began cleaning up his new room. He found garbage bags in a hall closet and filled it with stray papers, random things left behind by the last tenant, and finally, his old cell phone. He heard it ringing—Bunny's personalized ringtone—as he carried the bag into the hallway. Zander knocked on the door of the residential advisor.

"Hey, good to meet you," said the advisor. "You moved in okay?"

"Just need to know where trash goes."

"Trash chute. Third door on your left."

Zander nodded.

At the trash chute, Zander looked down. He grabbed the garbage bag and stuffed it down the chute. He could still hear Bunny's first single playing as the bag fell to the bottom.

Back in his room, Zander found the sheets his dad had

brought him from home and made up his bed. He peeled off his boots and jeans and sat cross-legged on the bed, his back against the wall with the summer session course catalog in his lap.

For two hours, he pored over the catalog, choosing classes and making up his schedule. When he was done, he closed the catalog, tapped his pencil on the cover, and stared at his new schedule until his eyes started to burn.

43

A nurse came into Birdie's hospital room and started her morning routine of poking, prodding, and drawing blood.

"Any word on when I'm getting out of here?" Birdie asked, staring at the ceiling.

"We're waiting for a clearance from the neurologist," said the nurse. "Your concussion was severe."

"I don't have amnesia," said Birdie. "I know my name. I remember exactly what happened. I'm ready to go."

The nurse smiled and packed up her supplies.

"Doesn't work that way. I'll be back a bit later."

Birdie grunted and then turned on the television. He started to fall asleep during a mindless sitcom and didn't hear the knock at his door.

Birdie opened his eyes and saw Alex standing in the doorway. He sat up as best as he could and waved her in.

"Hey," she said, sitting on the edge of his bed.

"Hey," Birdie said back.

"Are you okay?"

Birdie shrugged.

"Bruised ego mostly. One thing to get robbed. Another thing to get robbed by a gang of party chicks who prey on idiot celebrities who invite them to house parties."

"What'd they take?"

"Everything not nailed down," Birdie said. "Very organized."

Alex exhaled.

"Feeling better?"

"I'd be a lot better if I had my wife back."

"I just came to make sure you were okay."

"I'm fine."

Alex pulled loose threads off his blankets. They were silent for a long moment.

"I miss you," Alex finally said.

Birdie didn't respond. He knew he didn't need to.

"I haven't forgiven you," said Alex. "But when I heard about what happened, I had to see you."

Birdie nodded.

"And now what?" Birdie said. "You see I'm not dead. I'm going to live. Now what?"

Alex stood up.

"I guess now I go back home."

Before Birdie could protest, a doctor came into the room with a clipboard.

"We just heard back from the neurologist," said the doctor, flipping through some paperwork. "She's satisfied with your progress and she's referring you for discharge."

Birdie exhaled and sat up.

"Thank God."

"You're not one hundred percent yet," said the doctor. "You're going to need someone at home to help you out for a while."

The doctor glanced over at Alex.

"I have that taken care of," Birdie said.

"Good," the doctor said, smiling. "You'll have some papers to sign, one more round of observations, and you'll be discharged in the morning."

As soon as the doctor closed the door, Alex stood up.

"Who's going to take care of you?" she asked.

"I'm sure I can get Travis to come by once in a while. And Dylan is always showing up."

Alex nodded.

"I can take you back to Jersey in the morning," Alex said. "If you want me to."

"I don't want to go to Jersey," Birdie said.

Alex gave Birdie a look.

"You want to come to Brooklyn?" she asked.

"Yeah," Birdie said. "I do."

Everything about their old house was perfect. Birdie loved hopping over the missing step on the way up to the porch. He loved the etched glass windows and the little tiny foyer where he and Alex would wait for a rainstorm to slow down before venturing out. He loved the heavy banister leading up to the second floor. Everything in the new house in Jersey felt sterile and cold. This place felt like home. Tweet's drawings were tacked up everywhere. Her growth chart was scribbled on the wall near the kitchen. And dozens of Alex's cover stories were hanging up all over the house.

"Are you okay here all by yourself?" Birdie said, stepping gingerly into the living room and lying back on the sofa.

"I'm fine. Jennifer brings Tweet by sometimes when she needs a break."

"Wait," Birdie said. "My ex-wife brings my child to see my current wife? But she won't bring her to see me. That's insane."

Alex shrugged. She pulled some pillows out of a hall closet and propped them up under Birdie's neck. She pulled his shoes off and moved his legs onto the sofa.

"Birdie, I'm scared for you," Alex said. "People breaking into your house? With guns? What kind of life are you living?"

"Alex, don't concern yourself with any of that. Just know that when you come back home, you'll be protected. I'll make sure of that. This won't ever happen again."

Alex made a face.

"Just because I brought you back here doesn't mean I want you back. I love you. And I want to be with you. But you've hurt me one too many times. I can't go back there with you."

"So you're going to take care of me for a few days and then send me on my way?" Birdie asked.

"Yes."

"Why bother?"

"Because I feel like pretending," Alex said.

Birdie stood up and grabbed Alex's hands, forcing her to her feet as well. He picked her up and walked toward the staircase.

"Birdie!" Alex said. "You should be resting. And you should not be picking me up!"

"Did you put on a few pounds?" said Birdie, as he came to the top of the stairs, breathing heavily.

"Damn you, Birdie, I have!" Alex said. "You didn't have to say anything."

"I couldn't help but notice. You almost broke my back."

Before Birdie could come up with another joke about her weight, Alex was on him, pushing him back onto the bed and lifting him up just long enough to get his shirt off.

"Is this okay? Are you in pain?" Alex said.

Birdie shook his head.

"I'm okay, baby."

Her kisses were more intense than Birdie remembered. Usually, she didn't open up to Birdie until he forced her to let go. But this time, he had to hold her arms and tell her to wait so that he could get his pants off.

Finally, they were both naked and curled up in bed. Alex clasped her hands around Birdie's back and squeezed hard. He squeezed back and then turned her on her back and moved inside her.

Alex's moan was so low and guttural that it almost scared Birdie at first.

Birdie moved faster inside Alex, holding her shoulders and pushing in as far as she would let him. Alex rolled over onto Birdie and sat on top of him, rocking him the way she always did.

It was his favorite position and Alex knew it. She would sit up on him and just rock him back and forth. He'd feel himself moving inside of her and the sensation was always more than enough to make him come within minutes.

"Hold up, Alex," Birdie groaned. "Hold up one second—"

"No, baby," Alex said. She shook her head back and forth. "Let it go . . ."

Alex continued to rock, ever so slowly, until Birdie couldn't hold back anymore. They collapsed, falling asleep together almost immediately.

Three hours later, Birdie sat with his back against the headboard. Alex had her head in his lap. There wasn't a sound: no television, no music. Just the soft breathing coming from both of them.

"You trying to send me back to the hospital?" Birdie asked.

Alex sat up and chuckled.

"Are you sure you're okay?"

"I'm fine. It was a concussion. No big deal."

"I wish we could go back in time," Alex said.

"Alex, we can't. But you can move forward with me."

Alex was silent. They both fell asleep with their thoughts unsaid.

Birdie stayed with Alex for a week. On a rainy Saturday afternoon, he told her he was going back home the next day. Alex just nodded. The next morning, Birdie and Alex bumped around the house like they had a one-night stand the night before. Birdie tripped over the footboard. Alex threw him a towel that missed and hit the floor.

"So I'd better go," said Birdie, after he was showered and dressed. He rubbed the back of his head, where he still had a lump. "Travis is coming to take me back to Jersey."

Alex looked up from her laptop.

"Alright, Birdie. Take care of yourself."

"Take care of myself?"

Alex looked up.

"Yes. Take care of yourself."

Birdie paused. He wanted to drag Alex back to Jersey by her ponytail. But he was in the wrong and there was no way around it. They could have sex a million nights in a row and she still wasn't taking him back.

"Can I get you some coffee before I go?"

Alex smiled.

"I'd like that a lot."

Birdie whipped out his phone and began texting a message.

"What are you doing?" Alex asked.

"I'm getting Travis to bring some coffee," said Birdie. "Don't worry, I know how you like it."

Alex held up a hand and shook her head.

"I don't want coffee that you get someone else to fetch. I thought you were going to make me a cup. The same way you have for ten years."

"What difference does it make?"

Alex sighed.

"If you don't know," she said, "I can't tell you."

"Alex, let me ask you this," Birdie said. "Are you even considering coming back?"

"No," Alex said, with no hesitation.

"Because I won't make you a cup of coffee?"

"No! Because you don't even understand why little things like that matter to me. It just tells me who you are. And you're not the man I married."

Birdie thought better of defending himself. He began to walk toward the door.

"Alright," he said. "I'll see you later."

The house in Jersey seemed three times as big as the night of the robbery. While he was at Alex's house, he'd arranged for twenty-four-hour security and beefed up all the alarm systems in the house. There were cameras installed around the perimeter of the property. Anything over twenty-five pounds coming across his lawn would trigger a call to the local police department. Birdie felt safe. But empty.

He'd really believed that recuperating at Alex's house in

Brooklyn would bring them close enough to get back together. He wasn't done trying. But coming back to the house alone felt like a major setback.

Birdie walked throughout the entire house, stopping in each room and glancing around. Upstairs, he went into his daughter's bedroom and sat down on her bed. He'd barely seen Tweet in the past few months, except for a few awkward overly supervised visits at Jen's house. And he had never gone longer than a few days without seeing her since the day she was born.

Birdie took out his cell phone and flipped to Jen's number. He ended the call before it rang and turned his phone off. For the rest of the evening, he wandered around the house aimlessly, opening and closing bedroom doors and checking and rechecking the alarm system.

He felt the pain in the back of his head begin to throb. Birdie dug into his knapsack for his pain pills. He sat on top of the kitchen counter, head down, hands folded, waiting for the medicine to kick in.

R ight here," Jake said to his driver.
 "Are you sure you don't want security?" the driver asked
Jake. "I can have someone here in five minutes."

"I'm good. I'll text you."

The driver looked around warily.

"I'm going back into the city," said the driver. "Call me
twenty minutes before you're ready."

Jake smiled. He got out of the car and pulled his baseball cap
low on his head. He walked past a group of guys playing a dice
game in front of the nondescript building in Bushwick.

Jake never thought it would be so hard to find out where Lily
lived. Usually, he could give a name to a friend in the NYPD
and have an entire dossier on whoever he wanted within a day or
two. But Lily's name didn't come up in any databases. He finally
had to get someone to bribe her boss at the W to get her real last
name. With that, he was finally able to track her down to Bushwick.

Jake hadn't been this far up Knickerbocker Avenue in ten
years. Bushwick felt like another country, not just a part of
Brooklyn a few miles away from his penthouse. He checked his
phone, took a quick swig from his flask, and walked briskly into
the lobby. It was thrilling to be out in public with no bodyguards.
Just moving in silence, the way he did when his life was so much
simpler. He walked past a group of rowdy teenagers who didn't
even notice him, bypassed the elevator, and took the stairs up two
flights to apartment 202.

And then he wasn't sure what to do. Suddenly, he felt like an idiot, showing up unannounced at the apartment of some random chick he didn't know from a hole in a wall. A chick who had gone out of her way *not* to let him know where she lived. Or even her real last name. What if she was married? What if she had a bunch of kids? What if she lived with her parents? Jake stood in front of the door, trying to decide what to do. His hand decided for him and rapped on the door before his brain could protest.

Someone opened the door with the chain still on it. Jake saw an almond-shaped eye peek through the opening. There was a shriek and the door slammed shut.

"Lily," Jake said to the door. "Come on."

The door cracked open again.

"Jake?"

"Yeah."

"What are you doing here?!"

"I was in the area?"

"Go away."

Lily started to push the door closed and Jake pushed back.

"Are you married?" Jake asked.

"No," said Lily, still pushing the door.

"Then why can't I come inside?"

"Because I didn't invite you here!"

"But now that I'm here, you might as well let me in . . ."

Lily opened the door as far as the chain would allow.

"Jake, please. *Please*. Just go."

"Not unless you give me a really good reason."

"I don't have one," Lily said, her voice cracking.

Jake moved back from the door, turned up his flask to his mouth again, and then folded his arms over his chest.

"Then I'm not leaving."

For twenty minutes, Jake stood at Lily's door. First, he just leaned against the wall, head down, observing people entering and leaving their apartments. Every few minutes, he turned up his flask until it was empty. Occasionally, he would hear her come to the door.

"I'm still here," Jake would say.

"I'm calling the police," Lily finally said.

"Okay," said Jake. He sat down on the floor.

Lily unlocked the chain and opened the door.

"Get in here," she said, looking up and down the hallway.

Jake held out his hands. Lily put her hands in his and pulled him up to his feet. He stumbled into her apartment and rubbed his eyes.

"Why's it so dark in here?" he said, holding in a burp.

"Because it's late."

Lily turned on a light in her living room and led Jake to a sofa. She sat across from him in a red leather chair and sighed.

"So now what?"

Jake looked around. Lily's apartment was immaculate. The hardwood floors gleamed and there was a distinct smell of clean laundry. Her living room was tiny but expertly decorated. One wall was completely covered in vintage frames with black-and-white photos inside. A large painting of brightly colored sea life hung above the sofa.

"Did you do that?" Jake asked, pointing to the painting.

Lily nodded.

"You have anything to drink here?"

Lily shook her head. Jake licked his lips and took off his hat.

"So. I wanted to see you."

"You're looking at me," Lily said.

"I mean. Not like that. I wanted to spend time with you."

"So you track me down and camp out at my apartment?"

"That's not how I usually do it."

"How do you usually do it?"

Jake scratched his head.

"I guess I don't usually do anything."

"Yeah. I remember. You just dial a number and the women show up at your house."

"You want to get something to eat?" Jake asked.

"Are you seriously asking me out on a date?"

"Yeah. I am."

"Come in here," Lily said.

She stood up and walked into her kitchen. A small Formica table sat in the middle of the floor with two chairs with red vinyl seats tucked inside. Lily gestured to the table and Jake sat. She opened the refrigerator and began taking out Tupperware containers.

"You're serving me leftovers?" Jake asked.

Lily shot him a look and Jake threw up his hands. "I'll take it."

Lily bustled around the kitchen for a few minutes, finally coming to the table with two plates heavy with rice and beans, baked chicken, macaroni and cheese, and candied sweet potatoes.

Jake picked up his fork and Lily grabbed his wrist.

"That's not how it's done here," she said. Lily put her palms out and Jake took her hands. She bowed her head. She looked up at Jake and gestured for him to speak.

"Um, thanks, God for the . . . the food," Jake mumbled. "Amen."

Lily put a napkin in her lap and began to eat. She pointed to Jake's plate with her fork.

"I want your opinion," she said.

"You didn't make this," Jake said, stuffing forkfuls of food in his mouth.

"Not only did I make it all, I *grew* the sweet potatoes myself," Lily said. She stuck her tongue out at Jake.

"Whatever."

"I farm a little plot of land a few blocks over. Me and a few of my friends grow lots of stuff."

Jake nodded and continued eating. When he was done, Lily took his plate to the sink and washed the dishes while he watched.

"You really don't have anything to drink here?"

Lily threw up her hands and then got on tiptoe and opened

a cupboard over her refrigerator. She brought down a bottle of Hennessy, poured a shot glass, and set it down in front of Jake. He tossed it back immediately.

"You're not going to join me?" Jake said, reaching for the bottle to pour another shot.

"No."

Jake hesitated. Then he shrugged and drained the glass.

"Okay, Jake," Lily said. "You've had dinner. And drinks I shouldn't have given you. Now I need you to go."

"It's still early," Jake said.

"I have to get up in the morning."

"To work at a bar?"

Lily closed her eyes.

"I do more than just work at a bar."

"What are you going to do after I leave?"

"Some yoga. Meditate. Watch television. Then go to sleep."

Jake stood up from the table and carefully tucked his chair underneath. He felt something he couldn't quite name. It was the buzz of the alcohol as always. But there was something else. Being in this small space felt warm and comforting. He didn't want to go back to his own apartment, twenty times bigger with all its creature comforts. He wanted to stay in Lily's orbit for as long as she would let him.

"I wanna stay here," Jake said. "And do some yoga. And meditate. And watch television . . ."

Lily stared at Jake.

"And go to sleep," he said.

Two hours later, Jake and Lily were folded into the full-sized bed that took up more than half of the space in her bedroom. The walls were sky blue and there were fluffy white clouds painted on the ceiling. Lily's bed was all white—the wooden frame and all the linens, pillows, and comforters. The whole room was the size of a closet in Jake's apartment, but he was more than comfortable.

"Lily?" Jake whispered.

There was no sound. His entire body was sore from the stretches she'd put him through in their impromptu yoga session. He'd never known his body could move that way. And he wasn't sure he liked it. She tried to get him to meditate, but he fell into laughter every time they were silent for more than ten seconds. Lily said they would try it again when he was sober.

After watching late-night news, Lily went into the bathroom and came out wearing sweatpants and a tank top. She went into her bedroom without saying anything, leaving the door open. Jake took off his sneakers and laid on top of her bed in his clothes. She was asleep immediately. Eventually, Jake stripped down to his T-shirt and boxers and climbed under the covers. As soon as he turned to his side, he felt Lily relax her body into his. She wrapped his arms around her waist and held his hands.

"Lily?" Jake asked again.

"Hmmmmm . . ."

"The food was good."

"Mmmmmhmmm . . ."

"And I really like your place."

Lily opened one eye and yawned.

"Jake, go to sleep."

"Thank you for letting me stay here tonight."

Lily didn't answer. In a few minutes, Jake could tell she was back into a deep sleep. Jake held Lily tighter and tried unsuccessfully to fall asleep. Six hours later, the sun was peeking through the windows and his eyes were still wide open. He texted his driver and then felt Lily stir. He rolled over to let her out of bed.

"You sleep okay?" Lily asked, throwing her legs over the side of the bed.

"Like a baby," Jake lied.

"Good. I would make you breakfast, but I really have to go. And so do you."

Jake pulled on his clothes and slowly laced up his sneakers. Lily walked him to the door of her apartment and opened it.

"I know where you live now," Jake said.

Lily held back a smile.

"Good-bye, Jake."

Desperation was not a feeling Jake was accustomed to. It was so new to him that he had some trouble identifying it at first. All he knew was that he felt like Lily wasn't trying to see him again. And that wasn't an option he wanted to entertain. But he felt helpless. Was that the same as desperation?

"So. I'll call you later."

Lily didn't reply, nod, or even smile.

Jake took one step away from her door, and it closed firmly behind him. He heard several locks being put in place. And by the time he got to the stairwell, he was almost positive that Lily wasn't thinking about him at all.

His driver was right in front of the building when he stepped out of the lobby. He slipped into the back seat and watched the street as the car sped away.

"Stop at the first liquor store you see," said Jake.

The driver nodded and pulled over a few blocks later. By the time he got back home, Jake was comfortably smashed. Ian had to come down to the garage to help him up to the penthouse. He drank off and on for the rest of the day, skipping work and several meetings. That night, he called Lily. There was no answer. He called her several times throughout the night. She never picked up or called back.

45

The only sound in the hospital room was baby Reina babbling. Ras was slumped in an uncomfortable chair closest to the door, as if he wanted to be able to dash out at any moment. His legs were outstretched and crossed at the ankle. His eyes were shut and he looked like he was fast asleep, although he was far from it.

Josephine refused to sit, no matter how many times Ras told her she was making him nervous. She stood up, her back to Ras, playing soundlessly with the baby in her crib. She covered her eyes and then mouthed the words *peek-a-boo* over and over as the baby giggled. Next to the crib, Alex sat, her eyes on the ceiling. Ras had no idea why she insisted on coming to the hospital, but he hadn't been able to stop her. He was so grateful that she had helped him find Amelia and David that he didn't put up any kind of fight. Ras opened his eyes and took a quick look at Amelia. She sat facing the window, her back toward everyone in the room. The doctor had told her she could wait in another room until the blood test was completed. But she insisted on meeting Ras, Josephine, and the baby. Ras had been petrified. What if she took one look at Reina and decided she wanted her baby back? Even though it would be legally impossible, Ras didn't want Josephine to deal with any kind of drama. She'd been through enough. Alex cleared her throat and everyone turned around and looked at her.

"Sickle cell is not a death sentence," Alex said. "I have a cousin who was diagnosed at about this age."

Josephine nodded. Ras and Amelia were silent.

"The doctor said as long as she can get regular transfusions with the right blood type, she'll be fine."

Josephine kept her eyes on the baby but turned her head slightly to speak.

"Hopefully, Amelia will be willing to donate . . ." she whispered.

The young woman turned from the window and looked first at Josephine and then the baby.

"If I'm a match, I'll donate every day if I have to!" the young woman said, her voice strained and high-pitched.

Josephine put her hand to her mouth and moved across the room. She hugged the woman tight. Josephine pulled back and then put her arms on the young woman's shoulders.

"I want you to be a part of Reina's life."

The young girl shook her head.

"No," said Josephine. "I mean it. When Reina first came to me, I wanted to pretend I gave birth to her and I never wanted to acknowledge your existence. But I feel differently now."

Josephine stole a quick look at Ras and then turned back to Amelia.

"I'm going to be a single mother," she said. "I want Reina to have as much support in her life as possible."

"Don't start this, Josephine," Ras said. "Not right now."

Josephine didn't respond to Ras. She kissed Amelia on the cheek and went back to playing with the baby. Ras leaned back and closed his eyes again. First, he had to get Reina well, then he would work on getting his wife back. Ras thought about what Amelia said. *If I'm a match . . .*

"You have to be a match," Ras said out loud. "They already tested David. He wasn't AB negative. The doctor said it was a rare type and that one of her parents has to have it."

Josephine nodded and looked over at Amelia.

"Well, then, that's it. I'm a match," she said softly, going back to her seat.

Ras felt the hairs on the back of his neck stand up.

"Can I talk to you outside for a moment?" Ras asked. Amelia looked up at him, terrified. He held her gaze and then walked outside the room, holding the door open. Amelia walked out of the room and Ras grabbed her arm.

"That man who came here and got tested. Is he the father or not?"

"Yes!" Amelia said, twisting to get out of Ras's grasp. "I told you I've only been with one man."

"You're lying. Who's the father? And why aren't we testing him?"

"Get off me!"

Amelia pulled away and walked quickly down the hallway. Ras thought about going after her but he didn't want to make a scene. Alex poked her head out of the doorway and then came outside, closing the door behind her.

"What's going on?"

"She's playing with my daughter's life," said Ras, pointing at Amelia. "She knows something and she won't tell me."

"Let's just wait for the results before we flip out," said Alex. "She said she would help. I believe her."

Ras paced the hallway, checking the time on his cell phone for no reason and stopping every so often to think. The worst part was that Ras didn't even know what to obsess about. He just had this nagging, raw feeling that something was *very wrong*. It was more than just finding out that Reina was sick. She had a diagnosis and there was an encouraging treatment plan. That would work out. He was sure of it. As for his relationship with Josephine, it could very well be over. And though he hadn't given up yet, Ras wasn't worried about that either. What he felt was an unnamed dread. Something he knew would affect all of them— Josephine, Ras, and Reina. Nothing specific came to mind. Just the knowledge that it was Not Good. Ras watched a woman in athletic gear and running shoes walk toward him with a bulging folder of paperwork.

"Mr. Bennett?"

Ras nodded.

"I'm Dr. Campbell," the woman said, holding out a hand to shake. "Excuse my appearance. I was on my way out when I was asked to look over your daughter's results. Is your wife in the room?"

Ras couldn't find words to answer. He was completely choked up and fearful about what this doctor was going to tell him. He just opened the door and waved her inside. Alex excused herself as soon as the doctor walked in. Josephine picked up Reina out of the crib and held her close, as if the doctor had come to take her away.

Dr. Campbell spread out papers across the empty bed and picked up one.

"Reina's biological father is not a match," said the doctor.

"So Amelia's a match!" Josephine said. "She's already promised us that she will donate blood as often as we need her to!"

Ras felt his eye begin to twitch. He walked over to his wife and grabbed her hand. He was certain she would shake him off. But she did not. She smiled, squeezed his hand, and then held it tight. The doctor looked down at the floor.

"We can't use Amelia's blood," said the doctor.

"Why not?" Josephine whispered. "Is she . . . sick?"

"We can't use it because Amelia is not a match either."

"That's not possible!" Josephine said, looking from the doctor to Ras. "What are you talking about?"

Ras wrapped an arm around Josephine's shoulders.

"Dr. Campbell, can you just please be straight and tell us what you're trying to say."

"Amelia is not Reina's mother."

A heavy pulsing started spreading across Ras's forehead. He couldn't hear anything the doctor was saying, but he saw her lips moving. Ras felt as if he were shrinking, all the way down to a tiny dust speck at his wife's feet. He tried to focus on breathing in and out. When he felt the blood rushing back throughout his body, he opened his mouth to speak.

"My grandmother . . ." Ras said, trying to find his voice. "My grandmother told me that Amelia gave birth to my little girl in this very hospital a year ago. And now you're telling me that's a lie?"

"She did give birth to Reina here," said the doctor. "I checked the records."

Josephine clutched the baby and threw her head back, and screamed: "Then what the hell are you talking about?!"

The doctor jumped and Ras tried to calm Josephine down.

"Mrs. Bennett, I didn't treat Amelia during her pregnancy. And I didn't deliver Reina. I called the doctor who delivered your daughter, and we're waiting to hear back."

"What do you *think* is going on?" Josephine asked.

"I think Amelia was inseminated with a fertilized egg. She gave birth to this baby. But she did it for someone else."

Josephine sat down hard on the closest chair and put her hand to her mouth. She closed her eyes and rocked back and forth for a few seconds and then stopped abruptly. Her eyes popped open and she looked at her husband.

"Find her," she said to Ras.

Ras grabbed his jacket off the back of the chair and walked out.

46

Jake sat up in bed, his hands on his mouth to keep from throwing up. It was hot in the room, but he was shivering. He tried to call for Ian, but no words would come. It had been a full day since his last drink and his attempt to detox was not going well.

He tried to swing his legs over the side of the bed, but his hands were shaking so violently that he couldn't support himself. He dropped back onto his back and stared at the ceiling. The room began to spin and he closed his eyes to stop it. His stomach flip-flopped and he leaned his head over the side of the bed and vomited. He expected to hear it hit the floor but when he looked over he noticed a plastic-lined pail on the floor next to his bed. It obviously wasn't the first time he'd vomited that day.

He rubbed his hands over his face and then heard the door to his bedroom creak open. For a moment, Jake felt guilty about Ian having to clean up after him. He opened his eyes to apologize to him. But it wasn't Ian.

The door opened completely and in walked Kipenzi, dressed in a T-shirt and cut-off jeans. She was there as clearly as everything in Jake's bedroom. Jake blinked. Kipenzi was still there, her hands behind her, clutching the doorknob. Her hair was in a messy ponytail—no weave—and her face was flawless, clean and smooth without a drop of makeup. It was Jake's favorite look for her—raw, natural, and everyday.

"Baby . . ." Jake croaked.

Kipenzi shook her head.

"What are you doing to yourself?" she asked, as she made her way to the bed. She sat down on the bed gingerly and took Jake's trembling hand.

"I know you can stop drinking, Jake. I know you can beat this."

"I don't know if I want to," Jake whispered.

"Can you do it for me? Can you just try for me?"

Kipenzi leaned over and kissed her husband's forehead and then bent down and hugged him tight. Jake drank in her smell, a light blend of soap and baby lotion. That was one thing that had slipped away from him—her smell. He'd almost forgotten how wonderful she always smelled. And here she was, holding him.

"Can you stay with me?" Jake said.

"Of course, I will," said Kipenzi, kissing him on the cheek and again on his forehead.

For an hour, Jake moaned, his head leaning on his wife's shoulders. He threw up twice, the last time just bringing up bile and blood. Kipenzi stayed near, humming a song Jake didn't recognize and holding him tight.

"I missed you so much," Jake said.

"I know," said Kipenzi. "I missed you, too."

Jake's throat closed up and he held his wife tighter and began to cry uncontrollably.

"How could you leave me, Kipenzi?"

Kipenzi didn't answer. She continued rocking him and holding him tightly to her chest.

Jake's stomach suddenly lurched and he pushed Kipenzi over so that he could throw up again. Kipenzi stayed nearby, rubbing his back.

"I'm sorry," Jake said. "I don't want you to see me like this."

"Please," Kipenzi said. "You think I haven't seen worse from you?"

Jake smiled weakly.

"You have to shake this off," Kipenzi said, still rubbing his back. "You can't destroy yourself like this."

"If you're not here," Jake said, "then I don't want to be here either."

"What are you talking about? I am here. And I'm not going anywhere."

Jake turned away from Kipenzi and stared at the bedroom wall.

"Look at me, Jake."

Jake shook his head. He couldn't take the intensity of the feelings that came with Kipenzi sitting right next to him. He'd dreamt nightly about seeing her again. And now here she was, as clear as a bell.

"Are you going to spend the rest of your life like this?" Kipenzi asked.

"Like what?"

"Mourning. Drinking yourself to death. Sleeping with anything that moves."

Jake fell silent.

"Jake, I didn't just marry you for who you are. I married you for the man I know you could and would be. What you're doing right now? You're not honoring me. You're disrespecting me. Don't downplay what we had by invalidating it now that things have changed. We're not divorced, Jake. I'm just dead."

Jake opened his mouth to speak and a chill went through his entire body. He closed his eyes. When he opened them up again, Lily sat next to him on the bed, her hands on his hands, replacing Kipenzi's hands that were there, in the same exact spot, seconds before.

"What happened?" Jake asked.

"I think you were hallucinating. You were talking to me as if I were Kipenzi. I think that happens when you're detoxing."

"Lily, you have to get me something to drink. Anything. Immediately. Please."

"I can't," said Lily. "I promised you I would get you out of this. And you're almost there."

"I don't *want* to be there. I just want you to get me something to drink."

Lily shook her head vigorously.

"You called me. And I came. And now I'm not going anywhere."

Jake rolled out of his bed, steadied himself on his feet, and pushed Lily away.

"I'm not responsible for what happens if you don't go."

Lily crossed the room, sat down on a loveseat under a window, and crossed her arms over her chest.

"I'm staying and I'm going to help you whether you want me to or not."

Jake tried to remain standing and found that it was too difficult. He got back in the bed and tried calling out for Ian. He slept off and on, waking up sometimes to vomit and sometimes to scream out his wife's name. Hours later, he slept. When he woke up, Lily was still there, sitting on the loveseat and reading a magazine. There was a knock on his door and he stood up.

Jake limped over to his bedroom door and opened it. Ian stood on the other side with a breakfast tray.

"Mr. Giles," Ian said, "I didn't expect you to be up yet. Good to see you walking."

"I need a drink, Ian. Now. Bring me whatever we have from the bar."

Jake turned away and started walking back to his bed.

"There's nothing here, sir."

Ian's eyes darted over to where Lily sat and then he quickly looked back at Jake.

"What'd you do?" he asked Lily.

"There's no liquor in the house," said Lily.

Jake summoned all the energy he had—which was not much—and charged across the room, snatching Lily up by her shoulders.

"I'll stop drinking when I'm good and ready."

With his hands squeezing Lily's shoulders, Jake clenched his teeth and stared her down.

"Ian, get me something to drink right now," said Jake, not taking his eyes off Lily.

"Yes, sir," Ian said. He set the breakfast tray down on Jake's bed and quickly left the room, closing the door firmly.

Jake let go of Lily's arms and clutched his side, a stabbing sensation kept him from standing up straight. He limped to the bed and sat down.

"Abdominal cramps are part of the process, too," said Lily.

Jake tried to keep himself from throwing up again.

"When Ian comes back, I'm getting drunk as fast as I humanly can."

"Look at your hands," Lily said, pointing.

Jake looked down.

"They're not moving," Jake said, more to himself than to Lily.

"And you haven't thrown up in over an hour," said Lily. "You're almost there."

"I'm not ready to stop drinking, Lily," he said. "But thank you for trying."

"Wash your face," Lily said, pointing to the bathroom. "You'll feel better."

Jake went to the sink while Lily stood behind him in the doorway.

"Ian is going to bring you some alcohol. But you don't have to drink it. You can beat this."

Jake focused on brushing his teeth. He rinsed, spit, and then turned to face Lily.

"When I want to see you," Jake said. "You disappear. I call you. You never call me back. And when I don't want to see you, you won't leave. What is *that* about?"

Lily looked down at the floor and then raised her eyes to meet Jake's.

"Can we focus on the fact that I'm here now?"

"No," Jake said. "We can't."

Jake threw his toothbrush into a cup on the sink and dried his face with a towel. He moved past Lily and sat down on the edge of his bed. Lily sat down next to him and crossed her legs underneath her.

Jake held out his hand. It was moving, slightly. But it wasn't shaking violently anymore. Jake took his hand and put it on Lily's cheek. He bent down and kissed Lily on the mouth, slowly at first.

Lily pushed him away when Jake tried to ease her back onto the bed.

"I don't want to do this," she said, shaking her head.

Jake stood up.

"Then why are you here?" Jake asked. "Where the hell did you even come from?"

"I'm here because you needed me," said Lily. "Why can't that just be enough?"

Ian knocked and then opened the door slowly.

"Come in," Jake barked.

Ian brought in a tray. A fifth of vodka and a glass of orange juice was on the tray. Ian sat it down on the bed and then left.

"Don't do it . . ." Lily said, her eyes pleading.

"Leave me alone," said Jake. He grabbed the bottle of vodka, opened it, and brought it up to his nose and smelled it. Then he put it back down on the tray, clasped his hands in front of his face and begin mumbling to himself. To Lily, it looked like he was praying. When he was done, Jake took the bottle into the bathroom. Lily followed. Jake looked up at the bathroom ceiling, exhaled, and opened the bottle of vodka. He lifted the toilet seat and poured it out, shaking out the last drops until it was completely empty. Jake flushed the toilet and then closed the lid and sat on it.

"Congratulations."

"Lily . . ." Jake began.

Lily held up a hand.

"Don't thank me. I did what I had to do."

Lily led Jake back to his bed. He climbed in, and she pulled the covers over him and helped him drink some orange juice.

"I don't like this," Jake whispered.

"You don't like what?"

"Not being numb. I can feel stuff."

"Like what?"

"Missing Kipenzi. And not wanting you to leave."

"Sounds normal to me."

"I don't like it."

"Give it some time."

Jake rolled over to his side, facing Lily.

"Can you lay here with me?" Jake asked.

"Yes, I can."

Lily took off her shoes and slipped into bed next to Jake. She wrapped her arms around him and kissed the back of his neck. Jake turned around to face her and his heart turned over. He was still shivering uncontrollably and every so often he would hear himself babbling incoherently.

The next time he fully woke up, he felt like a new person. Lily was still there, in his arms.

"How long have I been asleep?" Jake said.

Lily opened her eyes and smiled. She leaned in and kissed Jake on the cheek.

"Off and on since yesterday," she whispered.

Jake went to the bathroom, washed his face and brushed his teeth, and then returned to bed. As soon as he got comfortable and rearranged Lily in his arms he felt something strange. Somehow, he missed his wife fiercely. But he also desperately wanted to move on and love the woman in his arms just as much.

"I miss my wife," Jake said. He choked on the word *wife*.

Lily moved closer to Jake and rubbed his back.

"I know you do."

"I miss her so much," Jake said under his breath. He put his hands up to Lily's face and pulled her close to him. He kissed her. And for the first time, he felt her kissing him back. Holding a woman while sober was an entirely new experience for Jake and he drank it in, smelling and tasting Lily as she kissed him. He knew it wasn't Kipenzi. She was never coming back. But here was someone right here, in his bed, who really cared about him.

Jake rolled Lily over to her back and pulled her shirt over her head. Her arms moved up to her chest and covered them. Her eyes were wide with what looked like fear.

"It's okay," Jake said, softly moving her hands down to her side.

"I'm not Kipenzi," Lily said.

Jake nodded.

"I just want you to be you. Only you."

Jake leaned in to kiss Lily on the chest and she pushed him back up.

"What did you say?"

Jake froze.

"I said I want you to be you."

"You really mean that?"

Jake looked at Lily.

"Yes, I really mean that. I want you to be exactly who you are. You are brave and smart and funny and interesting. I want you to be that person. And that person only."

Jake watched as Lily closed her eyes and sighed. Her body seemed to relax beneath his. He felt himself getting hard and Lily's eyes popped open when she felt it too.

"Is this okay?" Jake asked.

Lily didn't answer.

"Lily?"

Lily said nothing.

"Shit," Jake said. He lifted himself up with his hands so that he was hovering over her.

"You've never done this before have you?"

Lily stared at Jake, not speaking.

"How old are you?" Jake asked. "And don't lie to me."

"Twenty-one."

"Do you want to do this?" Jake asked.

Lily didn't answer. Jake moved her legs apart with his own and wrapped her legs around his back. He moved against her body until he heard her breathing harder. Jake took his time.

Twenty minutes later, he was still kissing her, holding her, and moving his hands up and down her body. Jake reached over to his bedside table, took out a condom, and gave it to Lily.

"Put it on me," he said, guiding her hands inside his boxers.

Lily rolled it on, her eyes closed tight. As soon as Jake started to enter her, he felt her whole body tense up.

"Am I hurting you?" he asked.

Lily shook her head back and forth.

"Are you sure?"

Lily nodded.

Jake kept pushing, as gently as he could. He watched Lily's face carefully to see if she were in pain. Her eyes opened wide and she looked surprised and in awe.

"Is it okay?" Jake asked.

Lily nodded and Jake pushed in deeper. He felt Lily's nails digging into his back as he moved inside of her. After a few minutes, he felt her cling tighter to him, locking her legs around him. Jake felt Lily begin to twitch.

"Ohmygod," she whispered.

"It's okay," Jake said.

Lily's body jerked several times. She sat up, Jake still holding on to her, and squeezed her eyes tight.

"Shit!"

"It's okay, baby. It's okay."

Lily collapsed back on the bed and took several deep breaths. Jake pulled out and laid beside her.

"Did I hurt you?" Jake asked.

Lily shook her head.

"But," she said. "We didn't finish. You didn't . . ."

Jake gathered her in his arms and kissed her forehead.

"Don't worry, Lily," Jake said. "We're not done."

Corinne paced the room while Lily cowered in the corner of the living room. She was getting angrier by the second and Lily wasn't entirely sure that her friend wasn't going to outright smack her.

"What were you thinking?"

"I wasn't thinking!"

"Are you trying to get yourself *killed*?"

"Please don't do this. I need your help right now."

Lily reached out a hand and Corinne smacked it away.

"What is the first rule, Lily?"

"Don't have sex with any man who doesn't know."

"*You* made that rule up, Lily. Not me. I didn't tell you how to live your life. *You* decided to set those parameters for your own safety. So why would you let this happen? *Why?*"

Lily pulled at her hair and then sat on the couch and put her head down.

"I don't know what happened. I just got caught up. And I started thinking—"

"You started thinking he never has to know. I'll just take what I can get right now because this feels so good and so right and so *normal*. Never mind how he would react if he found out. Right, Lily? Just live in the moment. Throw caution to the wind. Right?"

Lily kept her mouth closed. She had no defense and no excuses. Corinne was absolutely right. In that moment, when Jake asked her if she wanted to do it, she just didn't care. She didn't care if she never saw him again. Or if she had to move halfway around the world to make sure he never found out. She wanted it. She wanted him. And she was willing to pretend in order to feel that sense of normalcy she knew she'd never have.

"I just wanted to know what it would feel like to be a girl," Lily said quietly. "Not a trans girl. Just a regular born-this-way girl."

"What gives you the right, Lily?"

Lily covered her ears.

"I know! God!"

Corinne glared at Lily with a wild look on her face. She took her bag off her shoulder, dropped it on the floor, leaned down, and pulled out a handful of photos. She went over to Lily and dropped them in her lap. Lily picked one up and then dropped it. Her heart was beating out of her chest. Corinne picked up the photos and walked to Lily, backing her up to the wall.

"Look at her," Corinne said, tears streaming down her face. "Look at what he did to her."

Lily closed her eyes as Corinne tried to put the photos closer to her face.

"Open your eyes. Open your eyes, Lily!"

Lily looked at the photo. And then turned away and covered her mouth with her hands, willing herself not to be sick while Corinne screamed at her.

"My sister went out with him three times," Corinne said. "And she didn't let him so much as kiss her. She wouldn't even hold his hand. He said he was in love with her. He said that nothing she could tell him would change his mind. She believed him, Lily. So she told him the truth. And guess what? He said he was okay with it." Corinne smiled wistfully. "He said he did not care. Can you believe it? She came home that night and she was over the moon. She told me they had sex, it was amazing and he was completely fine with the whole thing. He told her to come over the next day so they could spend some time together and—"

Corinne stopped, dropped her head, and cried hard. Then she stopped abruptly and looked up at Lily.

"And this is what he did. He beat her with his bare hands. Then he grabbed a fire extinguisher and bashed her with it until she was completely unrecognizable. The coroner said my sister was *already dead* by the time he started beating her with the fire extinguisher."

Lily shook her head slowly, trying to stop crying.

"You think Jake can't find out the truth? Manny found out. What makes you think Jake couldn't find out? And what do you think he would do? Send you a dozen fucking lilies with an engagement ring inside? Fat chance, Lily. You're an *idiot*."

Corinne went to a bookcase in Lily's bedroom and came back out with a photo album filled with newspaper articles.

"Victoria Carmen White," said Corinne, holding up the album and pointing to a clipping. "She met two guys at a party and then went home with them. They found out she was trans and they shot and killed her."

Corinne flipped the pages quickly, her eyes on Lily. She stopped on a page and stabbed at it with her pointer finger.

"Myra Ical. Found in a field, beaten to death. She had bruises on her hands that show she tried to fight back. She belonged to a local trans support group." Corinne looked up at Lily. "Myra was the *tenth* unsolved homicide against a trans woman in Houston in ten years."

"Corinne, I know what you're—"

"Duanna Johnson, Nakhia Williams—" Corinne flipped the pages faster and faster. "Erika Keels, Ruby Ordenana."

Corinne stopped on one page and shook her head back and forth.

"Gwen Araujo," she said softly, moving her fingers along the page as she read. "She went to a party with two guys she'd been involved with. They had no idea she was trans. But two other guys at the party were suspicious. They'd heard rumors. They stripped her down and inspected her and discovered the truth. They choked her and then hit her in the head with a can of dog food and then a frying pan. Then they *left* and came *back* with a pickax and a shovel."

Corinne closed the book and tossed it to the side of the room.

"They beat her to death. Hog-tied her and threw her in the back of a pickup truck. Drove her body out to the Sierra Nevada Mountains and buried her there."

Lily stared at Corinne, praying she was done. She knew all the stories, practically by heart. She was the one who had created the scrapbook. Those stories informed all the choices she'd ever made about how she would carry herself before and after surgery. And she'd thrown everything she believed in away.

"I don't want to ever talk to you again," said Corinne, rising to her feet.

"Wait," Lily pleaded. "You're right. I messed up."

"Do you think I want to come here and clean your brains off the walls?! Do you?"

Corinne picked up her bag, stuffed the photos inside, and stalked to the door.

"Do *not* call me when this shit blows up in your face. You better hire a bodyguard. Or better yet, *move.*"

Corinne pulled out her keys, removed Lily's spare keys from her ring, and tossed them on to the couch. Lily followed her to the door, pleading with her to stay. Corinne never stopped or even slowed down. She pounded the button for the elevator and when it didn't come fast enough, she walked to the stairwell and disappeared.

In the middle of a quick nap on the living room sofa, there was a series of heavy raps at Birdie's door. He sat up abruptly and looked around. He wasn't sure if he'd been dreaming or if the knocks were real. When he heard more knocks, he got up and went to the door. He looked through the peephole and then swung the door open.

Gerald, Terrence, and Biz spilled into his foyer, laughing and talking. They made their way into the kitchen and continued talking about their evening the night before. As they talked about groupies and strip clubs, Birdie just stared.

The guy at the refrigerator was his new manager, Gerald. He had been his label rep for the past year and when Travis left, he offered to step in. Although they'd been working together for only a few weeks, he had quickly become a constant presence at the house and he and Birdie had forged a friendship of sorts. Gerald's assistant, Terrence, was sitting at the counter, swigging a cup of orange juice. Birdie wasn't sure how he felt about Terrence. He was just the guy who always arrived with Gerald. And then there was Biz, his bodyguard and permanent wingman. The three men he was now closest to were all on his payroll.

Just months ago, Birdie had been shooting his reality show with Travis, Daryl, and Corey. Now Travis had his own management company. Daryl was on the West Coast at Interscope, and Corey was trying to manage a few up-and-coming producers.

Birdie let himself out the patio door off the kitchen and looked out at the collection of cars parked outside the garage near the pool. There was the Mercedes Maybach he got as a present from Jake after his album sold a million copies. Next to it was his Carrera, a present he bought himself after the sales hit five million. Each car, barely driven, gleamed and reflected the rays of the sun. Birdie squinted his eyes and looked out at all that his music career had afforded him. The house, the cars, the trips, the women. It was all nonstop and dizzying. It was impossible to believe that a few months ago he'd been sitting next to Alex on the living room sofa watching his first video on BET. Birdie heard laughter from the living room and he dipped back inside. Gerald held his phone up in the air and waved it in Birdie's direction.

"Jake said he's going to rerelease *Fistful of Dollars* at the end of the year," Gerald said.

"So?" Birdie asked.

Gerald chuckled.

"So this means you're probably going to get to diamond status. Ten million records sold."

"Oh," Birdie said.

"Oh? What do you mean *oh*. Do you know how rare it is to sell ten million albums. The Diamond Life club is a small one—especially in hip-hop."

"OutKast, Biggie, Eminem, Tupac . . ." Birdie said.

"And now you get to add your name to that list. And all you have to say is *oh*."

Birdie thought about the club he was joining. Biggie and Tupac were dead. Eminem was still dealing with addiction and recovery. And OutKast hadn't recorded together in years. Was being in the Diamond Life really a blessing?

Birdie tried to smile, but it came out looking like he was in pain. Gerald shook his head and got on the phone while Birdie wandered back onto the patio.

"We got some girls coming over," said Biz, poking his head out of the patio doors.

Birdie nodded without turning around. A few hours later, Birdie was getting a blow job in his basement from a thick brunette with a tattoo of lip prints on her neck. After twenty minutes, he was no closer to an orgasm than when she'd first started.

He finally pushed the girl away, pulled up his pants, and walked her back upstairs. The house was full of people, dancing, singing, drinking, and having a good time. Birdie's was the only nonsmiling face.

When the last person left the house that night, Birdie locked up and climbed the stairs to his bedroom. In bed, he wondered what Alex was doing. Was she thinking about him? Did she ever? His mind raced through all of the possibilities until he fell asleep.

In the morning, Birdie shuffled into the kitchen scratching at his beard. As soon as the coffee stopped dripping, he poured a cup and went back into the family room. Birdie picked up the phone and pressed 1 on the speed dial.

"Hello?"

Birdie hesitated.

"Bird? Is that you?" Alex asked.

"Hey . . . I wanted to come by, just to say hello. Say Happy Fourth of July and stuff."

"Happy what?"

"I just want to say hello, that's it. I have a studio session in Brooklyn tonight so I'll be in the area."

Birdie could practically hear Alex turning this over and over in her head.

"I'll be here," she finally said.

Birdie slipped behind the wheel of his car and looked in the rearview mirror as he reversed out of the driveway. The fact that Alex would even agree to see him was encouraging. But he knew there were no guarantees.

Erika, the latest woman Birdie had been sleeping with, texted Birdie about his plans for the night. He didn't respond and drove off the grounds of his property.

The ride to Brooklyn wasn't long enough for Birdie to figure out what he would say to Alex to make her come back. He had tried to give up and let his new lifestyle take over. But he just couldn't do it. He couldn't let her just walk out of his life. Birdie drove down Atlantic Avenue toward the brownstone and watched a group of young kids playing freeze tag on the block. Miraculously, there was a spot right in front of the house. Birdie didn't get out of his car. He leaned back against the headrest, watching the children, and thought about what he would say to Alex. That he'd changed? That he would never cheat again? That he was the same person he'd always been? The truth of the matter was he *had* changed. The flashing lights of fame had permanently blinded him and he didn't know any other way to be. He had the numbers of at least a dozen models who would come over at a moment's notice and leave before the sun came up. He slept until three in the afternoon and worked through the night, usually while drinking and smoking with his new crew. Everything was different. And Birdie wasn't sure how to rein it in and make his life make sense again.

Birdie finally got out of the car and trotted up the steps to the house. He had keys, but he rang the doorbell anyway. As soon as Alex came to the door, Birdie's eyes widened. She was wearing the white tank top and a pair of his old basketball shorts. And she was smiling. Not hard. But enough.

"Come inside," said Alex, walking toward the living room.

"You look good," Birdie said.

"Thanks. How are you?"

"I just wanted to check on you. It's been a minute."

"You've been busy."

"Jake's rereleasing my album," Birdie said. "Trying to get it to diamond status."

"Nice."

Before she could say another word, Birdie rushed up to Alex and put his arms around her waist.

"Birdie, don't."

"Don't what?"

Alex pushed him away.

"Don't mess with my head. Why are you here?"

"I'm here because this is where I belong."

"You belong in that frat house in Jersey where anything goes."

"No, I don't," said Birdie. "I want to be wherever you are."

"Birdie," Alex said, her voice trailing off. "Do you really think we could start over again?"

Birdie thought about the times he and Alex were so broke that they scoured the couch for spare change so that they could split a pack of Ramen noodles. Alex still never gave up on his dream—ever. When Birdie wanted to quit rapping and get a job at UPS, Alex talked him out of it. She was usually the first person to hear his songs and the last to leave his shows—even the ones with only a sprinkling of people who had come to see someone else. She'd financed years of studio sessions. She'd encouraged him even when Travis and Daryl told him to give it up. And when he cheated on her with Cleo, she forgave him and married him.

"I do think we could start over again," Birdie said.

Alex kept her eyes on the floor.

"I . . . I have to tell you something."

Birdie froze.

"What is it."

"When you were on tour . . ."

Alex's face crumpled, and she buried her face in her hands. Birdie leaned down and grabbed her hand.

"What Alex! What's wrong?"

"I didn't have a miscarriage," Alex said, crying harder.

"What are you talking about?"

Alex stopped crying long enough to look up at Birdie's face.

"When I found out about the chick in Australia, I just . . . I fell apart. I could not see us getting back together and so I—"

Birdie felt a chill and he dropped Alex's hand.

"So you what?"

"I got an abortion."

Birdie backed away from Alex and began pacing.

"After all we worked for?" Birdie said, his voice rising. "The shots. The treatments. The transfers . . . And you—. You—"

Birdie felt nauseated.

"I was devastated," Alex said. "I wasn't in the right state of mind."

"You just wanted to hurt me. Like I'd hurt you."

Alex was silent.

"You didn't want to have a baby by me. Because I cheated on you. I can't believe I made you feel like you needed to—*Jesus.*"

Birdie sat down on the floor next to his wife and held her close. She sobbed as he smoothed her hair back over and over. For hours, they sat together on the floor, holding each other, forgiving each other. In the morning, they were still there, talking, crying—and making a plan.

49

Jake sat at the conference room table in the label offices. Alone, he held the telephone to his ear and listened closely.

"Sixty million for the clothing line," said Dominic.

Jake nodded.

"Ten million to buy you out of your contract at the label."

"What about my shares of the label?" asked Jake.

"Another twenty-two million."

Jake sat back in his chair and exhaled.

"Let's make it happen," said Jake. He hung up the phone and went back to his office at the end of the hallway. He nodded to his assistant, who got up and followed him into the office and closed the door behind her.

"I'm leaving in three weeks," Jake said.

Sydney nodded.

"I need you to make sure everything here is put into storage until I figure out what to do with it."

"I'll take care of that," said Sydney.

"What are you going to do after I go?" asked Jake. "Whoever they bring in is going to can you immediately."

Sydney shrugged.

"Don't worry about me. I'll be fine. What are *you* going to do?"

Jake walked over to his window and looked out to the street below.

"I'll still perform," he said. "When I want to. Make an album if I feel like it . . ."

"Jake?"

Jake turned around to face his assistant.

"What's up?"

"You look good. Rested."

"Sober?" Jake asked.

Sydney smiled.

"I was trying to be tactful."

"I'm getting better. Thanks for noticing."

"You're really walking away from everything," said Sydney. "Just like Kipenzi did."

Jake nodded.

"I've made a nice amount of money over the past few years," said Jake. "It's time to have some fun with it."

An hour later, Jake's driver pulled up to the building and looked back at his passenger.

"Do you want me to wait for you?"

Jake looked at his watch.

"No. I'll hit you up when I'm ready."

Jake took the stairs to the second floor. As soon as he opened the door, he heard screams. He stopped short and listened closely. Down the hall, he could see the door to Lily's apartment was slightly open. And the screams were coming from inside. Jake jogged down the hallway to the door and pushed it. There were at least three guys in the doorway to Lily's bedroom. He couldn't make out what was going on. All he knew was that Lily was screaming and he needed to act.

"What the hell are you doing?" Jake yelled out.

One boy, no more than fifteen, jumped when he heard Jake's voice and ran past him and out the door. Jake barreled into the room and saw a tall young man with his fist high in the air. He had the other hand pinning Lily to the bed. Jake flew over to stop him, but the boy punched Lily in the jaw just before Jake landed on his back. The two of them scuffled. Jake was finally able to overpower him and punched him in the chest hard enough to send him falling backward back into the living room. He landed with a thud and began groaning about his neck.

Jake turned around to face the two guys left in the bedroom. He scanned the room and saw Lily in a corner, half-dressed and crouched down low. He felt sick to his stomach. Jake was no angel. He'd run trains on girls as a teenager. But he'd put that world so far behind him that he had almost managed to convince himself that it never existed.

"Y'all can't get no ass on your own?" he said to one boy who had his belt buckle undone.

"That's Jake . . ." said the other boy, whispering to his friend.

"What are you doing here? With . . ." The boy looked over at Lily, who was lying in a still heap in the corner. "With *that.*"

"I'm giving you exactly one second to get out," Jake whispered. "Take your friend with him before I break his neck for real."

The boys scrambled out of the bedroom and picked up the friend who was on the floor. One of the boys whispered "freak" as they dragged their friend out of the apartment.

Jake rushed over to Lily's limp figure in the corner. Her eye was turning purple and she had a split lip and a few deep cuts on her cheek and forearm.

"Let me help you up," Jake said, taking her arm.

Lily was silent. Jake watched a droplet of blood fall out of the side of her mouth and down her chin.

"Shit," Jake whispered. He picked Lily up, unsure if he was doing the right thing, and placed her gently on the bed.

Jake took out his cell phone and called 911. He gave his location and her name and then sat on the edge of the bed, holding Lily's head in his lap. Every five minutes, he placed his hand over her heart to make sure it was still beating. Although she was unconscious, she was still alive.

"What happened!"

Jake looked up and saw a young woman, out of breath and panting, standing in the doorway.

"I don't know," said Jake. "Who are you?"

"What did you do to her . . ." the girl said, walking slowly in his direction.

"I didn't touch her," Jake said calmly. "I came over and some guys—"

"*Ohmygod, ohmygod, ohmygod . . .*" the girl said, whimpering. She sat down on the bed next to him and stroked Lily's forehead, moving her hair and placing a lock of it behind her ear.

"She's dead."

"No. She's just unconscious. Ambulance is on the way."

The girl seemed to wake up from a dream.

"You called an ambulance? Then you need to get out of here," she said. She went to the window of Lily's bedroom and looked out.

"And you need to go *now.*"

Jake didn't move. He didn't know who the chick was. But he was going to make sure that Lily was taken care of. And he was going to make sure his face was the first one she saw when she woke up.

"I'm not going anywhere," Jake said, shifting his weight so that Lily could fit more comfortably in his lap. "You go."

The girl clapped her hands under her chin and closed her eyes. She looked like a small child about to say her nightly prayers.

"Please listen to me," she said. "My name is Corinne. I'm Lily's friend."

"So?"

"So. I—. I really don't think you want to be here when the ambulance gets here. There's a crowd of people outside. Reporters, cameras, all of that. You do not want them to see you here."

"I don't care."

"You *will* care. Trust me."

"Corinne, I'm not leaving. Period. I'm staying here and I'm going with her to the hospital."

Jake watched Corinne carefully. Her mouth kept opening up and closing and she was breathing heavily. She only looked away from Jake when the sounds of the approaching ambulance filled the apartment. Jake could hear a commotion coming from the area right below Lily's bedroom window. Corinne knelt down next to him and put her hands on Lily's cheek. She leaned in and whispered something in her ear that Jake couldn't hear. As soon as she stood up, Jake could hear the bustle of EMTs rushing into the apartment.

Jake and Corinne moved back to the wall near Lily's closet as the men moved Lily onto a stretcher and shouted orders at each other.

"Jake," Corinne whispered. "Lily really can't have people knowing that you were here."

"Why? Is she married or something?"

"It's not my place to say why. I just really want you to know that it's not something she would want. If you care about her . . . and it seems like you do . . . you should *not* go to the hospital with her."

Jake turned to look at Corinne. She had her head down. The EMTs hoisted Lily out of the bedroom and started out of the apartment. Corinne grabbed a bag and walked behind them. When they got to the front door, Corinne turned around. Jake was still in Lily's room, watching her. She looked at him for a moment, walked into the hallway of the building, and then closed the apartment door.

Jake looked around Lily's bedroom and then out the window. She was being placed in the back of the ambulance while several people stood around gawking. Jake went into the kitchen and looked for a sponge. He wet it, squeezed it out, and took it back into Lily's bedroom. He knelt down and began scrubbing the bloodstains out of the floor. A few hours later, her apartment was as clean and neat as the day Jake came over unannounced and ate Lily's leftovers.

It was nightfall when Jake heard a key turn in the front door. He stood behind the sofa, his hands clasped in front of him.

"Watch your step," said Corinne. "Here. Give me your hand."

"I got it, Corinne. Just let me—"

Lily saw Jake and froze. Corinne turned around and her eyes widened.

"You're still here?!"

Jake ignored Corinne, walking slowly over to Lily and putting his hand on her back. He felt a tightening in his chest when he saw the two rows of black stitches on the side of her head. The skin beneath was red and puffy. Her eye was now dark purple, hugely swollen, and completely shut. Her left arm was bent at the elbow, close to her chest, wrapped in a plaster cast.

"You okay?" Jake asked, rubbing Lily's back.

Lily kept her eyes down.

"What are you doing here?" she asked softly.

"I never left," said Jake. "And I'm not leaving."

Jake saw Lily exchange a glance with Corinne. Corinne shook her head, dropped Lily's bag on the couch, and headed for the door.

"I'll be back in thirty minutes," she said, before walking out.

Jake took Lily by the arm and led her into the bedroom.

"You cleaned up," Lily said, looking around the room.

"Relax," said Jake, easing her down onto the bed. "Who were those guys?"

"They live in the building. They've been messing with me for a while now."

Lily winced as she tried to prop herself against a pillow.

"They usually just talk shit. But today I came up the stairs and they were hanging outside my door. I opened the door and they pushed their way in."

"Why would they—"

"Jake, I need to talk to you."

"I need to talk to you too."

Jake started pacing back and forth in the bedroom.

"I'm not saying that I'm, like, trying to be with you forever or anything . . ." Jake peeked at Lily to see her reaction.

She was staring at her lap. "But I am saying that I like you. A *lot*."

"Jake—"

"Damn, would you please let me talk?" Jake shook his head. "You're always trying to fight me off and it's annoying as hell. I know you want to take things slow. And I know you don't want me to treat you like a groupie. Which is easy because you don't act like a groupie."

Lily furrowed her eyebrows and then put her head back down.

"That didn't sound right. Forget about the groupie thing. Look, I just want you to let down your guard and let me *in*. I know it's hard. I never let a woman into my life until I met Kipenzi. I'm glad she showed me how to get in touch with my feelings and all that stuff. She would want me to do this. She would want me to pursue someone I'm interested in and see where it goes."

Jake stopped talking and pacing and waited for Lily to say something.

"Why'd you come over here? Earlier."

"I wanted to tell you that I just cashed out," said Jake. "As of next month I am no longer a CEO. Or a recording artist. I don't have a clothing line or a restaurant."

"Congratulations?" Lily asked.

"Yes. Definitely. Congratulate me. I'm looking forward to the rest of my life."

"I'm happy for you."

"Lily. I want to start this new chapter of my life with you."

"You don't even know me."

"I know enough."

"No, you don't."

Jake stood up and went to the wall covered with photos on Lily's bedroom wall.

"Who are these people?"

Lily put her head back on the pillow and closed her eyes.

"Family. Friends."

"Why don't you have any pictures of yourself up here?"

"I do. You just don't recognize me."

Jake combed the wall with his eyes and then gave up.

"I don't see you."

"You're not looking hard enough."

Jake shrugged and walked over to where Lily sat. He knelt down on the floor and put his hands on her face.

"I'm clean, Lily," said Jake.

"I know. I'm proud of you."

"You got me here."

"No, Jake. You got yourself here."

"You helped me."

"Because you were ready to be helped."

"Why won't you take any credit?"

"I don't deserve any."

Jake leaned over and kissed Lily on the lips. He felt her resisting him, but he didn't stop until she relaxed and kissed him back. Lily pulled away and pointed to her closet.

"At the top," she said. "Bring me the brown box."

Jake brought the box over and helped Lily up into a sitting position. She used her good arm to pull a photo album out of the box and onto the bed. Jake felt his pulse quicken. Lily wasn't making eye contact and her body language was awkward and distant. Lily picked up a photo book and leaned back on the bed, clutching the book to her chest.

"I'm from Ohio," Lily said.

"Yeah? What part?"

"Rendville. About an hour and a half from Columbus."

Jake kept his eyes on Lily.

"What's popping in Rendville?"

"Absolutely nothing," said Lily. "There's less than fifty people there."

"Word?"

"Word."

"Why are we talking about Rendville?"

"I lived in Jersey for a few years and then I moved to Atlanta when I was thirteen. Stayed with an aunt. Left there at eighteen and I've been on my own ever since."

Jake stood up.

"So, are you a serial killer or something? Why do you have to be so extra? Just come out with whatever you have to tell me. I'm not gonna flip out."

Lily handed Jake the photo album. He sat back down on the edge of the bed and began to flip through it.

"Who's this?" he asked.

"My mom. And that's my dad standing next to her."

"And who's that? Your brother?"

"I'm an only child."

"Damn? That's you?" Jake laughed. "You grew up into a beautiful woman. 'Cause you looked like a straight-up dude when you were a kid."

Lily raised one eyebrow.

Jake stopped laughing abruptly and looked down at the photo album and then back up at Lily.

"Wait."

Lily inched her body across the bed away from Jake. His nostrils flared. He swallowed hard and then looked back down at the photo album.

"This is you."

Lily nodded. Jake pulled out another photo album from the box. He flipped the pages quickly, his eyes furiously moving back and forth across the pages.

"These are all you."

"Yes."

Jake tossed the album on the bed and reached in the box. He pulled out a yearbook and started flipping the pages.

"Where?" Jake asked.

"Page 246. Bottom right."

Jake turned the pages quickly and then stopped. He saw a

young version of Lily, a serious look on her—no, *his*—face. The kid had a buzz cut and was wearing a striped, button-up shirt and a clip-on tie. Under the photo was a name: Joseph Michael Callahan. Jake felt bile rising up in his throat and then choked it down.

"You're—"

"I started hormones when I was sixteen. Had surgery a year ago."

Jake turned away. His head was spinning. He felt rage swelling up inside him and began walking toward the door of the apartment before it could escape. If he could just get out and get something to drink, he could deal.

"Jake?"

Jake stopped walking and turned around.

"I wanted to tell you. But I didn't know how. So I just avoided you as much as I could."

"This is a joke, right," Jake chuckled. "You're kidding. *Right*. I mean—I had—I had sex with you. You're joking, right?"

Lily shook her head and Jake tried to move but found that he suddenly could not.

When Jake was very young, he'd walked in on his mother being attacked by a man she was dating. He wanted to rush in and pull the man off his mother and clock him in the jaw. But he couldn't move. He was rooted to the spot. He finally yelled out for help, and their next-door neighbor came over and screamed until the man stop hitting his mother and ran out of the apartment. For weeks afterward, Jake felt flush with shame and embarrassment. He could run up on dudes twice his age and size on the courtyard and beat them bloody for no reason and with no help. But he couldn't help his tiny mother? Jake stared at Lily. Once again, his feet felt like they were encased in cement boots. His brain wanted to attack. He wanted to break Lily's other arm, punch her in the other eye. He started to hear a sharp ringing in his ears and when he put his hands up to his temples, he noticed that his skin was hot to the touch.

Jake felt his fists curl up and he fought hard to keep his hands at his side.

"Do you want to talk about this?" Lily asked.

Jake took a step toward Lily, his balled-up fists still tight at his side. Lily didn't move.

"Is this what you usually do? Date guys and then wait to tell them the truth?"

"I usually don't do anything. I just stay away from dudes."

"So why didn't you stay away from me?"

"I asked you to just leave me alone," said Lily. "But you wouldn't."

Jake walked to the doorway. Then he stopped, turned back around, and rushed over to Lily's bed. He looked at his hands, balled them into fists, and then punched the wall inches above Lily's head. She ducked down and put her head in her lap.

"You don't *do* no shit like that!" he screamed.

Jake pushed Lily onto the bed with his left hand and pulled his right fist back. He watched Lily curl up and prepare for his blow, covering her face with her hands. Jake noticed that she had a splint on her finger that he hadn't seen before. And from this angle, he could see that she had deep bite marks on the side of her neck. Jake's stomach turned. Something shifted, and he restrained himself from punching her in the face. He got up and quickly walked out of the apartment, slammed the door shut behind him, and ran down the stairs two at a time. At the bottom, he took several deep breaths while he sent a text message to the driver.

"Where to, sir?" said the driver, as Jake climbed inside.

"A liquor store," said Jake. "And then home."

Just a few blocks away, the driver pulled over to a liquor store with a flashing OPEN sign on the front door.

"What can I get for you, sir?"

Jake threw his head back against the car seat and squeezed his eyes shut. He thought about what he'd gone through to get clean. The detox, the hallucinations, the tremors, and shakes . . .

"Never mind. Just take me home."

*   *   *

Back at the penthouse, Jake squished himself into the corner of a living room sofa, brooding and mumbling to himself. More than anything else he was embarrassed. Humiliated. And what kept smacking him in the head was the fact that the main reason why he was pissed was because he actually *liked* Lily. If he'd found out that one of the nameless, faceless people he had sex with over the past year was a dude, he'd be grossed out. But he would be able to shrug it off. Shit happens when you're drunk and screwing anything that moves.

But Lily was different. He liked talking to her. She wasn't afraid to challenge him or call him on his bullshit. She didn't trip over his fame or his money. She had her own life and found her own joys in yoga and gardening and whatever else she was into.

Lily reminded Jake of Kipenzi and the woman she would have been had she not become a celebrity. Someone who took pleasure in planting vegetables and painting. Someone who loved to spend time alone. Someone who liked the company of a man but didn't need one.

Despite himself, Jake's mind kept going back to that night in her apartment. She was scared shitless. But nothing felt any different for Jake than the last time he had sex with a virgin—his wife Kipenzi. He had been careful not to hurt Lily and tried to take it slow. How could he not have known . . .

Jake shuddered. He looked at the ceiling. It was beyond what he could comprehend, so he stopped trying.

50

Corinne rubbed Lily's back with a wet washcloth and then ran the cloth under the running water in the sink.

"Are you sure he didn't hit you?"

"It's not something I would forget."

"Might be something you'd lie about."

"He did not hit me. I swear."

Corinne grabbed a towel from the back of the bathroom door and wrapped it around Lily's shoulders. She eased her up out of the tub and walked her back into the bedroom.

"So what did he say?"

"He yelled and screamed. And then he punched the wall and left."

"And that's it?"

Lily shrugged.

"That's it."

Corinne made up the bed while Lily tried to squirm into her clothes with the use of only one arm. The swelling on her eye had gone down, but she still couldn't see out of it and every inch of her body was achy and sore.

The nurse at the hospital had warned her that she would probably relive the attack over and over for a long time. She even told Lily to ask the doctor to give her a prescription for Ambien so that she could sleep uninterrupted. But Lily's thoughts never wandered to the attack. It was Jake's eyes she saw when she tried to go to sleep at night. That look on his face when the truth finally dawned on him. It was just like when she sat in the break room at the Waffle House with Rick and told him the truth. She knew Jake would be angry. That was easy to predict. But the first emotion she saw was pure disappointment.

"I wish he had hit me," Lily said.

"Why would you say that?"

"It would just be easier. I'd have a reason to hate him, too."

"You've been through enough. Where's your bag?"

Lily pointed to her open suitcase in the hallway and Corinne placed some folded jeans and T-shirts inside.

"I really think I should just stay here," Lily said. "The cops caught the kids. I'll be okay."

"And you think people are not talking about you? The jig is up, Lily. Everyone knows."

"So what am I supposed to do? Move, again? Am I going to be running for the rest of my life?"

Corinne stopped folding Lily's laundry and carried a pile of clothes to her closet.

"So what do you want to do?"

Lily's head began to pound and she could feel her painkillers wearing off. She grabbed a bottle of pills with her good hand, shook a few into her mouth. She had no idea how to even begin answering that question. She knew she didn't want to stay at Corinne's house. Now that Jake knew the truth, she had nothing to run from. She would never see him again. And she was confident that he wouldn't send anyone after her or try to hurt her in any way. He was just gone. And for Lily, that was enough punishment. She was ready to hunker down in her tiny apartment and ride out the rest of her life with Cat.

"I want to call Jake."

Lily was just as surprised as Corinne to hear those words come out of her mouth.

"Are you insane?" Corinne asked. "What makes you think he wants to talk to you?"

"I want to hear him say he never wants to talk to me again. He never actually said that."

"Does he need to?"

"Yeah. He does."

"Let me ask you this. Is he here right now?"

Lily closed her eyes.

"No. He's not."

"Have you heard from him since you told him the truth?"

"No. I have not."

"Do you honestly think a ridiculously rich and famous rapper would ever publicly admit to being in a relationship with a woman who was born a man?"

Lily stared at Corinne, wanting to punch her in the eye.

"No, I don't."

"Then that's that. You don't need to call him."

"I need closure," Lily said.

Corinne pointed to the hole in the wall where Jake's fist had landed.

"There's your closure right there. You try to contact him and he'll probably do that to your face."

Lily wandered into the kitchen and pulled down an ancient bottle of Hennessy from the cupboard, the same bottle she'd poured for Jake a million years ago. She twisted off the cap and lifted the bottle to her lips. The liquid burned her throat and chest, warming her from the inside out. She immediately felt better, lighter.

"What are you doing?!" said Corinne, reaching out to grab the bottle from Lily's hand. Lily pulled away sharply, almost dropping the bottle to the floor. She quickly recovered, caught the bottle in the crook of her good arm, and then used her shoulder to push Corinne away.

"Leave me alone!" said Lily, limping to the living room sofa.

"You're on *painkillers*! You can't mix those with alcohol!"

Lily turned up the bottle once more and took two long gulps. She shivered as the alcohol hit her stomach and then replaced the top on the bottle and set it down on the floor. She curled up on the sofa as best as she could and turned her face toward the cushions. Corinne sat down on the edge of the couch and smoothed her hair back.

"I can't pretend like I know what you're going through . . ."

"You'd better believe it," Lily mumbled. Her words were beginning to slur.

"But you have a lot of decisions to make. You have a life to live. It's not a perfect one and it comes with challenges. You have to find a way to make this work."

Lily pulled herself up and arranged her body against the cushions so that she could lean in close to Corinne's face.

"You know what really pisses me off? A woman could be a porn star and a prostitute and still nab a dude. She can say that's who I *used* to be. That's not me *now*. And they can live a perfectly respectable life. Criminals come out of jail and get a clean slate. You can be a recovering alcoholic. You can be an ex-*anything*. How come I can't be . . ."

"How come you can't be what? An ex-man?"

Lily and Corinne locked eyes and they both erupted into howls of laughter at the same time.

"I should call Jake and say, hey, I'm not a man, I'm just an ex-man! Like the X-men! I'm a mutant!"

They continued to laugh until Lily urged Corinne to stop because the sharp pains in her side were starting to come back.

"I gotta laugh to keep from crying, I guess," said Lily. She put the alcohol back up to her mouth, tilted the bottle back, and swallowed hard. Corinne shook her head and made disapproving noises.

"I'm getting very very drunk tonight," Lily said. "If you don't like it, leave now."

Corinne stood up and looked around the apartment.

"Try not to hurt yourself," she said, walking to the apartment door.

"Can't promise that," Lily yelled out, before turning the bottle up yet again. Corinne opened the door and stopped short. Lily heard her make a little sound like *oh* and Lily's whole body tensed up. She immediately began breathing heavily and there were beads of sweat coming down her underarms. The boys were back. They were pissed off that they got arrested and now they were going to kill her. Why the hell didn't she just pack a bag and go straight to Corinne's house? What the hell was she trying to prove? Lily could not bring herself to turn around, so she just listened. She heard the rustling of what sounded like paper.

"Who's at the door?" Lily asked, her eyes on the wall.

"Turn around," Corinne said. Lily slowly turned just her head toward the door. A delivery man stood in the doorway, struggling to balance what looked like a thousand lilies.

"What the—," Lily whispered.

Corinne led the man into the apartment and gestured for him to put the flowers on the kitchen counter. She signed a form and returned it to him. As soon as she closed the door, she rushed over to where Lily stood.

"Is there a card?"

Lily shook her head.

"I don't see one."

"What does this mean?"

Lily looked up at Corinne.

"It means he ordered these flowers a week ago and they've finally arrived."

Corinne ran to the front door and flung it open.

"Hey!" she shouted down the hall.

In the distance Lily could hear the delivery man answer Corinne. "What's up?"

"When'd you get this order?"

"What'd you say?" came the voice, sounding very far away. Corinne cupped her hands around her mouth.

"I said, when did you get this order?"

"It's on the receipt!" the man yelled out, just as the stairwell door slammed shut. Corinne smoothed out the receipt on the counter and ran her finger across the numbers. She held it up, peered at it closely, and then folded it carefully and pressed it in Lily's hand.

"Today," Corinne said. "The lilies were ordered this morning."

Lily walked to the trash can, stepped on the lever and threw the receipt away.

"It wasn't him. It was someone else."

"Someone else who sends you lilies from Holland?

"Maybe someone's just messing with me. Maybe—"

Corinne turned her head to look at the back of the flowers.

"There is a card!" she said, plucking it out of the vase. "It fell inside."

Lily moved away from the tiny envelope, as if it would burn her as soon as she touched it.

"I don't want it. Take it away."

Corinne moved closer to Lily, holding out the envelope.

"You know you want to know if they're from him. What could he possibly have to say to you?"

"That it's my last day on earth?"

"He wouldn't send you flowers and then kill you. Sounds like an episode of *The Sopranos*."

"I don't care what's in it. I don't want to know."

"You just finished saying you want to stop running away from everything." Corinne put the envelope down on the counter. "Put your big-girl panties on and open it."

Lily kept her eyes on Corinne as she slid the envelope off the counter. Still staring at her friend, she slipped her finger under the sealed flap and pulled it apart.

Finally, Lily looked down and flipped the card open. She could hear Corinne's breath as she read. She closed the card, inhaled, and closed her eyes.

"Lily?"

Lily didn't move. She stood stock-still, the card still grasped in her hand.

"What'd it say?"

Corinne waited for Lily to speak. But she said nothing. She just stood there, her head tilted toward the floor. She looked like she'd just fallen asleep standing up. Corinne waited. And she saw tears slide out of Lily's swollen eye. The drops came down faster and faster until they collected on her chin and began to drip onto her chest.

51

Ras pulled up to the large brick office building and threw the car into park. He opened the glove compartment, slipped out his Ruger, and tucked the gun into his waistband. He left the car running and trotted up the steps, pushing the doors open with the palms of his hands and heading straight to a receptionist's desk. He took out his cell phone and read the text message once more: "Meet me at Dr. Montague's office. 3PM."

"Ras Bennett," the woman said, her eyes wide. "So nice to meet you!"

"Dr. Montague," Ras said, ignoring her attention.

The woman looked down, embarrassed, and wrote out a visitor's badge. Ras snatched it and looked down at the suite number. He walked down the hall quickly, only glancing over to look at the suite number on each door. He came to suite 100 and read the sign on the door: Dr. Phillip H. Montague Metropolitan Fertility Center. Ras felt his stomach constrict, and he willed his knees not to completely buckle under him. A fertility clinic? *What the hell?*

Ras closed his eyes, drew a deep breath, and put his hands on the doorknob. Cleo was in the waiting room, sitting on the edge of her seat with her legs crossed at the ankle. Her eyes were closed and she had her hands clasped under her chin. Immediately, Ras flew across the room. Before anyone could stop him, Ras had shoved Cleo to the ground and was shaking her shoulders. Cleo struggled to bring her hands up to her face, but Ras was holding her wrists with one hand and trying to smack her face with an open palm with the other hand.

"What did you do!?" Ras screamed. Two women who had been seated next to Cleo dashed over to the side of the waiting room, their hands covering their mouths. Ras rolled Cleo over to her back.

"I said, what—did—you—do?" Ras said through his teeth.

"That's *enough*, Mr. Bennett!"

A tall man with a heavy build and a light Jamaican accent grabbed the back of Ras's shirt and yanked it hard. Ras fell backward and Cleo stood up and ran into the inner office. A receptionist grabbed Cleo and held her arm, leading her quickly into an examination room, closing the door, and locking it behind her.

"Inside!" the man barked, pointing to the door Cleo had just walked through. Ras rolled over to his knees and then stood up slowly. He walked into the inner office and past the door of the room Cleo had gone into. He tried the doorknob. It was locked and he shook it a few times before the man pulled his hand away.

"In my office, Mr. Bennett," the man said, pointing to a room at the far end of the hallway.

Ras threw open the door of the office and sat down on a leather couch facing an expansive glass desk.

"I'm Dr. Montague," the man said as he stepped behind the desk. He stretched out his hand in Ras's direction. Ras stared at him, not moving.

"Why am I here?"

"Ms. Wright told me that your daughter Reina is in need of a blood transfusion."

"Why is she telling you anything about my daughter?"

"Because she can help you find someone who matches her blood type."

Ras stood up.

"I don't know what's going on, but somebody better have some answers. Now."

"Have a seat, Mr. Bennett."

Ras sat down just as someone knocked on the office door. The doctor quickly went to the door and then turned to face Ras.

"Keep your hands to yourself."

Ras glared at the doctor and didn't speak. The door opened and Cleo stood there. Mr. Bennet motioned for her to sit on the other side of the office, away from Ras.

"Ms. Wright," the doctor said, motioning to Ras. "I think you have something you need to tell Mr. Bennett."

Cleo kept her eyes on the floor. Her left knee was bouncing wildly as Ras stared at her.

"Ms. Wright?" the doctor asked.

Cleo looked up at the doctor, taking care not to look in Ras's direction.

"You have to tell him. His daughter's life is on the line."

Ras leaned over to drop his head into his hands and felt the coolness of the pistol on his stomach. He jumped a bit, adjusting himself. He'd forgotten that he grabbed the gun, and now it felt like it was pulsating.

Maybe he could leave. Lure her into the car and drive her somewhere . . . Ras shut his eyes tight and dreamt of a world where Cleo didn't exist. Until that moment, he'd never considered it. Even after Josephine caught them at the hotel and he vowed to himself that he would never see Cleo again, he never really thought that he would ever be truly rid of her. He expected her to always hover around the outer edges of his life, popping up unexpectedly every so often and trying to get a rise out of him. Not once did he ever imagine a life fully free of the woman he'd tortured for over a decade. Ras tried to imagine what Josephine would do, say, or feel if she found out Cleo was dead—out of the picture forever. Would he have a better chance of getting his wife back? Would she be more likely to forgive him if she knew they would never have to deal with her again?

"He has a gun," Cleo whispered, pointing at Ras.

The doctor whipped his head around.

"Is that true, Mr. Bennett?"

Ras crossed the room, hooked an arm around Cleo's neck, and pulled out the pistol, holding it to her temple.

"Speak," Ras said. Cleo said nothing and Ras clicked off the safety and squeezed her neck tighter.

"I said *speak*."

Cleo's mouth was open, but nothing came out. Ras put his finger on the trigger. Cleo shut her eyes and her entire body tightened.

"She's been coming to me for several years," the doctor said quickly. Ras kept his arms around Cleo's neck and looked at the doctor expectantly.

"She's been having her eggs extracted and frozen. She can't have children and she wanted to be able to—"

"No," Ras said, shaking his head. "No."

"Mr. Bennett," the doctor said, "it is not my responsibility to double-check where my patients receive the sperm for in-vitro."

Ras blinked.

"The sperm?"

"Of course, I prefer that the sample is extracted here in the clinic. But if that's not possible, I do supply my patients with semen-collecting condoms that will preserve the sample long enough to bring to the clinic."

Ras could hear the words the doctor was saying. But he was unable to fit the pieces of what he was saying together in any kind of cohesive way. He replayed the doctor's sentences in his mind, still holding the pistol to Cleo's temple. Key words ran through his head on a loop: *eggs, sperm, condoms, eggs, sperm, condoms*.

Ras thought about the hundreds of times he had sex with Cleo. Most times he was drunk out of his mind. He was usually fanatical about using his own condoms. But there were nights that he woke up to her on top of him, riding him while he was in and out of consciousness. Did she use her own condoms then?

Did she leave right afterward? Is it really possible that she could have—Ras shook his head. One thing he was absolutely sure of was that Cleo was *not* pregnant at all last year. So how could she have—

"Mr. Bennett, can you please remove the pistol from Ms. Wright's head?"

"Only if you want me to turn it on you. If not, I suggest you keep talking."

The doctor seemed to consider this for a moment.

"Ms. Wright brought me several sperm samples a few years back. We used them to fertilize her eggs."

Ras dropped Cleo to the floor and stood over her.

"What did you do?"

Cleo stayed on the floor and propped herself up on her elbows. She looked directly at Ras.

"I paid someone to carry the baby—"

Ras dropped to his knees, the gun still in his hand, and stared at her with his mouth open.

"Reina is my child," Cleo said. "And yours."

Ras was a statue, his hand still gripping the pistol.

"I planned to raise her myself," Cleo said. "Just until you realized that you should be with me and then we could raise her together."

Ras looked down at the floor and then back up at Cleo.

"What were you thinking?" he whispered.

"After she was born, I—I freaked out. And I had the girl turn her over to your great-grandmother. I knew she'd make sure she was given to you and your wife. I thought I was doing the right thing."

Ras stepped closer to Cleo, rubbing the side of his leg with the nozzle of the gun.

"You did *not* think you were doing the right thing. You were trying to torture me and my wife because you knew I would never be with you."

Cleo held Ras's gaze and said nothing.

The ringing in Ras's ears grew louder and louder until he couldn't hear anything being said. He saw the doctor's lips moving and his arms flailing about. He saw Cleo, tears streaming down her face, babbling about something he couldn't hear. Ras opened the chamber of the gun, shook out the bullets and put them in his pocket. He knew if he didn't disarm himself, he would blow Cleo's brains out and deal with the consequences later.

Ras shook his head and walked toward the door.

"I'm going to donate blood," Cleo said. "As often as I need to."

Ras walked out of the office and closed the door behind him. He left the building, got into the car, and drove to the hospital where his daughter and his wife were waiting for him. The entire way there, he thought about how he would tell his wife the truth. And there did not seem to be any words he would be able to say to her that would make any sense whatsoever.

Back at the hospital, Ras walked slowly to his daughter's room. He stood outside the door for several minutes, listening to his wife sing to her in French. He pushed open the door and cleared his throat. Josephine turned around and stopped singing in mid-sentence.

"I need to talk to you," Ras said. "There's some things you need to know."

"She called," Josephine said, her eyes boring into Ras's head. "I know everything. We don't have anything to talk about. You can go."

"I had no idea that she—"

Josephine took a step toward Ras and her face was so full of rage that Ras was actually afraid of her. He took a step back.

"If you go now, this won't be messy. If you stay here . . ."

"Josephine, we have to talk about this. Reina is going to need several transfusions."

"I've worked that all out. It will be taken care of. Reina is my daughter. I will not let anything happen to her. But if you don't leave this room right now, I will do my very best to kill you."

"I know there is absolutely nothing I can do to make this right," Ras began.

"There's only one thing you can do that can make this right."

Ras's eyes widened. In that moment, there was absolutely nothing on earth Josephine could have asked him that he would not do. He'd cut off his pinkie toe and eat it if it meant she'd even consider taking him back.

"What is it?"

"I need you to get your stuff out of the house. Put it in storage or throw it out. Whatever. And I need you to leave. I need you to leave Kingston. I need you to leave Jamaica. I need you to leave me and Reina—forever."

Ras opened up his mouth to speak, but no words formed. There was a calmness to Josephine's words that chilled him. This was not a woman who was pissed off. This was a woman who was just plain through.

There was a knock on the door and it creaked open. A tall, thin man stood in the doorway, questioning Josephine with his eyes.

"It's okay," said Josephine. "Come inside."

The man crossed the room and hugged Josephine tight.

"Is everything okay? Is Reina going to be okay?"

"Yes," said Josephine. "They found . . . a donor."

"How did they find a match?"

Josephine took the man by the hand. As soon as she touched him, Ras felt an icy rage building up in his chest.

"This is Bobby," said Josephine. "He's a friend of mine."

Ras kept his eyes on Josephine, not daring to look in the eyes of the man who was holding her hand.

"I'm staying here in Jamaica," said Josephine. "With Bobby. And Reina. I want you to leave and never come back."

"You think I'm going to just walk away and leave my child?"

"You asked me what I wanted!" said Josephine. She began to march toward Ras, but Bobby held her back.

"I am this little girl's mother. And one day I will have to tell her how she came to be. How her biological mother created her just to make me miserable. She is still my baby. And I will love her and I will raise her. You don't deserve me. And you don't deserve Reina. I want you out of our lives forever."

Bobby pulled Josephine back and forced her to sit on the edge of the hospital bed.

"You should probably go," said Bobby.

Ras sized him up. The dude was slim but muscular. He gave some quick thought to going for broke and clocking him in the jaw but thought better of it.

"Josephine. If you need to talk to me . . ." Ras said.

Josephine sucked her teeth and waved a hand in the air dismissively. Ras came up to the bed and looked at baby Reina sleeping soundly. He put a hand out to touch her forehead. It was smooth, soft, and warm. Ras kissed his hand and placed it back on Reina's head.

"Daddy loves you," Ras said.

In the parking lot, Ras turned the car over and eased it onto the smooth road. The primary schools were just letting out and he passed dozens of young children in their crisp white shirts and khakis. The boys wore loosely knotted ties. The girls all had wild hairstyles that had escaped the orderly barrettes and braids that had been painstakingly fastened just hours before. Ras pulled his car over to the side of the road and watched the young people pick their way over the rocks guarding the ocean from the town. He got out of his car and followed, staying just far enough behind that the kids could not see him.

As soon as he made it over the wall of rocks, a feeling of warmth and comfort enveloped him. Beneath his feet was flawless and pristine white sand. And just beyond, the incomprehensible blueness of the Caribbean Sea.

Long after the kids had gathered their books and lunch boxes to head home, Ras sat on the secluded beach. His socks were tucked into his shoes, the same way he'd done it years and years ago when he was a little boy.

As the sun set, Ras focused on watching its every blood-orange move as it dropped lower and lower into the horizon. The wind began to increase and the breeze coming off the water chilled Ras. But still he did not move.

When he finally stood to leave, hours later, he went back to the home he'd built and shared with his wife. He unlocked the door for what would be the last time, went to their bedroom, and packed one small bag. He caught the first flight back to New York and went straight to the studio.

52

Is everything in place?" Jake asked Ian for the third time in an hour.

"Sir," said Ian. "The movers will be here at noon. Everything important has already been shipped out. Everything is in place."

Jake looked around the empty penthouse. He remembered how happy Kipenzi was the day she moved in. It had been her first real home. And their first real home together. They'd exchanged vows on the very spot where he was standing. He'd had the nerve to envision himself there for years, chasing kids up and down the hallway.

"You always looked out for my wife, Ian," Jake said. "I appreciate that."

Ian nodded.

"And you took decent care of me too."

"A pleasure, sir."

The two exchanged a few awkward glances and then found other things to do in the apartment. Jake realized that even with all of the stuff he owned, he could walk out of that apartment with one bag and never look back. He had his wedding album, a few letters from his mother, random mementos, and his laptop. That was it.

Five hours later, Jake was in Miami. It was one of the few cities that had areas where he could drive around in a convertible, wearing a T-shirt and shorts, no shades, and still not be hassled.

His first stop was a local barbershop. The shop went quiet when Jake walked in. He took a seat with the other guys waiting for a turn and opened up a magazine. He pretended not to notice that everyone in the shop was staring at him.

"Yo," said a teenager waiting nearby. "Can you sign my magazine?"

"No doubt," said Jake, signing the back page with a flourish.

In the barber's chair, Jake pointed out what he wanted done in the mirror. For the first time in months, he was getting his haircut. He almost forgot what it felt like to be well-groomed. As the barber edged up his line, Jake rubbed his hands on his thick, fluffy beard.

"I think it's time to let this go too," said Jake.

The barber nodded and took out a straight razor. When Jake stepped out of the chair, he was a completely different person than the grizzly man who had walked in. He stared at himself in the mirror for a long moment. The last time he looked this way, his wife was alive and he felt like his whole life was ahead of him.

Jake rubbed his now-smooth face. He paid the barber, tipped him with a hundred-dollar bill, and shook hands with the other patrons as he made his way out.

There was no driver there to whisk him away to the next spot. He'd actually driven himself to the barbershop in his own car. On the ride back to his rented condo, he opened up the sunroof and found a classic R&B station playing Aretha Franklin. He turned it up as loud as it would go.

Back at the condo, Jake poured himself a glass of lemonade and went out onto the balcony overlooking Biscayne Bay from his bedroom. Miami would be home. Indefinitely. And for the next year, at least, Jake had no plans to do anything except work on staying sober and figuring out the second act of his life.

Jake looked into his glass, as if there were answers in the ice cubes.

The doorbell rang and Jake remained still, his eyes in his cup. He took a deep breath and stood up when the bell sounded a second time. Jake went to the door, unlocked it, and stepped back without opening it. The doorknob turned and opened slowly.

Lily stood in the doorway. She was dressed in a simple button-up shirt and a pair of khaki shorts. She held an overnight bag in one hand that she placed on the floor.

"Hey," said Jake.

"Hey yourself," said Lily.

Jake turned and walked toward the kitchen and Lily followed. Jake went to a vase on the counter and took out a single flower. He walked over to Lily and she leaned her head down. Jake wrapped the stem of the flower around her bun and then lifted her chin up to face him.

"In the card," Lily said. "You said you wanted to talk to me."

"Yeah," Jake said. "I do."

"Well. I'm here. So talk."

Jake led Lily onto the balcony and they sat down together. Together, they watched the sun set over the water without exchanging a single word.

53

Z folded the paper into fourths and stuffed it in his back pocket, the same way he did every day since he got the results in the mail. A few times he opened it up. But he hadn't had the nerve to actually read the paper. Not yet.

Z walked quickly, making his way to the Brooklyn Diner for the last time. He tapped on the window and startled Alex, who jumped a bit and then smiled when she saw that it was him. As soon as he slid into the booth across from Alex, she slid a sheaf of papers in his direction.

"I finished last night," said Alex. "I made all the changes you asked for."

"Do you like it?" Z asked, thumbing through the pages.

"I love it. I just wish we had a title."

"It'll come. In the meantime, I want to thank you for everything."

"I was just doing my job," Alex said.

"I'm not easy to work with."

Alex sucked her teeth.

"Please. You were a dream."

Alex and Z shared a long look. It said everything and nothing.

"I'm going to miss working with you," Z said. He kept his eyes on the table and played with a straw wrapper.

Alex cleared her throat.

"Um, yeah, me too."

"I guess I won't have a reason to see much of you now that we're all done."

"Probably not."

Another awkward silence.

"You made it," Alex whispered. "I'm proud of you."

"Made what?"

"You made it out of the hell that was your life for thirty years," Alex said.

"I did."

"And you did it against all odds."

Z smiled.

"Thanks for giving me the title for my book," he said, scribbling the words across the top page of the book.

"*Against All Odds*," Alex said. "I like it. It fits."

"I think so."

"What about you, Alex? What's going on with you and Birdie?"

Alex closed her eyes and shrugged.

"We're going to try and work it out."

"I'm really glad to hear that. From what I know, he's a good dude."

"He *is* a good dude," said Alex. "But we have a lot of work to do. There are some things I just won't accept."

"My wife accepted a lot from me."

"Would you do the same for her?"

Z's hands instinctively went to his back pocket where the paper folded in fourths was tucked inside. He sat back down at the booth.

"Can I tell you something?"

"Of course," said Alex. "Anything."

"It's really personal."

Alex gave Z a look.

"You just spent the last year telling me your life story."

"Good point," Z said. He looked around the diner and back at Alex. "There's a good chance that my daughter is actually not my daughter."

"What are you talking about?" asked Alex.

"I think Beth cheated on me when I was with Cleo."

"Impossible."

"It's just a feeling."

"What are you going to do about it?"

Z pulled the paper out of his pocket and put it on the table.

"I got a paternity test."

"And?"

"I haven't opened it."

Z and Alex both looked down at the paper on the dinner table.

"What happens if she's not your child?" Alex asked.

Z looked up at Alex.

"I've cheated on Beth hundreds of times," said Z. "But when I think about her with someone else and then getting *pregnant*."

"You've gotten women pregnant. More than once."

"I'm aware of that."

Alex picked up the paper and turned it around and around in her hand. She held it out to Z.

"You might as well get it over with."

Z slipped the paper back into his pocket.

"I'm going to go."

Alex stood up and gathered her things. They walked out of the diner together and stopped at the entrance.

"Stay in touch with me," Alex said.

"I will."

"And whatever you find out . . ."

"I'll be fine, Alex. Don't worry about me."

At home, Z sat in the driveway in front of his house for twenty minutes. His hands, clutching the folded paper, were warm and sweaty. He folded and unfolded the paper dozens of times, never looking down to read it.

Finally, he put the paper back into his pocket and went to the door. Before he put his key in, he could hear the kids screaming and laughing. Z came into the house and Zeke and the baby flew past him, laughing hard and out of breath.

"Slow down, you two!" Z yelled.

He moved out of the way just in time to avoid getting knocked down by Zakee, who was chasing them. Z shook his head and went into the kitchen. Beth stood at the counter, chopping vegetables.

"Hey, you," Z said.

Beth smiled and looked up.

"Did you get the book from Alex?"

Z took the manuscript out of his bag and passed it to Beth.

"I want you to be the first one to read it."

"I'm honored. Your son is home for the weekend. He's in the family room."

Z fell silent and watched his wife as she began to read the book. Her hair fell down, covering her face as she read and every so often, she absentmindedly pulled her hair back and held it in place at the nape of her neck. Her lips moved quickly as she read, yet she turned the pages slowly.

Z went into the family room where all the kids were lying around watching television. Zander came up to his father and slapped hands with him.

"How's school?" Z asked.

"It's cool," said Zander. "I think I'm where I belong."

Z smiled and then noticed Zakee looking up at him with a question in his eyes that Z wasn't sure he could answer. They had barely spoken a word to each other since the day he did the test and saw him in the hallway. Z simply sat on the sofa and gestured for his son to join him.

Zakee sat next to his father. Z threw a hand over his son's shoulders and squeezed his arm. Zach and Zeke were on the floor, racing cars over imaginary tracks while their baby sister tried to steal the cars away.

Z stared at his baby girl. Many years before, his beloved

grandmother told him that a baby girl would save his life. She told him that at some point, he and Beth would have a little girl. And it would be then that he would finally get his life cleaned up. They had four boys back to back while Z slipped deeper and deeper into the abyss of addiction. And as soon as Beth got pregnant the last time, he started finding the strength to kick his habits. Long before the baby was born, he knew it was a little girl. And he knew that somehow she was giving him the strength to make all the changes he needed to.

And indeed, his life was much different. He was sober, clear-headed, and whole. And he was in love with his family—every single member. No matter where they came from or how they got there . . .

"Kipenzi, come to Daddy," said Z, holding out his arms.

The baby toddled over to Z and then giggled when she finally made it and collapsed in his arms.

"You know Daddy loves you, right?"

Kipenzi just laid her head on Z's shoulders and yawned. Z stood up, still holding Kipenzi and walked to the kitchen. He took the paper out of his back pocket and put it in the sink. He rummaged through the junk drawer for a lighter. He found one and lit the paper. Kipenzi watched the flames, transfixed.

Z turned on the faucet and the water doused the flames, leaving charred flakes of paper. He rinsed out the sink, sending the ashes down the drain.

He went back to the family room and looked out at his family, Kipenzi still on his hip. Beth looked up at him, smiled, and then went back to reading the book. Z stood in the doorway, not moving. Just watching. He felt hot, salty tears coming down his face and didn't bother to wipe them away. The baby fell asleep on his shoulder as he held her. He closed his eyes and let the tears continue to fall, a smile on his face.

ACKNOWLEDGMENTS

Much love, thanks, and respect to my agent Ryan Harbage, my editor Allegra Ben-Amotz, and the entire Touchstone team. And thank you to my early readers for encouragement and direction: Anita Johnson, Michael Arceneaux, Demetria Lucas, and Shydel James.

Touchstone

TOUCHSTONE READING GROUP GUIDE

Diamond Life
By Aliya S. King

Journalist Alex Maxwell's star is on the rise. And her husband Birdie is getting a bigger taste of fame as he joins the ranks of famous rappers, complete with McMansions, world tours, and tempting fans who threaten their marriage. Meanwhile, the industry's biggest players are overcoming their own demons and struggling to maintain their relevance in a world where the next big thing rules. This follow-up to the novel *Platinum* gives an inside look into a glittery industry where alcohol, sex, scandal, money, and betrayal can taint the reality of finally "making it."

FOR DISCUSSION

1. "It's beautiful. But it's so cliché," Alex says of the house Birdie wants to buy in New Jersey. How is Birdie's rise to fame, including leaving Brooklyn for a mansion in the suburbs, groupies, and staring in a reality show indicative of celebrityhood today?

2. Many of the artists struggle to maintain relevance within pop culture. Which character do you think is most afraid of losing his or her edge? Whose career is most in jeopardy?

3. What are the most important factors that led to Z's transformation? What event ultimately led to his redemption?

4. Discuss the treatment of women in *Diamond Life*. Why are the men so flippant toward women? Why do you think the women tolerate this behavior?

5. Discuss Alex as a strong, independent female in contrast to the other women in the book. Where do Josephine, Lily, Beth, Bunny, and Cleo show their greatest strengths and weaknesses?

6. What habits did Zander learn from his father, and how did this influence his relationship with Bunny? How does Z's transformation contrast to his son's setbacks?

7. Discuss the theme of forgiveness in the book, from Birdie's infidelity to Lily's lies to Jake. What actions do you feel are most unforgivable?

8. What do you think is the cause of Beth's distant attitude toward Z? Do you think Z is the real father of baby Kipenzi?

9. What was the breaking point for Alex in her marriage to Birdie? Discuss her rationale for having an abortion.

10. What do you think will be Cleo's role in the future of Josephine's baby?

11. Who is the most motivated by money? Who is most in search of the "diamond life"? Explain.

12. Why did no one intervene in Jake's self-destructive behavior following Kipenzi's death?

13. Discuss the gender stereotypes among the characters in the book. In this world, what are the differing attitudes about cheating, alcohol abuse, and violence for men versus women?

14. Why are Josephine, Beth, and even Alex so willing to turn a blind eye to their husbands' philandering?

15. Discuss the meaning of Z's statement, "Triumph and disaster are both imposters." To whom does this most apply in *Diamond Life*? How has it played out in your own life?

A CONVERSATION WITH ALIYA S. KING

While writing your first novel *Platinum*, did you always have this sequel in mind?
In the beginning, when I first began writing *Platinum*, I definitely did not have a sequel in mind. As it was my first novel, I had no idea it would ever see the light of day! I was just really excited about finishing the novel. But as I began to get closer to the end of the novel, I did start wondering what would become of my characters and how their lives might change in that fictional universe.

You've said you related to Alex in *Platinum*. Do you relate to any of the characters in *Diamond Life*?
I still relate to Alex quite a bit. We're both writers who cover the same beat and work for the same publications, so we have a lot in common.

As a woman writer, how difficult was it for you to portray female characters as objects of desire, or as scorned wives? Why do these women take such abuse from their partners? How much is this a reflection of the hip-hop industry as you see it?
It's not just a reflection of hip-hop. It's a reflection of celebrity, period. Gene Simmons from KISS just married his girlfriend of twenty-eight *years*. A lot of folks wondered why on earth she would stick around that long when she wanted to be married. I don't think that problematic relationships are hip-hop specific. Give someone fame and fortune and relationships may suffer, no matter what genre of entertainment they're involved in.

How difficult is it for celebrity journalists to keep their objectivity when writing about their subjects? Did Alex cross any lines in writing Z's memoir?
Good question. Going with Z to a twelve-step meeting could be seen as crossing a line. (Although I would do the same thing in her position.) If I'm writing someone's book, I want to see as

much of his world as I possibly can. It's a thin line, and I think many journalists cross it at some point.

What was the reasoning behind the inclusion of Lily's storyline, a character who did not appear in *Platinum*? How would the world of *Diamond Life* react to a relationship between her and Jake?
I really thought a lot about what would become of Jake after I finished writing *Platinum*. He loved Kipenzi so much. How could she possible be replaced? I wanted to see what it would take for Jake to open up and feel for someone again. And then what would he do if this woman was not who he thought she was? Also, I'm very interested in how the hip-hop world would handle a relationship between Jake and someone like Lily. Would they be accepted? Probably not. A bigger question would be: Does a relationship like Lily and Jake's exist right now? I'd love to know!

How "ripped from the headlines" is this book, in comparison to *Platinum*?
It's not as ripped from the headlines as *Platinum*. *Platinum* was heavily based on a real life article that I wrote for *Vibe*, so the similarities were heavier there. *Diamond Life* does have elements of real life. But it's more ripped from my mind than ripped from the headlines. I love answering those what-if questions!

When we pick up with the characters in *Diamond Life*, it seems that many of them have forgotten the sting of Cleo's tell-all book in *Platinum*. Why wasn't there more of an outcry? Who was the most hurt by Cleo's book?
I don't know if they've forgotten. I think it's more that they are trying to move on. It's been a year, and the damage has been done. Ras was the most affected by Cleo, in my opinion, and that continues to be the case in *Diamond Life*!

Were there any unanticipated reactions to *Platinum* you wanted to address in *Diamond Life*?
I never imagined that readers would be so affected by the outcome of one of the major characters in *Platinum*. I still get messages on Facebook and Twitter about it! So in *Diamond Life*, I almost wanted to change what happened to a major character in *Platinum*. But I couldn't do it. There was tragedy in *Platinum* and it had to remain so.

Whose book will be a bigger seller—Cleo's or Z's? Why?
Probably Cleo's. She was dishing dirt. Z is just coming clean about his own problems in life. Plus, everyone's already heard crazy stories directly from Cleo! She beat him to the punch!

Birdie's song states, "All I want is a fist full of dollars." What are the realities of sudden wealth for both the characters in the book and the players in the music industry?
In reality, does a fist full of dollars ever end well? How many of today's most successful rap acts remain so for the life of their careers? It's always a risk. And the sudden wealth is often very blinding. And when you're blinded by the diamond life, you don't always make great choices.

ENHANCE YOUR BOOK CLUB

1. Play some current hip-hop hits during your group's discussion. Think about how the lyrics of some of your favorite songs relate to the characters in *Diamond Life*.

2. Watch the movie *American Gangster*, the film adaptation of Aliya S. King's book *Original Gangster*, about Frank Lucas. Discuss the similarities and differences between the world of gangsters and the hip-hop artists depicted in *Diamond Life*.

3. Read Karrine Steffans's 2005 bestselling memoir, *Confessions of a Video Vixen*. Discuss how the book may be similar to Cleo's fictional tell-all.